HAMMERHEAD
RESURRECTION

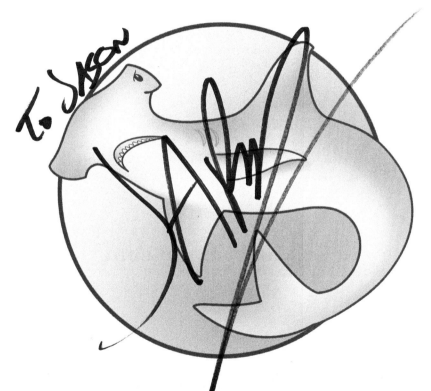

JASON BOND

For more about the author, future novels, and events please visit:

www.Jason-Bond.com

ACKNOWLEDGMENTS

I want to offer sincere thanks to all those who helped keep my fires lit during the arduous process of writing and editing *Hammerhead Resurrection*. As always, thanks are due my beta readers, who have saved me so much grief. I couldn't tackle the closing of a novel without their wonderful help. Finally, deep gratitude is due our veterans, who inspired the core of this novel.

In light of that, this novel is dedicated to those who've served in my family…

My father
Richard A. Bond
Major, U.S. Air Force

My step-father
John W. Spriggs
Petty Officer Second Class, U.S. Navy (Vietnam)
Captain, U.S.P.H.S.

My step-grandfather
Dorsel F. Spriggs
Seaman, U.S. Navy (WWII—U.S.S. West Virginia)

…and to all the men and women around the globe who have put their lives in harm's way.

TO THE READER

Before you begin reading *Hammerhead Resurrection*, I would like to offer you sincerest thanks. I appreciate your time as a reader more than I can express.

This novel is fully a year and a half in the making, and I hope you enjoy it. I do have one request. As I am currently an independent writer, word of mouth is the main engine I must rely on. In light of this, I humbly ask that, if you should find my work to your liking, please tell others and consider leaving a review wherever suits you best. I would also love to hear from you at jason@jason-bond.com.

For my part, I will continue striving to create the best stories I am capable of. If you see fit to recommend this new novel, even more will be helped.

All the best,

Jason

CHAPTER 1

The Earth winked out of existence as Leif Holt looked at it through the thick viewport glass. Narrowing his eyes at the place where the faintly blue spark of light had been, he touched the viewport's titanium frame, warm despite the temperature on the other side being close to 60 degrees above absolute zero. Beyond lay Europa's ravined ice, ranging away to the unnaturally close horizon. Above, Jupiter blocked out the stars in a great, convex sky of sandstone-hued bands.

Rubbing his palms into his eye sockets, he looked back. Earth's bright spark had returned.

Footsteps entering the room distracted him as Sarah's quiet voice asked, "Another bad night?"

A tickling kiss brushed the back of his neck.

"I'm fine," he said, turning to her. Even now, after months of close-quarters living, he found her beautiful with her red hair in a pony tail, and her bangs swept to the side of her face.

As she touched his cheek, her jade-green eyes searched his. "Your eyes say different." Her fingertips slid down his neck. "Why aren't you sleeping?"

"Don't know." After running his hand through his shaggy, blonde hair, he turned to the window. "Are any ships coming in today?"

"I don't believe so. Why do you ask?"

He shook his head. "I think something just blocked out..." Even as he looked at Earth's bright light he felt foolish.

"What is it, Leif?"

1

"It's nothing. I'm just tired."

"I know, and I want to know why you're so restless lately."

He shrugged. "I have no reason to be. Everything's great." Out on the ice, a fusion rover rolled away from the base on fat, wire-mesh wheels. "The cores we have are reaping wonderful data."

"...but you'd rather still be working on the singularities."

He looked over his shoulder. "No. It's not that. I've done what I needed to do. Now is *your* time." He turned back to the glass, his eyes lifting to the stars beyond Jupiter's wide curve. He didn't feel successful. The singularities should have taken decades to develop, but he'd stumbled on the solution to the unsolvable, like many leaps in science, through a tired mistake.

"You've done all you can."

Leif nodded, but said, "They're being put into service. I don't like that I wasn't there for the testing." But he sensed that he'd misstepped. Turning back, he found her glaring at him, her eyes luminous.

"If your work wasn't done, what the hell are we doing here?"

Leif held up his hands, "I don't want to fight about this again. We came here because you deserve to have a career too. My work was *almost* done when this opportunity came up. There are others on it who are perfectly capable. Okay?"

She watched him, clearly still ready to argue the point. He did not react to her anger because he understood its source. While she'd been grateful for his sacrifice, she felt guilty over it. Whenever that guilt was skinned bare, she immediately covered it with anger.

He took both of her hands in his. "I'm glad to be here because I love you and want this for *you*. For me, running the Ice-Core Lab is a good, easy job. I needed the rest."

With that her eyes softened, the storm passing as quickly as it had risen, and she moved closer to him. "The obsession complete?"

Leif let out a slight, insincere laugh. "I suppose."

Sarah took hold of the sides of his face, lifting his chin to look at her. "Even in a job you say is easy, you've been working too many hours. Why do you always push yourself so hard?"

He drew her hands from his face and kissed them one at a time. "I'm always trying to live up to my father?"

"Whatever," she said with a short, playful laugh. "You've never wanted to be like him." She sat down on his lap, putting her arms around his neck and settling her head on his shoulder.

He kissed the back of her neck, the slightly floral scent of her shampoo causing his mind to grow peaceful. "Maybe not like him, but as good as?"

She lifted her head. "I don't want you to be anyone other than who you are. You're the best man I've ever known."

At that, a tear ran down Leif's face.

Sarah brushed it away. "What is going on Leif?" Her voice held the vespers of anger again.

He shook his head. "I don't know. I'm just tired, and I love you very much."

She softened again. "There's more work to come."

"In what?"

She took hold of his head with both hands, kissed him. "We're going to finish this assignment and get back to Earth just in time."

"For?"

"For our child to be born."

Leif felt adrenaline flush through him. While his rational mind tried to check his words, his emotions overrode him. "What the hell?" He held his hand out to the miles-deep ice beyond the window. "You can't be pregnant out here."

Her eyes went flat. "Well, asshole, I am, and you sure didn't mind getting me that way."

"Sarah, I'm sor—"

She shoved herself to standing. "I do *not* want to hear it. You're not the only one who's sick of this place, and it's my stupid job that brought us here. I want to go home as much as you."

"Sarah, I—"

"Listen to me Leif Holt." She fixed him with a pointed finger. "Get your head screwed on straight. We're going to have a child, and you can't keep obsessing about death and war. I know you got screwed up by what King did, but you've *got* to let it go. Do I make myself clear?"

"Yes. I—"

"I'm not going to let you live," she said, her face flushing, "under her shadow, nor your father's once we bring this child into the world."

"I—"

"I'm late," she said as she whipped her lab coat from a chair back and walked out of the room. He heard the main quarters door slide open and shut. He was left in silence.

"I'm sorry..." he said to the empty room. He turned back to the viewport. She was, of course, right on all counts. He'd talk to her tonight. She'd be calmed down by then, probably already was. She had the temper of a fury, which cooled even faster... and God she was so beautiful when she was angry, face flushing, eyes narrow, glowing green. A shiver ran down his spine, and he smiled to himself. He loved her dearly and would do right by her... and the child.

Looking out on the ice, he thought how much he hated Europa, hated being trapped in steel cages for months on end.

In the silence of their quarters, the air vents hushing in the walls, he fell into his imagination, a simple house with white walls and broad, latticed windows, bamboo flooring and a dog. They'd live near the ocean and go for walks on the sand, the crab grass rough and spiking at their legs. The fresh breeze would swirl through her long hair as she held her rounded belly.

"When we get out of here," he said to himself, "I'm going to take her to the ocean and sit on the beach and watch the waves for a week."

He put his lab coat on and walked out the door.

...

"What the hell?" Simons said as Leif entered the Ice-Core Lab.

Leif glared at the young man. Phillip Simons found something to gripe about every day. At twenty-two and fresh out of college, he was an intelligent kid who'd had an easy life before coming here. If life on Europa station had been difficult for Leif, it had been much harder on Simons.

"You left the freezer door open yesterday."

"What?" Leif had done no such thing.

"The damn freezer door to the core samples."

"The main freezer?" Leif felt a shock rush through him as he imagined water dripping from the long core cases, all the mission's physical specimens lost. There would be hell to pay... but the main freezer had temperature alarms and backups. Those specimens were worth the cost of the mission.

"Not the main freezer." Phillip sat down, his shoulders hunching as he appeared to resign himself. "That would be the end of us. I don't think they'd even fire us. Probably would just leave us here when everyone else left."

"What melted, Phillip?"

"The samples we sliced yesterday. You left the freezer open."

"The wafer freezer? I didn't leave it open," but even as he said it, Leif doubted himself. He hadn't been thinking clearly in the last few weeks.

"*I* sure as hell didn't, and there are only two of us working here."

Leif held up his hands. "Okay, okay, I'm sorry. It must have been me. I haven't been myself lately. I'll slice new cores and redo the work from yesterday. You can move forward. If I have to work late to make up time, I will."

Phillip pursed his lips, nodded, and returned to his work.

Leif didn't need Phillip's attitude today. He went to the head-high, circular hatch where, on the other side of the thick plate of steel, the rover crews stored the core samples from the drilling operations in

5

a long, narrow airlock. Leif looked through the dish-sized viewport. New sample cores had been delivered.

"Phillip."

"What?"

"Did you know they delivered new cores this morning?"

"No deliveries were scheduled."

"Well, there's new cores in the airlock."

"There shouldn't be." Phillip pushed him aside and looked into the small window. "Hell," he said at having been proven wrong.

Leif walked over to the comm-panel and touched the icon for Coring Operations. The screen went live as Dennis MacAlpine moved into view, his face too close to the camera. "How can I help you Mr. Holt?"

"Hey Dennis. Did you folks deliver new samples this morning?"

"Yes."

"We weren't expecting them."

Dennis looked down. Leif heard fingers tapping on glass. "Yes. I apologize for the lack of warning." He held up a tablet and smiled. "Calling you was on my to-do list."

In the background, Leif caught sight of a beautiful woman, her long, red hair pulled back into a pony tail, which draped down the back of her white lab coat. Sometimes when Leif saw her, he could not believe he was married to her.

"...had an easy drilling session yesterday, so we stored two loads at the door."

"Got it, just wanted to make sure. We'll process them."

Sarah looked over to the screen. Their eyes met as Dennis said, "Check," and the comm-link went dead.

Leif touched the screen where she had stood. He put his head in his hands.

"You okay?" Phillip asked.

Leif looked at him, distrustful of the taciturn young man's caring tone.

One of Phillip's eyes narrowed, "What? I'm not always a prick."

"Know thyself," Leif said with a heartless laugh. He walked over to the airlock. "Sarah and I got into it this morning."

Pressurizing the airlock, he unlatched the door and opened it. As he walked in, the metal-cased cores crusted with a hoar of frost. His breath billowing in the chill air, he looked over the labels. He could already feel himself shivering in the super-cooled air.

"Phillip."

"What?"

"Dammit Phillip, just come over here."

"Jeeze. All right, man. I'm comin'. Don't take it out on me."

"Don't...? Are you—look, just gear up and bring me gloves and a coat. I need help bringing these in."

In a few moments, Phillip entered the small space wearing a thick parka. He handed Leif a similar coat and fat, mitten-style gloves. Sliding past Leif, he walked down to the end of the airlock, inspecting the far ends of the sample tubes.

"They didn't cap this one right." He twisted the cap with his gloved hands. It popped free. "Shit," Phillip said as the cap fell in the low gravity.

When the cap hit the floor, it rang out, and the floor began to shake. The walls rumbled. As Leif stared at the cores, shuddering under their straps, he tried to understand how the cap falling had caused the airlock to— The floor pitched and threw him into the sample tubes. With no gloves on yet, when his wrist touched the metal, it stuck.

A horrific cracking sound was followed by a hiss of air. Leif yanked his wrist free, tearing flesh away. In the lab, the air went white with mist as the area depressurized. The mist began flushing out the main doors. His ears popped. Jumping to the hatch, he punched the emergency-close switch, immediately frost-biting two of his knuckles. The airlock door slammed shut just as the walls, ceiling, and floor bucked sideways. Hard coldness cracked his head, and the metal walls went black.

...

When Leif came to, he felt weightless, which wasn't right. The gravity of Europa was light requiring frequent exercise and bone density training, but not this... not nothing.

A hand gripped him, turned him. Leif found himself facing Phillip, his face full with weightlessness.

Leif gripped the tough outer fabric of Phillip's parka. "What happened? Was there an explosion in the lab?"

His mind searched for where Sarah would have been. She was on the other side of the installation. At least five pressure doors stood between her and them. *She's fine.*

Phillip shook his head. "Not the lab."

Leif, dizzy from the weightlessness and a possible concussion, reached for a wall handle to turn himself. Before he could grip it, Phillip snatched Leif's bare hand away and slid a glove over it.

"Thanks."

Phillip nodded.

Gripping the handle, Leif felt coldness coming through the glove as he pulled himself to the viewport he'd stood on the other side of a few moments before. It should have been glowing with lab lights, but he saw only a black wall filled with stars and something glittering.

Pulling himself closer, he peered through the port. To the right, almost out of view, hung Europa, several miles away and shrinking. They were in orbit. As the airlock rotated, the moon's icy surface slid out of view to the right. In the new darkness, thousands of pieces of twisted metal glinted among chunks of ice ranging in size from pebbles to high-rise buildings. The viewport gradually rotated away from the wreckage. The distant spark of the sun drifted by followed by the hulk of Jupiter, its broad and dominating bands filling the port. It seemed impossible they wouldn't simply fall into it. When Europa came back into view, what Leif saw caused his jaw to go slack.

The surface had a long gash in it. At the end of the gash, a long, black ship with sleekly bladed lines shot a dazzling-green beam into Europa's ice. The impact of the beam sent up billowing clouds of vaporized water. Melting and boiling in the vacuum, it refroze in a crystalline fog, which caught the faint sunlight in glittering rainbows. The ship, the shape of a scimitar turned blade up, seemed a dark, faceless thing with no visible bridge nor windows.

"What is that?"

But even as the question escaped him, he knew the answer.

As the moon moved to the right in the viewport, Leif saw small ships begin to emerge from the front third of the large ship. Swooping around, they caught chunks of ice with mandible-like hooks and drew the blocks back toward the large ship.

He looked to Phillip. "They're mining ice?"

"What?" Phillip shoved him aside and looked out the port. "Yeah, it looks that way."

Leif's eyes scanned along the ice to where the base had been anchored. The only evidence of it having been there was a single rover, lying overturned beside the dark, seemingly bottomless canyon.

As the airlock turned away from Europa, Leif's view passed again over the field of wreckage. His gaze caught the roofline of the analysis lab where he'd seen Sarah walk by Dennis MacAlpine's camera. As it turned, the internal ceiling, tiles missing in a haphazard checkerboard, came into view. He understood with absolute finality that his quick glimpse of her over Dennis' shoulder had been his last. He closed his eyes and tried to remember every detail, the slight curve of her neck where it met her jaw, the delicate arc of her chin, her hair coming off the back of her head and caressing the lab coat between her shoulders. Grief rose up in him, and knowing it would be too much to face, he shoved it down. The terror at having lost her bored itself into his chest, cutting his heart in half as he swallowed it down.

"There's one, blinking light," Phillip said. "It's a survival pod."

Leif opened his eyes, scanned the wreckage, and caught the red pulse at the far side of the field. The base had housed 106 scientists.

The odds of the pod holding Sarah were remote, but he found himself staring at the strobing light with a will. It would be sending out an assistance signal. Help might reach it. Ships must be nearby.

The airlock viewport rotated away from the wreckage again, passed the sun, Jupiter, and back to Europa. Two additional monstrous ships, the same as the first, had come to fly to the right and left of the first. They had begun cutting their own canyons in the ice. Three great canyons, as if gouged by monstrous claws, grew across the surface. They would scar the moon's ice for millennia. As the bright curve of the moon slid away, the debris field came into view again along with the red flashing light of the survival pod. Something dark arced through the wreckage toward the pod. His eyes caught one… now two… and three small ships.

The ships curved around the section of roof where Sarah had worked, their nose cones and fuselages bristling with blasts from directional jets. Their main engines, glowing redly, faded to deep blue as they slowed in their approach of the pod. Blazing-white blasts struck out from under the nose cones of each ship. The pod blew apart in a magnesium-white flare, which snuffed out immediately in the vacuum of space.

Leif closed his eyes.

Phillip, who'd been peering over his shoulder, said, "They can't see us because we don't have a power source. That'll save us."

"Yeah, but without a power source, we have no air, no heat." He looked at the thermometer on the wall. "It's already negative fifty degrees Fahrenheit and dropping fast."

"Good thing I got these coats and gloves," Phillip said as he pulled the thick hood over his head.

"Those won't do us any good at negative three hundred and fifty, Phillip," Leif said as he pulled his own hood on. The skin of his face felt brittle, and his nostril hairs froze together as he inhaled. When he drew air through his mouth, ice crystals formed on the roof of his palate, and his molars ached. With only lab-duty scrub pants on his legs, the cold etched its way into the flesh of his thighs, cooling his groin.

"What should we do?" Phillip asked, sincere worry in his voice. "We'll be out of air in a few hours."

"We're going to be all right, Phillip," Leif said as he pushed off the wall. He didn't for a moment believe that everything was going to be all right, but he wasn't about to let the younger man become frantic. Drifting over to a panel with the word HEATED stenciled across it, Leif unlatched it and drew out two candy-green cylinders with O_2 written in large white letters on their sides. The bottles still held the warmth of the insulated compartment. He looked into the compartment. Six more bottles.

"Emergency supplies," he said to Phillip as he pushed one of the bottles over to him. Pulling open another panel, he found four bottles of water. "We have water." He floated one of the liter bottles over to Phillip. "Put that under your coat right now, so it won't freeze."

"What's the point?" Phillip asked. "We'll be frozen in a few more minutes." He held up the water bottle Leif had tossed to him. "It's already crystallizing, look."

Tendrils of ice crawled across the inside of the Lexan bottle.

"Get it under your coat."

"What's the damn point Leif?"

Leif pushed away and caught Phillip by the front of his coat. His face a few inches from Phillip's, he said in a calm voice, "Phillip, here's the point. We can simply let ourselves die, or we can try to live. If we try, we might succeed… or not. Would you rather die trying or die giving up?"

"Dead is dead."

Leif brought a sternness to his voice he didn't honestly feel. "Think of everything you've ever done in your life, every meal you've eaten, every heartbeat. This might be the last moment of your life. How do you want to live it?"

Phillip looked at the bottle for a moment, nodded, and stuck it up under his coat, wincing with the coldness of it.

Leif reached deeper into the cabinet and felt soft nylon. He pulled out the dark-red bundle of a cold-temp survival bag. The rush of success brought Sarah to mind as though his subconscious wanted to dash his hopes.

"Don't think about her," he said to himself. "Not right now."

"What?"

"Nothing, just get into this." Leif pushed the survival bag over to Phillip. Half folded and weightless, it twirled end over end to Phillip, who caught it, and pulled it open—its mirrored interior crinkling. He slid his legs into the long, pillowed sheath. Leif pushed a second water bottle over to him, and four of the eight bottles of oxygen. Phillip took each one. As Leif breathed in, the ice crystals on the roof of his mouth no longer melted fully with his exhalations, and his fingers felt stiff in the gloves. His groin ached with the cold, and the skin of his legs had gone numb. The airlock temperature now showed below negative seventy, the needle sliding quickly downwards. Dizziness fuzzed his thoughts, and he understood the oxygen in the room was already running low.

He pulled himself into the bag, clumsily holding the wall and took his two bottles of water and four oxygen bottles with him.

"What do we do if we have to pee?" Phillip asked through his oxygen mask, only his face exposed now.

"No matter what you do Phillip, do not open this bag. If you let your heat out, you're dead."

"But what if no one comes?"

"Someone will come."

"How do you know?"

"The only thing that's going to keep us alive is hope, Phillip," Leif said as he slid his oxygen mask over his face and zipped the bag up, leaving only his face exposed. "You think any other way and you're already gone. You understand me?"

Phillip nodded and zipped himself into the dark-red cocoon of pillowed nylon. Leif could hear the young man breathing through his oxygen mask in slow draws. Leif took one last look at the thermometer, negative eighty now, and pulled the zipper of the bag closed. The efficient insulation immediately began to warm with his body heat. The air in the darkness became quickly stagnant, and he felt his mind dulling, as if falling into a dream-state. Pulling the gloves from his hands, he followed the tube from his mask down to the cylinders tucked around his legs and twisted the valve open just enough to keep him alive. As he breathed in the dry air, clarity came to his mind.

Floating in darkness, castaway in orbit around the Jovian system, he finally allowed thoughts of his wife to well up and haunt him.

CHAPTER 2

Navy Special Warfare Commander Stacy Zack approached the war room in a wonderful mood. Her team had completed a week-long training maneuver with perfect scores. She'd never worked with as skilled and dedicated a group and understood she was probably living in the days she would later consider the pinnacle of her military career. The pressure sensitive electromagnetic plates in her zero-G boots clicked as they locked down and released from the decking. The carbon fiber calf supports kept her legs slightly bent allowing her to push herself forward into the next step.

When she entered the war room, Commander Adam Roth nodded to her and pointed to Captain Sharon Driskgill, who stood with her arms crossed scowling at the Navigation-Control console. On the Nav-Con's four-foot, circular base, lay the holographic crown of Europa, the image as clear as though the moon had been scaled-down and mounted in the floor. Three razor-thin scars grew across it.

Stacy came to attention a few feet away from Captain Driskgill, whom she had yet to meet in person as the captain had taken command of the Rhadamanthus only five days earlier.

After several minutes of silence, Driskgill, who wore her blonde hair as strictly short as her reputation, looked to Stacy with ice-blue eyes.

"Commander Zack?"

Stacy saluted. "Yes, sir."

Driskgill's almost soulless eyes searched Stacy's face as the Captain, fulfilling her reputation, said, "You don't have the appearance of an effective war commander Zack. Your frame is too slight, and," her tone became somewhat mocking, "those pretty, auburn eyes will distract the men."

Stacy drew a slow, temper-cooling breath.

Another captain, another chance to prove someone wrong.

Still, she'd grown tired of the seemingly endless need to prove people wrong.

"The men on my team know if they get distracted by anything, I'll kick their ass, sir."

A hint of a smile pulled a crease into the corner of Driskgill's mouth. She looked back to the image of Europa. "We have a situation I need your thoughts on commander."

Only then did the fact Driskgill had said *war* commander strike her.

Sweeping her hand into the holographic image, Driskgill moved the moon aside. The space above the obsidian black disk of the Nav-Con filled with glittering debris. Driskgill tapped her index finger into the dark space, and the image retracted. Now Stacy could see the debris field in relation to the moon.

"What is that debris from?"

"That is what remains of Europa base."

A cold shock ran through Stacy's shoulders to the small of her back. "What the hell caused it?"

Captain Driskgill swept her hand again. Europa rushed forward, the image centering on the end of the long claw marks. Three dark shapes hung over the moon, throwing long shadows. Brilliant-green energy beams lanced from under the ships' prows into the ice. Where the beams touched down, great plumes of pulverized ice and freezing vapor exploded upward. Small ships arced around collecting larger icebergs.

As Stacy leaned over the image, she did her best to keep the stark fear she felt from her voice. "Please tell me that's not them."

"Unfortunately, as far as we can tell… it is. They match the descriptions from the war. Analysts at the time had assumed the energy beams used to break Demos in half, had been a weapon. Now we might be looking at mining."

"Mining."

Stacy hadn't intended it to be a question, but still Captain Driskgill said, "Yes."

"Are you suggesting we're not considering them hostile?"

"Not at all commander. Our guests have clearly hostile intentions." Driskgill drew her finger across the open air above the Nav-Con, pulling a video frame with it. She tapped it, and the video went live. It was of an escape pod rolling end over end. As the pod rotated a red light pulsed at one end along with the sound of the emergency transponder's pinging radio frequency. Small black shapes came through the wreckage, bearing down on the pod. With a flare of light, the pod scattered into indistinguishable flack.

"Was there anyone in that pod?"

"Three distinct heart signals."

Stacy forced away the intense reaction that brought on by centering her mind on her job. "How do you imagine my team helping in this situation?"

"I need you to do a recovery."

Stacy stared at the blackness where the pod had been. "If they're dead, what's our recovery?"

"We've detected two more heart signals in the wreckage."

"Another survival pod?"

"Fortunately for them, no." Driskgill swept the video frame aside. She tapped the debris field, zooming the image in on a cigar-shaped structure, ragged at one end with a section of wall still hanging from it.

Stacy leaned forward, squinting, "What is that?"

"That, Commander, is an airlock."

"An airlock?"

"Yes. That's the source of the heart signals. These two must have been in the airlock at the time of destruction."

"They sealed themselves in."

"Europa base schematics suggest the airlock was stocked with emergency supplies, which explains why they haven't frozen to death or run out of air. Even so, they can't have much time left. We need to get to them quickly."

"I'm assuming this isn't just altruism."

"Not at all. We wouldn't risk your team and an unknown reaction for two lives." She pointed at the airlock. "However, we need to know what they know, specifically what happened in the moments before the attack. That makes them worth saving."

Stacy leaned in on the image again, "May I?"

The Captain held out her open palm as permission.

Stacy pulled the image back over to the alien ships.

She said to herself, "Three large cruisers, with support transports and fighters. May I see the video of the attack on the life pod again?"

Driskgill brought up the video.

As Stacy watched it, she said, "Fast and precise, but they haven't reacted to the two heart signals in the airlock."

"No. Either they don't care about the heart signals, or they're unable to sense them. I'm assuming, based on the aggression of the life pod attack, they cannot sense them."

"But a heart monitor is a basic instrument."

Driskgill shrugged, "Technologies develop differently."

"So the only way to go in," Stacy said, "is dark. We hook them up with a sling or a harpoon…"

"You can't risk piercing the airlock."

"Then we use a recovery net. Scoop it out of orbit. We have to carry enough momentum to come from the dark side there," she pointed beyond the curve of Europa, "orbit past the airlock, securing it as we pass, and freefall back around to the dark side before powering up and leaving."

Captain Driskgill smiled. "This is precisely why I asked for you, commander."

Stacy let the compliment fall unacknowledged. Whether the captain believed in her or whether she was capable or not did not enter in. For the first time in her career, she was facing war. She'd give it everything she had. "May I begin preparations?"

"Yes, what is your ETD?"

"15 minutes, sir," Stacy said as she walked away.

Captain Driskgill asked after her, "Is there anything specific you need from us?"

Stacy stopped at the hatch. "My team? No. What we all need is for someone to contact Jeffrey Holt."

"Jeffrey Holt?" Driskgill asked. "Who the hell is that?"

"He's a Hammerhead," Stacy said and left the room.

CHAPTER 3

Jeffrey Holt sat cross-legged on the back of a Mitsubishi asteroid miner eating a sandwich, unwilling to face what his life had become. The ship's rear thrusters towered to his left and right like massive haunches. Ahead, its sun-shining back stretched away in a broad, titanium plane, buckled halfway down from the force of the crash. A scent similar to burnt copper wires drifted by now and again on a capricious breeze. Beyond the ship's smashed prow, the salt-crusted dirt of the lakebed ran out to the mountains, which stood in clear relief against the pale-blue sky. It was rare to have no heat waves. In the cool, spring air stark shadows reached deep into the ravines.

Finishing his sandwich, he smacked the crumbs off his hands, stood, and turned to the gorilla, which sat hunkered down behind him. As he walked to it, his boots clanged on the back of the leviathan ship, which had been retired after thirty years of service.

Entering the shade under the gorilla, he climbed the ladder into the cab. Leaning into the back pad, he strapped himself in with the five-point harness. When he hit the close-cab switch, the doors swung shut with a thump, enveloping him in darkness. As he pulled on his VR goggles, the exterior cameras went active. As if a few inches from his face, one of the Gorilla's forearms came into view, a bullet scar across the paint directly in the camera's line of sight. Jeffrey could hardly believe it had been a decade since he and Stacy had survived the firefight in the gorilla. While the machine showed no signs of slowing down, he did. With his metal spine, modified vascular, muscular, and nervous system, he still felt strong and mentally sharp, but his life had gone still as though a windless lake in the twilight of his life. He'd never remarried. Working alone in the heart of Nevada hamstrung his social life. Now with Leif and Sarah hundreds of millions of miles distant on Europa, his house—even on weekends—was a quiet place he didn't care to be.

He went through the start up sequence. The gorilla stood, arms dropping away from the cameras. The broken back of the ship descended. Slipping on his gloves with the metal rings around each finger-joint, he put his hands on his hips. The gorilla mimicked him.

Where do I start on this beast?

While the Mitsubishi had come down yesterday, he'd spent the morning coordinating the final shipments of raw materials out of the scrap yard. The last ship had a large sphere at the fore and a brick of thrusters to the aft connected by a long, fragile body. The thing had come down sideways and blown apart into thousands of pieces. It had taken him far longer than expected to clean it up. Not that he complained. It meant he could work until the sun dipped below the western mountains and come out on Saturdays. Now he had this solid beast to rip down. At seventy years old, Jeffrey had Leif bugging him to retire, but from what? Demolition? Never. Aside from hope for Sarah and Leif's future, this was all he had.

But he couldn't spend time feeling sorry for himself. It had never been his way. The demolition of the miner called for removing the thrusters intact for repurposing. Everything else was to be broken down and recycled.

As he took a step, the foot plates in the cab went active, simulating the surface movement below the gorilla. He walked over to an engine nacelle. "Gorilla, kneel."

The gorilla knelt and tore into the skin of the ship at the base of the thruster. The titanium peeled away as if made from brittle lead exposing structural mounts beneath. He threw the strip of metal aside before repeating the motion with the gorilla's other hand.

"Gorilla, stand."

The gorilla stood, and he walked down several feet.

"Gorilla, kneel."

He tore another line of metal sheathing away, repeated the procedure all the way down both thrusters.

"Cutter," he said. The gorilla's right hand fell backward at the wrist, and a metal bar extended. When he pulled his finger in a trigger motion, blue plasma arced along the cutter's edge. He touched it to the first structural mount, and metal spattered away. When he shut the cutter off, he heard a rumbling. He looked at the deck of the ship, but the rumbling seemed to come from a distance. He looked to the mountains, but the sound didn't come from out there, it came from high up. He listened to the deep rumbling. Not Jet turbines. That was nuclear drive plates.

It had been ten years since he'd had unscheduled visitors. He thought of Stacy, now an eleven year veteran of Special Warfare. The last time he'd seen her she'd been confident, powerful, and unquestionably in charge. He felt a great deal of pride in who she'd become, but had to admit that he missed those last vestiges of the unsure little girl that had lived in her. While she hadn't grown into arrogance, she was now fully aware of her capabilities both mentally and physically. Small doubts can be endearing, and she seemed to have none. But she had become a strong woman, and Jeffrey could want nothing less for her.

As the rumbling grew louder now punctuated by heavy thuds, a dark point in the clear-blue sky grew into an orbital re-entry vehicle, the red glow of descent fading from the black tiles along its belly. Jeffrey's eyes followed the craft down as its nuclear drive shut down and liquid hydrogen/oxygen stabilization rockets lanced out with a faint blue light, shifting left and right. Landing skids extended from its belly. As it touched down about a three hundred feet away, the craft vanished in a cloud of salt-dust.

Kicking fresh footholds into the side of the ship, he climbed the gorilla down. As he walked over to the lander, which had set down sideways to Jeffrey, its rear ramp dropped open. A pair of gray and black fatigue-clad legs stepped out on the descending ramp. The hips became visible, the arms and chest, and finally a weathered face and gray hair. Sam Cantwell.

He's retired. What's he doing wearing BDU's and riding on a Navy re-entry vehicle?

He suspected he didn't want the question answered.

"Gorilla, shut down."

As the gorilla powered down, he pulled out his earpieces and removed the VR goggles from his head. In the darkness of the cab he smacked the glowing, green cab-close switch. The cab doors opened, flooding the space with shadowed sunlight. Jeffrey climbed down the ladder to the crunching dirt of the lakebed and stepped out from under the gorilla.

Walking toward him, Cantwell lifted his hand in simple greeting. He didn't smile, which was usual for the taciturn admiral. Under his arm, he carried a flat bundle. Jeffrey met him on the open lakebed.

"Sam, how are you?"

Cantwell nodded as a response to the pleasantry before saying, "You told me if they ever came back, you'd sign up and fight." He held out the bundle, a dark-gray Navy uniform.

A horrific rush rose up through Jeffrey's chest and pressurized the blood in his neck and face. Drawing a breath, he exhaled hard, puffing out his cheeks, and took the uniform from Cantwell, its fabric pressed and smooth.

Cantwell put his hand on Jeffrey's shoulder. "I'm sorry."

Jeffrey smiled against a sudden hopelessness. "I have the distinct impression, thanks to political pressure from conspiracy theorists, we're drastically unprepared for this."

Cantwell nodded.

Jeffrey said, "That means we die."

Cantwell's expression remained flat. "Then we die fighting."

Jeffrey nodded. "I'm fine with that, but I'm not shaving my beard."

Cantwell let out a slight laugh.

Jeffrey pointed his thumb to the gorilla. "I need to get this thing parked back at—"

"No time." Cantwell turned and walked toward the re-entry vehicle.

As Jeffrey followed, his initial hopelessness cracked. The volcanic pressure of something he hadn't felt in a long time brought Dylan Thomas to his mind.

Rage, rage against the dying of the light... I will and more.

He felt suddenly on fire and glad of the chance to fight for something meaningful one last time.

CHAPTER 4

Stacy stepped through the airlock onto the team's medium-sized transport/fighter, which on the outside, looked very much like its squat, snub-nosed namesake—a warthog. The ship was docked to the Rhadamanthus' gravity drum, its rotation creating a full G at its outer edge. Absorbed in the wonderful sensation of a natural G, Stacy sat in a jump seat next to Jacqueline, who packed bottles and packets into her Kevlar medic's bag.

Jacqueline had the sleeves of her dark-gray jumpsuit rolled up to her elbows, exposing the compass rose tattoo on the inside of her forearm. Her true north, as she called it, as an SW Medic, had come after losing her husband and infant son in a transport crash.

Stacy considered the airlock survivors. Two cocoon-like survival bags floating in the quiet, freezing darkness. She imagined the survivors as gray-haired scientists, perhaps a woman and a man. Today, Jacqueline had the chance to snatch those two from death.

Jacqueline zipped the bag closed. When Stacy had first met the taller woman, her ice-blue eyes had struck her as heartless. However, the woman who rarely smiled had proven to have a deep reverence for life, and a welling of sincerity that Stacy had come to rely on.

Stacy wondered if risking someone like Jacqueline was worth those two survivors. Seven lives for two... two drawing what they most likely considered their final breaths in a metal coffin.

She knew full well that *worth it* didn't factor in.

Their Vehicle Operator, Lieutenant Marco Fields, who once claimed he could fly a horse over short distances, came into the crew area from the cockpit. Stacy had only known one pilot better. Of course, in her mind, no one could outfly Jeffrey Holt. Marco and his generation had none of his modifications, which had facilitated the Hammerheads' victory fifty years ago. She wondered if these visitors to Europa marked the eventual death of Marco and most of his generation of pilots as it had for Jeffrey's.

"Marco," she asked, "Are you ready to keep two people alive?"

His constant smile faded. "I'm there O.C."

As Stacy looked over Jacqueline and Marco, doubt hounded her. Jeffrey had told her many times that no one could fully prepare for the real thing, but Stacy knew this team had trained hard, pushing itself as far as possible without killing someone. Each member had permanent scars from training. They'd get it done.

"Let's wait until the rest of the team is here," she said. "I only want to go over it once."

Lieutenant Xavier Riley, or X as everyone called him, bent his tall, thin frame to come through the hatch. His wide eyes, which held Stacy's for a moment as he sat, regarded the world with a hawk-like depth and clarity, looking in all ways the perfect fit for his sniper specialty.

As was his way, he sat in silence, nodding once to her. When Marco punched him in the shoulder, X put the tip of his index finger to Marco's temple and curled his middle finger in a trigger pulling motion.

Only Spacewalk Specialist Adanna Hammersmith and Demolitions and Breech Master Horace Sixtro remained absent.

Stacy looked to each member. When each avoided her gaze, she asked, "Where are they?"

X kept his eyes on the floor as Marco looked to Jacqueline. Jacqueline found something to adjust on her medical kit.

In a seething tone, Stacy asked, "Are you serious?" In her heart though, she wasn't surprised. She'd noticed the looks between the two over the last several months, looks which she'd dismissed as they suggested an impossibility. The player Horace and the frigid Adanna were as unlikely a match as fire and water. When they first began working together, they gave every indication of mutual hatred.

Running footfalls came clanging down the corridor. Horace, of average build and average size, jumped through the airlock out of breath. Adanna came in right behind him. She ran her fingers through her regulation-short hair, smoothing it.

Stacy stood and glared at them. "Really?"

They squared their shoulders at attention and locked their eyes on the far wall.

"We don't have time for this," Stacy said as she walked over to the hatch, swung it shut, and sealed it. She'd rip them down later. Right now, the team needed to go live.

"Sit down," she said, letting her lack of approval show in her tone. Looking over the six members of her team, she said, "The Europa base has been destroyed by unknown ships." She gave that a moment to sink in. Their quick looks to each other and slight widening of eyes let her know the news hadn't reached general population. "Three ships, approximately the size of Lacedaemon-class destroyers, are cutting canyons in the surface of the moon with high-energy beams. They appear to be mining ice. The base destruction may or may not have been intentional."

"Are they hostile?" Adanna asked.

"Definitely." She told them about the survival pod's destruction and the airlock.

Horace asked, "Are these... *them?*"

"That's... undetermined. There aren't a lot of people left alive who can visually identify the invaders and almost all images are highly classified. Our higher-ups haven't released them yet."

"Jeffrey Holt would know," Marco said. "He was in dog fights right next to their destroyers."

Stacy stared at him for a moment, letting him know this wasn't a game to get excited about. When she saw his shoulders drop slightly she said, "I agree, we need Holt, and I've told the higher-ups as much, but he's on Earth. We need to act now."

She could see questions forming in their eyes, but they kept their mouths shut and ears open.

"The survivors should be frozen or asphyxiated by now," Jacqueline said.

"I agree, but they're not. Two heartbeats are still detected by orbital sensors."

"Interesting," X said, leaning forward. "They must be in survival bags with a portable oxygen source, but what about radiation?"

"The airlock was built for use on the surface of Europa," Stacy said. "It has as much radiation exposure in orbit as it had on the surface. Its design should offer adequate shielding, but we still don't have much time to get to them. If we hadn't been here in IO's orbit, they'd have no chance. The next closest cruiser is orbiting Saturn, four days away."

"What advantages do we have?" Adanna asked.

"The aliens appear unconcerned with life forms or are unable to detect them. We assume they'd have sought out the airlock otherwise. The power source or the transmitter from the life-pod seems to be what triggered them." She summarized the plan to fly by without power.

Horace asked, "How much time do we have?"

"Unknown. They could run out of whatever resources are sustaining them at any moment. If the heart signals stop, we abort."

"That's going to be quite a fly by," Marco said.

"You think it's doable?" Stacy asked.

For the first time since she'd met him, she saw doubt in his eyes even as he said, "No problem O.C. I've got this."

"I don't need B.S. Marco. I need reality. If you think you can't do it, we abort."

"You want the truth?" Marco leaned his head back against the wall, sounding irritated by his own self-doubt. "I won't be able to tell you until we've come through it, so let's get out there and find out. But we can't go fully dark. X's gunnery systems must be powered."

"I only need power for the gunnery chair and trigger mechanism," X said.

"What about VR?" Marco asked.

27

"Don't want it."

Marco looked at X as though he were stupid. "You mean to tell me you're going to hit an object at a velocity delta of 1000 miles an hour *manually?*"

"Yes," X said flatly, as if it were nothing more than brushing his teeth.

"Okay then," Marco said as though he had no idea how to cope with the claim.

"We're running out of time," Stacy said. "Marco, get us separated and target-bound."

"Yes, O.C." He moved to a mini Nav-Con and tapped its dark base. A three-dimensional hologram of the Jovian system appeared, the banded sphere the size of a pea floating above the dark glass. The moons lay in a long chain of diamond-sparks around the planet. Even at that small size the moons extended beyond the range of the Nav-Con's viewer. On the dark side of the planet lay Io, it's sulfur-yellowed light contrasting with the brilliant white of icy Europa on the far side of the system.

Marco slid his finger along the glass causing a red line to leap away from Io, curve around behind Jupiter, and run away into open space.

Marco slid his finger along the line, turning the red to blue until it moved inward and curled around Europa. He pointed to the place where the flight path changed from red to blue. "If we begin deceleration here and go dark here…" the line went white and shifted to fall short of Europa. He adjusted the acceleration and deceleration times until the arc intersected with Europa again. It now pinned straight into the center of the moon.

"That's not gonna work, Fields," Horace said.

"I damn well know that," Marco said without looking up from the console. He increased the burn time until the line shifted back into a circular orbit.

"Our relative airlock flyby velocity will be…" he leaned over the read-outs, "1,000 miles an hour." He shook his head. "That's too fast. If we snatch it at that speed, we'll grease the people inside."

"We'll have to use a net pack," X said. "Hooks could pierce the sides, and a single line could collapse it. I don't trust the strength of that structure."

"Can you go slower?" Stacy asked.

Marco entered more information into the Nav-Con. The path shifted, again, pinning into the center of the moon. He made another adjustment. It missed the moon and dropped into Jupiter's broad bands. He returned it to wrap into an orbit again and shook his head. "No, we've got no hope of a slower flyby if we have to do it dark."

"We'll use a decelerating trailing-link then." X said.

Marco turned to look at the sniper with disbelief. "At a thousand miles an hour delta, X? No one can hit that with a net pack."

"I can," X said, and unlike Marco's claim, Stacy saw no doubt in X's clear, hazel eyes. He walked to the far side of the cabin, opened a panel, and slid out a knee-high spool of black cord. He unwound some of the pencil-thin line and held it up. It glittered in dark blues and purples in the bright light as if its surface were mica.

"If I use a free-fall bungee," X said as he slid the cord through his fingers, "it will absorb the extra energy and release it in an uncontrollable manner, shooting them either into us or past us." He unhooked the end of the spool and drew the line out. "Shooting past us in that mess of debris, they could easily hit something. Right now they're relative to the debris. When we change their course and speed, they could easily encounter collisions. We have to bring them out in a controlled manner behind us, so we clear debris for them." He held up the luminous line. "This is made from synthesized spider silk." It bent liquidly in his fingers. "As tough as a steel cable six times thicker, yet it's soft and pliable. With this as my trailing line on an air-bearing deployment system, I can make the shot."

Stacy took the end of the cord, sliding its cool softness through her fingers. "Okay, so how do we deploy the net?"

X said, "We'll have to use the standard rocket pack to vector and deploy the net. As we pull away," X held up the cord, "I keep this playing out, slowly putting the brakes on the spool, speeding up the target and giving the folks inside a somewhat smooth acceleration up to our speed."

"That's not going to be easy to pull off," Stacy said.

X shrugged. "Those folks are as good as home already." He looked over Stacy's shoulder. "Marco…"

Marco lifted his chin in acknowledgement.

"Get me as close as you can. I'll net it and bring them home."

A slightly doubtful scowl formed on Marco's face as he said, "I'll get you close…" He fell silent, but Stacy could see he wanted to say more. She felt the same thing. …*but there's no way you're going to make that shot.*

X lifted the spool onto its side and rolled it to the back of the cabin to the gunnery chair hatch in the floor. He opened the hatch, climbed down, and drew the spool in after him like a squirrel loading an oversized nut into the hollow of a tree.

"When do we need to launch?" Stacy asked Marco.

Marco turned back to the Nav-Con, tapped it a few times, and looked back to her. "We have to be en route in seven minutes."

"Let's get locked and loaded folks," Stacy said clapping her hands together. The other members of the team moved to the jump seats as Marco walked into the cockpit. As Stacy strapped herself in, she felt the docking couplers let go, freeing the warthog from the gravity drum.

Stacy braced herself as the flipping weightlessness came to her belly and shoulders and her feet floated free of the floor. No matter how many times she experienced it, she hated the first few seconds of nerve-thrilling weightlessness. Eyes closed, she let her breath out slowly as she tugged her harness tighter.

"You're not having trouble with the weightlessness are you O.C.?"

Turning to the voice, she found Horace giving her a ribbing smile.

"Apparently screwing a teammate keeps you from feeling the weightlessness so bad," she said to him, keeping her eyes flat. Horace paled as she heard Jacqueline chuckle from across the cabin.

The genuine hurt in the consummate player's expression surprised her. Perhaps Horace felt more for Adanna than she'd guessed.

Despite the moment, Stacy couldn't contain herself. "I don't need shit like this right now." She looked to Adanna, whose eyes dropped to the floor. "You both know that. We're up for review. A lot of eyes are on us, and you two are playing grab ass behind my back."

"There're a lot of men and women on the Rhadamanthus to blow off steam with. I mean what the hell?" But even as she said it, she understood that somehow the frosty Adanna and the hustler in Horace had gravitated into something that neither had experienced before, and it had been powerful enough to risk their positions on the team.

Horace said, "O.C., I just want to say that I wouldn't put my career at risk over something casual—"

A faint smile flickered on Adanna's lips.

"I don't damn well want to hear it right now, Horace," Stacy said, regretting having brought it up at all. "One of you is going when we get back, but…" Stacy let her frustrated anger fade, "I'm glad it wasn't just a casual fling."

When Stacy looked to Adanna, an uncharacteristically bashful smile crossed the young woman's face. "It hasn't been casual for months O.C."

Stacy shook her head. "Months? Wonderful." She looked at the other team members. They all looked away. Her accusing tone mixed with disbelief, she said, "You all knew." Before anyone could speak, she held up a hand. "I don't want to hear another word."

CHAPTER 5

Drifting in darkness, Leif bumped into something yielding, which he assumed to be Phillip, and floated back into nothingness. He could feel the cold, now surely nearing negative two hundred Celsius, leaching the heat from him. He turned the valve on his oxygen slightly, and the extra air, tinged with the fresh-vinyl smell of the soft-edged mask, allowed his body to warm itself.

More comfortable, his mind wandered again to Sarah. He recalled her green eyes, beautiful even in the final storm. Their argument had been such a foolish waste of that last moment. If only he'd known. If only he hadn't been so stupid about... What they'd argued about, forgotten in the heat of the moment, came back to him like a sledgehammer. A baby... a son or daughter... gone. He would never know what sort of child it would have been. Bold like his father? Quiet like him? Tears filled his eyes, pooling in the zero G. Wiping them away, he shoved the thoughts of the child out. His subconscious, seemingly intent on torturing him, brought him to the first moment he'd been captured by her storm-sea eyes. Such a fierce beauty. So sincerely herself.

His first day at MIT, two months after leaving the Army, he walked among the boisterous eighteen-year-olds wishing he'd chosen to live off-campus. He felt out of place in the pine-cleaner and sunscreen scented hallway. Reaching his assigned room, he pushed the door open. A tall young man, whose angled, gangly features would one day be considered ruggedly handsome, stood in the center of the small space.

He held out his hand. "I'm Ian."

Leif shook his hand, only then noticing a woman with pale skin and long, red hair sitting at one of the two desks.

Ian indicated the woman with his thumb, "That's my sister, Sarah."

As she turned to look at him, her hair drew over her shoulder, catching the light as if liquefied fire, silk infused with magma. When the illuminating heat of her jade-green eyes caught his, he knew he'd love her the rest of his life.

"She's a chem sophomore," Ian said with the dismissive tone of a younger brother.

Leif, feeling as though he didn't have the strength to stand, faltered onto the bare mattress. He'd long since forgotten what he'd said to her. He did, however, remember every detail of her, every shift and expression in those first few moments. His heart had hammered in his chest. It was as though he'd never seen a beautiful woman before that moment.

The day after he met her, he saw her walking hand in hand with an athletic man. As they parted ways, she kissed him on his unshaven cheek. Witnessing that small peck, Leif felt a crushing hopelessness. After a few agonizing days, he swore to himself he would put her out of his mind. It was an oath he failed to keep within a few moments.

On an early December night, as he left the physics department in the dark, his breath billowing in the cold air, he saw her walking across the courtyard. Snow-scented wind gusted her hair behind her. He jogged to catch up with her, and as he approached, she turned on him, her eyes wary.

"Hey," he'd said, "where are you going by yourself in the dark?" and felt as though it was the creepiest thing he'd ever said.

When she saw who he was, she smiled politely and said, "I'm going to my boyfriend's place."

Leif held out his arm, desperate to put her at ease. "We best make sure you get there safely then."

As she shoved his arm aside, her smile became a bit more sincere. She walked on.

He ran a few steps to catch up with her. As he walked with her, he stole glances at the curve of her hip and the delicate shape of her shoulders and scarf-wrapped neck. He could think of nothing to say.

The gusting wind flushed her hair around her face, and she drew it away from her lips with nimble fingers. With each step, with every word she spoke, his heart quickened until it pounded in his chest with hope and fear. They'd walked in silence for some time, until he—after glancing at her body again—found her staring at him with darkness in her eyes. He looked quickly to the path ahead.

Her tone now reserved, she asked, "Why did you come to MIT?"

"To study engineering."

"Which discipline?"

"Mechanical mostly, but particle physics will be important."

"Particle physics? Important to what?"

"I want to develop weapons systems."

The look she gave him was exactly why men go into poetry and arts majors; women don't dream of marrying weapons engineers.

She said, "Don't you think there's not much call for weapons these days?"

He nodded. "Yes. As long as they don't come back."

"*They* won't come back."

"I would love for that to be true, but we can't really count on that can we?"

She was silent for a few steps before saying, "No, we can't." Then she sighed, "I suppose even people like you have a place in the world."

People like me.

He considered challenging the comment but, knowing it would do no good, let it go.

They walked along in silence, seeming to have nothing more to discuss. In the gap he felt the urge to talk about his father, to justify his vision for a super-weapon based on the limitations of light speed,

34

which could prevent billions of deaths. He remained silent, afraid talking about his father would come across as bragging.

Instead he settled on, "What do you plan to do with your Chemistry?"

She shrugged, "Not totally sure yet."

He felt that she was the kind of woman who understood herself and what she wanted in life perfectly. In her lack of further discussion, he felt a clear message: she had no interest in him. Standing in dumbfounded silence, he felt something invaluable slipping out of reach.

"My dad was a Hammerhead." It leapt from him the moment his mind touched on it, and he felt like a kid on a playground, chest out, thumbs in armpits, one tooth missing.

She stopped walking. Her eyes narrowed. "Are you messing with me?"

"No."

"I thought they were all dead."

"He's one of the last."

"It's not... Holt?"

He nodded.

"Wait... You're Leif *Holt*?"

He shrugged, but she'd brightened, and in that smile he held his hope close.

"Oh my God," she said covering her mouth with her hands. "How did I not recognize you?" She touched his forearm, and he felt his face flush with that slight contact. "I remember seeing you on TV," she looked him over, and a brilliant smile came finally to her face, "I had a bit of a crush on you."

He thought he might fall over.

She blushed, and covered with, "But I was only sixteen. What do we know at sixteen?"

He let out a quiet laugh in the uncomfortable silence.

She laughed as well, and said, her tone had gone from a position of authority to unsureness, "But look at you now."

But look at me now? What kind of a mess do I look like to her?

"Where'd that skinny kid go? You look more like your father than yourself."

Whether it was a desperate attempt to keep the conversation rolling or the wash of emotions she brought out in him, he said, "I had a bit of a thing for Stacy Zack."

"The special forces woman you saved?"

"Well, I didn't really do the saving, that was my dad's doing."

"That's not how the newsfeeds told it."

Her easy smile returned at that, which made him feel wonderful. "You've seen her. She's a badass. So I started working out in the hopes of catching up to her."

"Did it work?"

He looked down at Sarah's delicate fingers, so much different than Stacy's more compact hands. He laughed with the kind of honest humor one has in the face of reality. "Not in the slightest, but it became a bit of a habit for me, and I stuck with it."

She scowled as she looked him over. "It suits you."

"Too bad you have a boyfriend I suppose." He couldn't believe he'd been bold enough to say it, but having done so, didn't really regret it.

Blushing, she looked away, shrugged, and said, "Well, I better get going."

Chiding himself for speaking so impulsively, he jogged to catch up to her. When he reached her, the look she gave him held renewed distrust.

He said, "I told you I'd walk you, and I will."

"I don't need a protector you know."

"I'm only here to protect you from boredom."

The wit appeared to fall dead on her, but after a time, they returned to simple conversation.

Approaching a gated complex of condominiums, she stopped and said, "Well here we are." She smiled and touched his elbow. "Thanks for walking with me."

A massive fracture of his life rose before him with two very different paths—one with her and one without. His heart pounded in his chest, and his arms and shoulders went light. He felt dizzy.

If you let her walk away from you right now, you'll regret it forever.

He reached out to her, pulled her to him, and kissed her. Her cold, soft lips parted. As the heat of her tongue brushed his, her fingers slid into his hair in tingling trails of nails on skin. For a moment, he experienced nothing save her, not even the ground under his feet.

She shoved him away. Out of the darkness, her hand cracked across his face. The quickness of his heart and the force of the slap caused him to stumble backward. His heel caught on a root, and he fell backward onto the wet grass.

"Bastard," she said through gritted teeth. With her eyes narrowed and lips in a slight snarl, she was even more stunning. She kicked his leg. "Don't ever touch me."

Putting his hands up, he said, "Okay, I'm sorry," and remained seated while she pressed the call box, spoke into it, and the gate clacked open. She glared at him one final time as she walked into the complex.

He made his way home, head down, hands in pockets.

Entering his room, he found Ian standing with crossed arms. "What the hell did you do to Sarah?"

All Leif could think to do was ask, "Why?"

"Why? She called me furious, said you were an asshole. When I asked why, she hung up the phone."

Leif felt sick. "I don't know; I'm sorry. I must have said something, but I didn't—."

"What did you do?"

"Nothing," Leif lied.

Ian stepped up to him, jabbed him in the chest. "Stay away from my sister."

Leif, taller and stronger than Ian, looked back at the door. He wanted to leave in embarrassment. "Okay, no problem, I never meant to do anything wrong. I'll give her all the space in the world. I won't say another word to her."

Ian shouldered past Leif and left the room, slamming the door behind him. Leif, feeling like a damn fool, sat down on his bed and put his face in his hands.

Falling back onto the mattress, he stared at the ceiling. It had been a stupid thing, and yet he considered that it was good to have taken the risk. He regretted making her feel uncomfortable, but now he knew. He didn't have to live his life wondering what could have been if he'd had the nerve. What could have been was what was. Sarah hated him.

He tried to accept that, but for the next several nights he drifted off to sleep thinking about the brush of her tongue on his. When her fingers ran through his hair, there had been a half-second in which she had drawn him to her. But a half-second wasn't enough.

Later in the week, while walking under the bare oaks of the south-quad, his attention on a wet leaf stuck to the toe of his boot, he heard a distant man's voice say, "There's your brother's roommate. Holt, right?"

He looked up to find Sarah, eyes livid, pulling her boyfriend down another path.

As she walked him away from Leif, her boyfriend gave an apologetic wave.

She hadn't told her boyfriend what had happened… but had talked about meeting him. That understanding tortured him as he couldn't understand what it might mean.

A week later Leif sat studying in his room. The sky framed in the window hung in an even slate of gray, darkening as night came on. A knock sounded on the door. Feeling irritated by the interruption, he tossed his tablet onto the bed and opened the door. Sarah stood in the hallway, arms crossed.

His heart raced.

"Is Ian here?" Her eyes leveled flat hate at him.

"No." Leif said trying to keep his eyes off of her, feeling as though he had done her a great wrong, but he couldn't keep himself from stealing glances at her storm-green eyes, and her hair, flustered by the wind.

"Where is he?"

In a quiet, defeated voice, he said, "He went to see a movie."

Her jaw tightened, and her face reddened. With her fury somehow renewed, he felt sure she would strike out at him again. Stepping back, ready to close the door, he said, "I'm really sorry Sarah. I never meant to—"

"To what?" she asked through her teeth as she stepped into the doorway, up close to him, "ruin my fucking life?"

"It was just a kiss."

"Everything was going great for Stephan and me."

Anger awoke in Leif. "I respect that Sarah. I—."

She balled her hands into fists and, looking up to the ceiling, said, "You don't get it, do you?"

"Hey look, this is—"

She shoved him backward, and he fell onto his bed. Kicking the door closed, she locked it and came at him. He held up his hands to protect himself. She caught his wrists, shoved his arms out of her way, and her mouth collided with his, hungry and searching. Her hands tugged at his clothes.

When his Industrial Physics professor asked him how an A student had failed to turn in three weeks worth of work and fallen to an F, he shrugged and said, "I fell in love."

The professor looked over the tops of her glasses. "A broken heart?"

"No, Ma'am, a full one."

She gave him an unsolicited incomplete.

Now Leif, with oxygen tanks as the measure of his life, lay trapped in a frozen cylinder orbiting a Jovian moon. The heat and joy Sarah had brought to his life would never return. The legacy of her in the child was also lost. They'd shared so many wonderful moments.

When he'd first met her, he knew he would love her forever. Just as surely, he knew that allowing her to end her life as he had—balking at the child she offered him—would be his greatest failure.

CHAPTER 6

Cantwell took Jeffrey to Houston where they joined a launch shuttle filled with military leaders and civilian delegates. When Jeffrey stepped aboard, he saw the vice president seated on the right hand side of the passenger area. With her shoulder-length, blonde hair pulled into a loose ponytail and askew bangs framing her graceful face, there was no missing her. Almost as tall as the Marine sitting beside, she held an athletic power in her posture.

As Jeffrey followed Cantwell up the rows of full-body launch seats, he couldn't help glaring at her. He didn't make a practice of holding grudges, but for her he'd make an exception.

When she looked up, their eyes met, and she gave him a disinterested smile before saying something to a thick, balding man with glasses.

As Jeffrey sat, he asked Cantwell in a whisper, "What the hell is she doing here?"

"While there are many women joining us today, I can only assume by your tone you mean Vice President Delaney."

Jeffrey nodded.

"Don't let her bother you. The president asked her to join us."

"He's no better. You know interference by people like them will bring no good."

"I do," Cantwell said with a sigh, "but they're the bosses. You have to take it easy Holt, or you'll give yourself a stroke. This is command life. We have the power of the world's destroyers at our fingertips and yet find ourselves with people like her holding us on a choke chain." He shrugged. "Just remind yourself that restrictions bring humility, which is important."

"You were always better at the ass kissing than I was."

"Dammit Holt. It's not ass kissing."

"So says you. When are you going to give me details on what's going on?"

Cantwell set his tablet face down and leaned his head back. "I suppose now's as good a time as any." He seemed unwilling to begin.

Hesitation from a man he'd never known to waver troubled Jeffrey. "It must be bad."

With a bluntness most surely driven by doubt, Cantwell said, "Europa base has been destroyed."

Jeffrey's hands began to tremble as adrenaline flushed through him. He shook his head.

"I don't understand. That doesn't make any sense."

Cantwell gripped Jeffrey's forearm. "It happened at 8:34 GMT."

As Cantwell walked him through the events, he closed his eyes, trying to remember what Leif had looked like the last time he'd seen him. Instead, the memory of an old Christmas photo came to him— Leif standing beside his mother wearing footie pajamas and holding up a model airplane. His smile was so much a reflection of hers.

In a quiet voice, he said, "I thought they were done taking from me."

"I'm so sorry Jeff."

Jeffrey tried, as he'd done so many times before, to wrap up the turmoil of emotion and shove it down. But it wouldn't settle, so he said in an unsteady voice, "There's no way it's a mining operation."

"Some are suggesting the destruction of Deimos fifty years ago could have been the same—a misunderstanding."

Tears began to well in Jeffrey's eyes, and he breathed deeply trying to quell them. "It wasn't. They cracked the moon in half."

"It's a small moon," Cantwell said flatly. "We attacked before any diplomacy was attempted."

Anger rose up through Jeffrey's sorrow. "You can't seriously—"

Cantwell held up his hand. "I'm not. I just want you to know what we're going to be up against."

As Cantwell told Jeffrey about the destruction of the life pod, Jeffrey's thoughts returned to Leif and Sarah. They'd had no children. In that the Holt line would end. He felt himself going numb. Nearly twenty years ago he'd lost his wife, and before that, so many others in the war. Now his only son... gone. It was the same brutality they'd faced fifty years ago.

He'd known they'd return, and all those who claimed the war had been a lie would be silenced by it. He also knew the return could mark the end of the human race. What he'd never guessed was that his son and Sarah would be among the first casualties of their final war.

Cantwell shoved his arm. "Jeffrey."

"Sorry, I was thinking about the pod."

"I said we have a Special Warfare team retrieving it now."

"The pod?" Jeffery asked, sitting forward, "You said it was destroyed."

"Were you listening at all?"

"No."

A countdown interrupted them as a digital timer on the front wall dropped out of the teens. "...ten...nine...eight..."

Even as part of him was disintegrating in grief, Jeffrey felt a thrill at the prospect of returning to space. He hadn't been off-planet in a long time. Imagining the depth of the stars and the limitless flight paths, he felt homeward bound.

The cabin lurched and vibrated as the huge trident engines far below fired and lifted them from the ground. The pressure in the seat felt familiar and welcome to Jeffrey, almost motherly.

"It's been awhile hasn't it?" Cantwell said to him over the rumble and vibration.

"I did miss it."

Jeffrey wondered for a moment if leaving the military fifty years ago had been the wrong decision. When he thought of the final years with his wife, the moments he'd spent with her before she'd gone and how military life would have cost him most of those, the doubt vanished. He'd lived as best he knew how, and the one thing that mattered most, the solitary evidence he'd been a good man and all the pain had been worth it, was now gone, blown into the black abyss by the same monsters that had taken most of his closest friends. When he thought of them returning, and he always knew they would, he considered it would mean his death. He never thought he'd outlive his son. Leif... loved... now missed so deeply that his chest began to burn, and he told himself to shut it off, bury it down as he had with so many other deaths in those days, but he couldn't get himself to do that to the memory of his son. Tears welled in his eyes and drew over his temples with the acceleration of the ship.

God, Leif... son, how did it come to this?

Cantwell said, "I was telling you that an airlock had come away from the lab."

The burning pain in his chest went cooler. "An airlock?"

"Yes, with two detectible heart traces in it."

"Two?"

"Yes."

"Are they retrievable?"

"We've got a Special Warfare team on it now."

And Jeffrey, drying his eyes with the back of his sleeve, let all hope for Leif and Sarah sit still. To hope meant going through the loss all over again. They were dead until he heard otherwise. He closed his eyes and imagined Leif alive before him, but as a little boy, six years old, smiling and holding up the model of a Delta Class Phantom. "This is what you flew, Dad! This is what you saved us with!" And with that Jeffrey broke down in tears and Cantwell was polite enough to pretend it wasn't happening.

CHAPTER 7

The Warthog accelerated away from the Rhadamanthus as if swept forward by the hand of Jupiter himself, the deck thrumming. As they passed into the darkness behind the great planet, Stacy and her team sat in silence, the thrust pinning them into their articulated, forward-facing jump seats.

When Marco throttled off, weightlessness came on without warning, causing Stacy's stomach to flip.

Dammit.

She drew a deep breath and closed her eyes, which made her head swim, so she looked out the side viewport. The stars spun, and the great, dark wall of Jupiter slid into view, blocking out all light. Marco had aimed the stern of the ship at their destination. Now flying backwards, Marco fired the engines, and Stacy sank into the seat's padding, the sensation of lying on her back under several G's a welcome respite.

When the burn ended, weightlessness returned. A lighter burn pressed her into her seat for a moment, then a bit more, and they were floating.

As they closed on Europa, the wall of Jupiter became a disk of blackness against a sea of stars. The bladed crescent of its terminator grew along the edge of that disk, glowing in sandstone hues, which blazed brightly after the darkness of the shadow-side transit.

Marco's voice came over the intercom, "Okay folks, we're on course to pass the airlock at a relative speed of approximately 1585 klicks per hour."

"That's going to be one hell of a shot," Stacy said to X. "You sure you can make it? You only get one chance."

"If I only have one shot," X said, unbuckling himself and shoving off his seat, floating toward the rear of the transport, "whether I can or can't doesn't figure in. I have to."

Stacy nodded her agreement.

Adanna unlatched her harness as Marco said, "Find a handhold folks. I'm turning us head on to Europa."

Adanna and X grabbed for handholds. As the Warthog turned, their bodies arced around and pressed against the wall. When the Warthog stabilized, Stacy unlatched and pushed her way up to the cockpit.

Marco looked over his shoulder at her.

She looked past Marco's glowing instrument panel, out the leaded, five-inch thick cockpit glass to the brilliant quarter crescent of Europa.

"How long?"

"Thirty minutes."

Stacy patted Marco's shoulder and pushed back into the rear cabin, finally settling into the sensation of weightlessness. "Adanna and Horace, you're my side gunners on this run, get 'em ready."

"Marco," she called forward.

Marco looked at her through the small passage. "Yes, O.C.?"

"How's our glide path looking for debris?"

"I can't do an active scan without painting us in the sky, but I think we're looking fairly good to avoid anything large. We're still going to make good use of our armor plating through the small stuff though."

"Okay." Stacy turned to Horace. "You and Adanna get the pulse-nukes prepped."

Horace and Adanna both nodded and went to work.

"X," Stacy called to the rear of the ship, "you ready?"

From down in the floor panels X called back, "I have the cable almost loaded." His head of coarse, dark hair popped up. "About ten minutes away."

"Get it done, X. I need you to have chair time to settle your nerves."

"Yes O.C." His head disappeared again.

"You need help?"

"Negative O.C."

Jacqueline had remained strapped in. Stacy said to her, "You're on when we get the survivors on board." She scanned the team members, glanced at Marco's shoulder in the cockpit and the hole in the floor where X was. "We won't have time for quarantine as we have no idea how much oxygen these folks have. They were in a clean environment, and we have to bank on that environment as having stayed clean. They're going to be cold and perhaps asphyxiated." She looked back to Jacqueline. "You ready?"

"Affirmative O.C., totally ready."

Stacy signed *okay* as she called up to the cockpit. "Time Marco."

"Twenty-six minutes thirty-five seconds until we pass apex on the airlock."

"You get that X?"

X's voice came muffled from the floorboards. "Affirmative O.C."

Stacy watched the hole in which X was working. What was taking so long? She felt the desire to check on him but knew she had to let him work, had to show trust, hell, had to *have* trust. They waited, Jacqueline looking at the floor as Horace worked with Adanna to prep the nukes. Adanna stole glances at Horace.

Stacy's anger at them reignited. Their selfishness would force her to tear apart the best team she'd ever worked with. But that was often the price of excellence. As teams gelled, that kind of thing could and did happen. Excellence was balanced on a blade. Get arrogant, fall; get too intimate, fall.

Silence filled the cabin as time passed.

Marco called back, "We got ten minutes O.C."

Five more minutes passed.

47

Stacy looked to the floor hatch where X worked. "X, where are you?"

No answer.

Damn it.

Kicking off, she drifted across the cabin. Coming over the hole, she looked down and saw X floating, his eyes closed, his index fingers touching his thumbs, legs crossed in a lotus, relaxed. The spool was loaded, and its green 'armed' light glowed.

"Go time X."

His wide eyes opened and trained on her. As he unfolded his legs, she looked back to Horace and Adanna, who each gave her a thumbs up. She pulled a cord on her jumpsuit, deploying internal, Kevlar-wrapped airbags, which turned the soft fabric into articulated, air-cushioned body armor. "Activate your armor and get your helmets on." Taking her helmet from the wall, she pulled it on. As each face disappeared behind a ruby-red visor and snub-nosed jaw plate, X rose up out of the hole.

Marco's voice came through the earpieces in her helmet. "Five minutes."

"Horace and Adanna, get yourselves strapped into the gunnery chairs."

"Yes, O.C.," they said in unison.

They moved amidships where two depressions in the floor held the gunnery seats. While they each faced blank walls, in their visors they would have a 280-degree view through the gunnery cameras.

"Marco, bring up a fifty percent ghost of the outer cameras on my optics."

"Yes O.C."

As she strapped herself into the command seat, mounted rear facing against the front bulkhead, the room flickered and dimmed. Now she could see, as if the ship were transparent, the Jovian system, the bright points of its moons, and the stars beyond. Looking over her shoulder, she saw Europa looming ahead, a disk of darkness in the stars with a thin blade of crescent light down the far side. She pressed the switch on her helmet to reduce the image of the ship's interior, and the moon became more pronounced. To her left, the banded face of Jupiter felt far too close.

"X?"

He gave her a thumbs up from the rear gunnery seat. "Ready O.C."

"Pulse-nukes Adanna?"

"Armed O.C."

"Horace?"

"Check check O.C."

"Marco?"

"Smooth as glass O.C. Two minutes."

"One shot X."

"On it O.C." His tone suggested: *with all due respect Zack, stuff it and let me do my job.*

In a whisper, Marco said, "Mother of God."

Stacy looked to Europa's surface. Three claw marks scarred it, running away to the horizon, beyond which the alien ships still cut into the ice. She reached absently for the scar on her own face. Her gloved fingers thumped on her faceplate.

"Going dark in five, four, three… shit *shit* SHIT." Marco said.

She quelled her inclination to ask what the problem was. She'd flown with Marco long enough to know when to let him be. Once it was go time, there were moments where each member's expertise caused them to become the most important individual in the group. Right now was Marco's time.

Beyond the crystalline outline of the ship, debris blurred by, now and again cracking off the armored hull. She saw what troubled Marco. A huge section of the base turned with a lazy rotation end-over-end directly ahead. One side was exterior metal, the other ceiling tiles. Now and again, chunks of wall stripped away with the rotation's centripetal force.

"It's just not my day," Marco said as the Warthog shifted. The straps of her seat hauled on her shoulders, pulling her downward as blood pressurized her head with the negative G's. When the ship clipped the end of the base section, her external view went to static. Her helmet's speakers lashed out with a deafening hiss for a split second before the volume cut out. When the image returned, she could only see outside. There seemed to be no cabin at all. Looking down, she saw no hands nor feet nor jump seat, only the vast darkness of space, the stars scattered infinitely in sharp points of burning light in whites and faintly tinted reds, blues and greens. As they passed under the huge turning section of the base, she saw a white lab coat snagged on a jagged arm of metal.

"X," Marco said, "I didn't get the angle I wanted. We're passing a lot closer than we planned, so I'll have to burn sooner and harder after we secure the airlock. We're vectored too close to the moon. No more time. Dark now."

Stacy's vision went black. As her eyes adjusted to the dim light, she saw the inside of the cabin. The side window, rear window and cockpit passage glowed with the hard light reflecting from Europa. Silence. Nothing.

X's seat shifted left, twitched, subtle adjustments. A thump came from the Warthog's belly. The cable spool howled. After a moment, the howl slowed with the soft whine of the spool brake.

He's got it.

She stilled her mind as she listened for the faint hints telling the story of their progress. The cable brake came on harder, the whine increasing bit by bit to a scream. She imagined the airlock, caught in the webbed net, accelerating hard. The cable slowed more and more, paying out less and less. A loud thump jerked the Warthog.

He ran out of cable.

That last moment would have been rough, but as long as the airlock's frame hadn't been damaged, the people inside might be okay as they would have already shifted to the far end with the initial acceleration.

Out the side window, Europa crowded in on them, the cracks in the ice blurring. Marco's shift in trajectory had put them on a collision course. There would be no time to orbit around to the dark side now.

"Horace and Adanna, be ready. I'm guessing we're gonna have company," she shouted into the dead air of her helmet. Powered down, they might not hear her, but Horace turned and gave her a thumbs up. Adanna appeared to be messing with her seat harness. Her left shoulder strap went loose, tight, and loose again.

What the hell's going on?

The lights flickered on, and the cabin went crystalline in Stacy's visor as Marco fired up the systems. The moon now ran as a wall of blurring ice.

Marco said, "Hang tight folks. I have to hit the throttle pretty hard here."

Adanna said, a hint of panic in her tone, "Wait, there's something wrong with my harness."

"There's nothing I can do, Adanna," Marco said. "I either hit it now, or we crash. Hold on as best you can."

"Okay," she said.

When the ship lurched, the straps on Stacy's shoulders and hips hauled on her. She felt as though she were strapped to a ceiling. As Marco accelerated harder, the G's felt as though they were trying to rip her from her seat. Marco must have been approaching ten G's, which meant Stacy would have the equivalent of 630 kilos hauling on her harness. Fortunately, her armor distributed the pressure evenly across her torso.

Adanna's arms went wide as her harness gave way. She fell, slamming into the back wall, where she lay motionless in a C shape. At ten G's, those twenty feet would be equivalent to falling two hundred on Earth. Stacy could only hope Adanna's armor had protected her enough from the impact.

"Marco," Stacy said, growling with the effort of holding her head up enough to see Adanna, "I need you to let off for a moment so I can secure Adanna and take over the gunnery seat."

"What's going on with Adanna?"

"Don't worry about it. Just don't let the throttle off all the way."

"I'll take you down to half a G in twenty seconds. But get strapped in fast, we have company."

Stacy could see nothing in the darkness beside the blurring surface of Europa. She looked to Horace, who had his focus fully on Adanna.

"Horace," Stacy said.

He didn't respond... exactly the kind of freeze Stacy didn't need right now.

"Horace, look at me."

The ruby mirror of his visor turned to her.

"Forget Adanna. We have to get out of this to help her. You got that?"

He gave no acknowledgement.

"Specialist Sixtro, confirm my order."

At that, his voice came over her intercom, "Yes, O.C. Forget Specialist Hammersmith."

"Good, now when the throttle comes off, I'll get Hammersmith secured. You keep your ass in that gunnery seat."

"Aye O.C. When the throttle's off, I stay in the seat."

Okay... he's back.

Stacy watched Adanna for signs of life, but her collapsed shape remained motionless.

Come on Marco, you gotta let off. Just a moment.

Her massive weight faded to perhaps less than a fifth of a G, what it would be on Earth's moon. She felt like she'd been set free from iron weights, which had been hung from her arms, legs and the top of her head. Slapping off her five-point harness, she let herself free fall toward the back of the cabin. The transparent back wall came up at her, and she sucked in a breath as her instincts told her she'd pass right through it and be left to fall to the moon's icy surface. But her boots hit the solid wall. Grabbing Adanna, who was limp and unresponsive, Stacy strapped her into a rear jump seat before climbing back up the deck to the gunner's seat and pulling the harnesses around her shoulders. Closing the center buckle, she found the left-shoulder latch wouldn't lock.

As she came to understand what had happened to Adanna, Stacy found herself in the same situation.

"Give me the green when you're ready," Marco said.

Saying anything might be confused for permission, so she let him have silence as she fought the clip a moment longer. Moving to a side jump seat was an option, but that would leave one side of the ship exposed with no gunner.

"Any day O.C." Marco said.

Stacy extended the strap, slid it around the buckle, wrapped it around itself in a half-hitch, tucked the tail of the strap in, and pulled it tight. After testing the hold, she looked to Horace, who gave her a thumbs up.

She said, "Marco, we're green. Go. Go. Go."

The throttle came on even harder than before. Adanna's head snapped back and cracked against the wall.

Thank God for that helmet.

Stacy held her gun controls to keep her arms from falling toward the back of the ship as Marco throttled on harder. She rested her head into her suit's neck bracing as it became too heavy to hold up.

How many damn G's is he pulling?

The top turret began to fire. X was engaging.

The moon's surface began to pull away.

"I'm going to throttle down." Marco said. "There's no way we're going to outrun these guys in the Warthog. You'll have to gun them down. Here's your HUD O.C."

The interior of the ship vanished leaving only an outline of her hands and the gun controls. A laser-thin, yellow crosshair appeared ten feet in front of her. She went lighter as Marco let off the throttle, and while her head still felt like a bowling ball being dragged to the side, she could lift it. Reaching up with her leaden arm, she grabbed the gunnery controls. The chair turned with the cannon. Behind them, two near-invisible black shapes, outlined in glowing green, closed fast.

As tracers from X's conventional rounds lanced at them, the ships hooked and coiled around the shots.

"If they get to us we're dead," Horace said, "These guys are one shot one kill."

X's voice came over the Intercom, "I can't land anything on them. It's like they're reading my damn mind."

Horace said, "The pulse-nukes are rigged to the left trigger O.C."

"Hold your fire," X said. "I need to reel the airlock in the rest of the way. Marco, get back on the throttle to preserve some distance while I bring them in."

Stacy felt the G's increase. The com remained silent for a moment before X said, "Back off about two G's, the winch can't take the load."

Her weight reduced slightly.

A moment later, X said, his tone still calm, "About one more G."

The ships were coming on fast as the airlock drew in. Stacy tried to bring the crosshairs to the ship, but the G's were too powerful to move her head smoothly, so she relented, waiting as the alien fighters closed in. Europa continued falling away, turning from a wall of white to a huge sphere, and then diminishing.

The two alien fighters had to be nearing weapons range. Perhaps they would play cat and mouse. Maybe, in arrogance, they would see the Warthog as a fat, low-tech ship to play with and kill, which if the pulse nukes didn't work, was exactly how it would play out.

The airlock, wrapped in netting, drew closer. A ragged section of the base's exterior wall hung from it.

Marco said, "Our range to fire without flooding us and the airlock with radiation is closing. You have to fire. The moment you do, we'll go dark. Throttling down... *now*."

The G's lessened, and Stacy grabbed the gun controls, brought the crosshairs to bear on the right ship, assuming Horace would go for the left, and pulled her left trigger. Her lower rail gun flickered with sparks as the torpedo-shaped nuke rushed away, vanishing into the void. Horace's cannon fired. It had no radar signature to speak of. If she couldn't see it, she hoped they couldn't see it. If so, they wouldn't be able to target it. Jupiter's radiation and magnetic fields might help as well, confusing their radar systems. She considered the high-energy electrons and ions coursing from the massive planet. The Warthog had extensive shielding to protect them, and while the airlock had similar shielding, the side that had been attached to the base troubled her. Were the people inside suffering fatal exposure even as they saved them?

A brilliant-white light sparked in the darkness near the outlines of the alien fighters followed by a second.

Her exterior view vanished, leaving her once again in the darkness of the cabin as Marco shut the ship down before the electromagnetic pulse passed them, invisible in the darkness.

When the cabin lights clacked on, Marco said, "Our bogeys are dead in the water. You want me to decelerate and take them out?"

Stacy asked, "What's their trajectory?"

"They're in orbital degradation with the planet."

"You think they've gone permanently dark?"

"Depends on how close those blasts came and how insulated they are," Marco said, "but they look pretty dead on my scopes."

"Then get us out of here. We've achieved our objective and have an injured team member."

"Yes, O.C."

The acceleration started more slowly this time, but grew and grew until Stacy was hanging from her seat straps again. She gripped her harness to keep her arms from hanging out.

"How long will you have to burn like this Marco?"

"Another thirty seconds. I want to gain another 20,000 klicks per hour on those ships."

With the acceleration hauling her against her harness, she stilled her thoughts. There would be time to attend to Adanna. Time to analyze the fighters. Now was the time to be still, to reload. Her thoughts trailed back to where they often did when she needed rest, a cove on a distant, unpopulated island in the South Pacific. In her mind's eye, she waded into the clear water, its bending surface warping the sunlight into tendrils, which played along the white sand. In that memory, she'd found respite from the loss of her father and deliverance from the stress of the career she'd chosen. It had brought her through the grief of her closest teammate dying in a pressure-lock blowout during a training exercise. The memory of her time in the Tongan Islands with Leif and Jeffrey was hers as much as the scar across her cheek was hers. It did not give her strength. It brought her something she needed far more... peace. In that peace, fears faded.

She hung from the harness of the gunnery chair, racing across the shoulder of Jupiter, imagining herself standing with warm water lapping around her thighs, and she breathed deeply of the sea-scented air.

CHAPTER 8

The acceleration waned and vanished, leaving Stacy once again with a weightless, flipping sensation in her belly and shoulders.

"There we have it." Marco said.

Stacy untied her left shoulder strap before unbuckling the rest of the harness. Horace was already making his way to Adanna, her head at an angle and arms floating away from her as though she were a marionette. Jacqueline unstrapped and kicked off toward her as well.

As Stacy aimed herself at the rear airlock and kicked off, she asked, "How long until we have to begin our deceleration burn Marco?"

"About twenty minutes O.C. Any longer, and I won't have the power to match orbit with the Rhadamanthus. If so, we'll overshoot Io and have to slingshot Titan to gain orbit again."

"Understood."

Horace was helping Jacqueline strap Adanna down to the emergency medical outline on the floor. Jacqueline, who had already pulled straps over her own thighs, securing herself in a kneeling position to the floor, leaned over Adanna.

As X unstrapped from the rear gunner seat, Stacy motioned for him to follow her and said, "Horace, help us get this airlock docked."

Without argument, Horace shoved away from Adanna and Jacqueline. He stopped himself on a hand hold with the expertise of someone who'd spent a career in zero G. Stacy looked at the blank mirror of his face shield. The snub-nosed jaw of his helmet gave him a furious countenance.

"You're doing well Horace. She'll get the best care from Jacqueline."

"Aye aye O.C."

X activated the airlock manipulator controls. Beyond the porthole, long, spider-like arms cut away the tangled netting. After cutting it free, he turned the airlock around to what would have been the outside end, aligned it, and flipped a switch. A loud clack-clack came through the hull as the holding clamps set into the locking ring. The view ports for the Warthog's airlock and the survivor's airlock were now aligned. Looking through them, Stacy could see two cocoon-like bags floating inside.

"Do we still have heart signature?" She asked.

Marco said, "Yes. Slow and steady."

Stacy looked over to Jacqueline. She'd taken Adanna's helmet and gloves off, and had her fingers on Adanna's wrist. Stacy resisted the urge to ask about Adanna's status. That had nothing to do with her responsibility. Jacqueline had it covered as best as it could be.

Stacy said to X and Horace. "Keep your helmets on. The air will be more than two-hundred degrees below zero in there. Keep your gloves on as well folks."

X and Horace both gave her a thumbs up.

"Breach it," she said.

X threw the lever, and the warthog's airlock irised open, exposing the base's. A hoar of frost grew across the metal as the ship's warm air contacted it.

Stacy asked X, "What pressure do you have?"

X said, ".89 atmos."

"Repressurize it to one full."

"Check-check O.C." He typed on the control panel. Air hissed beyond the thick metal.

X said, "Whoever's in there just felt their ears pop—if they're conscious that is."

"Crack the door," she said.

"Aye, opening the airlock inner door." He opened the main release cover, twisted the yellow and black lever below it, and the airlock door rotated open like a large, armored camera lens. She felt the cold wash over her even through her armor. In the space where the air of the Warthog and the airlock met, a fog formed. With no gravity to cause the heavier, cold air to drop low, the mist hung veil-like in the opening.

"Holy hell that's cold," Horace said.

"Blow it out," she said.

Fans fired up, and the fog rushed over them dissipating into the Warthog's cabin.

Marco said over the intercom, "Our overall cabin temp has dropped by twenty degrees."

As Stacy pulled herself into the airlock, her gloved hand brushed one of the tubes to her left, and she felt the cold immediately leach the heat from her. She did her best to avoid any further contact. As she gripped the nearest cocoon, a sheet of dusted frost lifted away from it. In the doorway, X held a square-toothed clamp attached to a spool of cord. With a flick of his wrist he sent the clamp floating down the airlock to her, the cord coiling away behind.

Catching the clamp, she attached it to the bag. Horace took hold of the cord, braced his legs on the airlock hatch, and pulled on the rope, drawing the survival bag out. As the clamp pulled the bag taught, Stacy could see the form of the person inside and wondered what that person was going through. Were they even aware they were being rescued?

As Horace gripped the bag, more condensed frost floated away. He drew it through the hatch. Stacy took hold of the second bag. The body inside moved, startling her.

Pressing the external com on her helmet, she said, "If you can hear me, stay calm. We have you. You're safe. Just a minute more. Please do not attempt to exit your bag until we have you secured." She heard a muffled response but couldn't make it out.

"O.C."

She turned to find X ready with the clamp. He tossed it to her. Catching it, she attached it to the bag. Horace dragged it out. She kicked off the end of the airlock, drifting after the bag.

When Stacy twisted the yellow and black lever, the airlock apertures curled shut. She left the airlock attached to the Warthog's locks. One didn't want to release an object until it was time to move definitively away from it. No need to go bumping along with it at a quarter million klicks an hour.

The survival bags floated in the center of the cabin, Jacqueline hovering beside one with a scanner.

"Jacqueline, what's Adanna's status?" Stacy asked.

Her eyes stayed on the scanner. "She's unconscious, but stable. I've done everything I can for her right now. She most likely has a fairly serious concussion. I have monitors on her."

Stacy nodded as she checked the temperature display. Holding up her hand, she said, "Give it a moment. The bag's exterior might not be safe yet."

"How's the heart signal Marco?"

"Strong in one, a bit weak in the other, but nothing I'm worried about."

"What do you mean by weak?"

"It's slow," Jacqueline said. "The occupant is unconscious."

"We'll open that first…"

Stacy asked, "What's the air temp in here now?"

Marco said, "Cabin temp is 63 degrees and rising."

Stacy nodded to herself and removed her helmet. The cool air hit her face, welcome after the intensity of the moment. She attached her helmet to a wall strap.

Jacqueline asked, "Permission to remove protective gear?"

"Granted," Stacy said.

The team removed their helmets.

"Temp?" Stacy called to the front.

Now Marco's voice came not intimately close through the speakers in her helmet, but far away, through the cockpit corridor. "64 degrees and rising."

When Stacy saw the frost, which had formed across the surface of the thermal bags, begin to go damp at the peaks of the quilting, she said, "Jacqueline, pull the unconscious occupant. I'll pull the one with the stronger heart signal."

Jacqueline unzipped the chrysalis-like bag, exposing the slightly blue face of a young man with tousled, brown hair. With eyes closed, he wore a clear rubberized mask over his nose and mouth. When Jacqueline pulled the mask from his face, a rosy color flushed through him, but he did not rouse. She unzipped the bag the rest of the way, and several oxygen bottles floated free. Drawing the bottle attached to the mask near, she inspected the gage.

"Almost empty." As she took the young man's pulse, she said, "Horace, give me a fresh O2 bottle."

Horace attached a new mask to an emergency O2 cylinder and pushed it over to her. Jacqueline fitted the mask on the young man's face and twisted the bottle full open. The young man's free arm floated in a limp arc as she checked his pulse again.

Stacy pushed off the wall with gentle expertise, sending herself in a slow flight to the second bag. She caught it as she passed. The mass of the bag slowed her. As the far wall approached, she extended a boot and stopped herself.

Gripping the bag's zipper, she pulled it downward. As the top of the survivor's head became visible, the zipper stuck. The mop of thick, pale-blonde hair reminded her of Leif, whom she hadn't seen in some time. As she fished the bunched fabric from the zipper track, she thought of how, over the years, Leif had grown distant from her, their lives diverging. After he'd met Sarah, they hardly spoke. She yanked on the zipper, but it wouldn't come free. Taking her knife from her hip, she cut into the side of the bag's fabric. When Leif had married she hadn't gone to the wedding, and he'd called her sounding hurt, and she'd been a bit... not rude... but quiet. Not talkative. He must have assumed she wanted nothing to do with him, but her silence came from not wanting to acknowledge how she truly felt.

Freeing the zipper, she pulled it down, exposing Leif's face. For a moment, she thought she'd become delusional. When his eyes met hers, she saw grief in them. A chilling understanding overtook her. The last time she'd talked with Jeffrey he'd told her that Leif had been stationed with his wife. She hadn't known where... only stationed with his wife.

Only two survivors.

"Sarah?" she said to him, and his chin pulled tight as he closed his eyes.

"O.C." she heard Marco say.

"Give me a minute, Marco."

"I would, but you got a comm from Admiral Cantwell."

"What?" She looked toward the cockpit. "Admiral Cantwell's retired."

"Apparently not anymore."

She turned back to Leif. "Are you hurt?"

"What are the odds that it should be you?" He said with a wan smile.

"Just dumb luck I guess."

In his hollow eyes, she saw the need to let what he'd been through be left alone.

"Horace, evaluate this man." She touched the side of Leif's face. "I've got to take care of this. I'll be close, okay?"

He didn't appear to care.

Kicking off the wall, she floated to the communications console.

"I'm at the console."

Marco said, "He wants a private channel."

Letting out a frustrated breath, she kicked off again, found her helmet, and pulled it on.

"I'm ready."

"Aye O.C.," Marco said, his voice now close in her ears as if he was sitting behind her, "I'm patching him through."

The connection clicked, and Sam Cantwell's aged voice asked, "Commander?"

"Yes sir, this is Commander Zack, Special Warfare."

"Do you have the survivors?"

"Affirmative, sir. Two."

"Are identities confirmed?"

In that moment, she understood; the old dogs of the war had been brought back, Cantwell from retirement and Holt from the wrecking yard. Cantwell was confirming if Holt's son was dead or alive and Jeffrey was in the room with him.

"We have two men, one yet unidentified. The other is confirmed to be Leif Holt."

"How is he?"

"He appears to be uninjured, but that's only my assessment. The medic has yet to finish her evaluation."

"Understood…"

In the following silence Stacy was unsure what to say so remained silent.

"Tell your team they've done well. Contact me immediately if any changes occur."

"Tell Jeffrey I'm sorry about Sarah."

"Understood. Thank you Commander."

The speakers clicked. Pulling her helmet off, she looked to the survivors being attended by X, Horace and Jacqueline. The unidentified man was still unconscious, but looking far healthier than the half-dead face they'd first found. Leif looked healthy, but in his eyes she saw darkness. When her father had been murdered, she went through hell privately. No matter how much Jeffrey had tried to help her, she'd never fully opened up about it. She saw the same closed-off grief in Leif's eyes now.

CHAPTER 9

As the launch vehicle finished its orbital burn and came into an intercept path with the U.S. Navy Space Station Elysium, acceleration let off, and Jeffrey went weightless, which came as a blissfully welcome and familiar sensation.

Cantwell took out a buzzing handset and held it up to his ear.

"This is Cantwell. Yes… Good… Connect me to the recovery team." He waited in silence.

Jeffrey watched him intently.

"This is Admiral Sam Cantwell. I need to speak with your O.C." He fell silent for a time before asking, "Commander?" A pause. "Do you have the survivors?"

Jeffrey held his hope close. In his impatience, he shoved his thumbnail at some loose paint on his armrest.

Cantwell asked, "Are identities confirmed?"

Jeffrey laced his hands together, the fingers going white.

"How is he?"

Jeffrey did his best to hold back a rush of assumption.

'He'. No mention of 'she'. Sarah…

Despite his attempt to keep his mind quiet, the truth shoved its way in. The woman he'd been so glad Leif had found was gone. Sarah had been wonderful—sincere, honest, beautiful, and intelligent. Everything a father would want for his son, and they'd been good together—really good.

"Understood…" Cantwell said.

Jeffrey thought how empty his heart had been after his own wife's passing, how empty it still was.

"Tell your team they've done well," Cantwell said. "Contact me immediately if any changes occur."

Jeffrey watched Cantwell's expression, but the old military man never let much show.

"Understood. Thank you Commander." Cantwell ended the call. He looked at Jeffrey and said simply, as a man used to loss in war will, "Leif's fine, but Leif and another young man were the only survivors."

The relief Jeffrey felt at the survival of his son was overshadowed by the loss of Sarah.

Giving a quick nod, he asked, to give himself something else to think about, "What's next?"

Cantwell let his tablet drift to Jeffrey. "We have an hour or so until we dock with Elysium. During that time, I have some files I want you to review."

"Files?"

"Pilots. Once you've been over the files and the summaries, I'll talk to you about what our next steps might be. I need you in a leadership role here Holt. I know you'd rather be blood and guts flying, but I need your experience. There are others who have *ideas* about how to deal with this situation, ideas I think you'll share my opinion on."

"I assume that opinion involves foul language."

Another rare smile passed over Cantwell's face. "The president and secretary of defense want to focus our fight with drones. Meanwhile the vice president," he pointed his thumb over his shoulder where Samantha Delaney sat, "while still seeming to be doubtful this isn't another conspiracy on our part, has been vocal that an accord to peace must be found."

"She's in for an awakening."

Cantwell offered a matter-of-fact grunt in response.

"…and drones won't work."

"I had a feeling you'd take that position," Cantwell said. "That's why I needed you back. We'll talk more on that point later."

He pointed at the tablet in Jeffrey's hands. "Right now you need to review those files."

"To what end?" Jeffrey asked, already knowing the answer. In his gut, he felt a wicked thrill mixed with dread. He was going to get to do what he was born to, what he'd been engineered to do. Most of the men and women whose files were in the tablet he held would be dead in six months. Maybe this time he'd be spared the pain of surviving them.

"We need to resurrect the Hammerhead program Jeffrey, and I need you to head it."

"I'm just a pilot."

"No," Cantwell said, anger tingeing his words, "get that humble-warrior bullshit out of your system. It's time for you step up and lead."

"I've never seen myself as a leader."

"Which is exactly the kind of leader I need."

Shrugging the comment aside, Jeffrey looked at the first name on the tablet, a Lieutenant Sebastian Grimstad from Norway. He tapped the name and looked over the stats, service record, and psyche profile, which while impressive, did not give everything he needed to know. Not until he'd met and worked with the man, would he come to understand him.

CHAPTER 10

     Stacy had been in the U.S.S. Rhadamanthus' sick bay checking on Adanna, who'd regained consciousness but could remember nothing from the mission. Stacy cut her from the team without making much of a scene. Adanna would be transferred to another Special Warfare unit when she'd been given medical clearance.

     Disconnecting her mag-boots from the deck, Stacy floated up the steep staircase-like ladder. As she locked her boots to the next deck and walked on, she felt dizzy and angry. Despite the convenience of the boots, who's carbon fiber calf supports allowed her to walk fairly naturally, the weightlessness still made her feel out of sorts. Her anger, of course, was directed at Adanna and Horace. Their reckless selfishness had fractured her team. Between the two, Adanna had to go. Their current situation required a healthy team *now*, and Adanna needed time to heal. Her injury had simplified the decision, but still it burned in Stacy's mind. Adanna had offered a strangely easy apology when Stacy told her she was out. Stacy kept her anger to herself as venting it on Adanna would have served no purpose. She'd save it for Horace.

     With no personnel nearby to collide into, she released her boots and, pulling on the railing, glided down the empty corridor. She understood she should enjoy the easy movements as long as she could. Soon the Rhadamanthus would be under acceleration, and Stacy would find herself under heavy G's wherever she went. Orders had come in: all destroyers would gather at the outer edge of the asteroid belt. Stacy had heard several countries were committing ships. Jeffrey's stories of the aliens from fifty years before caused her to worry about the tactics the higher command would commit the destroyers to. According to

Jeffrey, all large-scale engagements with alien destroyers had ended badly. Allied advances in the war had come solely through close-in fighting, which negated the aliens' more powerful weapons. The only close-in battles won had been fought by the Hammerheads.

Coming through a hatch, she found the sleeping decks busier with personnel, so she locked her boots down and, walking past her own cabin hatch, moved five hatches further down, coming to C-01-154. She knocked quietly enough that if the occupant was sleeping he would be able to remain asleep. A muffled reply came from the inside.

Pushing on the handle, which moved easily on freshly greased surfaces, she shoved the reinforced hatch inward. As she stepped into the dim interior, a switch clicked. LED lights over the bunk came on, glowing across Leif, who lay in a white T-shirt, his rack's sleeping sack zipped to his chest and zero-G straps over his thighs and chest. He had dark swaths under his eyes, the look of someone who wanted sleep but couldn't find it.

"How are you?" She asked him.

"Fine," he said, shrugging. He rubbed the palm of his hand with his fingers.

Stacy moved to the corner of the small quarters, near his feet. "I'm sorry Leif, sorry you lost her."

Leif kept his attention on his hands.

Stacy said, "I want you to know you can talk to me. I've been there. With my father."

Leif nodded as his face tightened, but he let out a deep breath, and his expression returned to blankness. Despite his defenses though, tears welled and filled his eyes in the weightlessness. He shoved them away with the back of his wrist. Stacy found it strange to see someone cry like that, no reaction of the face, only tears. After a moment, he said in a quiet voice, "I need to tell you something."

When he remained silent, she said, "I'm listening Leif."

He sighed again, "I need to tell *someone* anyway."

"You know you can talk to me, your dad too if—"

"No," Leif's voice became angry. "Promise me what I'm about to tell you will never be repeated to him. Understood?"

Stacy nodded but felt unsure of the bargain.

"I'm serious about this."

"Okay. It'll stay between you and me." She touched his blanket-draped knee. "You can trust me okay?"

A resigned expression tinted with relief came to his face.

"The morning she died, yesterday morning... God how could it have been only twenty-four hours ago? That morning she told me that she was..." He fell silent again, and fresh tears formed. He shoved them away and drew an unsteady breath. "...pregnant."

Not a lot could shock Stacy. She'd been through tough times and had the thick skin to show for it. Now, though, she found herself having to brace herself to avoid physically showing the impact of what he'd said. He would carry the scars of a lost wife forever, but to lose their child as well... Stacy could think of no words to face such a thing, so she sat in silence, her hand still on his knee.

"You can't tell my dad," he said, his voice falling to a whisper. "He's lost too much. To lose a grandchild..."

Leif's selflessness, protecting his father even through his own grief, caused tears to well in Stacy's eyes also. She bit her tongue to quell them.

After a long pause, she let out a small, heartless laugh, and said, "It's unfortunate life has to come with so much scar tissue."

He nodded. They sat in silence for some time before he pushed her hand aside and said, "Thanks for checking on me."

"I'm here for you Leif."

Leif released his straps, unzipped the sleeping sack, and floated free of the bed. As he put on his mag-boots, locking them to the deck, his shoulders trembled slightly. Stacy wasn't sure if he was crying or not, but she let him have his time. After a moment, he wiped his eyes with his sleeve.

Standing, he asked, "You hungry?"

She'd eaten thirty minutes before she'd cut Adanna. "Yeah, I'll eat with you."

CHAPTER 11

Jeffrey stood, or rather had the electromagnetic plates in his duty boots locked to the floor, as he surveyed the U.S.S. Lacedaemon's bridge in awe at how much Navy destroyers had advanced in fifty years. In his time the destroyers' bridges had been low steel-lined spaces with narrow windows... hard to see the stars. Here on the Lacedaemon, a lattice of carbon-wrapped titanium fitted with glass panels arced over the bridge. The structure seemed impossibly gossamer for the purposes of a warship. That latticed *ceiling* was, in fact, the nose of the huge destroyer, as the Lacedaemon's decks had been set perpendicular to its length, like the slices in a loaf of bread. When the main thrusters fired, the acceleration would create an artificial gravity as the floor panels pushed into the occupants' feet, rather than slamming everyone into the rear wall.

In the center of the broad space lay a shin-high disk with the appearance of mirrored, black obsidian—a Nav-Con imager ten feet across. A three-dimensional hologram of the fleet hovered above it. The ships at the edges of the disk were cut off in a sharp curve where the disk ended.

Walking to it, Jeffrey looked over the nearest ships. With finely detailed 3D resolution, each small ship appeared to be solid metal. The Nav-Con's of his day had shown ships in wire-frame outlines.

Behind him, Cantwell said, "The light transference and resolution has been greatly improved,"

"Incredible."

Cantwell moved to the Nav-Con's oval control panel. As he slid his fingers across its surface, the ships rushed closer, growing until only the Lacedaemon remained, hovering nose to thrusters over the entirety of the disk.

"The system uses drone cameras and solar positioning systems to monitor fleet status. These images are real-time. Critical for understanding positioning, battle damage, and so on."

Jeffrey sank his finger into the seemingly solid side of the ship.

With a sweep of his hand, Cantwell turned the image of the Lacedaemon until it's latticed nose, which reminded Jeffrey of a Victorian glass house, hovered before him. Leaning in, Jeffrey saw himself looking over the small disk in the center of the bridge where a small Lacedaemon floated.

Jeffrey looked to Cantwell. "A lot has changed."

"Not all for the better," Cantwell said pointing to the lattice. "It's a beautiful view but bad for war."

"There's no armor to it."

"None. That's what happens when lack of experience meets the desire for warships to look and feel fancy."

Cantwell swept his fingers across the control panel. The Lacedaemon slid away. The surface of Europa took its place, a curved arc blanketing the surface of the Nav-Con. The three destroyers, the size of pocket knives, continued to cut a three-clawed canyon into its surface.

Jeffrey hadn't seen one in fifty years, but he knew every detail from memory.

He said through his teeth, "Sthenos..."

"Yes," Cantwell said. "Some suggest that if we don't engage, they'll leave when they're done mining ice."

"These the same folks who said the war never happened?" Jeffrey asked, already knowing the answer. "They're not ice miners."

A woman's voice, efficient and direct, came from Jeffrey's right, "If you disagree, what is your assessment?"

Jeffrey turned and found himself facing Vice President Samantha Delaney, standing with her two Marine guards and the bald man wearing small, wire-framed glasses from the launch shuttle. She seemed to have adapted easily to the weightlessness and magnetic boots. Standing face-to-face with her, what struck him about her most was her height. Her blond hair caught the shine of the bridge lights as she gave Jeffrey a practice-perfect smile. Her beauty, which was much more intense in person, made Jeffrey feel defensive. Her gunmetal gray pant-suit opalesced as she held out her hand to him.

"Mr. Holt I presume."

"Captain Holt," Cantwell said.

She gave Cantwell a natural smile. "Forgive me," she said, "*Captain* Holt."

As he shook her hand, his eyes scanned her face, measuring her, and found her somewhat unreadable. Yet, he felt drawn into the delicate copper fans laced into her dark-amber eyes.

Tipping his head to her, he said in a reserved tone, "Vice president."

"The admiral warned me," she said as though cutting directly into his mind, "that you don't care much for my kind." She stepped closer and leaned in as if what she said next should be confidential. "I'll do what I can to not be a typical politician if you also agree to not be a typical meat head."

Jeffrey exhaled slowly through his nostrils.

"It would seem," she continued in a casual tone, "I was mistaken in the existence of these folks." She laughed easily. "Who knew?"

Cantwell's ability to remain expressionless gave Jeffrey the strength to keep from speaking his mind.

Delaney turned to the Nav-Con. "I need to understand as quickly as possible what we're dealing with here."

Something in her manner told Jeffrey that she'd already made up her mind on what she was dealing with. Her asking for his opinion was only showmanship.

"Ma'am," Jeffrey said, not willing to let her get away with using such a light tone, "imagine the worst thing you can, and you're only getting started."

The vice president's eyebrow lifted. "Interesting." She held her open palm up as if presenting Cantwell to Holt. "When the president asked the admiral to come out of retirement, he agreed on the condition that you be brought in as well. That makes a strong impression on me."

"Ma'am," Jeffrey said, "I don't want to be disrespectful, and I appreciate the compliment, but I don't have time nor use for it." He pointed to the Nav-Con. "This should bother everyone here."

"I would assume," Delaney said, "You don't mean the obvious."

Jeffrey shook his head. "No... not their presence... their *casual* presence."

As Delaney's eyes narrowed, Jeffrey's attention settled on the faint freckles scattered across the bridge of her nose.

She asked, "What about their demeanor troubles you?"

Pulling his eyes from her, he scowled at himself as he said, "They don't appear to care they have their backs exposed, but they *should*." He pointed at the ships. "This behavior doesn't add up. Fifty years ago, the first time they engaged us, we forced their local population to extinction. That should send a strong message to future visitors, but now they come calmly strolling back in? That makes no sense."

"They don't appear to care that we killed them," Delaney said in a matter of fact tone.

"Exactly. It would only make sense under three circumstances. One, they don't care about losing lives. I'm not buying that. Two, they're stupid—don't learn. That's invalid based on how dangerous they are."

"The alternative," Cantwell said, "is they're laying out a trap."

Jeffrey felt electrified in a way he hadn't since his conflict with Maxine King. "Exactly, and I'll bet my right eye that it's going to burn us if we don't figure it out fast."

"Perhaps," Delaney said as she turned to the balding man, whose face had flushed more and more as Jeffrey spoke, "they simply do not understand the impact they had on us."

As the man, his hands behind his back and broad shoulders set, stepped forward, he lifted his chin with an air of arrogance. His advanced baldness contrasted with his youthful face. In the dark eyes and thick torso, Jeffrey saw a man used to getting his way, be it through argument or intimidation.

We'll see how that works out for you today.

"Schodt," Delaney asked him, "what can you offer on these ships?"

The man coughed and tugged on the half-inch collar of his shirt, which encircled his neck somewhat tightly, before lifting onto the balls of his feet, settling down, and saying, "Madam Vice President, the alien race we encountered fifty years ago was classified as XTLF-A, or Extra-Terrestrial Life Form Alpha—the first we have encountered. While there are some subtle structural differences, analysis of these ships and their weaponry signatures suggests this is also XTLF-A; however, it is possible this is a different life form with similar technology. This life form must, of course, be classed in the Eukarya biological domain, and again assumed to be part of the Animalia phylum—"

"Excuse me," Jeffrey asked, "who are you?"

The man's thin lips pressed to nothing as his right eye twitched once.

"Oh, forgive me," Delaney said, "this is Gerard Schodt, the foremost expert on the alien race."

Schodt's lips curved downward as if his presence were a magnanimous gift bestowed upon Jeffrey.

"I don't wish to be disrespectful," Jeffrey said, "but I don't believe anyone can claim to be an expert on the Sthenos."

Schodt's expression went flat. "Captain Holt, I understand your attitude is to *kill 'em all* as it were. My intention is conversely to understand these beings as a species and a society."

Jeffrey said, "I think I understand them well enough."

"I would argue," Schodt said, rubbing his fingertips together as if testing their cleanliness, "your view is… bigoted." He offered Jeffrey a slight smile. "If you'll forgive me for being so direct. I do not believe we know enough to draw a conclusion of inherent hostility. It is possible the previous conflict erupted from a misunderstanding."

"Excuse me?" Jeffrey's anger sparked and crackled like gunpowder tossed over flames.

"I did not speak unclearly," Schodt said. "People like you, who call them *Sthenos*, create a barrier between worlds. The moniker Exteris Ignotum is far more—"

"Calling them 'extraterrestrial unknowns'," Jeffrey said, his pulse rising in his neck, "is equivalent to mistaking a pride of lions for house cats."

"Exteris Ignotum has been scientifically approved for the long-term health of our perception—"

"Please don't tell me," Jeffrey said to Cantwell, "that you're going to make me work with…" he held out his hand to Schodt and found himself at a loss, "…this." He squared on Schodt. "I know everything I need to know about the *Sthenos*—We kill them, or we die."

Schodt adjusted his glasses on his broad face. "That view is not acceptable to me, *Captain* Holt."

"Nor is it to me," Vice President Delaney said.

"Mr. Schodt, vice president," Jeffrey said, "if you live long enough, it will be."

Cantwell took hold of the back of Jeffrey's arm.

"To call this race Exteris Sthenos," Schodt said as his face bloomed fully red, "to equate it with Medusa's deranged, murderous sister, casts them permanently in a neg—"

Jeffrey held up his hand as he let out a slow breath. "I'm sorry. I believe we've gotten off on the wrong foot." In the shocked silence that followed, he drew another breath, letting go of the anger he felt toward this *expert,* who'd been born at least a decade after the war had ended and said, "Mr. Schodt, you and I are not going to be effective in this vein. I suggest we move beyond it."

Schodt glared at him.

"I'm going to make you a commitment."

The man's eyebrow lifted.

"I'll listen to what you have to say if you do the same for me."

Schodt turned his head and pulled at his collar as if the concept stuck in his throat.

Jeffrey said, "I am sure…" another deep breath, "there are many things I can learn from you and am willing to admit my view of the Sthenos is… biased."

Schodt held up a stubby index finger as he opened his mouth to speak.

"But," Jeffrey said, cutting him off, "I will also ask you to accept that, in many areas, I will have more experience. If we begin there, I think we'll find ourselves on higher ground."

Schodt's mouth turned down. He looked to those around him. While the narrowness of his eyes suggested he wished to argue the point, he gave a curt nod.

Vice President Delaney was looking at Jeffrey with what appeared to be slight surprise. She asked Schodt, "What is your assessment of the situation?"

Schodt pulled a tablet from his back pocket, looked it over, and said, "My guess, due to the mining we are seeing, is they have come for resources," he looked at Jeffrey over the rims of his glasses, "not war."

Jeffrey's anger flickered. The need for resources was the most common cause of war.

Schodt continued, "Because their weapons are so advanced, it is my assessment they do not perceive us as a threat. They attack us in the local area only to keep that area secure, and as long as we give them room to operate, it is possible we will have no further conflict."

Delaney looked to Cantwell. "What is your recommendation?"

Cantwell remained silent for a moment as if weighing his words before he spoke. "Rebuilding the Hammerheads is paramount." He pointed to the ships on the Nav-Con. "We should move the fleet to a position between Jupiter and Earth. We'll let them do what they want to Europa. If they move sunward, we engage."

Delaney asked Cantwell, "When could the Hammerheads be ready?"

Cantwell looked to Jeffrey, who said, "We have an acceptable list of pilots. The physical modifications will take a few days. The pilots already know how to fly, but we'll need to acclimatize them to their new limits. Depending on individual circumstances, that could take a few weeks, or a few months." He looked to Cantwell, "It's been fifty years since those modifications were applied to living subjects. None of the scientists who did the work can still be alive."

"None," Cantwell said. "However, I have a skilled team researching their academic papers and procedures now."

Jeffrey nodded as he said, "So we need to assemble the pilots on the list. That will also take time."

"They're already here on the Lacedaemon," Cantwell said in a somewhat apologetic tone.

"The list you gave me wasn't for selection."

Cantwell shrugged. "No. Those are the pilots you'll be working with."

Jeffrey held his hands up in supplication to the inevitable, "Well, if they're even close to what I see in their dossiers, you chose well. I should get started right away."

"But that still doesn't leave us with an immediate option should the," Delaney looked to Schodt, whose scowl deepened, and offered him a smile, "...Exteris Ignotum move in on us."

A man wearing the four gold bars of a captain, who'd been standing several paces behind Cantwell, stepped forward. "Ma'am, if I may interrupt." He stood at an average height, had an average build, and looked at Delaney with dark-set eyes under a heavy brow. Jeffrey thought he saw faint frustration in the look Cantwell gave the captain.

Cantwell said, "Madam vice-president, this is Captain Donovan, my second for this operation and captain of the U.S.S. Lacedaemon." He said to Donovan, "speak freely captain."

Donavan clasped his hands behind his back as he said, "For now I believe we should rely on our drones. They are highly developed, well-tested, and have been in service for several years."

Hearing the word *drone* did not sit well with Jeffrey. He asked the captain, "Automated or piloted from a remote location?"

Donovan's expression hardened, as though Jeffrey had broken a ceiling of decorum by addressing him. "We have both. Our self-directed AI is particularly excellent. In dog fight trials, they've consistently outperformed human opponents. They anticipate effectively and have no G limitations save those of the spacecraft." Donovan fell silent, seeming to invite Jeffrey to agree with him.

Jeffrey said, "Forgive me for saying so, but I'm of the opinion that the Sthenos will obliterate your AI hardware."

Schodt pinched the bridge of his nose, lifting his glasses.

Vice President Delaney scowled but asked with simple curiosity, "Why do you feel that way Captain Holt?"

"AI is good," Jeffrey said, "but beyond its basic programming, it must learn to be effective in new situations. There are two key learning methods I am aware of, the first being trial and error. When we try something, if we fail, we try something else. It's linked to classical conditioning, which is fine in most cases, but in fighter combat, failure equals death—or in this case, destruction—and a destroyed AI system can't learn."

Donovan said, "The AI systems learn from others' failures. They can capitalize on the loss of another unit."

Jeffrey nodded. "That's good, a nice addition, but it won't be enough, not if the systems are like what I've seen in the past."

"I think," Donovan said, "you'll find our systems much more advanced than *when* you served." A finality in the *when* gave Jeffrey a clear message. Donovan didn't perceive him as military, just an old man who'd done a few years long ago.

Jeffrey let the slight go as he asked, "Do they think abstractly?"

Donovan remained silent.

Delaney asked, "What is your meaning Captain Holt?"

"Artificial Intelligence doesn't typically run at what one would consider the highest levels of intelligence, not fifty years ago anyway. I'm simply curious what level of intelligence these new systems possess."

With clear irritation, Donovan said, "The intelligence is—"

"Creative?" Jeffrey asked.

Donovan's eyes narrowed. "Not creative. Not yet."

"Captain Donovan," Jeffrey said, "it's not my intention to tear down your work, but I have to base my opinions on my experience and—"

"Excuse me," Delaney said, "in less than an hour I need to offer my recommendations to the president. I either need to understand the relevance of this conversation or have it end so we can move forward."

Jeffrey was taken somewhat aback by Delaney's directness, but she'd not shown anger, simply stated a truth.

He said, "A moment longer and you'll see the importance, I hope. Basic analytical intelligence, the ability to discern from possible outcomes and learn from a set of trial and error situations, is not creative intelligence. An illustration of this comes from an experiment done with birds. A cup filled with seeds is set on a string and lowered into a hole. A bird with low intelligence might stuff its head into the hole, fail to reach the seed, and move on. A bit more intelligence would allow the bird to realize pulling on the string would bring the cup closer. However, one pull would not be enough to reach it. When the bird lets the string go, it falls back down the hole. The bird still goes without. An intelligent bird, say a seagull, might pull on the string—trial—realize it cannot reach the seed—error—and look back over the situation. Then the bird might lift the string, step on it, and pull again, successfully lifting the cup out of the hole."

Crossing her arms as though impatient, Delaney said, "I don't see what a seagull getting seed has to do with drones."

"It has everything to do with AI. The trial and error intelligence the seagull illustrated is not the highest level," Jeffrey said. "Creative Intelligence goes one step further, which is solving problems outside the boundaries of available information. A raven has this. Ravens tested in this way look over the situation, pull the cup up, and without hesitation, step on the rope."

In an irritated tone, Donovan asked, "How is that any different than the seagull?"

"It's a slight but critical difference. The seagull had to hit failure before realizing the situation needed another approach. The raven was able to see the failure abstractly," Jeffrey tapped his temple, "and create a solution in its mind, skipping the step of experimentation."

Donovan asked, "What does this have to do with AI-s versus living pilots?"

"One key trait we look for in Hammerheads is creative intelligence—fast, abstract problem solving. Quick reflexes and massive G-tolerance will do nothing against the Sthenos' main talent, which is attacking with relentlessly changing tactics. They never give lesser pilots, AI, etc., a chance to learn. An average pilot will repeat successful tactics, which the Sthenos will avoid or exploit. They do not repeat patterns no matter if they are succeeding or failing." Jeffrey sighed and said, "I sincerely don't disagree for disagreement's sake, sir, but I wasn't brought here to say what people want to hear."

"Well," Donovan said, "disagree if you must, but we have no other options until your epic Hammerheads are ready to fly."

"Easy Donovan," Cantwell said.

Donovan looked to the admiral, and his expression constricted. With a slight lift of his chin, he said, "Yes, sir."

Delaney asked Jeffrey, "You don't disagree with human piloted remote drones?"

"Not exactly," Jeffrey said. "With the right pilots, they're a better option than AI drones and can save lives—but therein lies the problem."

Donovan's eyebrow lifted, and Jeffrey felt him wanting to cut in, but to his credit, he remained silent.

Jeffrey said, "To give his or her best, a pilot has to have everything on the line, be totally committed."

Now Donovan did cut in, "The remote drone pilots are some of the best pilots in the—"

"It's not about best and worst," Jeffrey said, finally allowing some exasperation to show in his tone. "It's about alive and dead. Combat pilots in the seat know if they don't give their all, they'll die, or someone with them will. I can have a good feeling about a pilot and make a guess at how he or she will respond, but I'll never know what that person is made of until people start dying. That's when we find the hardcore—those who can perform even in the face of death. Training can't do that. No matter how intense the exercise, in the back of a trainee's mind he or she knows if things go really bad, the exercise ceases and medics come in."

"And how does that effect our drone pilots?" Delany asked.

"They'll never be at risk, not directly. In combat, they'll know if their ship's destroyed another will be assigned."

Delaney had her eyes on the floor as she said absently, "Interesting…"

Captain Donovan said, "Vice president, I—"

She held up a finger. After a moment, she asked, "What value does lack of fear play? I would imagine fear inhibits performance, and a lack of it could be a benefit."

Jeffrey nodded, saying, "In certain situations, that's true, but these aren't office workers. The average person will be shut down by fear, but the average person wouldn't be able to face the Sthenos. To take down something that vicious, one needs obsessively competitive people so driven to be the best they would rather die than capitulate. Only those obsessives will be able to stand a chance. Again, we cannot

82

truly know who they are until we put them fully in harm's way. Also, there is another issue…"

Donovan rolled his eyes as the vice president asked, "Which would be?"

"Their physical separation from the machine creates… problems."

"We have a system," Donovan said, "that lets them feel as though they are in the craft—"

"It isn't enough. It goes beyond visual clues, beyond gauges. It's…" Jeffrey thought for a moment before saying, "…harmonics. To fly right, a pilot has to be able to connect with the machine. A good pilot can feel if a nuclear drive has an imbalanced injector or a slightly misaligned drive plate."

Donovan said, "That's all well and good, but the systems we have in place are proven to work."

Jeffrey didn't enjoy poking holes in Donovan's work but knew that holding back to protect feelings could get hundreds, if not thousands, killed. "There's another problem."

Donovan let out an exasperated breath. "Which is?"

"Distance. At times, those ships will be several thousand miles away from their pilots. The milliseconds it takes for visuals to get back and commands to get to the drones is too much."

"I can't believe milliseconds would make that big of an impact."

"I'm going to make a believer of you on this one," Jeffrey said and motioned for one of the Marines standing behind the vice president to come forward.

Delaney scowled but motioned for the Marine to do as Jeffrey asked.

Jeffrey indicated the Marine should face him. "Fifty years ago the Hammerheads were subjected to modifications with two key ends: increased G-force tolerance and reaction time. The purpose of the G-force mods is clear, but the reaction time is even more critical. The difference between winning and losing a dogfight can happen in milliseconds."

Jeffrey patted the Marine, who stood a few inches shorter, at perhaps six-foot-three, on the shoulder.

Jeffrey asked, "Your background is in hand-to-hand combat?"

"Yes sir, among other things. I specialized in VIP protection after basic training."

"So you'd say you're at a pretty high level when it comes to striking."

His tone stoic, the Marine said, "Yes, sir."

Jeffrey held out his hand. "Hit my hand. Just tap it."

"Yes, sir." Stepping back into a casual boxing stance, the Marine flicked his lead fist out in a blur, touching Jeffrey's hand with a light slap.

"Again."

The Marine's fist fired. Tap.

Another position. "Again."

Tap.

"He's very fast, don't you think?" Jeffrey asked Delaney, who nodded her agreement, her expression somewhat bored.

"Human nerves carry impulses about 30 to 100 meters per second. This means, in the short distance from eyes to brain and then to muscles, targeting a punch only takes a fraction of a second, but as people train at skills, the pathways they use for those skills become more efficient. As we use pathways in the brain, myelin wraps those pathways, increasing efficiency as much as one hundred times. There's a big difference between one hundred meters per second and 10,000 meters per second. But that applies to the brain. The rest of the nerve structure stays fairly slow even as we train. The increase in speed is developed in the brain. One of the key modifications beyond vascular strengthening to the Hammerheads is corporeal nerve enhancement. Nanites lace graphene into the nerve structure. The inefficient nerve no longer carries the signal, the graphene does. Graphene is an excellent conductor, so electrical impulses move along it at close to the speed of light. The impulse is slightly slowed over synapses and so on." Jeffrey touched his arm. "My nerve fibers translate messages not at the highest human capacity of 100 meters per second, but at nearly 300 million meters per second." That means, while I am much older, I can see his strikes and process and deliver a reaction far faster. By the time his hand is one-quarter of the way to my face, I have processed the strike and am adjusting."

He looked to the Marine again and said, "Hit me."

The Marine stared at him.

"Hit me," Jeffrey said, motioning with his hand for the Marine to come at him.

Delaney, her expression unimpressed as if Jeffrey were only trying to prove he was still strong in old age, asked, "Captain Holt, is this truly necessary?"

"Give me this moment. I guarantee no one is going to get hurt."

"I can't give that same guarantee, sir," the Marine said. "I won't hit you."

Jeffrey smiled at the Marine and said, "That's true. Now throw a punch, or I'll have you down for insubordination."

"Captain Holt," Delaney said, anger tinting in her words, "we do not need to see this."

"Yes," Jeffrey said, "you do. The point I'm about to make will illustrate why the drones won't work. He looked to the Marine, "Now hit me Marine."

The Marine squared on him and shot out a slow jab at Jeffrey's chest.

Jeffrey slapped the jab aside. "You call that a punch? How'd you make it into VIP protection?"

The Marine's face reddened.

Jeffrey smiled. "Make it real."

The Marine fired his fist harder, and Jeffrey slipped the punch past his right ear. He pushed the soldier backwards. "Come on kid, go for it. What's the problem, don't have the stomach for it?"

The Marine's eyes narrowed.

That's right, get mad. Let's do this right.

The Marine threw a fast jab at Jeffrey's face.

As Jeffrey slapped it aside with his right hand, he touched the side of the Marine's face with his left.

The Marine, tightening his fists until the knuckles whitened, threw a hook at Jeffrey's left ear. Jeffrey ducked under it and slapped the Marine's belly. The Marine threw another hook, which Jeffrey caught with his forearm. The Marine's teeth showed through his slightly parted lips as he chucked an uppercut, which Jeffery leaned away from, the fist brushing his nose.

The Marine now threw a frenzy of punches, jabbing, crossing, hooking. He growled as he put his weight behind the strikes. Jeffrey reacted to none of the Marine's feints while slipping or checking every real strike. After a few moments, the Marine, appearing to understand he would land nothing, stepped back as a runnel of sweat ran from his hairline.

Jeffrey held up a hand, saying, "That's more than enough for now. How old are you?"

Through breaths, the Marine said, "Twenty-four, sir."

"A highly trained and athletic twenty-four-year-old soldier can't hit a seventy-year-old man." He smiled at the Marine. "Don't worry, it's no fault of yours, you've got the skill and the speed. He," Jeffrey pointed to the Marine, as he addressed Delaney, "is an apex fighter, top of the food chain. But one of the best the U.S. Military has to offer can't touch me. The difference in performance will be the same between your drone pilots and the new wave of Hammerheads."

Donovan opened his mouth to speak, but Jeffrey held up his hand as he said, "When a drone is 1,000 miles away, the data must travel from the fighter's sensory gear, to the receivers on the ship, through the system, and to the pilot. The pilot must react, inputting changes, before those changes are broadcast, travelling the 1,000 miles back to the fighter. Because of the inherent delay, your drones will find no success in a Sthenos engagement."

Donovan said, "Those impulses travel at the speed of light, which is faster than from a person's fingertip to their brain and back based on the numbers you just gave us."

"Yes, but a delay is a delay. Any delay at all can cause huge problems. I've seen nerve-shined Hammerheads blown out of their cockpits because they had a slight head cold. In my experience, it isn't the big things that kill good pilots. Big things are easy to avoid. It's the stupid little things that take them down—a head cold or a secondary circuit going out."

Donovan, clearly furious with Jeffrey, had probably spent years developing and championing the drone program. Jeffrey didn't enjoy pouring water on his fire, but it was the wrong system and would fail.

Delaney said, "I'd like to hear your recommendation Captain Holt, but first I want Captain Donovan's." She looked to Donovan. "How might Captain Holt's alter your recommendation?"

Donovan squared his shoulders. "I do not believe Captain Holt's thoughts…" he looked over Jeffrey as though he were gum on his shoe, "…reflect our current state of technology, and so have no impact on my recommendation. We should attack without hesitation. With an international host of destroyers we have the Sthenos outnumbered twenty to one. We have thousands of drones ready. We should be decisive," he glared at Jeffrey, "not pensive."

Delaney, nodded and turned to Schodt, "Your thoughts?"

Schodt crossed his arms. "The *Exteris Ignotum* are clearly on a resource gathering expedition. We should wait and study them as much as possible. If they do not aggress the Earth, we let them take what they want."

Captain Donovan, jabbed his index finger toward Schodt as if he'd like to punch it through the man's sternum, "Of course it's about resources, all wars are about resources, whether they be land, fuel, water, or citizens."

In a dismissive tone, Schodt said, "They are taking resources we have no interest in."

"What if they're here for more than water?" Donovan asked. "What if they need gold, or sodium?"

"Nitrogen," Jeffrey said.

Donovan looked at him as if shocked that any support would come from him. "Yes," he held out his hand to Jeffrey, "nitrogen. Thank you. The most readily available supply of pure, gaseous nitrogen is Earth's atmosphere. If they need resources which are not as abundant or not found elsewhere in the solar system, then Earth is next."

"We should cross that bridge," Schodt said, "when we come to it."

Jeffrey said, "You might find that bridge destroyed when you run to defend it."

Schodt, his jaw set, glared at Jeffrey.

"All right gentlemen… all right," Delaney said holding up her hands. "I asked for his recommendation, and I have it. Captain Holt, your recommendation please."

"I think we can throw something new at them. While AI has its faults and we've discussed the limitations of remote drone pilots, the Hammerhead solution presents a key problem."

Donovan's expression became distrustful. "Which is?"

"We don't have enough time to prepare a significant number of pilots."

Donovan crossed his arms and watched Jeffrey, seeming to wait for another slight against his proposed solution.

Jeffrey looked to Delaney. "We should be smarter with our resources by using them all. We can't come at them with the same tactics we used fifty years ago. We simply aren't prepared to play that game. If we try, they'll grease us, then roll over to Earth and destroy it."

In a doubtful tone, Delaney asked, "You really think that's their plan?"

"They still need what they came for fifty years ago."

"How can you know that?"

"Because in the last engagement we killed *all* of them. Whatever they need must be of great value. Ice isn't rare enough to hold that kind of value. It simply wouldn't be worth the risk."

"And if," Delaney asked, "they haven't come for war? What if we follow your lead and attack? Who's at fault then?"

Jeffrey'd had enough, and the volume of his voice showed it. "They've already killed eighty-seven people." *One of which was a daughter to me.*

"I don't—"

He got into her face, and the two marines stepped close. "You listen to me Madam Vice President. The Sthenos have mastered inter-solar travel. We haven't. They've mastered weapons systems that cut the hides out of moons. We have to be ready for what we can't expect. The AI drones can't do that, and we need greater buy in from the skilled pilots we do have."

To her credit, she did not react to his anger. Her voice calm and eyes flat, she asked, "So what would you have us do?"

"We prep as many Hammerheads as we can and send them out with the drones. The Hammerheads will serve as the risk to the pilots running the drones here on the ship. Having their own asses on the line isn't possible, but we need their expertise and the hardware they can bring to the fight. So we sit them down, and we show them a small group of pilots. We tell them, if you screw up, these men and women die, so don't screw up."

"And you think that will work?" she asked.

"I don't know. But it's a better option than drones alone."

"So you're proposing a three-wave system."

"Not three... two. The Hammerheads and remote live pilots."

"No AI?"

"AI would be a waste of hardware." Jeffrey glanced at Donovan, who was staring at him as though he'd like to cut his skin off.

"My gut tells me," Jeffrey said, "we shouldn't engage until we can get a decent contingent of Hammerheads ready to fight. We have high-end pilots, but we need time with them."

"Are the Hammerheads a serious option?" Captain Donovan asked. "You said the scientists who developed the Hammerhead modifications are all dead."

"My team tells me," Admiral Cantwell said, "they are a few days away from beginning human application."

Delaney looked at the floor, appearing to fall into thought for some time. The men around her stood in silence watching her. Finally, she said, eyes still on the floor. "We'll discuss this all with the president in," she looked to the ship's clock, "thirty-six minutes. Until then, I have other business to attend to." She walked out of the room followed by the two Marines and Gerard Schodt.

CHAPTER 12

When Jeffrey entered the room, the others were already seated in chairs arranged in a half circle. Gerard Schodt did not look up from his tablet. Captain Donovan gave him a scowling glance as though he were a server offering an unacceptable distraction. Admiral Cantwell pointed to the last empty seat. As Jeffrey sat, Vice President Delaney gave him a brief, somewhat heartless smile.

Centered at the head of the room, lay a four-foot black disk.

"Gentlemen," Delaney said, "Shall we?"

Schodt nodded, and Donovan said, "Absolutely."

Jeffrey said nothing, feeling his consent wasn't needed.

Cantwell pointed to Delaney, giving her control of the room. She looked back to her bodyguards. The one Jeffrey had used for his demonstration touched a control panel. The space above the black disk went bright, and United States President John Moore formed out of the brightness and clarified, sitting with his arms folded on a half moon of desk, sharply cut off where the viewing disk ended. His right leg, extended outward, ended just below the knee. The image was of such high quality, Jeffrey almost expected gore to be exposed by the amputated limb, but it simply ended at the upper calf in a dark-gray cross-section.

President Moore's eyes scanned the room, settling on Jeffrey. "Captain Holt, I presume."

Jeffery understood that each of them must be sitting on black pedestals before the president. He did his best to keep his feelings out of his voice as he said, "Yes, sir." He hadn't liked the man when he ran for office, and he didn't like him now. While he'd never seen

Moore lose his temper or act out, something about his demeanor struck Jeffrey as the type who bullied to get what he needed.

Moore said, "Admiral Cantwell lauds you highly. It's a pleasure, sir."

"You as well, sir." Jeffrey hated to lie to be polite, but there it was.

Moore looked at the other faces in the room. "The rest of you I know. How shall we begin?" His right leg reformed as he drew it back under the desk.

"I have," Delaney said, "recommendations from Admiral Cantwell, Captain Donovan, Gerard Schodt, and Captain Holt. Would you like to hear directly—"

"Summarize for me."

"Absolutely, sir." Delaney gave no indication if being cut off bothered her. Jeffrey suspected it didn't as long as what needed to get done was done.

With his elbows still on the desk, Moore folded his hands together. Index fingers making a steeple, he touched their tips to the end of his nose. He closed his eyes as he listened to her detail the recommendations of each man. She ended on Holt's.

When she'd finished, Moore remained with his eyes closed. Jeffrey expected him to ask for her thoughts, but when he didn't, Jeffrey understood that he didn't respect her. He wondered if that came from a bigotry on Moore's part or a fault on hers.

Moore said, "I appreciate each of your positions on the issue, but we do not have the luxury of time. This threat cannot be allowed to reach Earth." He looked to Schodt. "I reject that they are peaceful. They have destroyed an international base, killing all but two inhabitants. The destruction of the survival pod is telling. They kill the innocent..." he looked to Holt, "so we kill them."

Delaney's face flushed slightly, Jeffrey assumed, because her hug-it-out war policy was coming off the table.

She asked, "Do we wait for the Hammerheads to be—"

"Absolutely not." Moore waved his hand with unmasked irritation. "I also do not agree with Captain Holt. Our drones are not inferior solutions." He locked his dark eyes on Jeffrey. "You, sir, are living too much in the past. Our new technologies are better than the options we had before. We have thousands of drones. Those coupled with our new weapons systems have made the Hammerheads obsolete. Please reassign your pilots to Commander Holloway. Your services are no longer needed."

"No longer be—" Jeffrey began, but Cantwell's fingers lifted a quarter inch off his knee. Jeffrey fell silent, and Cantwell offered no argument to Moore.

With the president ending the Hammerheads with a few words, Jeffrey felt uselessness creep in on him.

At least give me an old Phantom and let me fly out to meet them. Let me end that way.

While Jeffrey found relying on the drones unsettling, there was one hope in the new weapon. Before he'd followed Sarah's career, Leif had been part of the team to develop them. Jeffrey knew a bit more than he should about the classified systems. Perhaps it was true, perhaps the drones, coupled with those weapons could be the deciding factor. Maybe the Hammerheads were an obsolete concept—the age of blood and bone coming to a close in his lifetime. Still… Jeffrey couldn't fully accept that. Perhaps that put him in the wrong.

"Captain Holt?"

The question had come from Delaney.

Jeffrey looked to her. "I apologize. My thoughts were elsewhere."

Moore scowled. "Captain Holt, I need everyone here to be on the same page, I asked you and the others if you are willing to support the assault plans as laid out by Captain Donovan."

"If my services are no longer needed, then my support doesn't factor in. True?"

"Well said." Moore looked to Delaney, who watched Jeffrey as if measuring his reaction to being slapped down.

"Samantha, I'll leave it in your capable hands. Keep me informed."

"Of course sir."

Moore turned to the empty wall to his right. "Cut the fee—" He and his half moon of desktop vanished leaving the black disk empty.

Gerard Schodt stood, tucked his tablet under his arm and walked from the room, his voice fading down the corridor as he said, "We are dealing with an intelligent race. I refuse to take part in the idiocy of..."

Seeming pleased with the meeting's outcome, Donovan said, "It would seem, Captain Holt," he weighted the word *captain* as if it were humorous to him, "that you are relieved from the trouble of having to work with Schodt after all."

Jeffrey tried to keep the anger from his voice as he said, "Yes."

Donovan's smile held a malicious edge. "I doubt Admiral Cantwell will allow that. You're a thorn in my side Holt, but we find thorns keep us on our toes."

Jeffrey distrusted the comment, which he'd most likely made to appease Cantwell.

Standing, Admiral Cantwell smoothed the front of his uniform. "Well said, Donovan. Holt, the president did not give me a direct order to relieve you."

"I'm sorry?" Jeffrey asked.

"Until someone tells me directly to do otherwise, I'm holding you to your commitment." His looked to Delaney, who's eyes had gone wider, lips parted as if to argue. "Do you take issue with that?"

Snapping her mouth shut, she offered no agreement nor challenge.

Jeffrey looked to Donovan. "I'd like to discuss tactics with your flight commander. May I be involved in that arena?"

Donovan gave him a flat look. "Not if you continue to espouse your distaste for our course of action. I don't need dissenters."

"Now that the decision is made, you'll get no such unprofessionalism from me."

Donovan seemed satisfied with that. Standing, he said, "I'll introduce you to Commander Holloway."

"Thank you, sir." He followed Donovan out of the room.

CHAPTER 13

Sitting in the officer's lounge, Jeffrey sipped lemon-tinged iced tea. Under the heavy G's of deceleration, the glass, his hand, and his arm felt as heavy as his heart. He'd be seeing Leif in less than an hour, and he had no idea what he'd say. Nothing would help. He felt powerless and, as it was his way to know what to do, unsettled.

He set the glass down with a solid thump on the table. After accelerating to nearly a quarter of the speed of light, they'd reached their median distance to the rendezvous point two days ago. After turning tail-on to their target, their deceleration had been constant. The thrust, shoving through the cross-mounted decks, caused the weight of objects to triple.

The motors of a passing sailor's support frame whirred. Even with the frame, Jeffrey, who'd remained strong as he'd aged, felt exhausted from the constant exertion of simply moving about the ship.

"Finish up your food folks," a CS called from the kitchen in a tone that echoed the same tiredness. I want all dishes in the next five minutes. I have to have everything washed and secured before we cut burn."

Jeffrey drank off the last of his tea and stood, his frame's motors spooling up. As he walked, he kept his arms crossed. Lowering them caused swelling and tingling. The constant acceleration put strain on his heart as well. Even in the best circumstances, the human body could only handle such high deceleration for a few days before exhaustion began to break people down.

He made his way to his quarters, where he sat on his bunk and unstrapped the frame from his shoulders, hips and legs. Just to see how it would be, he tried to stand, knowing it was the equivalent of weighing over seven hundred pounds. He couldn't lift himself from the bed.

An announcement came over the intercom, "Cutting deceleration burn in two minutes. As additional adjustments nearing two G's may be required, maintaining mag-boot connection to the designated floor surfaces is required."

As Jeffrey put on his boots and connected them to the floor, the announcer returned. "Cutting deceleration in one minute… fifty-nine seconds… fifty-eight sec…" When it reached zero, the crushing force Jeffrey had become accustomed to vanished. His mattress decompressed, pushing him to standing as a knock sounded on the hatch.

He opened it to find Sam Cantwell.

"We'll be rendezvousing with a shuttle from the U.S.S. Rhadamanthus in less than ten minutes. I thought you'd like to be present."

A jolt of nerves rushed through him. "Yes… thank you."

As Jeffrey followed Cantwell down the passageway, he could think of nothing to say. Leif's deep emotions had brought him great joy and sorrow over his lifetime. They would be crushing him now. Jeffrey remembered Leif as a baby, small in his arms, heart quick in a little chest, eyes clear blue, lungs powerful. But Leif had been a man for well over a decade now. In that quick jump of memory, Jeffrey felt overwhelmed by loss. He felt as though he'd done nothing but lose throughout is life, his friends to war, his wife to cancer, his little boy to time, and now Sarah.

Reaching the airlock, they stood facing the yellow and black striped wall, waiting. Jeffrey swallowed and shifted his feet.

It had taken him decades to so much as get his head above water. Through the process though, Jeffrey had found a strength he hadn't expected. His mind had become like a storm scrubbed sky, quiet and clear.

Right now, Leif was caught in the storm. Jeffrey knew his son's heart must be rent wide, a wound which would never fully heal. Jeffrey grieved, not for Sarah—her pain was over—but for Leif. Jeffrey could only offer to be there for him, offer understanding, and he understood too well how little that would seem to Leif at this early stage.

The light beside the airlock began to pulse red as air rushed on the other side of the armor-thick doors. When it faded, the light pulsed yellow, then green. Locks thunked, and the doors separated at the center black stripe.

The retracting door panels exposed men and women dressed in black Navy Special Warfare jumpsuits. As he scanned the faces looking for Leif, profound shock overwhelmed him when the door exposed Stacy. She offered him a subdued nod. Now Leif came into view to the left. A younger man, no more than 20 years old, stood beside him. Both wore generic green jumpsuits, and woeful tiredness underlined their eyes. Leif's expression did not change when his eyes met his father's, remaining dead, shut down. Jeffrey made no motion and said nothing, letting his son know that everything could wait.

Stacy saluted. "Permission to come aboard sir?"

Returning the salute, Cantwell nodded. "Granted. Welcome to the Lacedaemon."

"Thank you sir." She stepped out of the airlock, walked up to Jeffrey—her boots clacking on the deck—and saluted him. As he returned the gesture, he fought the urge to hug her in front of her team and lost to it.

Wrapping her in his arms, he said quietly, "Thank you for bringing him back to me."

When he let her go, she tried to smile. Failed. To hide the redness that had bloomed in her eyes, she did not turn as she spoke to her team. "Let's go folks. Time to debrief."

"Yeoman," Cantwell said to a man standing beside him. "Show the Special Warfare unit to my ready room. We have a great deal to discuss." He looked to Stacy. "Commander Zack, I will be with you shortly."

"Yes sir." She saluted and followed the yeoman out. Each member of her team saluted, and when the Admiral returned his salute, they walked out.

"Son," Admiral Cantwell said to the younger man from Europa base, "I'll see you to your bunk." He motioned for the young man to follow him.

"Okay," the young man said, stepping out of the airlock. Jeffrey could see he was unsure, scared, but not in mourning. He'd lost no one. His family, and anyone else close to his heart, was safe at home… as safe as anyone on Earth was at the moment.

Jeffrey listened to their footfalls fading down the passageway. Stepping out of the airlock, Leif came to stand before him, stony eyes on his father's chest.

"I'm sorry Leif."

Leif gave a curt nod.

Jeffrey didn't want Sarah's death to root down in Leif as the deaths of those close to him had, but he'd been through it too many times. It had to be this way. Death's natural order required it to dig into the soul, sinking into the dark soil to grow a dismal weed, which would have to live its course before withering away, leaving behind a scarred stump. Leif had always been a bit more like his light-hearted mother in his youth, but as he'd moved through his twenties, his seriousness and focus had intensified. At this moment, Jeffrey wished Leif could have stayed more his mother's son. She'd always been able to express her emotions more readily. When her own mother had died, she had sobbed openly, letting the grief pour out of her. In his hardened stare, Jeffrey understood Leif would cultivate Sarah's death, hold it close and let it grow deep… but she deserved no less.

Jeffrey took hold of Leif's shoulders and watched his face, feeling uneasy. There was something else there. Something more had happened on Europa base, but now was not the time for badgering.

He said, "If you need to talk, I'm here, but that's the last I'm going to bother you with it… for now."

As Leif's eyes rose to meet Jeffrey's, Jeffrey said. "Let's get you to your quarters so you can clean up. They have a lot of questions for you."

Concern formed in Leif's eyes. "What happens next… with them?"

"You mean the Sthenos?"

"Yes."

"We kill them."

"Good."

CHAPTER 14

Laying in his bunk in the more comfortable 1.5 G's created by the fleet's acceleration toward Jupiter, Jeffrey's thoughts turned to the war fifty years before. Sthenos destroyers had appeared on the shoulder of Mars and shattered Demos, obliterating its observation base and raining debris across the planet's surface, battering a Russian facility. An international declaration of war had been made within the hour. A global mobilization for war hadn't occurred in over two centuries. Before World War II commanders and kings could recline in the safety of their cities far from the front as their young men—mostly poor and underprivileged—did the fighting and dying. The nuclear age changed everything. The apocalyptic warheads had unexpectedly brought peace. The destruction of Nagasaki and Hiroshima had not just ended the war in the Pacific theater, it had marked the end of all major national conflict. Unable to attack their enemies without putting themselves and their own families in as much risk as the young soldiers at the front, world leaders, sane or insane, had been forced to find new, better methods.

Nagasaki and Hiroshima had been leveled, as many as a quarter million people killed in just a few days, because Japan needed oil, and the U.S. had stopped supplying it. Jeffrey had been to the conflict's point of origin—Pearl Harbor. He'd looked into the translucent water where trigger and convict fish drifted and darted through the half-disintegrated hulk of the U.S.S. Arizona. Looking across the calm water through the floating monument's white beams, he imagined a prop driven Mitsubishi Zero, one of the most deadly weapons of war yet built, coming in slow and loud. Yet, despite the destruction of the attack, Japan had missed her mark. The carriers had been away December seventh...

Jeffrey sat up and said into the darkness, "The carriers were away..."

Leaping from his bunk, he threw open his hatch and sprinted down the corridor, his old knees aching against the additional half G. As he approached a cross-corridor, a sailor came around the corner. Jeffrey tried to dodge him, but the sailor side-stepped in the same direction, and they crashed into each other. Jeffrey caught a support beam as he snatched the sailor's shirt, keeping him from falling.

Without a word to the sailor, Jeffrey sprinted up the ladder to the broad expanse of the bridge, where he stood huffing, sweat dripping from his forehead.

The night watch commander turned to the commotion as a yeoman called out, "Captain on Deck."

In a shocked tone, the commander asked, "Captain Holt," her eyes scanned downward, a slight flush blooming in her cheeks, "why aren't you in uniform?"

"It's an ambush."

"Excuse me?"

"It's the only thing that makes sense. They know we're dangerous. They wouldn't just show up and start mining."

"We've been through this, captain."

Holt waved the comment away. "They want us to think they don't care. They want us to mount an attack. It's Pearl Harbor in reverse."

She looked at him as though she thought he'd lost his mind. "I don't follow y—"

"They know we're afraid of them. They *knew* we'd overreact."

"Overreact?"

"Yes," Jeffrey said. "They want us all together, moving toward Jupiter. Out here, we're sitting ducks, and the Earth is unprotected."

"For three Sthenos destroyers? They're good, but not—"

"There's not three, I guarantee it."

102

At that, the watch commander blanched, looking upward, out the latticed bridge windows as if her eyes might tell her something that the instruments couldn't. She looked back to Jeffrey with disbelief. "The long range scanners..." but she trailed off.

Jeffrey said, "Fifty years ago, they arrived at Demos without warning. We never sorted out how they did that."

"They can stealth x-ray scanners."

"Yes."

"Oh my God..."

"Exactly."

The watch commander turned to the man beside her. "Yeoman, get Admiral Cantwell."

"Yes ma'am."

...

Admiral Cantwell stood in the center of the bridge looking out on the depth of space. "How many do you suppose there might be?"

"No idea," Jeffrey said, his eyes on the Nav-Con where the Lacedaemon hovered in the center. Behind it followed the motley array of battle cruisers—many of the same cruisers he'd helped save ten years earlier. Some had only recently returned to service after the damage of ejecting their reactor cores. The ships' drive sections glowed in various fission hues, thousands of lives on each ship. He'd seen destroyers cut in half by the Sthenos. He'd seen them shot through—rammed through.

Cantwell put his hand on Jeffrey's shoulder. "Fifty years ago, with only ten of their own destroyers, the Sthenos demolished or disabled over 90% of the Earth's militarized fleet."

"Sam, we're not facing three, and not ten. There are more... I'm sure of it."

Cantwell said, "Jeffrey, I know you feel convinced of this, but I can't turn back or disperse the entire fleet on a hunch. We'll need new orders from the president."

"Perhaps I can help with that," Vice President Delaney said as she came up the ladder onto the bridge. She looked half-asleep to Jeffrey, the first time he'd seen a frailty in her otherwise bulletproof demeanor.

Admiral Cantwell gave Delaney a summary of what Jeffrey had told him.

Her brow furrowing with skepticism, she asked, "So this is based on a hunch?"

Jeffrey said, "A hunch and one other thing. Sam, I wanted to save this until the vice president was with us."

He said to the Nav-Con officer, "Please bring up Europa."

With a practiced motion, the Nav-Con officer swept the fleet aside. The Jovian system came into view with Jupiter about the size of a marble surrounded by a chain of bright sparks. The planetary system shifted to the right as one spark centered itself and grew until Europa was four feet in diameter, suspended over the Nav-Con's surface.

The moon's pale, cracked surface shone bone-brilliant in the distant sunlight. A blade-thin scar ran across its face.

The Nav-Con officer asked, "Did you want to see the Sthenos ships?"

"Yes. Thank you."

The moon lowered as its dome expanded across the Nav-Con's disk. The scar grew into three ragged canyons. At their termini, the Sthenos destroyers cutting cannons still tore into the ice, illuminating it a pale-green.

When Delaney moved to Jeffrey's side, he could feel warmth from her arm near his. He suppressed an impulse to move away from her.

Delaney pointed to the Sthenos ships. "Ma'am," she said to the Nav-Con officer, "can you zoom in more?"

"Absolutely Ma'am."

The center ship grew until its midsection had filled the Nav-Con. The gnat-like ships still arced around the destroyer, ice caught in insect-like mandibles. As they approached the destroyer, they released the ice to freefall toward the dark opening on its back. However, the ice fell past the opening, crashing down to mix with the other debris misting the surface.

"It's all a show," Delaney said.

Jeffrey nodded. "I'm not sure of their true intention, but this," he pointed to the ships, "is a sham. We're walking into a trap."

"You assume it's a trap," Delaney said.

"Ma'am I—"

She raised her hand to silence him. "What do you propose we do about it?"

"We arrest our approach. My guess is, we're doing exactly what they want us to. If we change that behavior—"

Cantwell cut in, "We can observe their reaction to it."

"What," Delaney asked, "if they don't react?"

Jeffrey said, "We continue on to Europa and hit them with everything we have."

Her expression darkened. Motioning for her guards to stay put, she walked toward the exit ladder saying, "Captain Holt, walk with me please."

Jeffrey looked to Cantwell, who shrugged.

With suspicion, Jeffrey followed her as she descended the ladder from the bridge and walked down a quiet corridor. After rounding a corner, she turned to face him. When her eyes, the color of autumn leaves, met his, his heart rate accelerated. He exhaled to suppress what he dismissed as an instinctual reaction to a physically beautiful woman.

"I don't think," she said in a quiet voice, leaning close to him, "the president will allow the attack to be called off, but I wanted you to know, off the record, that I think there's something to what you're saying."

"Why does it have to be off the record?"

When she took hold of his forearm with gentle fingertips, Jeffrey scowled. She stood perhaps only six inches shorter.

"You don't have to distrust me Jeffrey. I'm not like them," she said as she slid her fingertips down his arm. "I have a sincere appreciation for... experience."

Her charm could not get Jeffrey to forget that she and President Moore had both made campaign promises to dismantle the military machine. Once, in an interview with News Source's Terri Blakely, she'd called military commanders *fear mongers* and those serving under them *minions of an outdated and socially detrimental system.*

"I thought people like you had written off my experience as implanted hallucinations."

Her smile vanished. "I can admit I may have been... wrong. Can you?"

"Wrong? In what way?"

"Jeffrey," her easy smile returned, "I don't need saber rattling right now. I need everyone to take a step back, and consider the possibility that we aren't facing a villainous race here. So many wars in our history have been based on cultural misunderstandings. Those people up there believe very much in you. Every time you get them riled up to fight, my job becomes more difficult. I need support from *all* areas if we're going to effectively face this situation."

Jeffrey watched her for a moment before saying, "Vice President—"

"Call me Samantha."

Disinclined to do so, he said with a sigh, "Samantha... I understand that you want to believe that life makes sense and everyone has intrinsically decent hearts. However, for every war fought over a misunderstanding, ten are founded in boundless greed. There was no misunderstanding when the Nazis murdered eleven million civilians and prisoners of war. Nearly every culture on Earth has been guilty at one time or another of allowing self-serving gluttony to flare into cold-blooded brutality. Societies seem to have a natural tendency to descend into egocentrism and bigotry even if they begin with the best intentions."

"Those were *human* societies. We're not dealing with humans."

Jeffrey removed her hand from his arm and took hold of her shoulders. "I need you to believe me when I say the Sthenos are far worse."

"But we've had more than 200 years of peace. Surely…"

Jeffrey let the flash of anger he felt show in his tone. "We've had *fifty* years of peace Vice President Delaney." He glared at her, daring her to step back into her old beliefs. When she seemed to falter, he said, "In our own history, moments of long-term peace have come and gone many times. Those periods seem to be an exception to the natural order rather than a progression."

Crossing her arms, she said, "That strikes me as a dismal world view."

"I'd be happy to give it up, but the memories I have," he touched his temple, "which are founded in my experience with the Sthenos, won't let me."

"What if that experience was based on a misunderstanding? What if there is a better solution?"

"It wasn't, and there isn't."

She flushed with anger. "I won't accept that."

"Madam Vice President, I'd like nothing more than to be wrong. If we could solve this without death, I'd be the first one in line, but we can't. Blood's already been spilt."

"Is that what this is about? Your daughter-in-law?"

Jeffrey went still, unable for a moment to believe she'd bring Sarah into this. "Don't."

"Don't what? State the obvious? Don't be like this Jeffrey."

"Like—what?"

"Don't make this about revenge."

"I'll make it about what I will."

Her jaw flexed. Drawing a deep breath, she appeared to succeed in bolting her anger under a professional blankness. Straightening the front of her shirt, she said, "Mark my words *captain*, I won't allow you to pour gas on this fire." Without another word, She walked away leaving a cooling, empty space.

"Where are you going?"

As she disappeared around the corner, she said, "To get a message to the president. Despite your stubbornness, I'm still willing to back the testing of your theory. While we believe in different ends, I think we both agree that our current course is wrong. We'll convene in the admiral's conference room in one hour."

...

Jeffrey sat beside Cantwell in the conference room. Delaney sat across from him. Cantwell, in good military fashion, looked well-rested despite having been stone asleep only a few minutes earlier. He sipped from a pale ceramic mug before saying, "I don't think I'm going to enjoy the next few minutes."

Delaney said, "Our messages from Earth are currently some twenty minutes one-way. Despite that, we already have a response from the president. I've viewed it and will share it with you in its entirety, but first I'll show you the message I sent to him. I want you all to have a complete picture."

Jeffrey tried to guess at the president's response based on her expression, but her expression remained neutral as she asked one of the Marines to call up her message. She appeared on the pedestal, sitting with one leg crossed over the other. Jeffrey's eyes drew up the length of her leg and along the curve of her hip. He closed his eyes, and when he opened them, he kept his gaze focused on the image's face.

"Hello, John," her image said, looking as real as the woman who sat across from him. She smiled beautifully with a practiced measure of humility. Jeffrey sensed insincerity in the perfection of that smile and wondered how much of her behavior was honest and how much manipulation.

"We have a possible complication to discuss. Captain Holt has suggested the Sthenos ships are baiting the fleet. He feels that somewhere, nearby, more ships are waiting to ambush us. He bases this on his previous experience. I'm not sure if he's correct." She offered this with a slight smile as she shifted in her seat, her chest stretching her shirt.

As her message continued, Jeffrey felt he understood her as a legislator. Politicians wanted one thing above all else, influence over others. Of course, looking as she did, she would have used every tool at her disposal from her intelligence to her beauty to rise to the position she held. He recalled how close she'd stood to him at the Nav-Con and her fingertips on his arm in the corridor. She'd attempted to use her guile on Jeffrey, but he was no one's puppet.

Delaney's message to the president detailed Jeffrey's deceleration tactic. When she'd finished, she gave a final, perfect smile and signed off.

Delaney said, "I'm sorry to have mentioned you Captain Holt, as you're technically not supposed to be involved, but I needed to lend the credibility of your experience to influence his decision."

I'm sure you're sorry. Jeffrey saw through her mention of him. *I won't allow you to pour gas on this fire*, she'd said. Instead of arguing with Cantwell directly, she intended to illustrate Jeffrey's involvement and let the president do her dirty work for her.

Quelling his anger, he said, "You did what you had to do."

She held his gaze for a moment, a slight smile in her eyes, before facing Cantwell. She glanced back at him as she said, "Admiral, I'm afraid I created a bit of trouble, but there's not much I can do about it."

Cantwell asked, "What sort of trouble?"

"I'll share his response with you as explanation."

The admiral nodded his consent, and the Marine called up the message.

A half-circle of desk and a leather chair appeared on the disk, blurred for a moment, then resolidified. The president was nowhere to be seen.

"Samantha," the president's voice said, "Admiral Cantwell."

He materialized as he stepped in beside the chair holding a tablet. He wore no tie and his shirt collar was lifted on one side.

Reaching beyond the area of the viewer, his arm and the tablet disappeared. His arm drew back, reforming, the tablet gone. As he sat, he crossed his hands on the half circle of desk.

Tapping its surface, he said in an irritated tone, "Midnight."

The Lacedaemon's clock, which ran on GMT, read 5:38 A.M.

The president propped his elbows on the desk and pinched the bridge of his nose. "I have to meet with the secretary of defense at 6 A.M." He looked into the room, his eyes meeting no one.

"Samantha, as you stated in your message, you are there to support me. I would expect no less. After all, the fate of your career is tied to mine. I understand you want to be cautious, but I cannot have you going off half-cocked due to some old man's delusion."

Old man's delusion?

Jeffrey's hands gripped into fists.

President Moore said, "Admiral Cantwell, I understand how I slipped during our last communication. I'll be clear now. I'm giving you a *direct order.* If Holt's theory proves to be wrong, we will have wasted time and resources. In that case, which I am *sure* it is, Jeffrey Holt is to be removed from military service. Keep him away from your staff, and Samantha, you'd damn well better stop listening to him. Still..." He fell silent as though it pained him to admit that anything Jeffrey offered could possibly be correct. "...if I ignore his suggestion, and his hunch proves correct, I'll be the biggest fool to have ever served in this office. Proceed with your deceleration. See what happens. If there's no change in status, continue with the attack per Donovan's recommendation. If I hear nothing from you, I will assume all is well and Holt is back in retirement... where he should have stayed."

He nodded to his right and vanished from the view-pad.

Jeffrey clasped his hands together, leaning forward on his elbows. Having a man like President Moore making decisions was bad for war. Reactionary men concerned more with popularity than prudence could cause the deaths of millions. Jeffrey felt sure something horrific was about to happen, and that only those with

110

definitive souls, those willing to sacrifice themselves for others, would be able to stop it.

In a flat tone Delaney said, "I think that went well."

Jeffrey looked at her with a coldness.

She gave him a perfect smile. "Something troubling you Captain Holt?"

"I'm fine." He stood. "I suppose we should find out if I stay in service."

"I don't give a rat's ass," Cantwell said as he slapped his hand on his armrest and stood, "what Moore tells me to do. For all I care, he can throw me in a cell. He won't pull me from command until this is over. Holt, you stay, no matter the outcome. That's an order. Clear?"

"Crystal, sir."

Delaney came to her feet, dropping her tablet as Captain Donovan said, "Sir I—"

"I won't have dissent on this Donovan."

Donovan's chin lifted. "Yes, sir."

Delaney's eyes widened with disbelief as she said, "Admi—"

"Ma'am, if you want to pull me from service, do it now, but unless you plan on leading this fleet yourself, I suggest you consider your next words carefully."

Her eyes blazing with anger, she said, "I won't pull you right now, but you must know this could end your military career."

"Don't make promises you can't keep madam vice president. My military career was already supposed to be over." He looked to Jeffrey, "Walk with me *Captain* Holt," and left the room.

As Jeffrey followed Cantwell out of the room and down the corridor toward the bridge, he said, "I don't think that played out to her expectations."

With anger in his tone, Cantwell said, "Well then, she and her boss might want to reconsider whom they're dancing with."

•••

111

Jeffrey stood beside Cantwell as he asked, "Am I linked to the fleet?"

Captain Raeburn, a stocky, balding man with a heavy bristle across his face, which Jeffrey considered had probably grown there in the last few hours, said, "Yes sir."

"Fleet," Cantwell said, "cut acceleration."

The men and women at the helm began inputting information and communicating in hushed tones. The subtle vibration in the deck plates vanished. The stillness and ensuing weightlessness felt like death.

"Initiate turn."

Above, the star field came to life, sweeping the Jovian system's bright chain of sparks away. The carbon fiber shin and calf supports of his mag-boots allowed Jeffrey to stay upright as his mass accelerated through the turn with the ship, but he did have to widen his stance to brace himself. Above, which really was *out ahead* relative to the Lacedaemon's bow, the small, brilliant disk of the sun slid into view from the right, settling a few degrees past center. The ships of the fleet, which had been behind the Lacedaemon, now hung among the stars, long blades of metal, all different constructions, some silvery, others glistening white, still others like dark iron.

"Begin deceleration burn of 1 G on my mark," Cantwell said. "Mark."

The vibration returned to the ship as the Lacedaemon came back to life and the weight returned to Jeffrey's feet. Out among the stars, fifty-six sets of engine thrusters erupted to life in reds, oranges, and white-hot blues.

Jeffrey looked to the Nav-Con where the Sthenos destroyers' green blades of energy still cut into the ice.

"No change," he said.

Delaney came to stand beside him. "Don't give in so readily, captain."

With Cantwell's surprising resistance, she was now playing nicer. He felt the subtle warmth of her nearness again and caught the lightly floral scent of her. A flourish in his chest rose up his neck, warming his face. He moved around the Nav-Con until the disk stood fully between them. He looked up to the thruster glow of the fleet.

After a moment, she moved to stand beside him again. "Are you all right?" Her hand touched his back. The other moved gently to his forearm.

"Please," he said quietly as he took her hand from his arm, "don't try this with me."

"Excuse me?" Her dark-amber eyes narrowed.

He said quietly, "I know what you're doing. I'm not a chess piece to be moved around where best fits your purpose."

She kept her voice low, "Are you suggest—"

"They're moving!" The Nav-Con officer said.

Jeffrey looked to the Nav-Con. The Sthenos ships had shut down their beams, and were lifting away from the gouged surface of Europa where shattered blocks of ice descended slowly through the fog of frozen vapor.

"Nav-Con," Admiral Cantwell said, "keep them on the viewer." His voice remained calm as he said, "Unfortunately Holt, it seems you're to stay in service."

"That is unfortunate," Jeffrey said. "Looks like we're in for hell."

"Navigation," Cantwell asked, "from this position and velocity, how long would it take us to reach Earth?"

"Earth?" Delaney asked incredulous. "What are you suggesting?"

Cantwell held up his hand to silence her. "If you get underfoot vice president, I'll have you removed from the bridge."

"Admiral, I will not be spoken to in that way"

"Ah," Cantwell said, "you just were. Now stay out of the way."

Eyes narrowing, she said nothing.

A male officer, his face still holding hints of the boy he'd been only a few years before, ran his fingers over the panel at his workstation and said, "At 3 G's of deceleration we'll have Earth-relative full-stop in ten hours 31 minutes. At that point, under full acceleration and deceleration we'll be four days and two hours from Earth orbit sir."

"What thrust percentage can the entire fleet match?"

"Eighty-five percent, sir, but that will put us at 4 G's."

"We can't sustain 4 G's for that length of time," Cantwell said. "Get us prepped for deceleration at 3 G's. We need to be Earthbound *now*."

"Yes sir." The officer's fingers flew across the console, pattering on the glass surface like fat raindrops. After a moment, he said, "The figures are away sir."

"Fleet," Cantwell said, "prepare for deceleration burn at 3 G's A.S.A.P. Report when you are prepped." He looked out to the myriad of glowing thrusters hanging among the stars. Jeffrey felt he could read the admiral's mind.

How many will be with us in the end?

Cantwell said, "Notify the ship to prep for burn."

"Yes sir."

As the message came over the loudspeakers, Jeffrey went to the back wall, strapped a support frame onto his legs, and returned to the center of the bridge, the frame motors whirring with each step. The rest of the crew took turns putting on support frames as Cantwell reclined into his command seat, kicked back so he could look up at the fleet.

"All ships have reported in ready to decelerate, sir."

"Fleet," Cantwell said, "begin 3 G deceleration burn on my mark." Cantwell looked to Jeffrey with a gravity in his expression as though the command to decelerate was the moment of engagement in the war. "Mark."

The myriad of ships' thrusters intensified. Some began to grow closer, some further away.

Cantwell said, "The Lacedaemon is on point, synch your burns to us." The ships that appeared to be pulling away were actually slowing down faster than the Lacedaemon. As the burns synched, they became still again. However, one ship continued to move closer. It would soon slip past to starboard.

"Navigation" Cantwell said, "identify the ship failing to match deceleration."

"The H.M.S. Halcyon sir. They've recently reported faults in their thruster systems."

"Contact them and report on their situation."

"Yes sir."

Cantwell looked to Jeffrey, who nodded to him, knowing full well what was going through Cantwell's mind. If the Halcyon had mechanical problems, it would have to be left behind, exposed to the Sthenos destroyers. The fleet could not delay the defense of Earth for one ship.

"Navigation," Cantwell asked as he leaned back, looking up at the thrusters among the stars, "identify our lead ship."

The young officer scanned his screen. "The R.O.C.S. Mogui Gou, sir."

"Chinese?"

"Yes sir."

Cantwell said. "Fleet, when we have all-stop and acceleration is on, the R.O.C.S Mogui Gou will be on point. Come gradually to a delta formation behind her. She will set pace."

"Sir," a navigation officer said, "The H.M.S. Halcyon has been able to increase thrust. She's now holding with the fleet."

Cantwell gave him a quick nod. Celebrations would wait. Small victories could turn tragic with a moment's bad luck.

On the Nav-Con, the Sthenos destroyers' shadows diminished on the ice as they lifted away, their formation widening. The swarming mining ships had begun docking in landing bays in the destroyer's prows.

Delaney stood on the other side of the display, eyes locked on the Sthenos destroyers, her expression dark.

With the Nav-Con centered on the destroyers, Europa drifted out of view. For some reason, that made Jeffrey think of Sarah.

Trapped in Jovian orbit, her corpse floated in the near absolute zero, abandoned. He imagined her face, a frozen death mask framed by her hair, which had been flowing and beautiful, now an icy mat. Unbidden tears began to stream from his eyes.

"Jeffrey..." Delaney said. She touched his shoulder. Pushing the tears away with the back of his sleeve, he let out a growling huff as he forced the image out of his head. He looked to her and saw, what appeared to be, sincere concern in her eyes.

The Nav-Con officer looked up from the podium. "Their course is settling out, sir."

Admiral Cantwell asked, "And it is?"

"Coming to bear on empty space. At their current acceleration, they'll come into a trailing position on the fleet, sir."

Silence descended in the room as Jeffrey saw many of the young officers glance at him and Cantwell. He knew his eyes were still red from that moment of weakness, and he chided himself. He had to be stronger. Everyone around him would be looking to him, Cantwell, and the other senior officers to understand how they should feel.

The next words Jeffrey heard, spoken by a female navigation officer, took him a moment to comprehend, as if his mind wouldn't accept the reality he had already guessed at.

Leaning forward over her display, squinting, she said, "There are more."

"More what?" Jeffrey and Admiral Cantwell asked at the same time. Jeffrey knew in his gut what the answer was, but he had to hear it.

She shook her head as if she couldn't understand what she was seeing. "More ships... I think." She looked to the admiral. "Sir, request permission to contact other fleet navigation officers for assistance in reconciling this data."

"What," the admiral said in distinctly separated words, "are— you—seeing?"

She looked at him, eyebrows twisted upward with doubt. "I- I'm not sure, sir."

"You have permission."

"Thank you, sir." Her fingers flew across the black glass, creating a storm of fluid light. Leaning into a microphone on her workstation, she said, "This is U.S.S. Lacedaemon contacting all fleet navigation officers. Please confirm location, trajectory, and nature of Saturn proximal and Mars proximal signatures."

Saturn proximal?

Jeffrey walked over to stand beside her as did Cantwell, Donovan, and Delaney. The young woman made no acknowledgement of their presence as she listened to the reports coming in.

After a few moments, she looked to her left. "Nav-Con, please split screen, show Saturn proximal and Mars Proximal formations for the coordinates I'm sending you." Her fingers scattered across the console.

On the Nav-Con two groups of long, dark shapes appeared. The shapes were blurred, but Jeffrey could clearly make out... eight in one group and nine in the other.

Cantwell asked, "What trajectory?"

The navigation officer said, "If we follow our planned acceleration and deceleration curves, their trajectory will intercept us halfway to Earth."

"They're not targeting Earth?"

"No sir. They're definitely targeting our flight path. With Saturn in opposition to Earth's orbit and Mars nearing conjunction, their acceleration curves will intercept our flight path at the same time."

Cantwell asked, "If we move to attack the three Sthenos ships coming from Europa?"

Her fingers blurred on the keyboard. "They'll reach them before we can. The Saturn ships are coming fast. They must be pulling five G's."

In a quiet voice, Cantwell asked, "How is that possible?" His eyes locked onto the fuzzy images of the ships. "We have to get back to Earth *now*."

Delaney's voice sounded incredulous, as she said, "Surely you can't be suggesting taking the fight to Earth?"

Cantwell walked over to her, took her by the arm, and pulled her aside. Jeffrey followed.

Cantwell said to her quietly, "Fifty years ago we faced the Sthenos with six-to-one odds and barely survived. This morning we thought we were at nineteen-to-one. Now, by my count, we're less than three-to-one. If this goes down even close to what we've experienced in the past, they'll walk through our fleet. Without us, we have to assume they plan to move on to Earth. The only hope I see in this situation is to get hardware to the planet's surface. We can't match them out here. We have to take the fight atmospheric where we don't need life support to stay alive. In approximately 100 hours we'll be fighting a guerilla war."

Delaney's eyes glowed with anger as she asked, "How can you possibly know that?"

"I've seen what those destroyers can do. I've seen three of our most advanced ships chewed apart by one of theirs. Now they have us in a shooting gallery, which we walked right into. We're in a tight group in the middle of nowhere. If we stay together, they destroy us. If we split up, they split up and destroy us."

"If what you say is true," she said, "then we're doomed no matter what we do."

"Not true," Cantwell said. "Might doesn't always make right. An early 21st century political scientist by the name of Ivan Arreguín Toft analyzed warfare between countries with more than a ten-fold discrepancy in militarized power and came up with a surprising conclusion. When the significantly smaller military used irregular tactics, guerilla warfare, that smaller force outstripped the larger nearly two out of three times."

"That doesn't make sense," Delaney said. "With that many fewer resources, the smaller side should always lose."

"If they use conventional, or matching, tactics, they would... three out of four times."

She looked back up to the stars. "So if you get creative—"

"Our odds of surviving almost triple… at least by our historical perspective."

She fell silent for a moment before asking Cantwell, "What the hell am I supposed to tell the president?"

"We'll decide that in a few minutes. Right now we all need to be on the same page." He took her by the shoulders. "Are we?"

"Are you so sure they'll do that much damage?"

Jeffrey said, "We have fifty-seven ships facing twenty Sthenos cruisers. They didn't come back to the bar with two friends, they brought twenty heavyweights."

She watched the Sthenos destroyers on the Nav-Con for some time before looking back to Cantwell and Jeffrey. "I'm not buying it. You want to sell me on how frightening these Sthenos are, but I can't see it. There isn't simply an evil race of murderers among the stars bent on our destruction. We'll discuss tactics with the president, but my recommendation will not include a return to Earth."

"Sir!" a navigation officer called out. "Four more, sir."

"Four more?" Cantwell asked, "Where?"

"A few hours from Earth Orbit sir."

...

Thirty minutes later a young woman looked up from her console. "Admiral Cantwell, a text-based message has come in from the president."

Cantwell, Holt, and Delaney all walked over. She pointed to her screen.

All ships return to Earth.

They would prove to be the final words of John Moore's presidency.

CHAPTER 15

Jeffrey walked down the corridor wondering what Delaney's next move would be now that President Moore was out of communication. A few moments after the president's message had come in, the four Sthenos destroyers reached Earth, and communications had immediately gone dark. Jeffrey had waited on the bridge for an hour, but when no responses came after the expected message delay, he'd left. With the Sthenos closing in, he felt the need to find his Hammerheads. No matter what Delaney and Moore wanted, he wasn't about to put that talent in useless, virtual-reality drone seats.

As he approached the officers' quarters, two female pilots, who'd stood talking in quiet voices, fell silent. Looking at his list of names, he asked, "Can either of you tell me where I might find a Lieutenant Sebastian Grimstad?"

One of the women asked, "The big Norwegian guy?"

"I think so."

"Last I saw, he was in the lounge."

As he walked away, he heard the other woman say, "You realize you always know where Sebastian is?"

"Shut up."

The sound of, what Jeffrey assumed to be, a fist hitting a shoulder, brought a smile to his face as he made his way to the officers' lounge. He found it empty save a few men playing cards at a corner table and, in the center of the room, a man, almost as tall and broad-chested as himself, sitting with his legs extended out on a table. He had his hands clasped behind his head of slightly unkempt, white-blonde hair. When Jeffrey approached, he did not open his eyes, but said in a thick Northern European accent, "Is that you Brooks? Leave me alone or I hold you down and nookie you."

"I sincerely hope you mean noogie."

The man's eyes came open, and seeing Jeffrey, he jumped to his feet, knocking the small table over. "Captain Holt. My apologies. I thought—"

"It's fine," Jeffrey said, indicating that Grimstad should sit. Jeffrey sat across from him and held up his tablet. "I've been looking over your stats."

Grimstad leaned forward. "Are they acceptable to you?"

"Yes, very good, but," he set the tablet down, "I need to understand the man behind these numbers." He leaned back into the soft couch. "Tell me what brought you to flying."

Grimstad frowned as though confused. "A bus?"

"No…" He thought for a moment. "What motivated you to join the Luftforsvaret?"

"Oh, yes… I see," he said with a rich laugh that showed both rows of squared teeth back to the molars. "I was not intended for this." He held his hands out to the lounge. "In my youth, I resolved myself to a fisherman's life."

...

Quiet fog lay over the water and long docks, which extended into pale nothingness, fishing boats tethered alongside. Sebastian's father sat in the stern of his worn fishing trawler wearing a salt-infused wool sweater, green rubber boots, and heavy duck-cotton pants with reinforced knees. His father's old hand, the last pinkie permanently curled shut, moved around a hole in the net, mending it with a large needle.

Enveloped in the mist, a distant thunder rose, but did not fade. It grew and grew still more until it ripped overhead and was gone, leaving growling echoes to dance in the close cliffs.

"Time to work in the world boy, not stare at it," his father said.

Sebastian, not yet as tall as his father, walked over to the old man and helped him fold the net, his hands passing over the pitted floats, which were crusted with bits of bull kelp. Their rights to fish the protected area required use of the old, difficult way—small nets, checked often—the wrong fish and other beasts freed by hand. He could have chosen an easier life, as his brother had, but in the hard work, he felt a connection to his forefathers. He would someday teach his own son to pull thrashing, silvered life from the dark waters.

His father fired the trawler's fusion engine. Sebastian unwound the lines from the cleats and set them aboard. As his father pulled away from the dock, Sebastian stepped over the widening gap with the ease of a young man, who'd grown up on the water.

As they moved through the inlet, their wake coiled out across the mirrored surface to lap against the stony cliff face. He knew the peaks, towering beyond the mist, well enough to envision their invisible ridge against the sky. Moving forward, he lay on his chest, head hanging over and watched the water bend around the prow as if a sheet of melted glass. Here it lay cold, sometimes crusted with ice, but deep and alive.

They'd almost lost everything, but as being good shepherds of the world became paramount to the human race, it voluntarily cut its numbers back. Now, deep under him, the world ran wicked with big-scaled life—healthy, strong, and plentiful.

He sensed its pulse in the depths and loved his place in it. He held profound gratitude in his heart for his family; to his father for the strong hands he'd passed down to him; to his beautiful mother with her white-blonde hair for the laughter she'd brought to their home; to his sister, whose short life had taught him to hold each day with care; and to his older brother for the rough years that had toughened his heart.

As they made their way to the fishing grounds, the mist evanesced revealing cloud-draped peaks against a pale-blue sky. The air remained still. Ahead, a black blade rose from the long, flat sheet of water. The surrounding surface bent and poured from a shining, gray back. A plume of hot breath exploded upward as another black blade rose and another, each followed by the bending back and plume. The brume of breath touched his hands and face, and he breathed deeply of the air from the whales' lungs.

When his father shut off the engine, the boat drifted into stillness. The two men went to work in silence, their actions serving as the conversation between them. As they laid out the net at the back of the boat, preparing it to be played out into the depths, the thunder returned. Sebastian looked to the northern end of the fjord where it opened to the ocean. The thunder grew louder as five sharp shapes came into view, raced toward them, and ripped by overhead so close he could read the warning markings on their bellies.

Sebastian watched the aircraft disappear up the fjord and cursed aloud, not because he felt anger, but because he felt it was what his father would want to hear. He looked down at the net in his hand. It suddenly seemed foreign. He didn't understand the sensation at the time, but that night his thoughts were consumed by the memory of the jets streaking through his limited world.

He spent the winter working the frigid waters, obsessed. In the spring, as they mended nets, he told his father he wanted to join the Luftforsvaret, that he'd talked with a recruiter, and they would take him.

His father's old hands went still, weathered eyes rising from the net, and he said, "Men of the same blood climb the same mountain."

In that Sebastian felt his father was angry with him or somehow disappointed.

"But," his father said, "You cannot fulfill yourself following another's path. Each man must find his own route to the summit if he wishes to have satisfaction on his deathbed."

With those few words, his father had set him free, and he, as always, had loved him for it.

His father had died while he was in flight school. When the news reached him, he lay in his bunk, the dark pipes of the carrier K.N.M. Andøya overhead, smiling as the memories of the old man and the fjord filled his heart. He took comfort in knowing his father had found satisfaction on his deathbed, and in his wisdom, the old man had assured Sebastian would find satisfaction on his.

CHAPTER 16

Later, Jeffrey found Lila Okoye in the empty gym. Very few would exercise during acceleration and deceleration, but still, there she sat on a bench, sweat soaked into her gray T-shirt. The dark skin of her delicate neck glistened, and when she turned to look at him, efficient muscle flexed along her thin arm.

Standing, she saluted.

"Please," Jeffrey said, indifferently returning the gesture. "Sit."

She wiped her face with a rough, white towel as she sat.

"Looks like you've been hard at work while everyone else is taking it easy."

Seeing her dark eyes glittering with intensity, Jeffrey understood there was more to her than her middle-of-the-pack stats suggested.

"I have less talent than the others," she said in her slightly lyrical East African accent, "so I have to work harder."

"I'd say you're average among the best in the world. That's pretty damn good."

A gravity drew over her expression. "Not good enough for me."

Jeffrey nodded. "I like that."

"You came here to vet me," Lila said in an almost challenging tone, as though she'd prepared for it.

Jeffrey shook his head. "I need to understand my pilots, not their stats but what makes them tick."

"I appreciate that, sir. You want to know me?"

"Yes."

"Then you have to understand two things."

"Those would be?"

"The scars of my homeland and the spirits that haunt it."

...

She'd grown up in an Africa filled with wonder, watching herds of elephants tearing branches from trees, trumpeting in the early evening and springboks bounding over the savannah as though on imperceptible wings. She could hardly believe her great grandmother that it had all once been gone—all the elephants, the lions, and the antelope hunted to extinction by starving men. According to her Granny the population of Africa had exploded, overrunning the supplies of water and land, leaving barren dust. Mass starvations became commonplace as warlords kept food and supplies for themselves.

"Many of my friends," her Granny had said in her rich, calming voice, "died when I was young." Lila sat on her lap in a room chilled by water cycled through pipes buried deep underground where Lila imagined diminutive miners with stumpy legs and ice-filled packs walking along frosted tunnels.

Lila's mother and grandmother scolded the old woman, telling her it was wrong to scare the girl.

Granny snapped back at Lila's grandmother, "I raised you with truth in your heart. That is what made you strong." And then to Lila's mother she said, "I gave truth to you as well. In that," she tapped her crooked finger to her temple, just below her tightly-curled, snow-white hair, "you learned to think. We cannot think clearly without fear, for it keeps us careful and humble."

As Granny turned her iron-dark eyes on Lila, Lila touched her creased skin, which looked like stone but felt as soft as log-hidden moss.

"Now I give my final gifts to my great granddaughter."

Granny sat with her hands over Lila's lap, weaving sweet grass, showing Lila how to make it strong. As she wove, she told the stories of warlords, of murders and rapes, which frightened Lila the most—

young girls brutalized, infected, and left to die. Lila had nightmares of infections burning in her belly.

She told of a young man, handsome and strong with skin the color of rich coal. At this point tears would brim in Granny's eyes. Lila loved to hear stories of her great grandfather even as Granny's tears made her cry as well. The stories of him filled her heart up so high, it spilled out. He'd been kind, full of love and hard work, but had been killed when he happened upon a young girl being assaulted by a group of men. He did not walk on as most did. He paid with his life, but Granny said he had kept his soul. His son, Lila's grandfather, her mother's father, had been born a month later. Right away, all those who met him agreed he seemed to be his father come again.

The warlords had continued to ravage the land, even as the rest of the world improved, but as her grandfather came to be a man, and her grandmother grew heavy with her mother, the Great Understanding had come. While some refused to believe such a thing could be true, the warlords, who had narrowed their eyes at each other, looked up to the sky. Beyond the blue, monstrous black ships were killing men and woman by the thousands. If those warriors failed, the ships would descend to Earth.

Her grandfather, now a pilot, was asked to go fight the horde in the sky, and they'd called him the Sand Tiger because he was fierce and skilled.

Drawing a deep breath through her nose, Granny said, "He was a Hammerhead."

"What is that, Granny?"

"Protectors of the innocent, infused with the spirit of your great grandfather and, like him, they gave their lives so you and others like you—the young and the fragile—could live in peace."

Granny had been left without a husband or a son, but she had Lila's grandmother, full belly stretching with life. As the war ended, Lila's mother came into the world.

The last time Granny told her the genealogy, Lila—then nine years old—had asked her, "Can women fly, be a shark?"

At that her mother had told her to hush, there was no need for such things any longer, but Granny fixed Lila with a severe intensity. "Lila, you can have what you earn. If you want the name of a shark, you go and you take it."

When the war ended, in deference to the Hammerheads, the warlords raked their chests with sharks' teeth, binding them to those who had saved them, and to each other. Africa found itself in a unified peace it had never known. Lila's mother had grown up in one Africa, one nation, one people.

Lila had taken great strength in this, which did little to quell an even greater fear. On dark nights, she would sit in her room looking out through the window, up to the glittering universe. When a shooting star streaked across the sky, leaving a faint trail of smoke in the upper atmosphere, her heart would jump and pound against her ribs. Each bit of rock burning in a flash, reminded her of what she knew in her bones—they would be back.

When she was fifteen, she told her mother she wanted to be a Phantom pilot. Her mother had laughed so hard tears came to her eyes. She had said, "My little gazelle is no warrior."

That angered Lila, who shouted a rude name and ran from the house. Hiding beyond the ridge, in the meadow where the lake formed in summer, she sobbed until her fury ebbed.

She stayed under the tree, finches flitting in its branches, until the sun began to redden. Hearing her mother calling to her, Lila hunkered down in the grass. Her mother's head rose over the ridge, and her large eyes found her. Lila curled up, bracing for her mother's venom. Her mother sat down next her, her skirts sounding like the dry grasses she moved aside. She put her still-youthful hand on Lila's and said, "I'm sorry to have hurt you. I did not mean to laugh. I thought you were telling a joke."

Lila pulled her hand away, and turning aside, said, "It's not a joke."

"Lila, my sweet, you have the heart of an elephant, patient and wise, but when you find your will, just like the elephant, nothing can hold you back. We'll find out if you can fly."

Despite not having a great deal of money, her mother took her to an airfield and paid for a flight. Lila found herself sitting in the right-hand seat of a tiny jet with two small engines. Using a metal handle hooked to the front landing gear, the pilot pulled the jet out of the hangar's shade. Lila's heart raced, and her legs felt numb. The pilot climbed in beside her, shoulder to shoulder in the small space, closed the cockpit's tight, plastic dome, and with a hiss of compressed air, fired the turbines. As the jet's whine rose, he handed her a headset. When she put it on, the sound of the turbines muffled down to a whisper.

His voice came tinny through the headset, "Are you ready?" He gave her an easy smile.

She nodded.

"Let's get free from this rock."

He taxied the plane to the end of the runway, squared on it, and said, "Tower, this is Alpha—Foxtrot—One—Two—Seven—X-ray, requesting permission to take off."

The voice from the tower came into her ears, clear and close, "Roger Alpha—Foxtrot—One—Two—Seven—X-ray, you are cleared for takeoff."

Sliding the throttle forward, he hurtled them down the runway, the seatback pushing her on and on.

The nose of the plane lifted, the rumbling vanished, and the ground fell away fast. As the roads, cars, and houses grew small, and the huge trees became toy-like, she felt her heart go light in her chest with wonder, as if she'd come home and found everything she'd ever lost sitting on her bed. She laughed out and clapped her hand on her thigh.

"Beautiful isn't it?"

But Lila couldn't answer with her heart in her throat.

"Your mother says you want to fly a Phantom."

She nodded to the pilot, feeling a bit foolish in the face of his experience.

"Let's see if you can handle what they do up there."

He shoved the stick to the side and the plane rolled upside down, coming to a crisp stop with Lila hanging by her shoulder straps, blood rushing to her face. Looking straight up at the ground, she felt nothing short of fierce joy. The sun, catching on the dials and Plexiglas, seemed to glow with a deep energy, which inundated her, burning through every joint and muscle.

The instructor turned the plane up right and said, "How do you fall?"

Lila did not understand, but didn't have time to form a question before he shoved the stick forward. Her guts thrilled up against her lungs. Her whole body came horrifically alive—groin, nipples, the gullet of her neck. Her face hurt from the smile as she let her arms go limp, her hands floating before her. Her braids hovered around her face, tickling at her cheeks. She screamed, not in fear, but with absolute, pure joy.

The instructor turned the plane upside down and pushed down again, and the blood rushed to her head as the shoulders straps hauled on her. She felt as though her head might pop. When they crested to the top of the outside loop, she felt as though she could see the whole of Africa stretching away in shades of dark green and pale tan.

He flew on, and all the while, she laughed and shouted out, calling for him to turn again, loop again, turn harder, fall again.

When they landed, the wheels rumbling along the runway, she felt her heart drop. They taxied to a stop, and she climbed down to the tarmac, feeling the weight of the ground under her feet. Looking up into the blue sky, she knew she'd never feel content standing on the ground.

CHAPTER 17

The next day, Jeffrey found the last of his pilots, J. Nathan Brooks, in the hangar. He stood under a Wraith, which had been converted for VR flight.

"I get the impression you're trying to avoid me."

Brooks turned to Jeffrey with distrust in his eyes and offered no acknowledgment of rank as he said, "I know what you're doing, and I don't like it."

"Care to explain your issue?"

"It's a waste of time."

Jeffrey looked around. "I don't see anything that requires your attention."

With a shrug, Brooks turned back to the Wraith.

"So you don't want to talk?"

"No, *sir.*"

"If I ground you?"

"Then I'll talk, but only enough to get me back in a seat."

"Have it your way," gripping his shoulder, Jeffrey spun him around, "but if you turn your back on me again, you'll be worse than grounded. Is that clear?"

Brooks swallowed as he came to attention. Eyes wide, he finally saluted. "Yes, sir. Clear, sir."

Jeffrey walked away infuriated. Any other time, he would have axed the punk without hesitation, but Brooks' stats put him at the top, and he needed someone like that more than he needed compliance. Still, a man with a chip on his shoulder could cause more problems than he was worth, even in desperate times. He had to know more about this kid.

Returning to the pilot's quarters, he asked a group, "Who knows Brooks best?"

"Wahls does, sir. They're both from the Midwest."

Jeffrey found Wahls. "I need you to tell me about Brooks."

"Yes, sir. I'm guessing he didn't want to talk to you."

"No. Knowing you might be his last hope of remaining with us, what can you tell me about him that will make me want to keep him?"

...

J. Nathan Brooks grew up Justice N. Brooks living five miles from the middle of nowhere Nebraska watching crop dusters fly over the barn, their shadows racing across the hot gravel before rolling out over the corn as white mist coiled away on the vortex of their wingtips. At the end of the field the gangly yellow planes would rise sunward, turn on a wing, and descend out of view until they thundered over his head again, disappearing over the farm house.

He'd sit on the fender of his grandfather's Ford tractor, which had been in one place, dead to the world, his entire sixteen years. As the planes passed and arced around, he'd try to imagine the Earth from inside the cockpit. He thought it would be simpler, smaller—the fields laid out in order and the trees like broccoli on his plate at supper. The flaws of the world would be too far away to see. He imagined himself sitting on the fender of the tractor, just a speck of denim and T-shirt on a rusted blue lump. In the distance, the crop duster turned again, the sun flashing off the tall canopy.

His father yelled from near the house, "Justice, get over here!"

Justice—He hated the name Justice. He told his friends at school to call him by his middle name, Nathan. Justice had been his grandfather's name, and sounded to him like something a drunk would name his son, which was true in his case. Grandpa Justice had served in the war as a ship's cook and come home to die a few years later in a bottle. *Justice*. As if there was any of that in the world. If there had been justice, he would have been born to a family that wasn't a dead end. His friend Coret, a year older, was leaving for the Naval Academy in Annapolis in the fall. He had Senator McCreedy's recommendation and was a damn eagle scout.

Years ago Coret had asked Justice to join the cub scouts with him. He'd asked his father, whose expression closed off as he said, "We don't have money for that. Besides, I need you here on the farm after school, not building jackass derby cars."

That moment struck Justice as a point of divergence between himself and Coret. With each of Coret's successes, Justice hated his own father more.

As Justice walked back toward the farmhouse, his father's voice echoed from its far side. "Dammit Justice, quit spacin' out and get over here. You need to learn how to service this."

Justice came around the side of the house to find his father crouched beside the mini combine. It had failed to follow it's GPS track. His father had bitched about it all supper. Justice was sick of hearing about farming. Now the bull-sized combine sat with its side panel open, its circuitry and servos in shadow.

Justice stared at the back of his father's sweat stained T-shirt. Scowling over his shoulder, his father motioned with his hand as he said, "Well, get in here boy. You can't learn nothin' bein' a wallflower."

Justice crouched down beside his father, the sickly sweet smell of sweat and alcohol wafting from the old man. He didn't like being this close to someone who'd so often thrown him into walls.

"Undo that frame piece," his father said, holding out a wrench.

Taking the wrench, Justice loosened the bolt. As the bolt came free, and he moved onto the next, he imagined he wasn't working on a corn-stained combine, but one of the yellow crop dusters. It would be his father's plane. Not this man, but someone like Coret's father—a man who would teach him, not to fix combines, but to fly.

The day after the end of his senior year, Justice's father said he needed him to stay and work the farm. Justice nodded, having learned at an early age that deceit was far easier than confrontation. The next day he found his way to the Navy recruitment center.

Justice said, "I want to fly."

The recruiter smiled, "Well, there's lots of jobs need doin' to get those fighters spaceborne. What if you end up as a plane captain?"

That *sounded* good to Justice, who asked with a bit of distrust, "What do they do?"

"Well, it's a damn important job. The plane captain makes sure everything is right with the fighter. The craft is yours, and you're responsible for it. Your name's on the side."

Justice remembered the wrenching he'd done on farm equipment. While he felt the recruiter already shuttling him away from flying, he imagined a Phantom thundering over head with his name below the cockpit. His Phantom. That would do. Hell, he'd take anything but ship's cook if it got him away from the farm.

"Okay," Justice said. "What's next?"

The recruiter took out a tablet. "What's your legal name?"

"Justice Nathan Brooks, but I go by Nathan."

"Okay." He typed on the tablet for a moment before sliding it across the worn desk. He held out a stylus. "Sign here Mr. J. Nathan Brooks, and we'll get you processed."

When he told his father, the old man fell dead silent. His mother had cried, which he'd expected, but his father, who he felt sure would blow up, had simply sat staring at his plate. After several moments, what his father said would drive Justice for years to come.

"You'll fail," the old drunk said as he looked up, "and when you do, you don't dare bring your ass back here." His voice became louder as the anger Justice had expected arrived. "I break my back raising you, and the first chance you get you walk out on me…" He held up his hand to his mother, who was now sobbing, "out on her." He pointed his calloused finger at Justice. "You leave this house, you don't never come back. Understood?"

Justice nodded and left the table. In his room, he packed his bag as the front door slammed, and his father's truck tore down the dirt drive.

"You give it your best."

Startled, Justice turned to find his mother standing in the doorway.

Her eyes red, but her voice sure, she said, "You give it your best, and when you've got nothin' left to give, you give 'em more. You understand me?"

He nodded.

She took her son in her arms and held him tight, saying. "You don't come back here. You're biggern' him, biggern' your grandfather too. You're not like them… never were."

...

In the last week of basic he'd been jogging back from mess, when a severe looking master chief came out from the staff building and shouted at him. "You Seaman Brooks?"

He nodded.

"Get your ass in here." The master chief went back inside, the screen door slapping shut. Justice walked into the white room, bracing to get chewed out for God knows what. The master chief, now sitting at a stainless steel desk, held out his hand to a chair.

Justice sat.

"Master Chief Widmore."

"Master chief."

"What do you want to do for the Navy?"

"I'm slated for ordnance."

The master chief's eyes narrowed. "Did I ask you what you were slated for?"

"No, master chief."

"Well?"

The truth made his heart race. "I want to fly Phantoms."

"Fly *Phantoms*? More likely you could train unicorns for us."

Justice's anger flared, but he remained silent.

The master chief looked over the screen to his right. "We don't fly *Phantoms* anymore." As if ready to offer Justice everything he'd ever wanted, the master chief asked, "You want to fly a Wraith?"

Justice nodded, feeling distrustful. "Sure."

"Let me understand you," the master chief said, "you don't even know what we're flying these days, and you think you've got what it takes to get in them?

"My grandfather served in the Navy. Used to tell me stories about the war."

The master chief's eyebrow lifted. "Did he fly?"

Justice felt trapped. He let a possible lie go. "He was a cook."

The master chief's eyes went flat. He looked at the screen and said absently, "A cook." He typed on his keyboard. "We can try you out for the mechanic's route. Looks like you have some experience there. You can fix Wraiths, and you'll get a bit of back seat time."

Unfamiliar boldness rose up. "I want to fly."

The master chief's eyes shifted to him, narrowed. "And I want to have a piece of your girlfriend, but we can't have it all can we? That's life. Don't bitch about it. You have to be an officer or have a college degree and be E-5 to even be considered to fly. We start with shitty jobs and hot girls, and if we work hard, we end up with decent jobs and fat wives." He shrugged and smiled for the first time. "I do love her though." He handed him a tablet. "Maybe you can learn to love this job."

Justice took the tablet.

"It's the mechanic's exam. You pinned the basic tests, so we've got to do something more with you. Can't waste talent. Go over there," he pointed at a small corner desk, "and take it. Keep your head down and your mouth shut."

When Justice brought the exam back, the master chief looked over the tablet, his bored expression darkening to anger. His eyes rose slowly to Justice before tracking to the desk where he'd taken the exam.

He came around the desk fast. Catching Justice's arm and spinning him around, he shoved him up against the wall and went through his pockets. "If you're screwing with me, I'll have your ass in the brig for the rest of your service years. You got me?"

"What the hell's going on?"

The master chief turned Justice to face him. "Take off your cover and your shoes."

Justice did as he was told. The master chief looked into the shoes and ran his fingers around the inside rim of his cover. He handed the cap back and sat at his desk, with a defeated expression.

"What the hell seaman?"

"Master chief?"

"You scored 100%... Nobody scores 100%."

Opening a drawer, the chief took out another tablet. "You think you're slick? Here's your one chance." He handed the tablet to Justice. "That's the pilot's exam. Sit down. If you don't nail it to the wall, you're gonna be running a wrench for the rest of your life."

Justice walked over to the desk dizzy, the tablet feeling like lead.

When he'd completed the exam, he approached the master chief but didn't want to hand it over. Once it was scored he was done, locked. The chief snapped the tablet from him. After entering something on its surface, he sat back in his chair, it's wooden frame creaking.

"I'll be damned. Looks like you'll get your chance to step up to the physical exam. Pass it at the top of your group, and you *might* get a consideration for an academy slot. That happens, and I'll be calling *you* sir. You won't fly though. I doubt you'll be able to take the G's."

Justice felt a rush of possibility, and years of frustrated anger came rising with it as he said, "I'll take down anything you throw at me."

The master chief waved the comment away. "Get your rucksack Brooks. Basic's over for you."

CHAPTER 18

Jeffrey lay on his bunk waiting. The fleet had been accelerating back toward Earth for two days. Samantha hadn't spoken more than a dozen words to him in that time. He'd waffled back and forth from feeling justified to embarrassed. He'd only recently settled on the conclusion that he probably should have simply let her be. Not responding would have been the higher, more cordial road than calling her out.

He let his thoughts of her go, and considered the Sthenos, who now closed in from all directions, save the four nearest Earth. War was imminent, but the two silent days of waiting had gotten under everyone's skin. The Sthenos would reach them in perhaps six hours.

The shade of his reading lamp threw a pattern of ellipses across the ceiling. He stared at them, considering the ovals of light against the chaos of the stars. What patterns existed here and now? He found himself again in a situation in which discerning patterns from chaos was the only way to scrape life away from certain death. He had to find weaknesses and exploit them in fractions of a second. His thoughts turned to his pilots, those who were to become the new Hammerheads—unmodified, unprepared. When the Sthenos attacked fifty years ago, the Hammerheads had been an experiment already in the final stages of development. He and the first wave were just coming on line when Demos had been destroyed. 50,000 dead in the first few moments of that war.

Over a quarter million men and women had fought and died to keep the Sthenos from Earth, and despite all odds, they'd succeeded. Those dead would be nothing when held in the light of this. He thought of the people going about their days in New York, Tokyo,

Moscow—millions in each, some sleeping, some committing crimes, others holding high a grandchild. He paused as the memory of Leif stepping out of the airlock, soul gutted, came to mind. There had been something worse than the loss of a wife in his eyes.

"A child," Jeffrey said quietly to himself.

Sarah had been pregnant.

He gritted his teeth against the shock of that realization, under which fury began boiling up. As he wondered if the gluttony of the Sthenos had any boundaries, he slipped into a self-preserving daydream of a final dogfight. Flying a Phantom, a ship long since retired, he imagined himself arcing above the last Sthenos destroyer as its hull cracked wide, its guts spilling into the vacuum of space. He wouldn't have delivered the final blow, as a Phantom couldn't possibly take down a destroyer, but would have cleared the way. In the end, a Sthenos fighter would get one last shot in. He'd see it too late.

As his windscreen spider-webbed and blew open, he'd watch one of his Hammerheads run the Sthenos fighter down. With his ship falling to pieces, a moment of searing pain would be followed by an enveloping serenity. What would he find? His wife? The other pilots, gone now fifty years? Mako with his narrow shoulders and hawklike nose? Finally smiling? Finally at peace?

That's how he'd like it to be.

A tapping sounded on the hatch.

Jeffrey came out of his thoughts, seeing the dark room again, the pattern of light on the ceiling.

The tapping sounded again.

Jeffrey shoved the blanket off, exposing his T-shirt and uniform slacks, now wrinkled. He went to the hatch, his support frame whirring. Opening the door, he found Vice President Delaney alone in the corridor.

"Vice President."

She stared at him, no smile, no pretense, just a matter of fact look. "Can we talk?"

Jeffrey leaned on the hatch-frame as he crossed his arms. "Yes."

She waited. When he said nothing more she sighed and said, "In private."

Jeffrey backed away, sweeping his arm into the small quarters. As she entered, he flicked on the main light and closed the door.

"Please," she said as she motioned toward the switch, "I prefer the dimmer light."

Jeffrey turned the main light off and crossed his arms again, balancing himself on his feet, shoulders squared. "What can I help you with Ma'am?"

She put her hands on her hips. "You clearly have a problem with me."

"Yes."

"What the hell have I ever done to you?"

Jeffrey saw sincere and uncharacteristic frustration in her expression. "Nothing." He said and left it at that.

"Nothing? I don't un—"

"It's what you did to all of us. You and those like you wanted so badly to turn your nose up at the military that you not only destroyed many veterans' sense of self worth, you left the entire human race exposed and unprepared for what we're facing today."

Her hard glare faltered.

"I understand," Jeffrey said, "you want to live in a world in which you feel safe, but saying there are no threats doesn't make it so. Telling yourself the war was a lie or we're somehow beyond it denies a fundamental truth. If you convince yourself there is no gravity before jumping off a building, you won't float. Not only do you stand against me and those like me, you're a very successful politician. That means you want and enjoy power. You might kid yourself that your desire for power is to make a positive impact, but I've found that those who make the real difference in the world do it quietly from the inside, not from the top."

"There are good people in politics Jeffrey," she said, her tone exasperated. "Thomas Jefferson said the tallest a man stands is when he stoops to help a child. You shouldn't judge me on what you assume I am either. There's a lot of macho bullshit in the military, but I don't think of you as a meat-head."

"Ma'am, I—"

She held up a hand to silence him, "I could have. Trust me, with your stony attitude, and physical stature..." She regarded him for a moment, "How tall are you anyway? Six-five?"

"Six-six."

"I'm six feet tall, Jeffrey, and I don't meet a lot of men whom I have to or wish to look up to, but I do look up to you, if you get my meaning. You should hear how the men and women out there talk about you. You're their anchor."

Jeffrey said, "I didn't ask to be—"

"Shut up and let me have my say."

Something in her eyes, some hurt, something fearful behind the strength caused Jeffrey to remain silent. The muscles of her jaw flexed. Her expression, coupled with the patches of lamp light across her neck, brought out the full depth of her beauty.

"You all but accused me of being a whore on the bridge."

"I never said—"

"*Shut*—" she balled her fists, her eyes on the floor, "*up*—and let me speak, will you?"

He glared at her, her commands restoking his anger.

"You," she said, pointing her finger at him, "may doubt me. You may think I'm no better than any of those other *fuckers* out there." When she hit the word her teeth bared and Jeffrey felt himself wanting to step back. "You may think I'm just here for myself, but I'm not. You want to know how bad politicians are? *You* try being a single woman near the top surrounded by wolves. These bastards don't care about anyone but themselves and which of their buddies can get elected in their wake."

Her eyes fairly blazed now, but her voice cracked when she said, "I am here…" She drew a deep breath and her arms came stiff to her sides as she collected herself. "I am here to help. I always have been, and I've given up more than I'll ever gain. And I don't care," she fairly growled her next words, "if you ever come to believe that. But I will *not* be called a whore." She stepped close to him, her anger fully unmasked. "I do *not* use sex to gain power. I *never* have, and I *never* will." She jabbed herself in the temple with her index finger. "This is what got me where I am today," she unceremoniously gripped her breasts, "not these. Anyone who suggests otherwise can go to hell."

Jeffrey had had enough. "What the hell then," he leaned in on her, letting her know he wouldn't be backed into a corner, his nose now a few inches from hers, "do you call what you've been doing to me? Sliding up beside me, touching my arm?"

At that her anger faltered. She turned halfway back to the hatch.

"I'm sorry," she said in an unsure tone, "I…" Her eyes narrowed as her face flushed. For a moment, Jeffrey thought she would strike out at him, but her gaze faltered as it traced his face. Without another word, she opened the hatch and left, shutting it with a resonating thump.

Jeffrey felt bewildered.

CHAPTER 19

Admiral Cantwell held his frustration close, offering an outward appearance of absolute calm. But still he found himself shifting too often in his command seat. Earth had been dark for two days. The message detailing their plan to land on Earth had gone unanswered.

"Communications," Cantwell said across the broad expanse of the bridge. "Any status from Earth yet?" He'd asked the same question an hour earlier. Knowing he should trust the officer to speak up when new information was available did not keep the worry from catching up with him from time to time and slipping out.

The young man looked up from his console and said, "Sir, I'm still attempting to hack into a satellite. The systems are all non-responsive. It's possible the Sthenos used electromagnetic pulse weaponry. I have a faint signal from a geostationary satellite in the Clarke belt. I'm attempting to bootstrap it now."

Cantwell shifted in his seat. "Keep at it sailor."

"Yes, sir."

Pushing himself out of his seat under the heavy G's, Cantwell walked over to the Nav-Con. Their transition from acceleration to deceleration, which they had to make in a few moments, would afford the Sthenos destroyers a perfect window of attack. "Bring up our trailing Sthenos ships."

"Yes, sir." She swept her fingers across the control podium.

The fleet whisked away, and the twenty Sthenos destroyers, came into view. As the groups from Saturn, Mars, and Europa approached, they hadn't converged on the fleet; they had vectored together into a large group trailing it. The ships grew in size on the Nav-Con until each was perhaps seven inches long.

"Are they still matching our acceleration?"

"Yes, sir. No loss or gain of distance."

They can easily outpace us. So… what are they waiting for?

"Nav-Con, please zoom in on the destroyer on point." The lead ship expanded, extending nose to tail across the disk of the Nav-Con. The image was badly pixilated.

"No higher resolution is available at this time. A drone camera wouldn't be able to follow our acceleration curve. These images are from the Lacedaemon's telescopes. Would you like me to drop a camera for a single pass?"

Cantwell shook his head. "Not at this time. Take the view out again."

"Yes, sir. How far?"

"Show me the Sthenos position relative to ours."

The Sthenos ship shrank away, shifting to the left. When they grew too small to see, brilliant yellow sparks of light took their place. Soon, to the right, the blood-red markers of the fleet slid into view.

"Distance?"

"50,000 miles, sir."

As Cantwell walked back toward his command seat, the communications officer he'd tasked with obtaining updates from Earth caught his eye and touched the console in front of him. His face was pale.

Understanding the young man wanted to keep what he had on his screen quiet, Cantwell walked over. A video from a low-mounted angle of a yawning blast crater played on the officer's screen. Debris ringed the crater—flipped cars, cinder blocks, twisted I-beams—all strewn outward. Now and again, windswept smoke obscured the camera's view. Based on the amount of debris, Cantwell guessed the crater had once been an immense building but couldn't discern which. In the crater, a torn pipe spit the near-invisible, pale-blue flame of hydrogen gas. Beyond the crater and a green body of water, stood a white spire.

In a quiet voice, the navigation officer said, "I now have access to several camera systems through the satellite sir. This image originated from a parking security camera."

"Where?"

"It's the Pentagon sir… what's left of it anyway."

As his mind adjusted to the knowledge, the white spire across the river became familiar—the Washington Monument. To the left of the monument, a knotted pillar of smoke rose several thousand feet into the air.

Cantwell pointed to the smoke. "Is that…?"

"The White House, sir."

Cantwell fell silent.

The officer said, "Cheyenne Mountain's gone as well." He swept his finger across the screen changing the image to an aerial view of a mountain range with a city at its base. At the southern end of the mountain range, one of the many peaks had been gutted, it's massive walls strewn outward to land among the surrounding housing developments.

"Colorado Springs," Cantwell said in a near whisper.

"Yes, sir," the navigation officer said, his voice still quiet. He swept his finger and the image changed to a city, sprawling across a broad plane, structure after structure.

Cantwell said, "The only area still that built up is China."

"Yes sir. Shandong province. These were recorded before nightfall."

The heart of the city appeared to have been cut out, leaving a bowled pit. Around the pit, tall columns of smoke threw shadows over the rooftops and streets. The crater had consumed a large portion of a runway.

"The headquarters of the PLA, sir."

"Overall status?" Cantwell asked.

"No status sir. I only have images, but all major military installations I've checked are gone."

"One hundred percent?"

"Affirmative, sir."

Cantwell stared at the image. "How deep would you say that crater is?"

"It's more than two miles across, so the depth must be… perhaps half a mile."

As Cantwell stared at the crater he felt himself faltering.

Half a mile deep? The singularity warheads could theoretically deliver that much damage. Had the Sthenos used similar tech? Could they defend against the singularities?

Cantwell squared his shoulders. "You stay on this full-time. I want to know if you hear anything new. Keep searching imagery and put together a last known picture as completely as you can."

"Yes, sir."

"Sir," the Nav-Con officer said in a dazed tone with a slight tremor, as though she'd cut her hand badly and, watching blood pouring from the wound, had yet to fully feel the pain.

Cantwell held his voice calm and confident with a hint of support, as he said, "Yes, what is it?"

"The Sthenos have begun to close on us."

Cantwell's gut went cool as his pulse rose in his neck. He took a half second to check himself before saying, "At what rate?"

"They are…" the Nav-Con officer looked at her display. "This can't be right."

"What is it officer?" Cantwell heard his irritation slipping into his voice.

"They've doubled our acceleration curve."

Six G's of acceleration?

Cantwell let out his breath. He'd have preferred to swear and slam his fist on the podium.

Well… let it begin. We'll do everything we can to end it.

He said, "Battle stations folks; this is it. Communications, get me a channel to the flight control deck."

CHAPTER 20

Jeffrey walked down a corridor, his steps heavy, his mind wandering.

A voice came over the corner mounted speaker ahead. "Captain Holt, please report to the flight command center immediately."

Turning, he walked down the corridor as quickly as possible under the heavy G's. The call could only mean one thing.

As he entered the control center, lights pulsed in dark-red arcs from the corners of the ceiling.

The flight boss, Commander Holloway, a stocky blonde woman with no nonsense eyes, regarded the room with her usual thin-lipped scowl. She asked her miniboss, "Distance from the Sthenos destroyers?"

"They've stopped their approach at twenty-five hundred miles and holding ma'am."

"When we stop acceleration, watch those Sthenos ships closely. If they launch, we launch."

"Captain on deck," a yeoman called out.

Holloway looked to Jeffrey, pursed her lips, and nodded to him, saying, "If it isn't Captain Holt, who doesn't think we're good enough." She touched her forehead in a relaxed, screw-you salute, before turning to the row after row of flight stations where pilots pulled on VR helmets. "Shall we prove him wrong?"

Several of the pilots nodded, but none duplicated Holloway's hard look at Jeffrey.

Jeffrey moved a respectful distance away from her. They had to live with each other, and Jeffrey knew how to make that happen.

He would pick his battles with the hardnosed flight boss. If ever there was a time to keep his mouth shut, it was now. Holloway was correct to say that Jeffrey believed they'd fail. What she didn't realize was how much he wanted to be proven wrong.

As the moments ticked by, Jeffrey shifted his weight from side to side, hating having nothing to do. He could do more if they'd let him strap into a fighter. But these new fighters, Wraiths as they were called, had their seats pulled and replaced with servo motors, cameras, and sensors.

The faint rumble of the Lacedaemon's main engines vanished along with Jeffrey's weight. His boots auto-locked to the deck. He braced himself, as the navigation officer called out, "Beginning turn." With no windows, the sudden side force of the turn was nothing more than a shoving sensation. The force faded as the engines came to bear on their destination.

"Ma'am," a flight control officer said, "The flight groups are ready for launch."

Holloway leaned toward the Nav-Con where the Sthenos destroyers hovered. "Watch 'em folks."

"They've stopped their acceleration ma'am. Holding at twenty-five hundred miles."

"They'll launch fighters soon."

As if Holloway's comment had initiated it, a blur of yellow sparks marking Sthenos fighters began to pour from the sides of the destroyers.

Holloway clapped her hands together with a sharp crack. "That's it ladies and gentlemen. Get 'em spaceborne."

"Yes, ma'am," her miniboss said. "First wave, launch."

Jeffrey's frame instinctually locked at the command. So many launches had slammed the seat into his back, compressing his chest, forcing his breath into short huffs. One of the VR pilots sipped from a sealed mug of coffee. With that, Jeffrey felt he was watching the end of the world in slow motion.

The flight control center had two Nav-Con's, each half the size of the ten foot goliath on the bridge. To the right, brilliant-green pinpoints of light emerged from the sides of the Lacedaemon and the other destroyers, moving away in tight fingertip formations. On the left, high-res pinpricks of yellow continued pouring from the Sthenos destroyers.

As the fighter markers swarmed on each Nav-Con, Holloway looked to Jeffrey. "Each destroyer has fielded, give or take, 100 piloted drones. Each of those will be wingmanned by two A.I. drones."

Fifty-seven destroyers, each fielding three hundred fighters give or take... Is that possible?

A slight sneer crept into the corner of Holloway's thin-lipped mouth. "Something troubling you Captain Holt?"

Jeffrey's curiosity overrode his pride. "Are we actually fielding some 17,000 fighters today?"

Her smile broadened, seeming to Jeffrey to be filled, not with humor, but derision. "Might that change your assessment?" She held her hand out to the VR pilot stations. "This method allows for far greater numbers. You beat the Sthenos with what, 1,000 Hammerheads at your best?"

"No, never that many—at the most seven hundred. We lost too many to maintain headcount."

She gave a dismissive laugh. "Today we overrun the Sthenos with sheer numbers."

Jeffrey watched the right-side Nav-Con as the fighters began to pull away from the fleet. The pilots in the room were now focused on their jobs, hands on the controls, VR visors down, quiet comments into headsets. He did not share her confidence. The Sthenos had proven to be formidable against larger numbers... but not this many. Perhaps he had been wrong.

"Engagement in four minutes, ma'am."

"Good," Holloway said before turning to Holt. "Would you care to put on a helmet? Take over one of the wingman AI drones?"

"No," Jeffrey said in a tone he hoped would come across as polite. *Not yet anyway.*

He looked across the sea of helmets at flight stations, pilots reclined in their seats…

"Holloway," he asked, "are these seats taken directly from the Wraiths?"

Looking at him as though she found the question's simplicity offensive, she said, "Of course. We contracted standard fighters, removed the seats and controls, and built them into these flight stations.

Jeffrey looked back to the pilots… so relaxed. She no doubt saw men and women at ease, ready for the fight. He whispered to himself, "17,000 fighters and not one heart fully committed."

No one might die now, but the dying will begin after the fighters are gone. Might that be enough to keep these pilots fired up?

He doubted that. The human mind could too easily build separation from trauma.

On the left Nav-Con, yellow sparks continued to mist from the sides of the Sthenos destroyers. Jeffrey watched the fighters come, hundreds and now thousands, but not tens of thousands.

The room fell silent as the two forces closed on each other.

"Give me a view of the engagement field on Nav-Con 1," Holloway said. The left Nav-Con, where the fleet had been, went empty.

Jeffrey realized he was gripping his tongue with his teeth.

After a few minutes of silence, green sparks appeared on the left Nav-Con moving with slow determination toward center. Now, yellow sparks emerged on the far side.

"Engage at will flight leads," Holloway said.

"Yes, ma'am," came several responses.

Stacy Zack had reported the effectiveness of the pulse nukes, but under full acceleration, the warheads would be unable to pull away from the Wraiths. The Wraiths accelerated so hard, they would actually leave the fired warheads behind. Due to this, Donovan and Holloway had decided not to include them in the Wraith's armament. They did, however, have singularity warheads, but due to the scarcity of early production, only in one third of the ships.

As the sparks of light came close to each other, Holloway said, "Zoom in. Set the perimeter at the outermost fighters."

As the Nav-Con zoomed in further, the sparks of light remained only that, but the space between them magnified until Jeffrey could see separate flight groups. Jeffrey gripped the railing as he willed them to hold—stay on course until the last possible moment, but the flight leads committed to maneuvers too early, and the Sthenos read them. In coiling arcs, the Sthenos bore down on the pilots. The green sparks began winking out.

As the fighters engaged, a few Sthenos lights winked out as well, but Jeffrey estimated it was twenty to one in the first few moments. They would have to do better, much better.

Curses and grumblings began to come from the pilot stations.

Above several of the pilots' heads, the green connection lights flicked to red.

"Stay in the fight folks," Holloway said, "Your flight coordinators will assign you to AI drones as your fighters are destroyed."

As more of the green sparks flicked out on the Nav-Con, Jeffrey felt as though he could see the ranks already thinning.

A green spark curled around the outside, chasing a Sthenos fighter. It was in a good position. An excellent position. An AI fighter came arcing toward the same Sthenos ship.

As the AI drone and the piloted drone rushed into the same space Jeffrey said under his breath, "You have to let it go."

Of course, if the pilot had been in the cockpit, he or she would have let it go, or the pilot would have died, but here the stakes were lower. The pilot would simply be switched to another fighter, so holding on risked only hardware. As the two green sparks met, joined, and winked out, a pilot slammed his fists on the console.

"There's a delay," he shouted as he pulled off his VR helmet. "I can't keep up."

Holloway yelled, "Stay in your helmet Lieutenant!"

With faint anger in his eyes, the pilot pulled his helmet on. The light above his console switched from blood red to brilliant green. As he re-entered the dogfight, a river of obscenities immediately coursed from his mouth. His light turned red.

"Shit!" he screamed.

"Take another one pilot," Holloway said.

Jeffrey moved to Holloway and touched her arm.

Holloway, obviously frustrated, glared at Holt. "Yes captain?"

"Give him a minute to center himself or you'll lose another fighter."

Holloway's eyes narrowed. "We're losing fighters anyway."

Jeffrey stepped back. "As you will commander. I meant no disrespect. I'm a guest in your house."

Holloway kept her eyes on Jeffrey as she said, "Pilot! Take another drone!"

The pilot made it a full thirty seconds before his connection light flicked to red again. It stayed red this time.

"Take… another… Lieutenant," Holloway growled.

Jeffrey had been watching the count screen, so he already knew what Holloway didn't. There were no more free drones. The Lacedaemon's contingent of fighters, which had been at 300 was now down to less than 100. The dogfight had been on for all of two minutes. The fighter contingents from the other ships appeared to be fairing no better.

The pilot Holloway had been brow beating offered no response to his commander. He sat still, his right hand holding the flight stick.

Jeffrey touched Holloway's arm again. Her eyes snapped to him. She separated each word in a furious staccato. "What—is—it—Captain?"

Jeffrey, keeping his face neutral, pointed to the flight status display screen.

She looked, and her anger melted to shock. She whispered, "Eighty-seven?" When she looked to Jeffrey, he shrugged his shoulders.

Her eyes hardened, and she turned, seeming ready to shout more commands, but her expression faded like fog in hot sun. She looked back to Jeffery. Her voice quiet, just between him and her, she asked, "What do we do?"

"We have no manned fighters?"

"None."

"Then we die."

Jeffrey knew too well, after the fighters, the Sthenos destroyers would come for the fleet. Without fighters to trouble them, the Sthenos would be methodical. First, they would make high speed passes, shooting away the fleet's gun batteries. With those gone, they'd take out the main engines, leaving the destroyers floating dead in space. At that point, the Sthenos destroyers would close distance and blow the Lacedaemon and the rest of the fleet apart with their main guns. Without fighters, there were no singularity warheads. Those had been—as the Hammerheads had so many decades ago—the crux all hopes hung on. Now all but gone... unless.

"This is going to be over quickly commander," Jeffrey said. "Request permission to take command of the strike force."

Holloway stared at him with unabashed disbelief. "You want command?"

"We need to move fast, ma'am."

Holloway glanced at the flight count display, which continued to drop.

"There's no shame in it," Jeffrey said, as gently as he could, "We have to move quickly though. It would take too long to explain. I need you to trust me."

Her expression was closed off, face reddening.

Jeffrey guessed that her anger wasn't directed at him, but at the devastation of having lost so much so fast. Her eyes softened as she nodded absently. When she said, "You have command, sir," he heard abdicated failure in her voice.

He was glad she'd capitulated. He would have ordered it if necessary, but better to preserve her sense of self worth as much as possible. If they lived through the next hour, they'd need as many officers at the top of their game as possible, including Holloway.

The pilots with no ships to fly had turned sideways in their seats, watching their commanders.

Jeffrey said, "I need you to announce the transfer."

"Yes, sir." She moved to a microphone. "This is Commander Holloway, turning command of the strike force over to Captain Holt."

Admiral Cantwell's voice came over the comm. "Acknowledged."

Even though she hid it well, Jeffery saw the admiral's shortness drown the remaining embers of her spirit. She took the railing in her hands as if for support.

No time for it now. You'll have to help her with that later.

Jeffrey pushed the comm link. "This is Captain Holt." He looked at the status displays. Less than 5,000 fleet fighters left.

12,000 fighters lost in four minutes.

He'd never seen anything this bad, but he reminded himself, no one had died… yet. He looked over the pilots in the room. Each was identified by the ship's name, Lacedaemon, and a number from one to one hundred. "Commander," he asked Holloway, "are the other strike forces organized with the same identification system?"

"Yes, sir."

He looked to one of the flight controllers. "How many fighters have singularity warheads?"

"Forty-three of the remaining seventy-one, sir."

"Bring thirty-three back home right now."

"Yes, sir."

Jeffrey said into the comm, "Strike force commanders, we have to split solutions here. We need to preserve our key advantage, namely the singularity warheads. I need you to get ten on target. Get any remaining fighters with singularity warheads back to your ships. Divide your remaining fighters to protect those ten with singularities. We're going to disengage the fighters and make a run at their destroyers."

We never should have engaged the fighters directly. With weapons this powerful, we should have gone for broke from the first moment.

He said both into the comm and to the room of pilots, "We're going to do some suicide runs kamikaze style folks. Let's do as much damage as we can. When the lead attack ships are within range, don't release the singularity warheads, just set them off."

The comm became a mess of voices again, some capitulating, others angry.

"I don't have time for questions or comments," Jeffrey said. "You've agreed to follow the Lacedaemon command for this maneuver, and I am the voice of that command at this time. Get your fighters on target."

The comm fell silent.

Jeffrey turned his attention to the Nav-Con. Most of the green markers formed up and began moving away from the dogfight toward the destroyers. A smaller group turned and headed back toward the fleet.

Well done.

"Keep your motion up folks. Don't be an easy target," he said and turned to Holloway. "Commander, I need your help."

At this, the shadow over her lifted somewhat. "Yes, sir."

"I need you to analyze the fighter groups. Get the individual flight groups I've just created on target for disparate Sthenos destroyers. Get the other fleet flight bosses doing the same. We need even coverage, understood?"

"Yes, sir." Holloway moved down and began talking with her miniboss.

Jeffrey leaned into the comm again. "Strike force commanders. You'll be receiving adjustment instructions from Commander Holloway. Please follow them quickly and to the letter."

Holloway sat down at a station, looked over the screens, and said into the desk mounted microphone, "Strike force Kobayashi 55, redirect to target Sthenos 6. Flight group Rothschild 85, redirect to Sthenos 14…"

On the Nav-Con the yellow Sthenos markers trailed after the fleet fighters. The green lights continued to wink out both on the Nav-Con and around the room. The pilot's who had lost their final drones had removed their helmets. Some sat at their stations, eyes dazed. Others unstrapped and came to stand on the far side of the Nav-Con, watching the final moments of the fight.

Realizing he was holding his breath, Jeffrey let it out and breathed in deep, slow draws as he watched more lights wink out. As the recalled fighters returned to the Lacedaemon, the ship's main guns began to thump, firing at the pursuing Sthenos fighters.

Jeffrey's attention turned to the fighters closing in on the Sthenos destroyers. The next minute was an exercise in self control. The wheels had been set in motion—now he could only watch and wait. Jeffrey clacked his teeth together as an irritated twitch ran through his right calf.

"Come on, just get me a few there." He was gripping the command station rail as if he could somehow squeeze extra speed for the fighters out of it.

More lights winked out. Only 2,000 fighters remained. On the status display the friendly counter continued to scroll downwards, the right-most digit a blur. 1900… 1800… 1700… down to 1500.

On the Nav-Con, the groups of lights had grown small. He only needed one to get through to each destroyer. They were close. He looked back to the counter 1100… 1000… 800. The fall accelerated as the Sthenos had fewer targets to focus on.

Fifty years ago the Hammerheads had been described as a chain saw on wood. Now he knew how the Sthenos had felt, smaller numbers killing larger numbers to the man, but what the Sthenos had just done in five minutes, had taken the Hammerheads a year of bloody fighting.

Jeffery had often wondered what the Sthenos' intention had been fifty years before. They might be close to finally finding out... if they lived.

Whole fighter groups had now disappeared from the Nav-Con. Sthenos destroyer 8 had no fighters on course to strike, nor Sthenos 17, or Sthenos 2. Those were now guaranteed to make it through the fight.

Three healthy destroyers is already too many.

Three green sparks very near Sthenos 12 caught his eye. One winked out. Two sparks. Now one.

He said, "Nav-Con, create a small zoom field on Sthenos 12."

As a small circle zoomed in at the point of the Sthenos 12 destroyer, a green marker came into view, it's distance displayed above... 8 miles... 7... 6... 5. A hoard of Sthenos fighters closed in on it, but the ship rolled and jigged and spun in an amazing, patternless chaos as it closed on the destroyer. In that chaos Jeffrey saw the hand of a brilliant pilot. 3 miles... 2.

As the fighter, Lacedaemon 15, reached the nose of the Sthenos destroyer, Jeffrey said under his breath, "Fire it."

But the fighter did not initiate the singularity. The pilot continued down the ship, corkscrewing and jigging. The green light winked out. Jeffery's heart sank.

Yet, even as his hope died, the side of the Sthenos ship began to peel away. The metal rushed to where the fighter had been, compressing there in an impossibly small sphere, which continued to reduce in size. Metal rained away from the Sthenos ship in ribbons and sheets until the ship seemed to have been bitten almost completely through by a great, jagged-toothed maw.

Jeffrey let out a relieved breath.

The reaction stopped just as quickly as it had begun, leaving some metal sheeting and reinforcement to float past the point of singularity. A haze of metal and outgassed ice crystals vented from the side of the Sthenos destroyer as though it were bleeding to death. Having been cut nearly in half, at its thinnest point, the hull twisted and ripped apart as the ship separated into two monolithic sections, bow and stern.

"Lacedaemon 15," Jeffrey shouted into the room where almost all the pilot's connection lights had turned red, "get your ass up here." He looked back to the Nav-Con. A few green sparks remained, and one by one winked out.

He scanned the Sthenos destroyers. "How many did we get Holloway?"

Holloway looked up at him as the last green sparks of their fighters vanished from the screen. "Just the one, sir."

Jeffrey felt his heart sink as if burrowing down into his belly with hard claws. Nineteen Sthenos destroyers against fifty-seven of theirs.

Not even close to enough.

A young woman, with shockingly deep-blue eyes and short blonde hair, looking no more than nineteen, walked up the three steps of the command tower stairs and saluted Jeffrey. She couldn't weigh more than 95 lbs and barely broke five feet tall.

Jeffrey said, "Yes?"

"I'm Lacedaemon 15 sir, the one you called for."

"Oh… yes… of course. Well flown pilot… very well flown."

"Thank you sir."

"What's your call sign?"

"Call sign sir?"

"Holloway," Jeffrey asked, looking to the commander, "You don't have call signs?"

Holloway spoke with a quiet tone, as if everything she'd done, every decision had been an error leading up to this catastrophe, "Too many pilots sir, no time for them."

"You," he said pointing to the young pilot, "are pale."

Her eyes narrowed. "Yes, sir?"

"Your call sign is Whitetip now."

"Whitetip, sir?"

"It's a shark; as of this moment you're the first fully-fledged member of the resurrected Hammerheads."

She stared at him, her mouth falling slightly open.

"Now," Jeffrey bowed his head to her, "I have to get up to the bridge, please forgive me." He turned as a blast rocked the ship and smoke poured from the hatch to the exit corridor. Jeffrey looked back to the Nav-Con, but it had gone dark—now just a flat, dark disk. Beams from the emergency lights hung in the smoke.

Someone yelled from behind him, "The corridor's blocked, the entire thing buckled shut."

Jeffrey ran to the hatch where something large and dark blocked the corridor. He had to stare at it for a moment before he could understand it was the far wall, crushed down.

"Commander Holloway, is there another way out of this area?"

Holloway shook her head.

Jeffrey closed the hatch and spun the locks. He touched its surface as he asked the sailor beside him, "This isn't a sealed hatch is it?"

"No sir," the sailor said. "It's good for only a few hours of fire control. If the ship loses pressure on the other side, that hatch will let our air right by."

"Let's do what we can to keep that from happening." Jeffrey turned back to the pilots and to Holloway. He pointed to the ceiling. "What's up there?"

"Air handling. Why?" Holloway asked, her expression bewildered. "There's no way out of here. We'll have to wait for..."

Jeffrey stepped close, speaking into her ear so no one around them could hear. "Ma'am, I need you to change your mode of thinking and fast. You must accept this one thing, odds are this room is going to be ripped in half when those Sthenos destroyers get into range. We have to get out and get to escape pods on our own. No one is coming."

Holloway's brow furrowed. "There's been no command to abandon ship."

"True ma'am, but we need to prepare as if it has. We have 19 Sthenos destroyers bearing down on us, and," he pointed to the closed hatch, "that is only from one of their fighters."

Holloway raised her voice to him now. "We don't know—"

"We don't know what commander?" He'd had enough. Until that moment he'd been uneasy with outranking key officers. He wasn't used to it. When he was a Hammerhead, a commander had been well above him. Coming back, he'd fallen into old habits of deferral—*sir's* and *ma'ams*. He knew too well his deferral categorized him in the minds of those like Donovan and Holloway at a lower social strata. He hadn't cared, until now.

"Commander Holloway, are you unsure of the hostility of their intent?"

"No," in the intensity of his tone, she faltered, "I—I wasn't suggesting—

"Are you suggesting they're ineffective in their intent?"

Holloway looked down.

"I'll no longer argue with you, commander. We must evacuate this area now if we are going to preserve pilots for the fight, and believe me that's all we're preserving them for." He leaned in on her. "You find yourself in a new world Holloway. If we don't work together, we all die. I don't just mean the men and women in this room. Do you understand me?"

Holloway lifted her chin and squared her shoulders, eyes professionally blank, "Yes, sir."

"You've got a lot of value Holloway, and I'm trying to offer you some respect, but I swear to God, if you don't stop swinging machetes at my knees, I might start taking it personally. Is that clear?"

"Yes sir, crystal clear sir."

Jeffrey let his tone quiet as he said, "Welcome to war Holloway, if you live through it, you'll never be the same."

"Yes sir."

As Jeffrey looked up to the air duct grating, the ship shook again. A few of the pilots lost their footing as their mag-boots jerked free from the deck. Air hissed around the hatch seams, and Jeffrey's ear drums strained against the depressurization. The hissing fell silent. With all eyes on the hatch, Jeffrey knew everyone in the room was thinking exactly what he was. *Will they lose their air?*

Holloway said, "We lost pressure somewhere. Blast doors must have sealed off the affected area."

Jeffrey motioned for Whitetip to come over to him. "You're small so you'll make a good scout." He looked to the rest of the pilots. "I need something to pry that grate off." He heard the clank of a metal panel, and an object was passed toward him through the pilots. The pilot nearest him handed him a yellow and black crowbar.

"Perfect," Jeffrey said and handed it to Whitetip.

She unlocked her boots and kicked off the floor, floating up to the grating. Jamming the end of the crowbar under its edge, she ripped it from the ceiling. It floated end over end, clattered to the deck, and rebounded toward the pilots. One caught it and jammed it into a gap between two stations.

Reaching up into the duct, Whitetip pulled herself into the darkness.

After a bit of shuffling and the crumpling of metal, she said, her voice sounding far away, "It appears to run parallel to the crushed corridor." Her face appeared in the opening with a slight smile. "You'll fit Captain... barely." She moved out of view again.

CHAPTER 21

"All but a small number of fighters have been destroyed," the Nav-Con operator said.

Cantwell turned to the communications officers. "Get me Captain Holt in flight control."

"Sir, we've lost communications with flight control. A Sthenos fighter struck the hull in close proximity to that area."

Vice President Delaney came up the ladder. "What's going on? Was that a collision?"

"Yes," Cantwell said, "but with all due respect ma'am, I don't need distraction right now."

"What are you planning?"

Cantwell sighed hard, freely showing his exasperation with her. "We have to stick to our plan to land on Earth and disperse hardware."

She shook her head. "I know you think it's the right choice, but the more I think on it, the more the thought of landing the destroyers troubles me. Their armaments will be useless. There must be another way."

"Madam Vice President, I appreciate your concern, but it's based on an overly optimistic perspective. We have two options, stand or retreat."

"Have we tried to communicate—"

"Are you still on that vein? Haven't you been paying attention to what's happening here?"

"I've seen a lot of destruction, but no *reason*. Why haven't we been trying to communicate?"

"It won't do any good."

"How do you know that?"

Cantwell turned away from her to swear under his breath. He masked it by walking to his command seat.

She followed him saying, "I've been discussing the conflict more with Gerard Schodt, and he feels if we can simply discover some of their basic language—."

"Gerard Schodt's advice is useless."

"Why do you say that?"

"He lacks a key understanding."

"Which is?"

"What it means to kill a sentient being. It's not a damn touchdown. Don't make the mistake of thinking combatants are blood thirsty. We're not. Yes, young soldiers may posture and run their mouths, but I've never known a single combatant who wasn't scared shitless in the moment, nor one who didn't want peace afterward. Let me make this clear, no one wants peace more than those who've lived through war. It is, by an extreme degree, the worst thing they'll ever experience. When men like Gerard Schodt think we actually *want* to go to war, that we ignore other options, he can't imagine what we've been through. When I say we must engage, I need you to believe that I absolutely see no other viable option for the best outcome in the long term. We either face the Sthenos or let them run us down."

Her eyes narrowed as she squared on him. "I refuse to accept that with fifty-seven destroyers to their twenty-three we only have running as an option."

Cantwell, not wanting to get into a shouting match, calmed himself as he said, "It's the only way to generate possibilities in the future."

"I don't believe that you can kno—"

He fairly yelled, "I can and do," and calmed his tone as he said, "We cannot face them head to head. We must retreat, but if we do so anywhere but Earth, we'll leave it defenseless and put ourselves at greater risk. I will not allow either."

"But you've beaten them before out here."

164

"We *won*, if you want to call it that, due to far better odds and unique tactics. Currently we have a third the advantage, and our new tactics have proven useless. The old, successful tactics aren't available to us." With a sigh, he said, "I need you to appreciate what happened here. We've lost the first battle of the war. Not simply lost it… we've had our main method of fighting obliterated. If we face them out in the open 2 to 1, we'll be cut to pieces just as those fighters were."

"But can't these destroyers at least somewhat stand up—"

"We've been through this, ma'am. In the past, when our destroyers went head to head with the Sthenos, not once did we come out ahead."

"What about the singularity warheads?"

"Our only method of delivering the warheads has been destroyed."

"I can't believe you won't consider a better solution. I'm going to have to ask you to come up with some other options for my review."

"Other options for…?" Cantwell walked right up to her. "I've had enough. Get off my bridge."

"Excuse me?"

"You're interfering with my command. Get off my bridge or be removed."

She opened her mouth as if to yell at him, but no sound came out as though she were so angry she couldn't form words.

"Nothing?"

"How dare you," she spit the words at him. "I'll have you—"

"Masters at Arms, remove the vice president from the bridge."

As six large sailors approached, she looked to her security detail. "You will allow no such thing."

Cantwell said to the two Marines, "You may assure her physical safety, but do not intervene with my order."

"Sir," one of the Marines said, "Our orders are—"

"Your *new* orders," Cantwell said with the confidence only decades of experience can bring, "are to stay out of my security team's way. Is that clear?"

The Marines looked to Delaney and the Masters at Arms. They moved aside.

As the masters at arms took hold of her upper arms, she said, "This is treason."

"Ma'am," Cantwell said, "You may feel free to throw me in the brig when this is over. However, until that time, you *will* stay out of my way."

She struggled for a moment against the Masters at Arms, but when she failed to stop them walking her toward the ladder, she relented and allowed herself to be taken off the bridge. Her security detail followed.

"Navigation," Cantwell said, "get the fleet decelerating for Earth orbit."

"Yes, sir," the navigation officer said, but sounded unsure.

"Concerns navigation?"

"If we begin deceleration for Earth orbit now, the Sthenos will run right through us."

"I have a feeling," Cantwell said, "their final attack isn't coming right now. If so, when we begin deceleration, they'll match us." Cantwell looked out the latticework to where the Sthenos destroyers lay among the stars. "For whatever reason, they aren't ready for us yet."

After a few moments the navigation officer said, "Sir, I have the fleet prepared for deceleration burn."

"Excellent. Begin."

The ship came alive again as the subtle vibration of the massive thrusters returned and Cantwell's weight pressed into the deck. Beyond the glass, the thrusters of the visible ships glowed.

The navigation officer said, "Deceleration burn begun."

"Nav-Con."

"Yes, sir?"

"What is our estimated time to Earth arrival?"

She looked at her display. "At current deceleration—two days, five hours, and ten minutes from orbit sir."

"Our distance to the Sthenos?"

"They are decelerating at a higher rate. Distance is now over 4,000 miles, sir." She stared at the display for some time before saying, "They're now holding at 10,620 miles, sir."

"Let me know if that changes in any way."

"Yes, sir."

Cantwell looked across his bridge, to the younger officers, many new from training, lives just beginning, and thought of the similar officers on the other ships in the fleet.

CHAPTER 22

Most of the pilots and support staff had made their way into the duct. Jeffrey looked at the few personnel still with him on the flight control deck. A young woman, a petty officer 2nd class, stood near him. She was pretty, in a awkward way, with wide, nervous eyes.

"Are you all right?"

She gave him a quick nod.

Jeffrey could see she was definitely not all right.

Personnel continued to kick off the deck and disappear into the darkness of the vent.

"What's your name P.O.?"

In an unsure tone, she said, "Isabel Ellstrom, sir."

He took her gently by the shoulders. "Everything's going to be okay, Isabel. I just need you to take a deep breath and trust me. Can you do that?"

Closing her eyes, she let out her breath. When her eyes came open, she still looked terrified.

"Are you ready to go?"

Looking up to the vent, she nodded, but did not release her boots.

Now only he, the young woman, and a male pilot remained. The pilot could have moved into the vent, but he clearly was waiting for Isabel to be on her way. In that selflessness, Jeffrey immediately liked the man.

Jeffrey said, "Isabel, here's what we're going to do. I'm going into the vent, you'll be next, and… What's your name pilot?"

"Lieutenant Kessler sir."

"First name?"

"Morgan."

He said to the girl, "Morgan will be behind you. We'll be right with you the whole way. Okay?"

She nodded.

Unlocking his boots, Jeffrey kicked off the deck, floating up to the opening. As he pulled himself in, a sharp metal edge scraped his forearm. Tilting flashlights outlined the last airman's silhouette, legs relaxed in the weightlessness.

After entering the coppery-scented duct, Jeffrey realized the space was too narrow for him to turn around as Whitetip had, so he waited, looking under his arm to see if the girl would appear.

He heard Kessler say, "You'll do fine, Isabel."

After a moment, she peeked into the duct. She pulled herself in cautiously, a flashlight in her hand, looking as though she might be sick. Jeffrey moved forward to make room for her. Behind her, Kessler entered the duct.

"You all right?" he asked her.

"Yes, somewhat, sir."

Jeffrey pulled himself forward along the duct, the air growing hot as he moved away from the opening. The thump of boots and shoulders bumping the ductwork echoed down the narrow passage. Isabel's flashlight played over his shoulders, throwing his shadow out ahead of him. Far ahead, Jeffrey could still make out the boots of the last pilot. The metal walls began to vibrate and Jeffrey had just enough foresight to brace himself as the floor of the duct, slammed into him. He found himself pinned to the metal. The Lacedaemon had begun deceleration. With the ductwork groaning under his weight, he wondered if it would hold. He began crawling, his body heavy.

Moving forward, he found places where the ductwork had bent downward with the weight of the others. A concussive bang made him brace for a fall, expecting to drop out of the ceiling. His ears rang. Out ahead of him, he could no longer see the lights of the pilots. Isabel's light still shone behind him.

She let out a long, drawn out moan, sounding like a breeze catching the mouth of a bottle, but with a living, phlegmy rattle. He looked under his shoulder.

The flashlight caught him in its circular beam. Looking into the small circle of light, which reflected off the bare metal walls, he could see the duct had been crushed shut. The space where the flashlight came from appeared far too narrow for hope. Still, the light moved a bit.

"Isabel, are you there?" He asked.

There was no answer.

Jeffrey, twisted himself, jamming his shoulder and hips into the walls, forcing the duct to bend so he could turn. The metal crinkled and groaned as he got himself shoved around. He crawled back down the duct, until he had to turn onto his side to fit.

The flashlight, now a foot or two away from him, turned over to shine on her frighteningly pale face. Her eyes were wide with fear, tears wetted her face, quick in the excessive G's.

How can she still be alive in that small space?

He barely kept the thought from his lips.

"Help me," she said in a whisper as tears fell from her chin, crystal clear and magnifying the light of the flashlight. "Please don't let me die."

Jeffrey knew, based on the narrowness of the duct behind her, that most of her body was crushed. There would be no way for one man without tools to free her. Even in the best circumstances she might not live. Behind her, Kessler was surely dead. If he'd told the pilot to take the lead… The flip of a coin had once again left Jeffrey alive.

Jeffrey stilled himself before saying in a calm, friendly tone, "Easy Isabel. Take slow breaths."

I've been here too many times.

He thought back to finding Stacy Zack on the bridge of the crashed Jules Verne, remembered how thrilled he'd been when he realized she was going to live, remembered how hard he'd fought to keep her alive. This young woman would have no such chance.

"Please help me," she said and began to sob, the convulsions obviously causing her severe pain.

"Isabel."

Her crying lessened as she asked in a quavering voice, "Yes?"

"It's a beautiful name."

A smile hinted across her face before pain furrowed her brow again. Her eyes went glassy, and she fell silent for some time. Jeffrey thought she might have gone.

It would be so much better to go quickly.

However, her eyes opened, widening with fear. "Are you real? Am I dreaming?"

"It's not a dream. I'm real."

"Help me…" her voice faded to a whisper, "please."

Jeffrey wanted to tell her he would, but he was unwilling to be dishonest to the dying. "Can you hand me the flashlight?"

She extended the flashlight toward him. He had to shove himself forward to reach it. He hung it's lanyard on a rivet, which had been pressed out of the ductwork. It now illuminated the space without shining in her face. Shoving himself further in, he felt a sharp edge of metal cut into his shoulder. He kept shoving despite the cutting sensation until he could take hold of her hand, which felt death-relaxed until she registered he held it and gripped down. She pulled on it with a ferocity he hadn't expected and screamed out in pain. Tears streamed from her eyes.

"Isabel, I don't think we can get you out."

"Oh God, please don't say that." Her sobs cut her words up. "Please don't leave me here."

"I'm not going anywhere Isabel." Jeffrey fought to keep his voice even. "I'm going to be right here with you the whole way. Do you understand?"

"Please don't go." She fell silent, her eyes waxing vague again.

It's okay to go. Let yourself pass.

171

At that Jeffrey's own breath trembled in his throat, and a hot tear spilled down his face because it wasn't okay. She hadn't even started living yet.

When Isabel's eyes clarified and focused on Jeffrey, he brushed the tear away.

She gave him a distant smile. "You're still here."

"Yes, I'm not going anywhere." He squeezed her hand. She squeezed back, her fingers narrow and delicate, cold.

Her eyes clamped shut with pain.

"There's nothing to be afraid of, Isabel."

The corners of her mouth turned down, and she said, "I finally got a date out of him."

"What's that?"

"He works in the machine shop." She smiled slightly. "...pretty eyes." Letting out a sigh, which clearly hurt, she said, "But I suppose he wouldn't have much interest in me now."

Understanding her, Jeffrey said, "Isabel, you're gorgeous. You understand that? Beautiful."

At that her mouth turned down, and she said, her voice no more than a tremoring whisper, "I told the other girls I was going to marry him."

At that a possibility of Isabel's life flashed through his mind. Her standing in an elegant, white dress beside a lean young man by the sea. He saw her kissing her first son's forehead, his hair soft on her nose, and her as an old woman, looking out a window, her delicate hands wrinkled.

In those thoughts Jeffrey felt the sore, stabbing guilt at having survived when so many others had died.

Isabel's hand had gone limp again. Her eyes were closed, but Jeffrey could feel her breathing through a slight draw and release of her fingers. Every so often they twitched as if she were dreaming.

After a few moments her eyes opened and traced the space before her until they found him. She smiled, seeming far away.

"I'm right here, Isabel."

"Dad?" Her tone was easy.

Jeffrey had no idea what to say.

Her eyes went wide and searched, seeming not to see him. She said again, now worried, "Dad?"

"I'm with you," Jeffrey said, doing everything he could to keep his voice even.

She began crying quietly.

"Don't cry."

"I'm so sorry Dad. I didn't mean to die. I'm really sorry."

Jeffrey hushed her and said, "It's okay, you didn't do anything wrong."

Her brow furrowed. "I tried dad."

"I know you did," Jeffrey whispered.

An easy smile spread across her face. "I love you." The light in her eyes faded as her hand relaxed.

Jeffrey held her soft hand. It didn't pull with breath nor twitch with dreams.

"I love you too," he whispered to her, the sound of his words caught and muffled by the narrow walls he lay jammed between.

He held her hand for some time, limp and delicate, before letting it go. It dropped out of reach. Shifting his weight backward, he felt metal stab into his shoulder. Reaching to his shoulder he found a tear in the metal ducting. The tear protruded to a point behind his shoulder blade. He could not move forward to free himself.

He pulled backward again, the metal slicing into his shoulder with a deep pressure. If he wanted out of that space, he'd have to cut muscle to pull himself free, and if the metal turned far enough inward, it could slash deep. He could bleed out here beside Isabel.

Maybe that's for the best. I'm so tired of outliving others.

But the idea didn't stick. When he thought of Isabel, he didn't want to be here beside her. He didn't suffer despair. What he felt glowed like an ember, a smoldering thing which had been dormant for decades. The ember stoked up and ignited. Like a boxer who can't fire up until he's punched hard, Jeffrey found his purpose. In that

173

moment, he didn't care why they'd come. He wanted only to kill them, all of them, not for the sake of death, but because he didn't know how many more like this girl he could stand to lose. He felt himself on a precipice, kill or lose his mind in grief. With or without warheads or fighters he'd do it. If he had to, he'd rip their arms off with his bare hands.

He pulled on his shoulder again and the metal cut deep, pinning him. Yelling out, he hauled on his shoulder again.

CHAPTER 23

Cantwell asked, "Distance to Earth?"

"Five hours, six minutes on the current deceleration curve, sir."

Leaning forward in his command seat, elbows on knees, he stared at the decking in front of him. He closed his eyes, imagining the distance between the fleet, the Sthenos, and Earth. For two days they'd matched the fleet's deceleration perfectly.

What do they have planned for us?

He felt as though he were trapped at the bottom of a pit with a boulder leaning over the edge high above.

"God damn you Holt," he said under his breath. "Why did you have to be so right?"

Holt and the flight crew had been missing for over forty eight hours. While he knew what that probably meant, he still didn't want to acknowledge it. Large sections of the ship in that area had remained pressurized, but were cut off by damage, so hope remained, no matter how thin.

Taking his mind from Holt, he thought back over the last few years. If he hadn't been in retirement maybe he could have prevented the removal of manned fighters. He opened his eyes. On the Nav-Con the fleet lay out before him, engines glowing off the cowls that seemed tiny and delicate but were, in reality, armored arcs of metal fifty feet high.

"Communications," he said, "Any transmissions from Earth?"

"Nothing sir."

"Nav-Con," Cantwell said, "give me a visual on the Sthenos fleet."

"Yes sir."

He moved to stand beside the Nav-Con officer. "That's a strange configuration."

The ships, flying thrusters backward with their deceleration, were arrayed out in a vertical disk, flying face on to the fleet, each ship slightly staggered. Their engine housings glowed a deep blue. Two hours earlier, the Sthenos destroyers which had laid waste to Earth's military installations and communications infrastructure, had come out of orbit, gone around the incoming fleet with astounding acceleration, and joined the larger Sthenos attack force.

Cantwell pointed to the ships. "What do you suppose this staggering is for?"

"I'm not sure, sir." She rotated the image side-on and scowled at it. "There is this." But she fell silent as if in thought.

"What?"

"Each ship has its front quarter clear of the others in a vertical plane. If they fire their energy cannons in the manner they did at Europa, they wouldn't strike each other.

Cantwell nodded. "That's good Lieutenant, very good. I'm thinking you're right. It's some kind of attack formation. It's close now."

Cantwell walked out to the center of bridge, under the great lattice the stars sharp and bright overhead. Turning to the bridge crew, he said, "Ladies and gentlemen, this is the time that I should offer a wise speech. I have none. Nothing I say will change what you know to be true. I can't armor our ships with words, and I can't steel your hearts. That is up to you. I *will* tell you we appear to be Earth's last line of defense. We must be decisive. There are four billion souls planet-side, all relying on us. I won't dress it up; this is going to get much worse before, and if, it gets better. In the next few hours, days, and months, our actions will steer the course of human history. You must find your strength even in the face of near-certain failure. We may not live through the day, or even the hour, but I do know this one thing: each one of you who sets self aside for service moves us that much closer to achieving the impossible."

Not waiting for their reactions, which was something between them and themselves, he walked back to the command seat and sat down, feeling tired.

CHAPTER 24

Stacy Zack walked onto the bridge with her team. Indicating that Marco, Horace, X, and Jacqueline should remain at the back of the room, she approached Admiral Cantwell.

"Sir, you asked for us?"

Cantwell, his eyes exhausted but his voice strong, said, "Commander, we're dealing with large scale warfare, but if we're lucky enough, we'll need your small scale operational expertise in the near future. I want you and your team to be here from the beginning to assure a full understanding of our situation.

The navigation officer looked up from her console, saying, "Deceleration reduction for orbital entry will begin in ten minutes, sir."

"Excellent."

Cantwell briefed Stacy on what had occurred up to that point. When he'd finished, the deceleration maneuver was a few moments away.

The navigation officer said, "Reducing deceleration on my mark. Three... two... mark."

Just at the edge of her perception, Stacy felt the ship go quieter, less alive. Her weight reduced to a now incredibly light-feeling, single G. Above, the stars seemed more still, despite the ship's high velocity. The sense of stillness at such staggering speeds could be deceptive. She'd once completed a space walk at a solar-relative speed over one million miles an hour. Floating in the deep dark, the swath of the Milky way ranged broadly over her left shoulder as she drifted in a state of profound peace.

"Sir," the Nav-Con officer said, but fell silent as she watched her podium screen.

"Yes?" Cantwell said.

"I'm sorry, sir, just a moment please."

After what seemed to Stacy much more than one moment, the Nav-Con officer said, her face glowing with the light of her podium, "The Sthenos ships have not reduced deceleration curves. They are falling behind quickly."

Cantwell said, "Keep me informed."

"Yes, sir."

Cantwell said, as if to himself, "If they aren't going to enter Earth's orbit, what the hell are they—"

The Nav-Con operator cut him off. "The Sthenos have cut deceleration completely now. They're turning… into an acceleration configuration." After a moment, she said, "They're accelerating."

"At what rate?"

The Nav-Con operator looked to Stacy and Cantwell as though she couldn't believe what she was about to say. "Eight G's sir."

"Eight?" Cantwell moved to stand beside her. "How is that poss—," but he let the comment go. "They're most likely going to make a strafing pass. We're going to catch some hell. Bring up the battle group, and Sthenos positions. Collapse accordingly."

The Nav-Con blurred before the sharp red and yellow lights swept into view over the display. Near the center of the battle group, the Lacedaemon glowed a more-intense red.

As Cantwell stared at the narrowing gap between the Sthenos ships and the fleet, he said quietly, "What the hell is your game?"

"Velocity delta is already 2,500 miles an hour sir," the Nav-Con officer said.

"This makes no sense."

Stacy shared Cantwell's confusion. The more the Sthenos accelerated, the more they would overshoot Earth and the less time they'd have to take shots at the fleet. Visualizing the black destroyers blurring by at thousands of miles an hour, she tried to understand what they had planned.

Cantwell asked Nav-Con, "What will our relative speeds be at current velocity deltas?"

She ran her fingertips across the podium. "If our deceleration and their acceleration remain constant, our relative delta will be 15,000 miles an hour sir."

"15,000 miles an hour?" Stacy said. "They'll be lucky to get one shot off at that speed."

"Nav-Con," Cantwell asked, "are any of the trajectories on collision courses?"

Without delay she said, "No, sir. There are no collision avoidance warnings. All trajectories are clear."

Stacy stared at the Nav-Con with Cantwell, the display zooming in as the Sthenos closed. Soon Stacy could see the small shapes of the destroyers.

Cantwell said, "At that speed, they'll overshoot the Earth so far we'll have more than enough time to touch down... but it can't be that simple." He returned to his command seat. "Fleet, it appears the Sthenos are going to strafe us. Be ready for Sthenos course changes related to collisions. Nav-Con."

"Yes sir?"

"Time to Earth orbit?"

"One hour, sixteen minutes, sir."

On the Nav-Con, the Sthenos and the fleet seemed to be nearly on top of each other. Stacy looked up through the broad lattice.

"Is that what I think it is?" Stacy asked, pointing at something dark among the stars. As she squinted at it, it grew into the glowering prow of a Sthenos destroyer.

Cantwell asked, "Nav-Con, are you sure they aren't on a collision course?"

"Not at this time sir. That ship will pass by starboard. It's highly unlikely, with their current velocity, they have enough time to redirect to strike any of our ships."

"They seem to live in the realm of highly unlikely."

"Yes, sir."

The Sthenos destroyer, aimed to pass by their starboard side, began to rotate in a slow barrel roll. The rotation accelerated to a spin.

"What the hell?" Cantwell asked in a quiet voice.

The destroyer increased the speed of its roll to a near blur. The Nav-Con officer, her voice incredulous, asked, "How can they roll like that and not crush everyone inside?"

"I have no idea," another officer said.

To the port side, much more distant, another Sthenos ship came into view, spinning up as well, faster and faster, also blurring. Even further away, another ship came into view.

"Holy hell," Cantwell said. "They're going to run us through a blender." He jammed his finger on his com button. "All ships cease deceleration and turn ninety degrees to port *now*! Get yourselves perpendicular to the Sthenos approach vector."

Weightlessness returned as the stars began to rotate above. The conn had responded quickly to Cantwell's order.

"I think it might be too late sir," the Nav-Con officer said.

"Let it be as it will," Cantwell said and shouted to his right, "Fire control! Engage at will as they pass."

The Sthenos' bright-green energy beam lanced out from the prow of each ship, and their long axis spin caused the beam to sweep into a corkscrewing sheet, filling the field of stars.

"Brace for impact," Cantwell called out.

The Sthenos whipped by leaving a green swath in front of the bridge glass just missing the Lacedaemon's bow. A moment later, the deck shuddered and pitched, throwing Stacy in the air as her mag-boots jolted free. Tucking her shoulder, she rolled over, and hit the lattice with her back. She braced herself for another impact, but none came.

The Nav-Con officer floated a few feet off the deck, struggling. Kicking off the lattice, Stacy landed beside her, boots relocked to the deck, and pulled her down. Red emergency lights pulsed. The main lighting in the bridge flickered, and everything fell into blackness.

Had they returned fire? Even one shot?

In the darkness, the stars overhead became brilliant and immeasurable. Stacy noticed a glow on the edges of the lattice work. It seemed to be coming from port side. Moving to those windows, she saw the S.D.F. Naraka drifting in three sections. From each cut, a crystallizing fog of atmosphere escaped into space. The Sthenos had cut down the largest and most powerful Japanese destroyer in half a second. Here and there, the orange burn of life pods streaked away in solid-rocket-smoking lines.

"I need fleet status Nav-Con," Cantwell called out.

"I have no power, sir."

As if the Nav-Con officer's words had triggered it, dim emergency lights flickered to life. The Nav-Con podium lit up, but the display remained empty.

"Nav-Con," Cantwell said, "get me status on the fleet and the Sthenos *now*."

"Yes, sir," she said. Her fingers flew over the illuminated podium and went still. She stared at the panel for a moment, tapped on it once. Eyes wide and mouth slightly open, she turned to Cantwell and said as if confused, "They're gone sir."

"Gone? Who? The Sthenos? Do you mean gone to a distance or gone entirely?"

The Nav-Con officer looked back to her screens. "I... I'm not..." She looked back to Cantwell and shook her head as if trying to clear it. "The fleet sir... our fleet, every ship is... destroyed."

Cantwell looked to the Nav-Con's empty disk. "That pass was too fast. They can't all... Are you sure?"

"Yes, sir."

Stacy said, "Forgive me sir, but the Naraka is off our port side."

Cantwell looked to her, his eyes hopeful, and she hated to tell him what she saw, hated to confirm and even believe it herself.

"It's in three pieces."

He stared at her only a moment before saying, "Navigation, make sure we stay with them. We have to collect life pods."

"Main thrusters went offline when we were struck, sir," the navigation officer said. "I have no control."

The dead feeling in the decking and the weightlessness bothered Stacy more than it had before because she knew the ship might never come alive again.

"Are we maintaining position with them?" He asked the Nav-Con officer.

"Yes, sir."

"Get pinging for survivors." He looked to the communications officer closest to him. "You're the point. Give me any messages that are relevant to main tactics. Route all other communications to relevant commanders."

"Aye aye, sir."

He looked to Stacy. "Any thoughts, Zack?"

"Nothing relevant to our current situation, sir."

He nodded, seeming to appreciate her brevity.

"Nav-Con, does your data still maintain that all ships are destroyed?"

"Yes sir," she said, the color somewhat returning to her face. "I show all fifty-six ships were at a minimum completely bisected, some trisected. We were the only one that turned sideways enough... and were lucky enough to avoid a major hull breech."

"What do you mean by that?"

"The U.S.S. Theras had completed its turn, but was cut down the middle."

"Completely down the middle."

In the woman's closed off expression, Stacy understood she was stuffing something down into her heart that was too hard to deal with. "Yes sir, all hands lost, no life pods ejected."

"Stay on task folks. Our job is to get planet side," Cantwell said. While Stacy felt certain the loss of a thousand men and women, most the ages of his grandchildren, crushed him, he gave no indication of it. He seemed to have switched off any part of himself which might get in his way.

Cantwell said to one of the communications officers, "Send out a signal to all life pod computers to autopilot themselves into our hangars." Then to navigation, "The moment they're collected, get us decelerating for orbital insertion again."

"Yes, sir."

"What's the status of the Sthenos ships Nav-Con?"

"The ships have begun their deceleration, but were travelling far too fast with their attack acceleration to obtain orbit. They'll pass the orbital plane by a significant margin."

"Estimated time?"

"Based on the physics of our ship's limitations, they should be delayed beyond our own orbital timeframe by twelve hours."

"Let's cut that in half for a safe measure and consider our window at six hours." Cantwell said. "That still gives us enough time to get to ground." He looked around the room. "Does anyone have a damage report? I know we got hit, I felt it."

CHAPTER 25

Stacy stood beside Cantwell's command seat staring at the dead Nav-Con as the minutes passed without information.

Finally Cantwell said, "I feel like I can't see at all without that thing on. Fire control, did we get any shots off?"

"I have no information on that at the moment, sir."

"Let me know when you do."

"Yes, sir."

"Comm, do you have the life pods directed to our landing bays?"

"Coming in now sir."

"Good man. Tell me when they're in."

"Yes sir."

"Keep the communication channels clear of chatter folks."

Cantwell turned back to the Nav-Con. His finger tapping on his armrest. Standing, he walked out under the lattice of bridge windows and looked up at the stars.

"Engineering," he said, his eyes still on the jeweled swath of the Milky Way.

"Yes, sir."

"Any information on why we've lost thrust?"

"I have inconsistent information coming in, sir. I'll update you the moment we have enough detail for an accurate report."

"Thank you. We need to complete our deceleration very soon if we want to touch down." He went back to watching the stars.

What Stacy was seeing in him now she understood to be what separated him from a non-war commander. His experience had taught him to keep his mind clear, *go to the void* as Jeffrey had called it. The fate of the survivors in life pods, the men and women on the Lacedaemon, and the human race as a whole might rest on his next few decisions, decisions which had to wait until he knew more. In the waiting, he could yell at people to hurry, remind them delays meant death, but Stacy saw in his silence that he understood he had the best people in the right positions. They needed nothing but time to do their jobs well. They knew the urgency.

A shatter of sound filled the bridge as the entirety of the Nav-Con display filled with a cylinder of static. The static faded, leaving behind the sparks of the fleet, pulsing in a deep-red light save the Lacedaemon's single, constant identifier. Brilliant-orange life pod markers swarmed the Lacedaemon.

"We have positioning now sir, but no visual," the Nav-Con officer said.

"Get a camera launched."

"Yes, sir."

"Damage control," Cantwell called out, "Do we have any information on thrust?"

"Coming in now sir," an efficiently gray-haired officer to the right of the navigation stations said. He watched his screens a moment longer before approaching the command seat. "Sir, we have a problem."

Stacy could see Cantwell didn't care to hear of more problems.

"Name it sailor."

"We have no drive plates, sir."

"What?"

"The damage reports indicate the rear quarter of the ship is gone... cut away."

"Cut..." for a moment Cantwell appeared visibly shaken. His expression stilled as he asked, "Do we have emergency thrusters?"

"Yes sir, side maneuvering thrusters used in tandem at the correct vectors can decelerate us effectively. However, within that solution lies our trouble."

"Which is?"

186

"The fuel required to achieve a degrading Earth orbit, which will effectively deplete our hydrogen/oxygen reserves."

Cantwell said with understanding, "We have to use all of that just to drop into degradation. Then…"

The gray-haired officer continued his thought, "we won't have enough fuel for a controlled descent."

Cantwell motioned for the officer to come closer. The officer leaned over the left side of Cantwell's command seat.

"Are there any other options? Any fuel-use scenarios, which might work?"

"I'm sorry, sir," the officer said, "There are no other scenarios, and if we don't implement in the next few moments, we won't have enough distance to achieve degradation. We'll slingshot past Earth and enter a solar impact trajectory."

"Damage control," Cantwell called out, motioning for a woman with short red hair to approach.

She walked with stiff steps to the command chair, her eyes strict, but her face young. "Admiral," she said with a slight nod of her head.

"Officer, paint me a picture of the drive plates. Is there any way they can be repaired?"

"If the reports are accurate, there are no drive plates, sir."

The Nav-Con officer said, "Sir, we have a visual coming in now."

On the Nav-Con, the marker of the Lacedaemon blurred into the actual ship, life pods swarming into the landing bays. The rear half of the ship grew until it filled the display. Stacy's heart sank. The last hundred feet had been sliced away at a steep angle, deck after deck flayed open to space.

"That's a definite no," Cantwell said.

The red-haired officer nodded. "Yes Admiral."

Cantwell said, "It's amazing the isotopes didn't collide. We were lucky."

"More than you know, sir." She walked over to the Nav-Con and pointed to the open decks where small bits of insulation and metal still floated away from the hulk of the destroyer. "The weapon cut right through both containment vessels. A secondary explosion here," she pointed to a crater in the low center of the mess that had once been the aft section, "caused by environmental oxygen, blew the material in opposite directions. Note how the damage spreads outward? That's all secondary damage from the blast."

"All of the emergency environmental oxygen—"

"Is gone, sir."

"So we won't have air in how long?"

"We will be breathing pretty thick in less than a day."

Cantwell tapped his fingers on his armrest. "So we have no nuclear thrust, fuel enough for about a thirty minute burn, there are twenty-three Sthenos destroyers bent on our destruction, and we're the only surviving destroyer in a fleet of fifty-seven."

Falling silent, he stared at the floor. Stacy felt certain what would happen in the next few seconds might be one of the most important moments she'd witness in her lifetime.

Cantwell's head came up, "Helmsman."

"Yes, sir." The team lead of the four women and three men who sat at the helm controls said.

"Status."

"Helm is responsive sir."

"Good," Cantwell said before trailing off. He sat for some time, and Stacy saw him drawing slow breaths, as if in meditation. Despite the situation at hand, his calm suffused her own thoughts.

"We're still receiving life pods sir. If we decelerate now, we'll lose over a thousand."

"Navigation, when is the latest we can begin burn and achieve degradation?"

"Fifteen seconds."

Cantwell's tired, pale-blue eyes came open. "God speed to those we leave behind." He paused as if he couldn't get himself to say what needed to be said but, after a moment, did what must be done. "Cease rescue efforts, secure landing bays, and begin deceleration burn now. Adjust course. Set a glide path for the Amazon."

One of the helmsmen looked over his shoulder, his expression sincerely surprised. "The Amazon sir?"

"Central delta. Make it happen."

"Yes sir." The navigation officers went to work at their station. The ship began an unharmonious vibration, and light gravity pushed into Stacy's feet. The navigation officer looked back to Cantwell and said, "Atmospheric contact in forty-three minutes."

On the Nav-Con the main maneuvering thrusters had come on full-burn shooting out clear-blue flame to the rear at forty-five degree angles. The life pods, still swarming the ship, fell away as they continued on their slingshot trajectory past Earth. Stacy imagined the people in those pods looking out the small, circular viewport as the wall of the Lacedaemon slid away, leaving the glass filled with stars. She bit her tongue to stifle the emotion the thought brought up.

"Commander," Cantwell said. A moment later, he repeated in a calm but insistent tone, "Commander."

She looked to him to see who wasn't responding and found him looking at her.

"Yes, sir. Sorry, sir."

He looked to his right, saying, "Captain Donovan."

The captain looked to him.

"Come here please."

When the captain had come to stand opposite Stacy, Cantwell said, "If we succeed in getting to the ground, we'll have to evacuate this ship and get as many resources and personnel into the rainforest as we can. We'll need food, water, and weapons. You," he pointed to Donovan, "are to begin coordination of that movement now. You have approximately forty minutes before all personnel must be strapped down. Get started with assigning stations. This must happen fast. After we touch down, we'll have a four to twelve hour window before the Sthenos return. I don't know what they're planning, but I'm

189

guessing they'll want to assure the Lacedaemon is dealt with. We must assume demolition is imminent and get a safe distance away. A quarter mile is an absolute minimum."

"Yes sir," Donovan said. "We can move the supplies one-half mile off, then have the personnel move further out until we establish a safe-zone and return for supplies."

Cantwell nodded. "Excellent."

Cantwell looked to Stacy. "Zack, this is Captain Walter Donovan. He's served under me many years. You can trust him, understood?"

"Yes, sir."

"Captain, this is Special Warfare Commander Stacy Zack. Jeffery Holt holds her in high regard, and so do I. You can trust her. Clear?"

"Crystal, sir."

"As we've not heard from Holloway nor Holt in two days, I have to assume they're dead."

His coarseness caused Stacy's stomach to flush with acid.

"If something happens to me, you two are the commanding officers of this group. You," he pointed to Donovan, "are logistics and large troop movement. Understood?"

"Yes, sir."

"You," he pointed to Stacy, "are guerilla tactics, which will be our main method of assault. We cannot face this threat head on."

Stacy asked, "How do you imagine us dealing with it, sir? As you mentioned, if something happens to you, I'd like to know your thoughts now."

"Our way, is your way, Zack. I have no guidance beyond that. You are the lead and the expert. Get in the forest with the singularity warheads we have left. Use them to play hell with the Sthenos."

Stacy felt unsure at that. "How big are these warheads?"

Cantwell held up his hands shoulder wide. "Just under fifty pounds."

"I can work with that."

Cantwell nodded. "But first we have to get this dying heap planet side without killing everyone. Donovan, get your people coordinated. When we stop moving I want every single man and woman on this ship carrying gear. Get any vehicles we can salvage obscured before the Sthenos obtain orbit."

"Yes sir." As Donovan walked away he shot Stacy a side-long look.

"Don't let him bother you Zack," Cantwell said. "He's harsh but solid and sure."

"Which is why you told him to team with me."

Cantwell nodded. "If he gives you any trouble, you remind him of that. It'll keep him aligned, but I expect you," his tone became sharp as he pointed at her, "to play ball with him as well. Clear?"

"Yes sir, but I'm sure that you'll assist us."

"Laying everything on one person's leadership is a low odds bet. We must prepare a contingency if and when our own deaths finds us. I expect you to do the same with your own team."

"Yes, sir."

"People are going to die. Are you ready for it?"

Stacy looked to Marco, X, Horace, and Jacqueline, who stood near the rear of the bridge. She imagined them in a firefight, not marking lasers but live rounds, tracers flying through smoking air. "I have no idea sir, but we'll do the best we're able."

"That," Cantwell said, his expression flat, "is the only true answer." He pointed to the row of jump seats along the curved, rear wall. "Get strapped in."

"Yes, sir."

As Stacy walked away, the navigation officer said. "Thirty-five minutes to atmospheric contact, sir."

CHAPTER 26

Stacy strapped herself into a jump seat with Jacqueline to her left and Marco to her right. X sat on the far side of Marco.

Jacqueline said, "O.C. I—"

Stacy held up her hand to silence her and pointed to Cantwell, who walked up to the row of helmsmen. "Ladies and gentlemen, this is exactly what you've trained for, do you understand me?"

"Yes, sir," they said, some with conviction, others with unsure quietness.

"You will save thousands of lives today, do not think otherwise." Then his voice boomed out, "Do I make myself clear?"

The helmsmen all shouted back, "Yes, sir."

"Good." Leaning down, with his hand on the team lead's shoulder, he said something into the young man's ear. Facing the rest of the bridge, he said, "I want every single body in this bridge strapped down *now*."

Staff began running for seats. Essential personnel drew five point harnesses from their station seats while non-essential personnel ran to the jump seats along the wall near Stacy and her team.

Stacy said to Marko, "I wish you were at the controls of this thing right now."

Horace nodded. "You got that right."

"Me? Hell no. My skills are with small craft. These folks are experts with a monster like this. I've never so much as pulled one out of orbit." He pointed to the helmsmen, "They'll get the job done."

X's eyes narrowed. "I think that's the first humility I've ever seen from you Fields."

At the command seat, Cantwell pulled a harness over his shoulders. He touched a switched on the armrest. "All personnel, prepare for crash landing. This is not a drill. Repeat, this is not a drill. Do not attempt to use escape pods. We are going to ride the Lacedaemon down to the planet. Repeat, do not use escape pods. Strap in and ride the ship down." He paused for a moment before saying, "God speed everyone."

One of the navigation officers said, "Reaching degradation orbit with alignment to the Amazon basin in three... two... one... Deceleration burn cut."

"Engines responding nominally," another officer said.

Cantwell nodded.

"Turning for reentry," navigation said. The stars above spun and the broad Earth, sunlight glittering off the Indian Ocean came into view from the left. The rotation stopped with the planet impossibly brilliant before them, the terminator of night cutting the globe in half. The ship lifted its bow slightly.

Marco said to himself, "Keep us belly on folks, nose up." He lifted his chin as if willing the ship to raise its bow to the correct glide path. The growing Earth reminded Stacy she'd been here before. For the second time in her life she would ride a disabled ship out of orbit. She'd been the only survivor the first time.

The Earth swung slightly to the right as if a great pendulum hung from the bow of the ship. As it centered, Marco said, "There you go. Now get that nose up a bit more and let's ride it in." As if Marco's quiet coaching had found an ear, the bow of the ship rose.

"Just a bit more," Marco said, but the ship remained steady.

"I've lost the vertical bow control," a helmsman called out as he looked to his left, "Can you shove the back end down?"

"Adjusting aft pitch," another helmsman said.

In a few moments, the lattice framing between the glass panels began to glow as a faint rumble grew. When the rumbling became a trembling in the deck, a panel of glass near the center of the lattice gave a sharp, crystalline crack. A line ran, spider quick, across its surface.

Another cracked, and another. The lattice frame glowed bright orange now, and the stars began to fade behind a faint violet-blue. As the violet turned to pure blue, and the vibration in the seat became extreme, the first glass panel window shattered inward. The next window let go and the next.

Wind coiled around Stacy, whipping her hair into her eyes and buffeting around her neck. Bits of glass nipped at her face. The air moved so fast past her nose and mouth it sucked the air from her lungs. She had to fight to draw breath. The bridge, bathed in the orange light of the glowing windows, vanished in acrid smoke so thick she couldn't see her knees. The smoke tasted acidic in her throat. She coughed in spasms. The smoke coiled away from her, whatever fire had caused it seeming to have been snuffed out as quickly as it had formed. As the smoke dissipated, she drew another coughing breath. Through the eye-watering wind, she saw a low mountain to their right, draped in trees. Her eyes squinting, she could see Cantwell, the veins in his neck standing out, screaming commands to the helmsmen, who probably were unable to hear him.

Something's very wrong.

They hung from their straps now, as if on a vertical wall of metal, out over the blurring valley floor. The dark-green trees of the rainforest came on fast, blurring. She smacked Marco's knee. He leaned his head close to hers and she screamed at him, "How fast you think we're going?"

He watched the trees rushing by for a moment before leaning back to her. She knew he was yelling at the top of his lungs but could barely made out, "More than mach one."

Then we're going to die.

There was no way a crash landing deceleration from that speed was survivable. That's what had killed the others last time. She had lived only by the fortune of having her seat mounts break, easing her deceleration just enough to live. Now she was strapped to the nose of thousands of tons of metal with only a lattice frame between them and their point of impact.

One of the helmsmen lifted her fist in victory as torrents of brilliant, yellow flame raged out from the sides of the bridge windows, the roar of rockets overrode the rush of the wind. Stacy's shoulder straps hauled on her, and blood pressurized in her skull as her vision tinted red.

The trees below the ship slowed more and more as the retro rockets burned. The ship lurched as a loud crack was followed by green leaves billowing into the bridge, swirling around the men and women at their stations. The green seemed unreal to Stacy. Moments before they had been in orbit and now a leaf, smacked free from a branch, slapped across her face.

She watched the leaf arc and spin down the row of jump seats, past each man and woman. As it touched the back wall, the deck heaved. Stacy's head snapped to the left and her vision tunneled and returned, filled with tracing stars. The ship lurched and shook, and Stacy felt at any moment her seat would rip free. The scent of broken wood and rich soil filled the bridge. With unnatural suddenness, the ship went still, her ears rang in the silence, and sunlight warmed her face.

As the haze of dust and smoke cleared, she found herself hanging from her harness at the top of a two hundred foot vertical, metal wall. The window lattice had been crushed down, now perhaps only ten feet away from her. Halfway down the wall, where the navigation crew, the Nav-Con officer, and Cantwell had sat, tree tops lay against the decking, and the lattice had been smashed flat.

Marco looked a bit punch drunk as he reached for his buckle. Slapping her hand over his, she said, "Watch the drop Fields."

Marco looked down the wall, and said in a dazed tone, "Thanks O.C."

"We need some way to climb or rappel down." Stacy said.

"We have no rapping gear," Jacqueline said, "so climbing's the only way." Locking her boots to the deck, she pulled on them. They released as they were designed to do. "These won't help us here. They'll let go as our weight pulls away from the wall."

Down the rack of jump seats, near the tree tops, some had unlatched and were climbing into the branches, using the seat frames as a ladder. Here the wall of jump seats were inverted, so when Jacqueline unlatched herself her feet swung out.

Stacy grabbed her wrist, but Jacqueline said, "Thanks O.C. I've got this."

Swinging her hips forward, she hooked her feet into the seats further down and, with her back at a forty-five degree angle to the ground, climbed down the seats. Stacy unlatched herself and followed Jacqueline, her arms burning in the short time it took to reach the vertical portion of the wall. Halfway to the tree tops, she heard a scream from above, which dopplered past. Branches cracked. Below her, tree tops tussled back to stillness as a thump rose from the forest floor. Looking up, she found Marco and X still above her.

Putting the falling man out of her mind, she climbed down the rest of the jump seats to the tree tops. Instead of climbing down though, she moved horizontally along the crushed lattice work, through the branches until she reached Cantwell's command seat. She had an unreasonable hope to find it empty, him already safely descended to the forest floor.

Reaching the command seat, she shoved a heavily leafed branch aside, exposing Cantwell hanging from his shoulder straps, head slumped forward, a tree limb speared through his belly. She felt his neck. Still warm but no pulse.

Looking at his gray head, she felt a sudden sadness for the old man. While his passing marked the loss of invaluable experience, it was something more for her. She hadn't known him well, but he'd been a connection to Jeffrey for her. With them both gone—

"That's no good."

She turned to find X, his arms draped over a branch, his feet planted on what had once been the hand rail of the command station.

"No," she said. "We don't have a lot of these guys left. We need to do a better job of protecting them."

196

"I don't know if we have any left at all," X said, but Stacy didn't want to think about Jeffrey being gone. She couldn't believe it had happened so soon in the war. He'd been the survivor of the impossible. If this engagement had taken him so readily, how could they hope to survive?

"Come on O.C., let's get down from here."

As Stacy climbed down the branches, consoles, and lattice work, she felt warm wetness on a seat's headrest. Holding up her hand, she found it slick with blood. Down, ten feet lower, she saw blonde hair. Past the hair, where shoulders should have been, she saw only leaves and smaller branches. Lowering herself around the seat, she found the headless torso of a female navigation officer still strapped in. Looking down the row of seats she saw that all of the helmsmen had paid for their efforts with their lives.

Another scream sounded above her and a body came crashing through the branches to her right. She saw a blur of legs. The sound of cracking branches raced to the forest floor.

She began descending again. When she reached the place where the branches ended and fifty feet of trunk should have remained until the forest floor, she found a tall berm of soil, dug up by the energy of the crash. She dropped onto the berm and climbed down the steep, loose slope until she stood on solid forest floor. The air felt heavy, and sunlight fell in a shattered mosaic across hanging mosses and bladed leaves.

Fighting the desire to crouch down and place her palms on the dirt, she turned to Marco and Jacqueline as X hopped down the berm. X looked up to the trees, pressed up into the lattice of the bridge. Several more had been driven forward, now hanging at steep angles over their heads. He said, "So we stand until the Great Birnam Wood rises against us." He absently kicked a broken tree limb.

"What the hell are you talking about?" Jacqueline asked.

"MacBeth," X said.

"Who's in charge here?" An exhausted but authoritative woman's voice called out.

Stacy turned to find Commander Holloway walking from around the side of the wreck. She had a nasty cut across her temple, which had soaked her shoulder red. A large group of pilots followed her, all covered in dirt, and grease.

Stacy felt a wave of relief at seeing the woman who had been with Jeffrey. "Commander Holloway, I am so glad to see you. Do you have Captain Ho—"

"I'm in charge here Commander."

Captain Donovan gave Stacy a withering look as he approached. He asked Holloway in a hard tone, as if being trapped in the belly of the Lacedaemon had been a shirking of duties. "Where have you been?"

"We were trapped behind a bulkhead. When we..." she fell quiet looking at the ferns and broad leafed plants. Somewhere a frog cricked. "Where the hell are we?"

"The Amazon," Donovan said without emotion.

Holloway looked slightly taken aback as she said, "We were trapped by a crushed bulkhead. When we crashed, the side of the ship ripped open, affording us an escape route."

Donovan nodded as though it was an acceptable excuse. "Your pilots will join the others in cargo. We must get supplies moved out as quickly as possible."

As Stacy scanned the pilot's faces, she asked, "Where's Captain Holt?"

Holloway shrugged her shoulders. "No idea. He was one of the last into the duct work we used to evacuate the flight control center. He and two others didn't come out the other end. We'd hoped they'd found another way out."

"No one's seen him."

"That isn't important right now," Donovan said.

Stacy's eyes snapped to Donovan as her heart thumped at the walls of her chest. Remembering that Cantwell had told her to team with him, she checked herself from speaking her mind. She huffed her breath out her nostrils.

"Get your people to the cargo hold," Donovan told Holloway.

"Yes, Captain Donovan, right away." She turned to her pilots. "All right folks, let's get around the side of the ship and start moving equipment."

Stacy said to her team, "We'll search for survivors."

"Moving supplies is the priority right now," Donovan said.

Stacy glared at Donovan. Drawing a deep breath, she felt the desire to play the card Cantwell had given her, but having to use it so soon did not bode well. "I feel some members of the team should be tasked with locating survivors. My team—"

"I am in command at this point. Commander Zack, unless your opinion is requested, you will do as you are told. Is that clear?"

Stacy squared on Donovan. "Captain, with all due respect, Cantwell instructed us to take joint command, and I—"

"Cantwell gave you command of guerilla warfare tactics, not large troop movements. Were you not listening?"

She said through her teeth, "I was."

"Then there is no need for debate."

Stacy said, "I will take my team and search for survivors."

"Those who cannot clear the wreckage under their own power should be considered a secondary priority to keeping those still able to fight alive commander. Your team will go to the holds with Commander Holloway, or you will be considered in a state of insubordination. Do I make myself clear?"

Glaring at him, Stacy felt anger so great that, for the first time in her career, she considered not only insubordination, but outright attacking a commanding officer. X and Marco took her by the upper arms and walked her away.

CHAPTER 27

Petty Officer Third Class Braden Whitman set his case down beside the towering side of the Lacedaemon. At the base of the sun-heated metal lay a large berm of deep red soil turned up in thick blocks. As he wiped sweat from his forehead with his sleeve, he said, "This sucks Tanner."

"Yeah," Russell Tanner said as he set his case down beside Whitman's. "It's okay though, because it's a wet heat."

With a half-hearted laugh, Whitman looked back to the narrow hole in the hull they'd made with plasma cutters to gain access to the medical supplies. The corridor to the infirmary had been smashed shut. The cases had barely fit through the blade-sharp edges of the hole.

"We need a hand truck or something. They expect us to carry this stuff half a mile out?"

A deep voice, which sounded exhausted, came from inside the dark medical supply area, "If you take branches, you can build a litter, and drag several boxes at a time."

Whitman shaded his eyes but couldn't see past the bright sunlight reflecting off the silvered hull-plates.

A tall, gray-haired man with a short-cropped beard, shifted sideways through the hole.

"That's a good idea," Whitman said absently, trying to figure out where the man, who now stumbled down the large berm of soil, had come from.

The shoulder of the man's shirt had been ripped open, and a flap of skin hung down several inches from a gash on his shoulder.

Below the gash, dried blood blackened the fabric of his shirt and pants down to his calf.

Whitman, still not quite believing his eyes, asked, "Where did you come from?"

As the man walked up to him, Whitman saw the side of his face was smeared with grease mixed with metal shavings. One shoulder-board and his name badge had been ripped away. On the other shoulder lay a captain's four gold bars.

What captain wears a full beard?

"Gentlemen," the man said, "where might I locate command officers?"

"Last I saw," Tanner cut in, "Captain Donovan was in the main hold."

"What about Cantwell?"

"He's dead, sir."

The man dipped his chin in acknowledgement. "Who else is in command?"

"Don't know, sir. Captain Donovan gave us our orders, and we got to work."

The man looked up at the trees, multiple canopies of dark-green, waxy leaves letting only tiny patches of sunlight to the forest floor. "Where are we?"

"The Amazon basin, sir."

The captain pointed to the boxes. "Build a litter. Use the canvas from the medical racks. Work fast." He walked away toward the main hold.

Tanner looked at Whitman as though he'd just been told something he couldn't understand. "That was weird."

Whitman could only nod his agreement.

...

The ground beneath his feet felt as though it was shifting as he walked down the length of the Lacedaemon. His view of the emergency ramps, which had been lowered from the main holds, was blurring. His head ached, and the heat of the sun made him feel nauseated. Men and women moved supplies into the trees. Some pulled carts, some drove small forklifts, and others carried cases.

Just outside the ramp to the main cargo bay, several bodies had been lined up, their faces covered by a long tarp. One wore a non-military white shirt and slacks. The thick, densely-haired arms looked familiar. Crouching, Jeffrey lifted the tarp, exposing Gerard Schodt's face, his glasses missing. His unnaturally widened eyes gave him a shocked look.

"Well Gerard," Jeffrey said, "you might not believe it, but I'd rather you could have lived with your ideals to become an old, irritating man." As he lay the tarp back down, he wondered if the man had any change of heart in his final moments.

"But he didn't."

Jeffrey turned to find Samantha Delaney standing behind him, her face smeared with soot and the leg of her slacks torn open at the knee. Blood stained the fabric below it, and when she limped forward, she winced.

Jeffrey stood and took hold of her arm.

"I'm fine," she said pushing him away. "You look like more of a mess than I do." Her eyes searched his a moment before she said, "I thought you were dead."

He looked back to Schodt's body. "Not yet."

"He's been an advisor since I was governor of Pennsylvania. He was a good man…"

"I'm sorry."

"You'll forgive me if I doubt that." The look she gave him was not as much combative as it was searching, as if she were weighing his reaction to her harshness.

"You might find it difficult to believe," he said, "but I would have preferred it if you and Schodt were right about the Sthenos, that there was a simple misunderstanding that could be resolved by sitting down to tea with them."

"You still maintain that only war can bring a resolution."

At this he did become angry. He held his hand out to the hulk of the Lacedaemon. "Look around you ma'am. We're in a figh—"

"Walk with me Captain Holt." She walked off with a slight limp. "We need to find Captain Donovan and get ourselves moving in the right direction."

"And what direction might that be?" Jeffrey asked as he followed her, but she said nothing.

...

As they made their way up the grip-textured ramp to the hangar, Jeffrey caught several shocked looks from the personnel he passed. Stepping into the shade of the hangar, the only deck which lay horizontally along the Lacedaemon's length to achieve enough length for flight operations, he felt cool air still venting from the Lacedaemon's core. The space smelled of kerosene. Near the center of the hangar, beside the tied down Wraiths, he saw a man directing personnel. While he could not focus on the figure, he knew from his body language it was Donovan. He had his back to them as they approached.

Delaney said, "Captain."

Donovan kept his eyes on his hand-written notes. "What is it vice president?"

"Excuse me?"

"What do you want? I'm very busy."

Delaney put her hands on her hips. "I would appreciate a little less attitude captain."

Donovan looked up from his notes, but his tone remained dismissive. "Of course ma'am." He glanced at Holt and Jeffrey saw shock settle into malice.

If he's angered by my still being alive, he's more dangerous that I thought.

"Captain Donovan, is there an issue you'd care to share with me?"

"No ma'am."

"How many senior staff survived the crash?"

203

"We have three," Donovan said, "Myself, Commander Holloway, and Commander Zack."

Jeffrey felt a rush of relief at hearing Stacy was all right.

Delaney looked to Jeffrey, and said, "Captain Holt as well."

"The president said that he was to be—"

"Two things Donovan," Delaney said with authority. "One— he was to be removed from service *if* he was wrong about the Sthenos. He wasn't. Two—the president is *dead*."

She took a scrap of paper from her pocket. It looked to have been torn from a larger sheet. Her fingers trembled slightly as she opened it and handed it to Donovan.

She said, "Read this to me."

He looked at the scrap and said, "Madam vice president I—"

She yelled at Donovan, "I've had enough of you men treating me as though I'm an irritation to be ignored." Her voice quieted but still held anger as she said, "Now read that to me, or I'll have *you* relieved of duty. Is—that—clear?"

Donovan glared at her. "Yes, ma'am."

Several personnel had stopped and watched them cautiously. She said to them, "You men and women will serve as witnesses."

They looked uncomfortable, as though they'd stepped into a trap.

When Donovan began to read from the scrap of paper, Delaney held up her right hand. "I do solemnly swear I will faithfully execute the Office of President of the United States," he paused giving her time to repeat the words, "and will, to the best of my ability, preserve, protect and defend the Constitution of the United States."

She repeated the second half.

The men and women seemed unsure how they were supposed to respond.

"Get back to work," Donovan said.

"My first act as president," she glanced at Jeffrey, "will be to bestow the rank of Fleet Admiral on Jeffrey Holt."

Donovan's mouth came open as his eyes went wide with shock. "Fleet Admiral? You can't—"

"I can, and I did."

Jeffrey was as shocked as Donovan seemed to be.

"You—" But Donovan's anger appeared to shut his ability to speak down. He looked back to Delaney. "He can't— He's not Navy personnel—" He faltered again, drew a deep breath and continued, fairly spitting out his next words. "You can't seriously be considering handing the command of our last military resources to a junk recycler."

Coming out of his own shock, Jeffrey said, "Captain Donovan, I've had about enough of that shit as I'm going to take."

Donovan stepped up to Holt, stabbed him in the chest with his finger. "You're compromised Holt. You're an old man with post traumatic stress dis—"

Jeffrey snatched Donovan's collar and hauled him close, lifting the smaller man's heels off the ground. "Donovan, to me, you're a kid who's never had to face the real world." He pointed to the hull of the ship. "*This* is the real world, and you have no experience leading in it. I do." He let his voice soften. "This is only the second wave captain. There'll be more." He let go of Donovan's collar, who seemed dazed, not fighting mad anymore. "The only way we can make this the low water mark for us is to work together. I swear on my own life I'll do everything I can to keep us from ending up here again. Now are you with me, or against me?"

"Goddamn you Holt," Donovan said, anger boiling in his tone as he straightened his collar, "of course I'm not against you. Before Cantwell went to Nevada to get you, he told me to follow your lead, no matter what." He turned sideways as if wanting to walk away. "I don't trust you, but *he* told me to follow you to my own grave if need be. I would have followed him there, but you... When I do as you say, know that I'm following Cantwell, *not* you. I'll say this once and let it drop. Every time I tell you *yes sir*, know there's a solid 'fuck you' imbedded in it."

A smile drew across Jeffrey's face. "Then let's keep moving supplies. However, I'll have to redirect a few of your people."

"Yes sir, fleet admiral… *sir*."

Jeffrey stared at him for a moment longer.

"May I be dismissed, *sir*?"

Jeffrey nodded.

He walked away, leaving Jeffrey and Delaney standing alone in the center of the expansive hanger. She watched Jeffrey as though she expected him to yell at her.

"Is there something else ma'am?"

She nodded slowly as if buying time to form her thoughts. While her face was an unreadable mask, tears brimmed and fell from her eyes. Her jaw flexed and she said, "I feel as though I've been a damn fool my entire life."

"No. You wanted something so badly, you let your judgment falter. There isn't a man or woman alive who hasn't made that mistake to some degree."

She pursed her lips before smiling and wiping the tears from her face. "I suppose presidents don't cry."

Jeffrey let out a small laugh. "Neither do fleet admirals I've heard, but I suggest we do this our way, not the way they expect us to." He held out his arm to her and she took it.

As they walked he said, "I need two things."

Her tone became more businesslike. "Those are?"

"One, I need water."

"Okay, I can help with that."

"Two, I need to find Commander Holloway and the pilots. We have to get the drone gear ripped out of the Wraiths and fly them off this ship. We have a war to win and we need hardware to do that."

CHAPTER 28

By the end of the fifth hour a good deal of supplies had been moved to the waypoint a quarter-mile away. While some climbed the racks and lowered supplies on ropes and pulleys, others moved through the ship rappelling down the vertical decks seeking out items such as bedding and waterproof material for shelter.

Captain Donovan had organized two chains of five hundred sailors each, which led away from the cargo holds into the forest. The men and women passed containers and bundles one to the next.

In the hangar Jeffrey, the pilots, and the flight deck personnel had succeeded in pulling the AI gear out of the remaining drone Wraiths and loaded them with as many armaments as would fit under their stubby wings. The VR flight room had been destroyed, but the machine shops had enough remaindered seats, which were modular and bolted directly back in, to return the ships to their original configuration.

With the ships prepped, the pilots gathered under one of the nose cones. A humid breeze carried the scent of rich soil and sap through the yawning side doors, which only two days before had lain open to the vacuum of space.

Jeffrey said, "We have functional Wraiths, but we need true aircraft. Wraiths are only effective in a vacuum. They don't have broad enough control surfaces for atmospheric dog fighting. We need something like Kiowa for air-to-air combat…" He faded off in thought.

"Sir?" Whitetip asked.

"I have an idea, but let me think on it awhile. You," he indicated the flight deck crew who'd helped them remove AI gear, "collect as much maintenance gear as you can carry and get out of here. Pilots, we'll need to fly out the far hangar doors and come around well away from the supply lines."

They nodded. All understood the radiation risks of the nuclear drives.

"All right folks, get to a cockpit."

The pilots saluted and jogged to their ships. Jeffrey went up the ladder behind Whitetip and climbed into the empty space behind her where the navigation officer's seat would have been. He sat on a metal rise at the rear of the cockpit.

"I don't have a seat, so take it easy; I don't want to die before we even begin."

"Thanks for the vote of confidence, sir," she said with an easy laugh.

Jeffrey laughed as well, finding himself sincerely liking the young woman.

The cockpit glass lowered, and she fired the nuclear thrusters, horrendously loud in the atmosphere. The Wraiths ahead lifted off their landing skids, hovered down the flight deck, and moved out into the bright sunlight. When Whitetip's Wraith had a clear path, she lifted it off and hovered forward. Jeffrey hadn't flown in a nuclear drive fighter in a long time. It felt different than a turbine driven aircraft, which moved in smooth, analogue lines. The Wraith felt twitchy, as if it were a half-broken horse, still unsure if it was willing to take a rider. When Whitetip came out into the sunlight she accelerated out over the trees. The power curve felt unlimited, hydroelectric. Jeffrey squinted into the sunlight as she flew a few feet above the forest canopy, turning in a wide arc. The Lacedaemon looked like a great, titanium whale, its back flexed and creased as if swimming.

Reaching the landing zone, she hovered the Wraith between the crowns of two large trees and descended. Leaves shoved against the sides of the ship and branches cracked beneath. The light fell into jade-green dimness. The Wraith tilted slightly sideways as she set down on uneven ground.

The engines shut down, leaving them in deep silence.

Jeffrey said, "Now all we can do is hope these things cool down enough to avoid thermal detection when the Sthenos come through."

A switch clacked and heavy fans came on outside, blowing potentially radioactive materials away.

When the fans shut off, Whitetip said, "The radiation levels outside aren't great but they won't kill us. I wouldn't want to use Wraiths this way every day though."

The cockpit lifted as Whitetip asked, "You really think they'll hit the Lacedaemon?"

"Yes… at least I would."

She pulled a ladder from the side of the ship, and climbed down. Jeffrey followed. As he stepped onto the dark-red soil, he looked up at the rainforest canopy high above. In the distance, the last few Wraiths still searched for gaps large enough to land in, filling the air with a thunderous roar highlighted by popping shrieks.

Jeffrey and Whitetip made their way to the rendezvous point as the distant Wraiths fell silent. Jeffrey enjoyed the sensation of his natural weight on his feet again, but the heat and humidity felt even more oppressive due to the transition from the perfect environment of ship-borne life. The humidity made him feel as though his mouth and nose were packed with damp, oven-hot cotton. While he didn't like Cantwell's choice of landing sites, he understood why he'd chosen it. The rainforest was largely unpopulated and easy to disappear into.

When they arrived at the rendezvous point, he felt a rush of relief when he saw Stacy talking with a sailor standing over a backpack.

"…singularity is a remarkably effective weapon," the sailor said to her. "We found no portal effect as some had suspected. Once the reaction is done, all the matter drawn in is left as a super-dense mass, almost a perfect sphere. Very strange looking."

"Everything?" Stacy asked. Her eyes, with dark circles under them, had lost their usual illumination. As Jeffrey came to stand beside her, she glanced at him. Looked again. Her eyes went wide as she said with disbelief, "You're alive."

"I am."

"You're alive," she shouted with anger. Tears welled in her eyes, but her feet seemed pinned to the ground, as if she didn't know how to deal with her feelings and still be a military commander.

Jeffrey wrapped his arms around her, hugging her tight. Without hesitation, he felt her arms lock around him. One sob escaped her.

After a moment, she said into his chest. "I've already had to live through my father's death. I don't think I could face yours." She leaned away from him, and touched the side of his face. "You've *got* to be more careful."

He nodded as he let her go, and said to the man she'd been talking with, "I apologize for the interruption sailor. Please continue."

"This is Ensign Roth," Stacy said.

"I…" Roth said in an unsure tone, "I was describing their function."

Leif had detailed the function of the singularities to Jeffrey more than a year earlier, but he wasn't supposed to know them. He motioned for the man to continue.

"These singularity warheads are actually small light-speed drives and, as a result, time machines."

Stacy scowled. "You're joking."

"Not at all. A single atom of hydrogen is sent in an electromagnetically shielded loop." He made a small circle with his hands. "The loop's only this big. The hydrogen is accelerated up to the speed of light with electrical impulses."

Stacy's right eye narrowed with disbelief. "Light speed? What the hell powers it?"

"A fist-sized fusion reactor, ma'am."

"And what happens when the hydrogen reaches light speed?" Stacy asked.

"According to Einstein's theory of relativity, as a mass, in this case the hydrogen atom, approaches the speed of light, it should become infinitely heavy."

"Does it?"

"Absolutely," Roth said with a faint smile. "That's what creates the singularity, but not in the way we initially expected. It doesn't gain mass gradually as Einstein theorized. The moment it hits the speed of light, it begins slipping backward in time."

Stacy stared at him, her face slack. "You're messing with me."

"No ma'am, I wouldn't do that. It slips back in time. As it does, a second atom occupies the same space as the first. It does this over and over again, a trillion times in a billionth of a second. That one atom-sized space becomes infinitely dense, creating a singularity with an event horizon half a mile in diameter."

"I see why it did so much damage to the Sthenos destroyer." Stacy crouched down and touched the canvas exterior of the warhead's carrying case. "All in a backpack."

"Exactly, no amount of armor plating or shielding can resist it," Roth said. "If we could get one into a Sthenos destroyer, it would pull the entire thing in on itself."

Jeffrey said, "We have thirty three Wraiths with singularity warheads on them, but I haven't seen this portable type before. Are there more of these?"

"Yes sir, we have thirty of this style."

Jeffrey nodded absently. "Cool."

"Very cool," Stacy said.

"I'll have to talk more with you later Commander Zack," Jeffrey said as he walked away.

Stacy called after him, "Where are you going?"

"I've got a few things I need to look into."

...

Jeffrey had been vague because he didn't want to speak of what was troubling him. It was something that had been floating in the back of his mind since the attack had begun and had worried at his thoughts more and more as the situation had worsened. He'd successfully pushed it from his thoughts, but now, as he walked along the uneven ground beneath the tall trees, which were infused with the sounds of insects and birds, he searched the surrounding faces for the one person he had to find aside from Stacy—Leif.

As he walked among a few service people stacking water and food, he heard footfalls behind him.

"Jeffrey."

He turned to find Delaney walking up to him. "You haven't seen a medic yet. You need to get those wounds treated."

"I will soon."

"*Now.*"

He let out a breath. "I need to find my son first."

At that her determined look softened. "I'll walk with you." As they moved on, she asked, "Did you at least drink water?"

"Yes," he said and couldn't help but smile.

"What?"

"We fairly hated each other only a few days ago, and now you're after me like a mother hen."

"I… didn't exactly *hate* you," she said with a light laugh.

He stopped and faced her. "Samantha, I apologize for how I spoke to you on the bridge and in my quarters. My comments were unnecessarily rude."

"I'm sorry as well… for everything."

In the following silence Jeffrey became transfixed by her eyes, the color of leaves in autumn, glowing with sunlight.

Forcing himself to look off to the forest, he said, "I need to find Leif."

"After we've found him, I want you to see a medic."

He nodded his assent as a female sailor nearby said, "If you're looking for Leif Holt, he's right over there." Jeffrey looked to her. She pointed over his shoulder.

He turned and, searching the faces on the far side of the clearing, saw his son carrying a crate, his shirtfront dark with dried blood. Jeffrey jogged over to him, feeling as though he might lift him off the ground and swing him up onto his shoulder as he had done when he was small. Leif put the crate down with a thump and nodded to his father.

Jeffrey said of the blood on Leif's chest, "Not yours I assume."

Leif shook his head. "No. I'm glad you're alive. I wasn't sure for two days." He said it in a casual tone though, as though he'd always expected to find his father alive.

"It might not always work out that way."

Leif shrugged. "So far so good."

The other personnel had set their cases down and left. The breeze rustled leaves overhead. Jeffrey looked to Samantha, who nodded and walked away.

He asked Leif, "How are you holding up?"

Leif looked out into the forest. Jeffrey could see that he was at the edge of his ability to cope with the strain he'd been under.

"There's no shame in grief son. If we try to hold it in, it only hurts us more. We're safe for the moment, in a place you can let it out a little… if you can."

Leif gripped his hands together.

"Leif I want you to know—"

"We fought."

"What's that?"

Tears welled in Leif's eyes. "The last words we had… were an argument."

When he fell silent, Jeffrey said, "Sit, son."

Leif sat on the container he'd been carrying and Jeffrey pulled another one close and sat facing him. He took hold of Leif's shoulders. A subtle tremor ran through them.

Jeffrey said, "I know it's difficult to see now, but it will get easier."

Leif pushed Jeffrey's hands away. "I don't want it to *get easier*." His voice fell to a near-whisper, "I feel like if it gets easier, I'll forget her. I can't let that happen."

Jeffrey took hold of Leif's hands with a firm grip. "Leif, she knew you loved her in the end. You set the stars by her."

Jeffrey felt Leif's arms relax somewhat. With his head down, he looked exposed, his spirit broken. Drawing slow breaths that tremored in his chest, he shook his head slowly.

"She knew you loved her. You have to accept that."

"It's not that," Leif said quietly.

"What is it then?"

Leif said nothing, and in that silence Jeffrey took his chance. "She was pregnant."

Leif nodded, and his eyes rose to meet Jeffrey's, a helplessness in them, as if he had no idea what to do with the pain he felt. "How did you know?"

Jeffrey shrugged. "I put it together."

Leif's voice lowered, "How?"

"I know my son. I know when he's hurting and how badly." At this tears welled in Jeffrey's eyes. He tapped the center of his chest. "I've felt every bruised knee and broken heart you've ever had, felt it like it was my own." He shook his head. "You can't hold up the world Leif. You have to let those around you help."

"You'll help me kill them?"

"Yes."

Leif nodded. "Good." His emotions appeared to cement back over. "Then we have work to do." He stood and opened the container. Inside, set in black foam, lay a blank onyx disk about a the size of a man's chest. Kicking the case closed, he set the object on it.

Jeffrey asked, "Is that what I think it is?"

"Yes. A remote Nav-Con and communications console."

...

As the sixth hour from crash landing passed, Captain Donovan approached Jeffrey in a clearing. "I have the last of the troops moving to our location now."

"Good. Have you got those folks working on shelter?"

Donovan said, "I was tasked with getting supplies off the ship. I've done that. Maybe instead of glad-handing your pets you should have had some setting up shelter."

In that moment Jeffrey imagined hitting Donovan in the jaw hard enough to lift him off his feet. Instead, he drew a breath and said, "Captain Donovan, please task your men and women with setting up shelter. When you've done that, come back and talk with me."

Donovan stared just long enough to show resistance, but not long enough to be insubordinate, and walked away without acknowledging the order.

While he understood Donovan represented a danger to his command, he knew that forcing him to comply wasn't enough. He needed Donovan to believe in him and follow him.

Thirty minutes later Donovan returned, his expression closed off. As he came to stand in front of Jeffrey, he crossed his arms. "The shelters are being prepared."

Beyond Donovan, through the trees, Jeffrey could see the back of the Lacedaemon broken in three buckled creases. Sunlight caught the metal along it's welded seams in glittering lines.

"Donovan," Jeffrey asked in a matter of fact tone, "exactly what is your problem with me?" He felt the air supercharge between them.

"You want to know what my problem is?"

"Yes."

"Off the record."

"Sure."

"I've said it before. You're nothing but a pilot. Cantwell was a full blown military commander with experience leading a destroyer and a fleet. He had experience leading battle groups. You were in the military what… six years? That man served for fifty."

"So you respect experience."

"Yes."

"And you respect ability."

"Yes."

"Good. So here's how we're going to work this. We're going to need a lot of different experience and ability to survive, and I do sincerely believe the survival of the human race is on the line here. I'm operating on the assumption that the Sthenos have no desire to rule us."

At that, Donovan's expression softened. "We'd be better off if that was their goal."

"Exactly. We'd have more time. At least in that, we have a point of agreement."

Donovan's expression remained unreadable.

"Individually," Jeffrey continued unfazed, "we're each limited. To succeed, we're going to need Commander Zack's guerilla expertise, my flight group and dog fighting expertise, and your large-scale operations expertise. I agree when you tell me that we need applied experience, but tell me honestly, what is your area of proficiency?"

Looking out on the hulk of the Lacedaemon, Donovan said, "Destroyer and fleet operations."

"Captain, you've forgotten more than I'll ever know on fleet battle tactics, but," Jeffrey held his hand out to the Lacedaemon where a flight of white birds now crossed over the broken spars of the bridge, "what use is it to us now?"

CHAPTER 29

     Sofía Fields sat on the couch in her small apartment running her fingertips across its cross-hatched fabric. The sun glittered off the stainless steel patio railings. Beyond, the skyline of downtown Los Angeles stood against a broad, blue sky. Cool summer air blew through the open patio door carrying the scent of the pine trees from the hills. Her children, Emilia and Luciano lay on their bellies on the white carpeting playing with a fractal hologram.

     While such a beautiful day should bring contentment, she felt troubled. She hadn't received a message from Marco in two weeks. While long separations without explanation were part of the life of a Special Warfare spouse, he'd always been able to warn her when he'd be out of touch. In his last video message, all had seemed well. He'd said he was off the shoulder of Saturn on the Rhadamanthus, that he was bored, and he loved her. She recorded a return message, having both Luciano and Emilia show him pictures they'd drawn of him wearing his flight suits.

     At three years old, Luciano held no greater hero in his heart than his father, and to Emilia at four, there was no greater prince. While she felt equally proud of her husband, she had difficulty sleeping in a lonely bed. During the months-long deployments, dark circles would form under her eyes. When he returned, she would hold his shoulder in the quiet darkness of their bedroom and sleep so deeply her body ached when she awoke.

     Luciano looked from the toy to the patio as a faint rumbling formed at the edge of Sofía's awareness. The little boy went out onto the patio followed by his sister. Emilia pointed upward and said, "Mama, la astronave de padre."

"What are you talking about Emilia?" Sofía said as she rose and walked across the living room.

With high-pitched excitement, the little girl said, "He's come home! With his whole ship!"

As she jumped up and down, Luciano caught up in her excitement, punched her. She slapped him across the face, which made him scream in anger.

Sofía ran onto the patio, saying, "Stop it the both of—"

She fell silent, staring at the glittering black spike dropping out of the sky on a tail of blue flame. What looked like black smoke poured from its upper reaches, but as the smoke dispersed it was granular, individual small things, which began spreading out.

The rumbling grew as the ship descended. Struts extended from its sides as it set down among the dwarfed skyscrapers. The small, dark particles began flying over the city. Green bolts of power lashed out at buildings. One of the sky scrapers, perhaps shoved aside by the base of the ship, tipped sideways, dust trailing off its edges as it collapsed in a billowing cloud, glittering with shattered glass.

Despite having no idea what she was seeing, as she watched the building fall, two instinctual thoughts came to Sofía's mind. *Hide or run.* Her gut told her to run. She looked to the cabinet by the entryway where Marco, the consummate soldier, kept his bug out bag. She'd given him a hard time about it countless times, had called him paranoid. Now all she could think was how grateful she was for him.

Going to the cabinet, she pulled out the big pack and threw it on her back.

"Put your shoes on," she said to Luciano and Emilia.

"Where are we going?" Emilia asked.

"But," Luciano said pointing to the ship.

"There's no time to explain, mijo."

As if sensing her mother's fear, Emilia's eyes widened and reddened.

"All is well Emilia," she said with a warm smile, "but we must go *now*."

The children did as they were told, and they left the apartment thirty seconds later. With both children stacked in her son's stroller, she ran up the street, past the balconies of the wealthier homes with people pointing out into the valley. It took her twenty minutes to reach the last street.

"We have to play a game with your father."

"Hide and seek?"

"Yes, but we must be very serious. He will be proud of you if he cannot find you."

Luciano nodded with a definitive downward bend to his mouth, and they left the stroller at the curb, climbing the steep slope between two houses to enter the tinder, dry pine trees of Mt. Lee. When they were halfway up the hill, a ship unlike any she'd seen came racing by the edge of the street, spraying down a glittering liquid, which solidified as a cross-hatched barrier. If she'd hesitated a moment longer, they'd have been trapped inside it.

CHAPTER 30

Jeffrey set up a shelter in a hollow of trees with a partial view of the Lacedaemon. That night sparks of fire lanced across the star-deep sky trailing moonlit smoke—debris from the fleet and razed satellites.

The next morning, Jeffrey stood outside his shelter looking through the trees. The Lacedaemon's back glowed copper in the early light.

He'd set his shelter down a small trail to be off by himself. Footfalls came down that trail now. In a few moments Samantha emerged through the broad leafed plants.

"They never came," she said. "What does that mean?"

"It means they don't care. They know they've won. It tells me they're used to easy victories. It also means they've spent the last 12 hours focusing on other targets."

"What do you suppose they've done?"

Before he could answer, Jeffrey heard the thudding of boots and the rush of leaves as someone ran toward them. A moment later, Stacy leapt over the nearby teak roots. "Come quick, we're communicating with a space station."

...

In the command area they found an operations specialist sitting on a crate, leaning over a portable communications unit. He had headphones on with one ear uncovered. The command staff stood around him.

The young man looked at Jeffrey with exhausted eyes and said, "I've got a low frequency connection with the space station. I haven't attempted to communicate yet. My guess is that the moment they fire up their power, they'll be destroyed."

"That's a good bet based on what we know of Sthenos tactics." Donovan said. "Any idea how they've survived?"

"It looks like they're running on extremely low power. No lights, minimal life support." He looked to Jeffrey, "Admiral, may I send the message?"

Jeffrey waited for *the admiral* to respond. He felt Donovan, Holloway, and the other ranking officers' eyes all on him. Samantha nudged Jeffrey with her elbow.

"I assume," Jeffrey said with a start, only then realizing he was the *admiral* to whom the young man was speaking, "you aren't going to expose our position?"

"No sir." The officer pointed to a black antenna cone strapped high in the trees. "I'm using an x-ray laser transmitter aimed directly at the station, not broadcasting it. They however—if I understand their communications equipment well enough—cannot direct their signal back at us in a similar fashion. They'll have to expose themselves if they want to respond."

"Okay," Jeffrey said, "What's the planned message content?"

The officer read from his screen, "We are a military force in need of logistical information on invading forces. If you have anything of value, please send. If not, remain dark."

Donovan nodded his approval to Jeffrey. "I'm good with that."

"So am I," Stacy said.

"As am I," Holloway said.

Samantha also nodded.

Jeffrey looked up beyond the antenna. Clouds had risen in the morning's heat, stark white against the blue sky. "Okay, send it off."

The officer tapped his keyboard. "It's away, sir."

They waited.

A breeze, heavy with the scent of rubber trees and rain, rustled through the leaves above as branches all around them swayed. Jeffrey worried the antenna might be thrown off target by the movement.

The officer kept his eyes on his display.

"Anything?" Donovan asked.

"Nothing yet."

They waited for almost thirty minutes. Jeffrey was about to direct the O.S. to inform him of any changes when the console squawked, and the screen scrolled with black bars. The scrolling slowed, stopped, and the center bar expanded to reveal a woman's face lit by a dim lamp. She had short, gray hair, which floated slightly. The zero-G effect on her face, gave her a slightly humored look. Crow's feet framed her brown eyes.

"Do we have you?" She asked.

"Yes," the O.S. said.

She smiled sincerely, "A handsome man to talk with, I'm so pleased. It's funny when you know you're going to die what matters."

"You aren't dead yet."

"Son, you aren't seeing what we're seeing."

"And what's that?"

She looked to her side, saying, "I'm going to send you some details—images, maps... documented locations of attacking ships."

"So the ships have touched down?" Jeffrey asked.

The woman had kept talking, not having heard Jeffrey, "...had several updates from broadcast military recon satellites before they were destroyed. A ship simply entered the low earth belt and flew through them all. There's a band of garbage that's going to be raining down on you folks for many years. They came up here to geosynch orbit as well. We completely shut down as they passed through the Clarke belt. They had several fighters attacking targets. Apparently we shut down in time. If this station hadn't been placed in such a unique orbit, we wouldn't be talking now."

Jeffrey crouched down beside the communications officer and asked into the screen. "Have the Sthenos ships touched down?"

"Sthenos?" The woman gave a humorless laugh, "I suppose that's as good a name as any. Yes, all but one has touched down. They land, stern down and appear to root themselves to the ground. They've landed in the largest population centers." She looked for a moment as though she might cry but pursed her lips, smiled, and said, "You men and women down there need to be careful. Stay sharp and stay safe."

Jeffrey said, "We'll do what we can, ma'am." He felt obligated to say something more. "We might be able to get a transport up to you."

"Don't you dare waste military hardware on us," she said. "We knew responding would mark us. We delayed to come to a unanimous decision. We hope you'll understand."

"Of course," Jeffrey said.

She looked to her right. "We've had alien fighters enroute since the beginning of this communication. They're only a few moments away now." She looked back to the O.S. with a resignedly peaceful expression. "Young man, there's nothing left to say, and I have a death sentence on my head. Give me some hope. Tell me, do you have a girlfriend?"

"A wife. We've been married six months now."

That brought a sincere smile to her face. "Beautiful?"

The communications officer smiled. "Yes. Really pretty…" his voice faltered, "…dark hair… wonderful smile. She has a great sense of humor."

The woman pursed her lips before saying, "Tell her you love her. We have no idea how much time we have left. Ironically we never did, but our fate is clearly more immediate now."

The O.S. said in a quiet tone, "Yes, ma'am."

When the screen flashed to static, he clicked the keyboard, killing the feed. He remained with his head down too long.

Jeffrey put his hand on the young man's back. "Youre wife?"

"Was on the Oestres, sir."

"I'm sorry," was all Jeffrey could say.

"I'm fine," the young man said with a dishonest smile. He typed for a moment on his keyboard before handing Jeffrey a pocket sized tablet. "That has the files she sent over."

Jeffrey tapped a document icon, skimmed it, and said, "The remaining Sthenos destroyers returned to Earth twelve hours after destroying the fleet… just as we predicted. Twenty-two have touched down in major cities. Only one remains in a ten-hour transit Earth orbit."

"Why are they orbiting that high?" Commander Holloway asked.

"Probably," Donovan said, "so they can respond quickly to threats high and low as they just did with the space station."

"That's true, and it gives us an advantage," Jeffrey said, "a longer window without observation."

"Observation?" Donovan asked. "What are you planning?"

"We need different aircraft… namely not spacecraft. The Wraiths won't serve us well in atmosphere. We need to get our hands on different hardware to give ourselves a fighting chance."

"You're hoping," Commander Holloway said, her voice showing some of the mettle she had before the first battle, "the Sthenos fighters have similar limitations in atmosphere."

"Yes, absolutely. Look at their design." He tapped on the tablet and brought up a schematic on the Sthenos fighters and held it out. "They have massive directional thrusters for zero G, vacuum based dog fighting, but there are only cursory control surfaces. Directional thrusters can only help a ship so much at speed in atmosphere. Nothing takes the place of excellent, old-fashioned control surfaces—big wings and tail fins."

He tapped the stumpy shape of the Sthenos fighter. "I'm hoping these things will be as big a pig in atmo as our Wraiths are. If they are, and we can get our hands on good, dedicated aircraft, our pilots will eat them alive."

Captain Donovan shook his head. "What about the destroyers? We can't stand for long against those. The moment we begin attacks, they'll come right here, wipe us out."

"That's why we have to lay low and do it all at once."

Samantha asked, "Do what all at once?"

He turned to Stacy. "Commander Zack has that all worked out."

CHAPTER 31

Stepping forward, Stacy said, "I've been considering a grounded Sthenos scenario for some time. Now we have confirmation of Sthenos destroyers planted at the center of twenty-two major cities. The good news is, we've been able to recover the special warfare equipment, including active-camo suits."

Jeffrey asked, "You found enough suits?"

"Yes. The suits are such an important tactical weapon we generally carry a backup for each team member. I had fourteen, and found another ten on the Lacedaemon, which were slated for Saturn Base. If, and this is a big if, those suits are as good at avoiding Sthenos sensors as they are ours, then we should be able to move right up to those ships."

"That's a significant *if*," Captain Donovan said. "The Sthenos have already proven to have different sensory capabilities. They, for one, do not appear to have heart rhythm sensors." Something appeared to have caught his mind. He scowled. "Are you telling me your team was bringing armaments out? You'd been ordered to bring out food stores."

Stacy's eyes darkened. "Captain, if you want my respect you're going to have to stop saying stupid things right out in the open, okay?"

Donovan's face flushed red and his mouth opened, but Stacy beat him to the punch, saying, "We're not bakers, *sir*. We're special warfare, and we have, are, and will be at all times focused on that job. You should expect no less."

Donovan's eyes narrowed with anger as he said, "You little b—"

"All right you two," Jeffrey said, his booming voice overriding all other words. Quieter, he said, "Please relax... Commander Zack is correct to stay focused on tasks related to special warfare. She should also be reminded that insubordination will not be tolerated from a Navy officer."

Donovan crossed his arms, and Stacy's jaw muscles tightened.

"And you Captain," Holt said, pointing at Donovan, "Should remember that leaders lead because people follow, not because they have more stripes. Understood?"

Donovan's expression sealed off behind a cold stare as he turned to Stacy, showing that he was ready for her to continue.

Stacy said, "To address your first statement, yes it's a big *if,* but I think we have some good hardware here." She looked to Jeffrey and a slight smile drew over her face. "They've even solved the CO2 fault."

Jeffrey laughed as he said, "Glad they waited until now to do that."

"I don't think they even realized it was a fault until you exposed it. At any rate, we have thirty singularity warheads able to be carried. I suggest we send a single operative into each location—"

"A single operative?" Donovan asked as though he considered the suggestion ridiculous. "Why only one? A pair would have better odds."

"Agreed." Her tone now came slow and steady, and Jeffrey knew she was doing her best to respect his wishes. "However, we have only twenty-five active-camo suits. This destroyer was not equipped for guerilla warfare, so we have only the stealth gear my team brings with them."

Donovan stared at her, as if waiting for his next opportunity to object. Jeffrey saw Stacy's ire rising again.

"As I was saying." She stared at Donovan, who motioned with his hand dismissively for her to continue speaking. Drawing a slow breath, she said, "We should send one operative in with a singularity warhead in a back pack. We should position and detonate them at one time." She looked directly at Donovan, as if already taking down another complaint, "We could do half the job with two person teams, but if one warhead is discovered, the rest might be discovered. We would then lose our advantage of surprise."

At this Donovan pursed his lips and nodded as if her point was obvious.

Stacy continued, "We plant a singularity warhead near the base of the destroyers. The weapon's half-mile radius should destroy a significant percentage. The Sthenos ships are what…" she looked to Jeffrey.

He shrugged.

Donovan said, "They are 6,543 feet in length. That means a singularity warhead at its aft will destroy over a third of the ship. More importantly, their entire drive section and landing base will be gone. One would hope the rest of the ship would be useless at that point."

"Madam President," Jeffrey said, "I want one agreement from you right now."

Samantha shrugged, "I'm not in the position to offer much."

"If we succeed, I don't want any of these men and women," he pointed to those standing around him, "to have to live through the fifty years of political bullshit I did."

She flushed.

"If we succeed I want those destroyers left where they crash. I want a monument in each of those population centers, not a memorial, but a gutted out alien destroyer to remind us all they were and continue to be real."

"Okay," Samantha said. Her tone suggested she considered him a bit off for wanting such a thing.

"The first step is to get aircraft with better atmospheric qualities." He looked to Stacy. "Please prepare your team."

Stacy saluted and walked away.

"Stacy," Jeffrey called after her, "send Marco Fields to me. I need him and your Warthog to move pilots."

"Yes, sir."

Jeffrey said to Holloway, "Inform your pilots to assemble tomorrow at 1600 hours for a briefing."

"Yes, sir."

Jeffrey looked back to the others. "The pilots who go on the run for aircraft will need to be modified. We'll try to avoid engagement with Sthenos fighters but can't guarantee it."

Samantha said, "You mentioned the procedure is hazardous. Do we still need to take that risk?"

"Without question. We need Hammerheads to effectively face the Sthenos. They have one destroyer left in orbit, and thousands of fighters. At some point we'll have to dance with them in zero G. We can't do that effectively without modified pilots. The pilots who fly in atmosphere will be that much more deadly as well. We need every advantage we can get."

CHAPTER 32

As evening came on, heavy clouds rose in the west and covered over the sky, bringing early darkness. Under his tarp, which formed a comfortable space for a mattress propped up on containers and an area to sit where he'd laid out a section of fabric-like sheeting to keep the dirt down, Jeffrey sat on his mattress with his elbows on his knees, deep in thought. Rain began to fall in heavy drops on the tarp. A few moments later, it increased to a torrent. Someone ran up to his makeshift tent. The boots were smaller, a woman's.

Samantha called from outside, "Jeffrey, can I come in? I'm getting soaked."

"Yes, please," Jeffrey said as he stood and lifted the tarp and makeshift mosquito netting.

"Thank goodness," she said, ducking under the flap. Her hair and shoulders were wet, but the rain had yet to fully soak her. "I'm so glad I was near your tent."

Jeffrey motioned for her to sit on his mattress. He sat on a container.

"I wouldn't want to—"

"Please," Jeffrey said, "The rain might not last long, but you might as well be comfortable while you wait."

Smiling, she sat. Neither seemed to know what to say as the remaining light faded.

"Are you thinking about what I'm thinking about?" She asked finally.

"If you mean obsessing over what has to happen over the next few days, then yes."

"Exactly."

"Any good thoughts?"

"No," she said, pushing her hair from her eyes. "To be honest, I don't really want to think about it anymore tonight. I'm tired of it."

"Okay." Again, Jeffrey found himself with nothing to say.

"Tell me something."

"Something?"

"Anything… something about you, your past."

"I don't tend to spend too much time talking or even thinking about my past."

"Something about Leif then," she said. "Something about his childhood… a good memory."

Jeffrey let out his breath. That was something he was willing to think about. His life had been a series of tragedies, save his son.

He said, "Leif was an interesting kid. He was an only child, and we had a different relationship with him. We were parents surely, but we tried to be open and honest. Even in grade school, he'd call us *guys* as if we were roomates." Jeffrey laughed. "*Hey guys, come here and look at this*, he'd say." Jeffrey fell silent for a moment. "He had a really sensitive soul." Jeffrey laughed aloud. "Any… I mean any heartfelt moment in a movie would make him cry. I'd know it was happening because he'd snuggle up next to me in the theater."

"That's very cute."

"Once, in a restaurant, he started sobbing. I think he was about five. We asked him what was—" Jeffrey had to stop as the memory choked his words.

"I'm sorry Jeffrey, we don't have to talk about it."

"No, no, I'm sorry. It's not a bad memory. Just one that fills my heart up a bit too much. We asked him what was wrong, and he said *the music's just so sad*. Only then did I hear the piano music playing in the background. It was Beethoven's Sonata Pathétique, and it had brought him to tears. He was only five."

"That's beautiful."

Jeffrey wiped his eyes. "He's always had this monstrously big heart, since the day he was born. God, I struggled so much in being a good father to him. It was so easy to yell, so easy to lose my temper, and with a boy like Leif it felt like a sin every time I did. Kids can be so *frustrating* though. Every other day I felt like a failure, but he made it through, turned out okay. Not screwing him up has been the greatest triumph of my life, but he gets the lion's share of the credit in my opinion."

Silence fell between them. Darkness had come on so fully that Samantha was nothing more than an outline against the less-dark tarp hanging behind her. The rain's heavy spatter continued to muffle all other sounds. Water rushed down the sides of the tarp, pouring into the trench Jeffrey had dug around its perimeter.

He asked, "What about you?"

She laughed in an uncomfortable tone. "I never had kids."

"There must surely have been someone in your life."

"Yes… there was…" Her words faded off, and in that silence Jeffrey sensed something she didn't care to speak about. He had so many scars he didn't want touched, he fully respected those of others.

"Tell me something happy then," Jeffrey said. "What was your best memory as a child?"

"What? A child?" She laughed as though embarrassed. "That's asking me to go a long way back."

"Not nearly as long as I'd have to go."

He could just make out a smile crossing her face in the darkness.

"Childhood…" she said before falling quiet. "You know the memories that are strongest for me are of the Northern California coast. I grew up in a small town, well… spent a few years there. We moved a lot when I was young. When we lived on the ocean, we'd go down to the beach every chance we could. We didn't have a lot of money, and it was free. My favorite times came with the fog. A lighthouse near the bay had the most beautiful fog horn. It was an easy sound, as if it came from a huge conch shell. Those were peaceful times."

"It sounds wonderful. I have some very good memories of the ocean as well." He told her of his crash landing in the Tongan islands, being a cast away for a few weeks during the war.

When he finished, she said, "I thought the war didn't come near Earth."

"One engagement occurred right up on us, but didn't make it through. The powers that be didn't want people to panic, so they covered it up."

She said, as though to herself, "A bit of a mistake considering what's transpired over the last fifty years. People might have made better choices if they'd known how close they'd come last time."

"I agreed with them then because I didn't expect a movement would claim the war had been faked. I never could have seen that coming."

As they talked, the rain let up somewhat, but remained steady. Samantha yawned deeply.

"Come on then," Jeffrey said, "lay back."

"What?"

"It's late. You can't make it back to your tent without getting soaked."

"I'm not going to take your bed. Where will you sleep?"

"I can sleep on the ground."

"I can't—"

"You can and you will. I can sleep *anywhere*. We all need you well rested tomorrow." He motioned for her to stand. When she did he pulled open the blanket. "Now get comfortable."

With an acquiescent sigh, she lay back on the bed. He flourished the blanket in the air, draping it over her. As he straightened the blanket over her legs he said, "I never in my life thought I'd be tucking the president of the United States into bed."

"You're not."

"What do you mean by that?"

"I'm tired right now Jeffrey... really tired. Tonight I'm just Samantha, okay?"

Only then did he understand how much she'd taken. People in power are so readily seen as super human, but if they're good leaders, they're just people like everyone else, with hopes and fears and limitations. Bending over, he gently kissed her forehead. "Goodnight Samantha."

Her fingertips brushed his face. "Good night Jeffrey."

He lay on the ground, and the patter of the rain quickly lulled him to sleep.

CHAPTER 33

Early the next morning a millipede tickling across his wrist woke him. Sitting up, he looked to Samantha, who lay on his mattress with his blanket pulled up over her shoulder, her face peaceful. Jeffrey found her presence calming and felt grateful for her visit. Even on the dirt, and despite the rain or perhaps thanks to it, he'd slept quite well.

Moving quietly, he emerged from under the makeshift tarp. To the west, heavy clouds hung along the horizon promising more rain. From the east, sunlight angled in through the heavy canopy of leaves, causing them to glow in many shades of green.

Realizing he could smell himself, he resolved he'd find a body of water to wash in. He felt sure, considering the location, that a good water source might not be too far away. They'd need it for drinking soon enough anyway, having a limited supply of stored water but unlimited fusion power generators and UV purification systems. He picked up a makeshift machete, a section of ship paneling ground sharp with a handle of wrapped duct tape. Heading down a freshly cut trail, he absently hacked at branches here and there. Soon he came to the main area, supplies tucked into the coves formed by broad leafed plants and among tall tree roots. Donovan stood in the middle of the clearing watching sailors move supplies.

"He's not a bad guy when he has something to focus on," a voice said behind him.

He turned to find Leif looking well-rested.

"You slept all right?"

"Yeah," Leif said. "The first night in a long time."

Jeffrey felt glad to see the healing process beginning. Leif had grown into a much stronger man than Jeffrey had hoped. When he looked at Leif, he didn't see a shorter, skinnier version of himself, he saw a better version—not all fight. Leif had a poetry to his manner as if connected to something deeper. Jeffrey not only envied that, but hoped it would bring his son peace more readily than he'd found it.

"You think he's going to cause trouble?" Leif asked.

Jeffrey shook his head. "I'm not sure. He was dedicated to Sam Cantwell and Cantwell told him to follow me. I'm hoping all we're seeing is exactly what I need—someone willing to play the devil's advocate. Every good command needs one. He'll keep me on my toes."

Donovan yelled at a sailor carrying a heavy crate, "What the hell are you doing? Canteen supplies go to the *north*!" The sailor walked off with the crate, the back of his neck flushed red.

Jeffrey sighed. "Our greatest asset is often presented as an obstacle."

Leif pointed through the trees to the glinting spine of the Lacedaemon. "They really don't care about us do they?"

"It would appear not."

His eyes still on the monolith of the ship, Leif asked, "What do you suppose they're doing?"

"I have no idea." He put his hand on Leif's shoulder. "But I'm guessing they didn't finish the job on the Lacedaemon because they've settled into victory."

"That's good for us."

"Maybe. An opponent so accustomed to winning is one to be wary of. I can only wonder what tactics they have waiting for us."

"What if we've already seen their best?"

Jeffrey gave a resigned laugh. "That's already pretty damn good."

"But what if that's all they can do? Macro-warfare? The Hammerheads took them out fifty years ago because they couldn't stand one-on-one against the pilots. What if they have no skill in guerilla warfare either?"

"If they're colonists, I can't believe they haven't had to deal with insurrectionists before."

"If they aren't colonists?" Leif asked. "What if they're here to simply take, like the ice? A quick grab and go?"

Jeffrey put his hands in his pockets, his eyes travelling down the broken back of the Lacedaemon. "If that's true, they'd land where their target material was richest."

"They've landed in the main population centers."

"That would suggest they came here for us." After a moment's pause, he said, "I feel as though we're standing on Africa's west coast five hundred years ago."

"Slavers?"

"That's as good a guess as any."

CHAPTER 34

After a few morning showers, the afternoon came on hot and humid. Big bugs buzzed through the stippled shade under the trees. Jeffrey walked into the makeshift ready room—a cove of trees out away from the rest of the encampment. The pilots, just over eighty in total, sat on crates. He'd called together those Cantwell had gathered for the Hammerheads, minus a few who had died in the crash, and several of the top drone pilots. Seeing some of them again, and some for the first time, Jeffrey felt a welling of hope and regret.

Whitetip, perched on a tall crate to the right, winked at Jeffrey as though she understood and was telling him it would be all right. But he knew too well it wouldn't be.

In a loud voice, he said, "Ladies and Gentlemen." Conversations faded as all eyes turned to him. "Many of you may not survive the next few months." He scanned their reactions stopping on Lila. Her rich, pure-dark skin set off brilliant eyes, which held his in a casually predatorial way. "But your efforts could result in the salvation of the human race."

He walked forward, in among them. "We and a small unit of Navy Special Warfare are all that is left of Earth's defenses. However, you are the *best* pilots in the world, gleaned from *all* nations. We're going to take you further by shining your nerves, increasing the quality of myelin in your brains, and lining your major arteries with reactive tissues."

He had enough pilots to run the ground mission and the attack on the lone orbital destroyer, if he could call thirty Wraiths against thousands of fighters enough, but only one Wraith carrying a singularity had to make it through. Still, this time there would not be

238

expendable AI or servos at the controls. Now, when a ship was destroyed, it would take one of these men and women with it.

"Before I begin, I'll designate call signs." Going over his list, he gave Lila, Springbok, to which she smiled broadly. He gave Brooks, Soy Bean. He didn't seem to like that much, but he didn't seem to like anything. He gave Grimstad, Kodiak, which he responded to by slapping the pilot beside him on the back.

"You watch out for me," the Norwegian said, "I'll steal your picnic."

"Should have called him Yogi," Jeffrey muttered to himself.

When he'd read off the rest, he said, "Our assault will be a two-stage process. For stage one, we'll need Lakota."

Smiles formed among the group.

"I see some of you've heard of them. If you haven't, they're the newest and best of the VTOL fighters in the U.S. arsenal. Apparently, they make Kiowas look like farm trucks. Our intel shows several possible locations for these aircraft, which we're studying to determine state and feasibility. Most are no longer intact."

"Pilots assigned to the Lakota run must be modified should we encounter Sthenos."

Soy Bean asked, in a tone that suggested he wasn't quite willing to submit to the procedures, "How are we to be modified?"

"First, we coat your nerves with graphene, increasing their conductivity from a few hundred meters a second to nearly three hundred thousand. This will make the world seem more intense; you'll feel and sense more. Your reaction times will appear almost predictive. The next step is to extract myelin from your brain, genetically alter it to be more aggressive, and reintroduce it. Within 24 hours you'll experience a dramatic increase in your ability to retain information and perceive fast-paced situations. I'll warn you, however, the nerve coating nanites induce severe pain, and in a few documented cases, cardiac arrest or extreme vasovagal reactions resulting in death. The modified myelin is usually well received, but in one case it induced a sensory overload state similar to autism."

He watched them for a moment before saying, "I need you folks to understand, once you've been modified, there's no going back. If something goes wrong, it's done. If you survive the modifications, we'll strap your ass in a Lakota or a Wraith and send you off with terrible survival odds. I want each and every one of you to commit to that hard truth right now. If you can't, I'll wash you out. I can bring other pilots up. I'll judge no one who stands down. I understand better than anyone the extreme nature of what we want from you."

Whitetip asked, "If we agree to this, how many will you let us kill?"

In a matter of fact tone, Jeffrey said, "As many as you can."

"I'm in then." Her smile broke broad and beautiful across her face.

Others nodded their agreement.

Jeffrey did his best to keep the welling of emotion out of his expression. For decades he'd believed no one would fill the void men and women like Mako had left in his heart. Yet here they were.

"When we return with the Lakota, I'll test each of you. The testing will be fast, we have a war to fight. You'll each dogfight me. I'll determine if you've passed or failed. There'll be only one shot at the test. We have no time for retakes. I have little room for failure among these small numbers, but I will fail you if I have to. A weak pilot will kill other pilots. I won't allow that."

"When we're ready for our assault, forty-four paired Lakota will be sent to the twenty-two land bound Sthenos destroyers. One special warfare operator will travel with each pair. The operator will be dropped as close as we dare come to the destroyers. We cannot compromise secrecy in this situation. We think a distance of ten miles is theoretically safe. The specialist will go on foot from that point wearing an active-camo suit with a singularity warhead on his or her back. From disembarkation, the special warfare operators will have eight hours to place the singularity and attain a safe distance. There will be no means to disable the warheads. They'll trigger without fail whether in place or still on the operator's back. When the warheads activate, the Lakota pilots will go airborne. Their mission is first to focus attacks on any destroyers which were not successfully taken down. Only one of the pair of aircraft tasked to each destroyer will have a singularity warhead. If you have the warhead, your job is to get it on target and set it off. In that contingency, you'll be making a suicide run. The stronger lead of the two pilots will be given the warhead. The other pilot will wingman."

"Our secondary phase will be a group of pilots in Wraiths. A few moments before the singularities are activated the Wraiths will launch from here to intercept the Sthenos destroyer in orbit." Jeffrey pointed at the blue sky. "We'll time the singularity warheads set near the land based destroyers to activate when the orbiting Sthenos destroyer is overhead." As he neared the back of the group, the pilots in front turned to track him. "In that moment, there will be thirty Hammerheads against hundreds if not thousands of Sthenos fighters. The method will be to get one of our Wraiths, *all* of which will have singularity warheads, near enough to the orbiting destroyer to gut it. Most, if not all, of the thirty will die, there is no question in my heart of that, but in their sacrifice, they have the chance to save billions and once again put the Sthenos in their rightful place. Only one of you needs to make it to the destroyer, but one, at least, must."

He'd reached the back of the group and put his hand on the Norwegian's broad shoulders. "It's my hope," he said, "that our assault will happen quickly enough that the majority of Sthenos fighters will not be able to launch. If the destroyers are brought down without warning, most fighters should be trapped in their hangars."

"With us dead," Lila asked, her eyes calm as if her death was something she'd expected for years rather than something she feared, "who will deal with the remaining Sthenos on Earth?"

"That's a best case scenario problem, and we'll have to face it when we get there. We'll have to cobble together more aircraft and train more pilots. There's no time to do it now, and despite the excellent stealth capabilities of the aircraft we're aiming to gather, collecting too many at this point could raise unwanted attention. I do know this one thing—we won't make the same mistake they did."

"What mistake is that, sir?"

"They left some of us alive."

CHAPTER 35

After leaving the pilots, Jeffrey found Leif in the main clearing, a beam of evening sun slashed across his chest.

"What's this?" Leif asked when Jeffrey handed him a tablet.

"That," Jeffrey said, tapping its surface, "is everything we know about the processes used to modify the Hammerheads. The team Cantwell assigned to it is dead. I need a technically skilled person on this."

"And you think I'm your man."

"Yes."

Leif looked over the tablet. "This is genetic modifications and nanotech. I don't know anything about this. Doctor Monti might be a better—"

"She'll be on your team—"

"On *my* team? What the hell are you talking about?"

"I need you to lead this."

"I don't think that's a good idea."

"It is."

"I don't have any expertise in these areas." He tried to hand the tablet back to Jeffrey.

Jeffrey ignored it. "Leif, I don't know how you can doubt yourself. You're the one who solved the containment problem with the singularity warheads."

"That was a fluke."

"You really think that?"

Leif remained quiet.

Jeffrey asked, "In your graduate program, how did you earn such high grades?"

"I listened in the lectures and read the books."

"How many times did you read the books?"

Suspicion crept into Leif's eyes. "Once."

"Did you have to review for the tests?"

"No."

"You have to know it's not like that for everyone."

Leif shrugged.

"Do this for me," Jeffrey said taking the tablet from Leif. He tapped the screen, pulling up a document. "This is an introductory summary of the implantation of graphene across human nerve tissue using nanotechnology. Read it." He held the tablet out to Leif.

Leif eyed him suspiciously before taking it. "Dad, look, if you need me to help—"

"I don't need another helper, Leif. I need a leader. You may not see it in yourself, but I do. Solving problems like this," he pointed to the tablet, "is as easy for you as flying was for me. If we don't get the details right, the Hammerheads can't work. If the Hammerheads can't work, then we lose the war."

"Some would say," Leif pointed through the trees to the hulk of the Lacedaemon, "that we've already lost." His tone suggested he wanted Jeffrey to prove the point wrong.

"We've lost when we're dead. As long as I'm breathing I'm fighting. What about you?"

"I suppose I'll try if you need me to."

"Leif, I don't need *try*. You've never found your limits because you've never had to." He pointed at the tablet again. "Read it."

Leif began sliding his finger along the tablet. After a moment, he looked up to Jeffrey, "This is actually pretty straightforward, but there are a lot of factors."

"You just read five pages of text in less than a minute."

Leif shrugged.

Jeffrey's tone became incredulous. "You don't really get it do you?"

"Get what?"

"Look, how long would it take me to read that?"

"I don't know… longer?"

"Dammit Leif," Jeffrey grabbed the sides of his son's head and, with a frustrated laugh, said, "wake up to what you are."

Leif pushed his hands away. "And what is it you *think* am I?"

"You're a damn genius. That's why you've never had to try very hard at anything. Don't get me wrong. I'm glad life's been easy for you, but the truth of the matter is an easy life means you haven't come anywhere close to your potential. You have to know that's true."

Leif shrugged. "That means I'm lazy, and I don't like that."

"Not lazy Leif. You only lack purpose."

"But everything's been easy for you, right?"

"What's that supposed to mean?"

"You've got everyone trumped on physical talent. You've got your *modifications*. Everyone else is just a second class human right?"

"Jesus Leif, do you really believe I feel that way?"

The fate of Jeffrey's life seemed to hang on the silence that followed. If his son, the one person in the world he'd strived to do right by, considered him that kind of man, he'd utterly failed.

Leif's tone became apologetic. "No. You're not an asshole, but everything's so *easy* for you. You can fight, and you're strong, and you've got all this physical talent."

"For every scrap of physical talent I have, you got your mother's brains. How do you think I feel about your intelligence?"

Leif looked into the trees. "I don't know how you feel."

"I feel great pride and relief that my son is smarter than I am." Jeffrey gripped Leif's shoulder. "I'm your father. That means I love your successes and take your faults personally, which I shouldn't do, but there it is. I understand I've been, and probably will be, too intense at times, but I need you to believe, when I saw you come into this world my whole life's purpose changed to focus on you, to raise you well and help you fulfill your potential. With your mother's help I was able to hold back some of my intensity. I wanted to drive you all the way to what I believed you could become, but I had to let you find it yourself."

With as much sincerity as he could muster, Jeffrey said, "You are the most intelligent, quick-witted man I've ever known, and I need you on this. I don't need you to work on it. I need you to bleed from the eyes for it. Only then will we have a chance."

Leif nodded, "Okay, I'll do everything I can."

"I need more than everything."

He scowled at Jeffrey as though he didn't understand.

"Look Leif, I'm going to give you something to think about. It might be painful, and I apologize for that."

One of Leif's eyes narrowed with doubt. "Okay."

"Somewhere out there," Jeffrey pointed beyond the trees, "Is another woman like Sarah. She has a young husband and has a child growing inside her. If you don't give it everything, she and her baby will die. That young man will have to go through what you went through. The lives of that mother and child are in your hands, and you *can* save them. You'll never know them, and they'll never know you, but every day for the rest of your life, their being alive somewhere in the world will come to mean more to you than your own life."

Leif lifted his chin as he looked out on the valley, appearing to steel himself against what Jeffrey had said. "Tell me something."

"Okay."

"What's the name of this woman I'm going to save?"

"There's two billion out there... her name is every name ever given by a mother to a daughter, but if you want to help her, you have to get this," he tapped Leif in the center of his forehead, "totally clear. You think you can do that?"

Leif looked at the ground.

Jeffrey was glad to see him taking his time, seriously considering the question.

Leif's eyes rose to meet Jeffrey's. "To keep someone else like Sarah alive, to keep another man from having to go through what I've gone through... yes, I can get my head straight."

"Okay," Leif said. "Let's get this going."

"You're in then?"

Leif nodded, "One hundred and ten percent."

Jeffrey clapped him on the back. "Excellent. I need you," he touched the edge of the tablet again, "to go through this as fast as you can. I'll have Donovan gather your team and send them to you. If they give you any trouble—"

"They won't," Leif said.

CHAPTER 36

Sofía Fields sat under a silvered emergency blanket with
Luciano in her arms. Emilia lay alongside her watching the sky beyond
the pine boughs paling with dawn. The three nights they'd spent under
the stars had been cool, but they'd stayed warm enough huddled
together. The day before, she'd found a hose bib on the side of a
utility shack where she refilled their water containers. Marco had
packed the bag with survival rations. At first, the children had turned
their noses up at the chalky food bricks, but as hunger came on in
earnest, they'd eaten one and asked for a second. But Sofía, to make
the supplies last, had only allowed them one in the morning and one in
the evening. While the bricks were nourishing, they left her stomach
hurting. Marco had included no other food, presumably to preserve as
much room as possible for the dense calories of the bricks. Sofía
estimated she and the children could survive in the hills for several
weeks if need be, but she was unsure what she would do beyond that.

They'd spent the first night tucked into the ravine of a ridge
valley. She'd made them a nest of leaves, and when Luciano began to
cry, she told him they were playing hide and seek, which their father
had told her he wanted to do should his ship arrive. While she tried to
sound lighthearted, when she fell quiet, her mind wandered through
disturbing questions. What was that ship, and where had Marco gone?

At dawn on the second day, she made her way to the tree line
near Griffith Observatory where she found the same type of barrier the
ship had laid down surrounding the parking lot. Where the glistening
fencing crossed the road a pile of metal and chunks of rubber lay as
though a car had attempted to drive through the barrier and been sliced

to palm sized pieces by it. She did not approach the fencing. Beyond it, the parking lot was filled with cars, several with doors open. She saw no one.

The next day, she ventured east to find the barrier at the base of the hill and then north to find the barrier again. She continued west and found, as she'd guessed, a barrier running along Barham Boulevard. In the distance, moving along an empty freeway, she saw a large, black vehicle, perhaps as long and twice as wide as a tractor-trailer.

She and her children were cut off on the island of the Hollywood hills. They saw no other people. The human race seemed to have been lifted off the surface of the planet, and she knew that she could not allow her children to be found.

Luciano shifted next to her. Looking down, she found his clear, brown eyes on her. She gave him the best smile she could afford.

"'amá," Luciano said in a matter-of-fact tone.

"Yes my love?"

"I know papa is not looking for us."

She struggled to settle her thoughts at being caught in the lie. Finally, she asked, "Why would you think that?"

"He would want to hug you too much to stay away."

At this tears welled in her eyes.

The boy's little hand touched her face. "Do not worry 'amá. I will protect you."

CHAPTER 37

Leif had been working with his team for eight days. Each time Jeffrey checked in with them, they'd been either sitting over tablets reading, or in quiet discussion, drawing and noting with graphite pencils on sheets of paper. No matter how much he wanted to move forward, no matter how he wished he could leave with a transport full of pilots to get Lakota fighters, he forced himself to stay calm. When he looked out on the low hills, dense with rainforest, he felt sure, beyond that horizon, something horrible was happening to the human race. He had no idea what. When his mind attempted to imagine it, he shoved the thought away. This was a time for facts, not conjecture. Knowing what was happening would have to wait.

In the evening on that ninth day, Jeffrey made his way down to the river. The day had been hot, and he had several day's sweat and grime coating him. Near their camp they'd found a tributary roiling down from the hills, sparkling and bending over rocks before it joined with the muddy river lower down. At the base of a huge boulder, a waterfall had cut a deep swimming hole.

Jeffrey carried his kit down the trail tied up in a rough, Navy-issue towel. He'd walked barefoot down the trail often, until he'd gotten a beetle's jaw stapled into the side of his foot. Nasty little bastard wouldn't let go even when his body had been removed from his head. Nail clippers applied directly to the half-inch mandibles were the only thing which had set him free. Now Jeffrey wore boots wherever he went, even to the swimming hole.

The air hung muggy among the trees and plants along the trail, but when he came into the swimming hole's clearing, the temperature dropped as the sound of the waterfall filled his ears. The scent of the misting water, and sunlight catching the channels of the falls calmed his heart. Leif stood beside the water in his underwear, scrubbing his hair with a towel. A woman, whom Jeffrey did not at first recognize, stood beside him. She had olive-Italian skin, dark eyes, and long, raven-black, hair, which was towel messy. Her slim figure was striking. As they spoke to each other, Jeffrey saw in their easy smiles that they enjoyed each other's company.

As there was no one else in the pool, he decided to give them a few more minutes alone. He walked back up the trail, found a place to sit, waited, and returned perhaps ten minutes later.

He found them now, fully dressed, sitting on the long buttress-root of a kapok tree, their backs to him. The woman had her hair wrapped in a towel, which exposed the delicate arc of her neck. With an excitement, she touched Leif's leg and pointed to a place where ripples ran out on the calmer water below the falls. A fish had jumped. She turned to Leif and caught sight of Jeffrey. Heavy, upswept lashes framed her eyes, and with her chin held at an angle just high enough to be regal, but not so high as to be haughty, she had the look of a classical movie star.

In a thick Italian accent she said, "Admiral Holt, how are you?"

Only when she spoke did Jeffrey recognize her as the ship's surgeon, whom he'd only seen previously wearing glasses and a lab coat.

"I'm well, Doctor Monti, thank you. I came looking for Leif. I'm sorry to intrude."

"No, please," she motioned with her hand that he should come sit with them. "Please, call me Caterina."

"Thank you, Caterina," he said.

As he sat on a root facing them, the doctor took her hair from the towel. As it cascaded over her shoulder, he felt somewhat stunned. Here, sitting with the backdrop of the deep greens of the jungle behind her and her dark hair down, she was positively beautiful. On a normal day a father would love to see his son sitting with such a woman, but today—so near Sarah's death—her presence brought a primal uneasiness, as if she was somehow infringing upon decorum.

Leif looked very tired, but in his eyes Jeffrey saw the dark obsession, which he had sunk into after their conversation. The doctor seemed more at ease.

"How goes the project?" Jeffrey asked.

Caterina looked to Leif, who sat with his eyes on the river. She nudged his arm.

"I'm sorry?" Leif looked to them, almost surprised, as if Jeffrey and Caterina had just appeared before him.

Jeffrey asked again, "The project... how is progress?"

A genuine, if not weary, smile came to Leif's face as he said, "Very well. We should be able to begin tomorrow."

"Really?" Jeffrey asked with unhidden surprise and relief. "That's excellent."

...

Whitetip lay on a cot, which had been elevated to hip level on crates to give Caterina, Leif, and two nurses easy access to her.

Caterina placed her hand on Whitetip's shoulder. "How are you feeling?"

"I'm good," Whitetip said with an easy smile and a wink.

Jeffrey saw in the paleness of her face that she was definitely not fine. She was scared to death. He wanted to tell her she'd be okay, that it wouldn't hurt, but he couldn't bring himself to outright lie. If it went well, this would be the worst experience of her life.

Someone had to go first, but Jeffrey wished it wasn't her.

Caterina brushed a bit of dirt off the young pilot's face. "In the first stage we will inject nanites, which when triggered, will drill along the surface of the axon tissue of your somatic nerve fibers. They consume a layer of material and, in the space created, lay down a single sheet of graphene." She patted Whitetip's hand, "It isn't dangerous, but is apparently... painful."

"Painful…" Whitetip looked to Jeffrey. "You've lived through this. How bad is it?"

Why did you have to ask me that?

Flicking the air out of a vial filled with a metallic liquid, Caterina connected it to the IV attached to Whitetip's arm.

Jeffrey sat down on a crate beside her. "I'd love to tell you that you'll be slightly uncomfortable, but I can't. It's going to hurt like hell. Thousands of tiny machines are about to eat the outer layer off every strand of your nervous system. It'll feel as though your flesh is being ripped off and burned at the same time. When it happened to me, I thought my muscles were being eaten by rats."

Whitetip gave a nervous smile as she glanced at the needle in her arm. "So it's going to suck."

"Yes." He looked to Caterina, who stood starting at him, her lips somewhat parted. "What?"

Caterina's accent amplified her anger. "This will be difficult enough without you frightening her."

"She'll be fine," Jeffrey said. Yet, as he looked back to Whitetip's pale, worried face, he wished he could have lied to her, but he couldn't bring himself to tell her it would only pinch before sending her through hell.

She'll get through…

"I am sorry," Caterina told Whitetip, "we cannot give you pain medication as that would impede the function of the nanites."

Jeffrey took hold of Whitetip's hand. Fifty years ago, several recruits had gone into severe shock. A few had died. Caterina might be mad at him for saying it would hurt, but at least he hadn't said it would hurt so much she might die from the pain. He felt scared for the young pilot and proud of her as she'd insisted on being first. By doing so, Whitetip had put herself at severe risk. This process was not precisely what they'd used in the past. No one knew if the nanites had been properly engineered. If Leif's team had made an error, Whitetip had effectively agreed to be put to death. Jeffrey had been shoving that thought out of his mind ever since she'd laid down on the cot. He understood it was sexist to worry more about killing a young woman than a young man, but Jeffrey couldn't escape the truth that it bothered him more.

Caterina had agreed to have her go first because a smaller subject was theoretically better, as the machines would finish sooner. She also suggested women handled severe pain as a genetic prerogative better than men.

"Are you ready?" Caterina asked Whitetip.

When Whitetip gave her a quick nod, Caterina motioned to the nurses. They strapped Whitetip's legs and hands down. When they moved off, Jeffrey took hold of her cold hand.

Caterina opened the valve on the Y connector and pressed in the gunmetal-gray liquid, which flushed down the rubberized tube and into the needle in Whitetip's arm.

With a nervous laugh, Whitetip said, "Just a walk in the park, right?"

"Just a walk in the park," Jeffrey said.

Just a walk in the park if you were being electrocuted every step of the way.

Guilt washed over Jeffery at what was about to happen to the young woman. No matter how tough, she was about to have a life-defining experience. For the rest of her days, no matter how horrible things got, she could look back and say, at least it's not as bad as this.

Whitetip looked from one face to the next, all eyes on her. Her fingers twitched in Jeffrey's hand, and her lips pulled back as her eyes narrowed. She drew a seething breath and said, "It's starting in my arm."

Jeffrey slid his crate closer and brushed her hair from her eyes. "It's going to be okay. Just take slow, deep breaths."

She nodded and gave him a brave smile, no longer the tough military pilot, but a scared kid, only a few years out of public school.

Her grip crushed down on Jeffrey's hand as she screamed a sharp bark of pain. Caterina wiped her forehead with a white towel. Leif stood on the other side, arms crossed, biting his thumb.

Whitetip breathed in little huffs.

"Try to draw slow breaths," Leif said to her.

She closed her eyes and her belly rose in a slow arc and descended. Her jaw tensed as she let out a quiet growl. As she gripped fiercely on Jeffrey's hand again, her breath returned to quick puffs.

"It hurts," she said through her teeth.

"I'm sorry," Jeffrey said.

Her eyes came open and locked on Jeffrey's. "It's okay," she whispered. She screamed again. As her legs curled, yanking at the cot's restraints, she gripped down on Jeffrey's hand so hard her short fingernails cut into the side of his palm. Her mouth came open as if to scream again, but nothing came out. Her face began to tint blue.

Caterina came forward, leaning over her. She touched the monitor next to her, which read pulse 130, blood pressure 193/74. "She's okay."

Whitetip gasped for air, her face flushing red as her eyes widened in a primal fight or flight expression. "My right arm and shoulder," she said through her teeth, "feel like they're being melted with acid." Her eyebrows tented up as her eyes reddened with tears.

Jeffrey knew he couldn't keep the worry he felt from his face, so he simply let it show. "I understand. It feels like you're going to die. I've been through it. But you have to trust me, there's nothing physically wrong."

She arched up on her heels and the back of her head, straining against the strap around her chest. Jeffrey wondered if she'd heard him. As her pulse reached 185, sweat beaded across her forehead. Her face blued again. Jeffrey leaned over her just as she let out a horrific scream, sucked in as much air as her small chest would vacuum up and screamed again and again.

"It's reached her chest," Jeffrey said, "It's going to get bad fast from here. He pointed to a tray on a crate nearby. "Now's the time to get her tongue and jaw secured. Whitetip had begun to toss her head from side to side. Leif came around above her and gripped her head, but she thrashed free. He pinned her skull down with his body weight and Dr. Monti shoved the mouth guard in and strapped it around the back of her neck. Her breath now whistled through the breathing hole in the mouth guard. Her screams came muffled in her throat. She kicked viciously at the end of the cot, her boot bending one of the metal bars. As her eyes came open, she looked like the subject of an exorcism, her hair drenched and eyes rolling upward until only the red-traced whites showed.

She screamed and thrashed for ten minutes. In the past, some had lost consciousness, but with microscopic machines eating away at every nerve fiber, no one stayed out long. Whitetip though, stayed with it. Her pulse had spiked to 200 several times, and her blood pressure was moving above 230. If she had any vascular weakness in the brain, stroke was a real possibility.

After ten minutes, the screaming faded to groaning gasps of air. She lay drenched in sweat with her eyes clamped shut and chest heaving. Jeffrey soaked a towel with cool water and pressed it to her forehead so the water squeezed from it, running down her temples and the sides of her nose.

As Jeffrey draped the towel across her forehead, her eyes came open—blood shot and weary. She blinked at him as though she couldn't quite focus.

"Are you okay?" Jeffrey asked her. "The worst is over. You're going to be sore for days, but the burning will only get less from here."

She whispered something through the mouthguard, and Jeffrey unstrapped it and drew it out.

She whispered again, so quietly he could not make out what she said.

He put his ear next to her mouth.

"I hate you," came just over the sound of her exhaled breath.

As Jeffrey leaned back, she, despite looking as though she'd nearly died from drowning, winked at him. Her tenacity of spirit overwhelmed Jeffrey. Resting his hand on her belly, he felt the flat muscles rising and falling. She'd passed through the eye of the needle and would lead the way for the next generation of Hammerheads.

Closing her eyes, she appeared to drift off to sleep.

The doctor pressed another vial into her IV and said, "This chemical trigger will cause the machines to seek out the bile system. They'll collect in the liver and break down."

Whitetip's hand flexed as her eyes drew open. She looked up at the draped tarps above, which billowed on a slight breeze as spots of sunlight danced across them. The sound of wind shuffling through leaves filled the air. When she tugged on her restraints, Jeffrey unstrapped her nearest hand. Holding it up, she stared at it for some time, touching her fingertips one at a time to her thumb.

"Strange isn't it?" Jeffrey said as he unstrapped her other hand.

"Yes," she said as though absorbed in thought. "Incredibly strange."

"What do you feel?" Caterina asked.

"I feel..." Whitetip paused, lifting and staring at her other hand, touching each fingertip to her thumb. Now she pushed her palms together and slid them along, her eyes closing as if in pleasure. "I feel... alive."

A quizzical expression came to the doctor's face, and she turned to Jeffrey as if to seek clarification. Jeffrey shrugged and held his hand out to Whitetip as if to say, *ask her*.

In a gentle tone, Doctor Monti asked, "Alive?"

Whitetip's eyes came open, and she smiled with a casual easiness as people will after a few drinks. "You are the most beautiful woman I've ever seen."

Dr. Monti appeared somewhat taken aback by this.

"I wouldn't worry too much about that," Jeffrey said, smiling with relief. He drew a deep, freeing breath, let it slowly out, and said, "She's in the euphoria of it."

Leif said, "Euphoria was documented in all successful modifications."

The doctor nodded, "Yes of course, as we discussed. I'd forgotten that."

Jeffrey said to Whitetip, "You're in the afterglow of a massive endorphin rush and the new sensation of a nerve shine."

Her smile still faint as she continued to feel her own hands, she asked, "How long will this last?"

"The endorphins should fade shortly," Leif said, "but reports suggest the sensation of nerve shine will be with you the rest of your life."

"Yeah," Jeffrey said with a laugh, "Fun isn't it?"

With a reverent sincerity she said, "It's amazing."

"Yes, it is and will be."

He picked up a roll of medical tape and threw it at her.

She snatched it out of the air.

Leaning her head back as if basking in warm sun, she smiled drunkenly. Her chest rose with a deep breath. When she tossed the tape up in the air, Jeffrey caught it. Leif and the doctor unstrapped her legs and waist. She tried to get up right away.

"Please," Dr. Monti said, "you must have rest as we give you fluids."

"I'm fine," Whitetip said as she shoved herself up. Her arms trembled, and she tipped sideways.

Jeffrey caught her, and as he lay her back down, said, "You're going to do whatever Dr. Monti says. That's an order. Understood?"

She nodded, still appearing a bit disoriented.

Leif said, "I'm going to go see if our next pilot is ready."

CHAPTER 38

Donovan walked up to Stacy, his expression hard. "Commander, did you take Marines off my security detail?"

With a flush, Stacy realized she'd forgotten to involve him. This wouldn't go well. "I'm sorry sir, I needed more operatives. My team is only five including me. I—"

"—thought you could move my resources without my approval."

"No sir. Not at all. I had to move quickly, and I became a bit hasty. I apologize."

"That seems to be how you operate."

Stacy felt her eyes narrowing and squelched the urge to ask him what the hell he meant by such a comment. Guessing he'd make her pay for not asking permission over the Marines, she chided herself for not being more careful.

"I thought SW teams involved six personnel."

Is he going to argue every little detail with me? "I had six."

"What happened to the sixth?"

Seriously? "One was injured. I had to cut her from the team."

He nodded as though he could accept the reason as a pittance, which made Stacy's anger flare again, but she checked herself.

"I suppose taking the Marines back from you would look bad. Well played Zack."

Stacy couldn't help herself at that. "Are you telling me you wouldn't have let me have them?"

His face contracted into a slight smirk. "Do you think they'll be able to fill the shoes of such highly trained Navy personnel?"

She ignored the veiled insult. "We found more than enough who already had experience in stealth suits and demolitions. They've been a natural fit. I've selected seventeen to round out the rest of my team, and ten more for backups. We're checking them out in the suits now, running drills in the forest."

"Games," he said with a flippant wave of his hand as he walked away, leaving Stacy seething.

...

Each pilot reacted differently to the nerve shine. The African, Lila, had been the most stoic. She'd kept her dark eyes on the canopy above, her arms trembling against the restraints. Even when tears streamed down her temples, and her body shuddered, she'd remained silent, almost supernaturally so.

The Norwegian, Kodiak, had yelled, beat his head against the bed, and lost consciousness several times.

Every pilot approached the process with reverence and respectful fear, all save Soy Bean, the kid from Nebraska. He sauntered into the medical tent and flopped down on the cot so hard Jeffrey thought he might break it.

"Not too worried?" Jeffrey asked him.

"Yeah, I'm fine." He put his hands behind his head as if he were at the beach. "Let's get this show on the road."

Caterina explained the process, and he had no questions.

Jeffrey explained the pain.

He waved away the comments, saying, "It's no big deal. I got this."

Jeffrey shrugged his shoulders and motioned for Caterina to proceed. She pressed the metallic looking liquid into the IV, which flushed down to Soy Bean's arm along with the saline.

When Jeffrey took hold of Soy Bean's wrist, he pulled his hand away. "Whoa there chief. No hand holding."

Letting out a frustrated sigh, Jeffrey said, "We need to restrain you, so you don't get hurt during the process."

260

"Boss," he held his hands up in a defensive position, "I never let any of my girls tie me down, and I'm not about to let some old man do it."

Jeffery's anger quickened, but he said in a slow, calm voice, "This is no time for kidding around. The process is going to begin in less than a minute, and for your own safety, you have to be restrained."

"I'm not messing around with you. No one's tying me down."

Standing, Jeffrey brought his nose a few inches from Soy Bean's face. "Listen to me you little shit," his voice a low, quiet growl. "You may think you're slick, but if you give me even one more breath of flack you're out, not just out of the program, but out of this camp."

Soy Bean's blasé calmness faltered.

Jeffrey asked, "Are you on board or are you out?"

Soy Bean's expression became somewhat submissive. "I'm in, I'm in. Jesus Christ what's gotten into your ass?"

Jeffrey grabbed him by the shirt, lifting him a few inches off the cot.

"Are you in or are you out?"

"I'm fucking in! I told you that. What's wrong with you?"

Jeffrey was close enough to smell the meal Soy Bean had recently eaten. "Are you in or are you out?"

The kid looked confused, his expression now sincerely worried. With a sudden flush, he appeared to come to a realization. "I'm in... sir."

"Excellent," Jeffrey said letting Soy Bean drop to the cot. "I'll strap you down then."

As Jeffrey set the straps, Soy Bean's face tightened, his eyes going to the needle in his arm. "It's really starting to burn." He shifted to the left, straightening his arm and tugging at the wrist restraint as though he could pull his shoulder away from his arm.

"This is the part I was trying to tell you about," Jeffrey said, as he put his hand on the kid's arm.

Soy Bean bared his teeth, sucking in air and scowling at his arm as though it angered him. "I know you said it was going to hurt, but thi—" He shouted out with surprised pain.

"His heart rate is already close to two hundred beats per minute," Caterina said.

Soy Bean glared at her, looking as if he had something smart assed to say.

She put the palm of her hand on Soy Bean's chest, and he closed his eyes, his arm trembling.

"You must relax," she said. "Try to stay calm."

Tiny droplets of perspiration formed across his forehead as his body shook.

The monitor registered 203 beats per minute. Caterina shook her head subtly to Jeffrey. Jeffrey understood all too well. The records they'd reviewed showed that when it went bad, it looked just like this. Soy Bean had that charmed mixture of lack of pain threshold and excitability. A common thing for those insecure enough to have as big an attitude as he did.

"We've got to get his heart rate down," Caterina said to Leif.

"We've been over this before we started," Leif said. "It's all in their head. If someone can't handle the pain, they'll react in this way. The only key we have is to get him to calm down."

Jeffrey looked back to Soy Bean, who's shirt had spots of sweat forming. He had his teeth bared, eyes clamped shut, the veins in his face and neck standing out.

Caterina put her hand on his forehead, "You have to calm down. Your blood pressure and heart rate are too high."

He seemed unable to respond to her.

Somehow, in that moment, Jeffrey knew the kid was going to die. He couldn't define it, give it a medical reason, but he knew that, in his inability to cope, Soy Bean was a dead man, and Jeffrey felt, correctly or not, he was at fault. He should have registered the kid's attitude. Those with a lot of attitude were weak. They are screaming at the world that they are afraid, just like a dog barking. Jeffrey knew all too well there are two core emotions in the human mind, two drives all other emotions and reactions stem from—love and fear. Fear drives negative behavior, love drives positive. This kid couldn't cope, he didn't have the strength, and Jeffrey should have known it. He should have washed him out.

He tried to take hold of the kid's hand, but it was locked into a fist. His face was going red, and Jeffrey smelled something foul.

"I think he voided his bowels," Leif said.

Jeffrey nodded. The heart rate monitor showed 238 now.

"I need something to get that down," she said as she reached for a packet.

The heart registered 247, lofted to 254, and then the numbers blurred. The arcing line of his heartbeat under the monitor fell to nothing, and the monitor began to tone with an alarm. The screen pulsed with a red hue.

"He's coding," Caterina said with the detached tone only experience with emergencies brings. She ripped open his shirt and took the paddles from the defibulator beside the cot. She squirted a gel onto them, swirled them together, and pressed them on Soy Bean's chest.

"Clear."

A click sounded, and his body arched. The beat returned but ran so fast it seemed the monitor must be broken. The number showed 301 and the short pulses on the line looked like the teeth of a saw blade.

Dr. Monti shook her head and shocked him again. The line went flat. Watching the monitor for a moment, she mouthed a countdown before shocking him a third time. Nothing returned. Setting the paddles aside, she began doing chest compressions on him, her arms rigid, smashing his chest down.

"Leif," she said, not looking away, "give me a count every fifteen seconds."

Leif picked up a tablet. After a moment, he said, "Fifteen."

Caterina kept pumping on Soy Bean's chest.

Sweat began forming on her face, and as she huffed with each compression, the kid's body lurched. Jeffrey moved into her peripheral vision as she huffed and compressed.

Leif continued to call out fifteen second intervals. When two and a half minutes had passed, she stopped the compressions, took up the paddles, and pressed them to his chest. His body jolted. Lifting the paddles an inch off, she watched the monitor. The alarm tone continued as the line remained flat. The spike the paddles had created shifted off to the left.

Pressing the paddles to his chest again, she hit the thumb triggers. Soy Bean's body arched. The line twitched, and went flat again.

"Dammit," she said. For a moment Jeffrey believed she was going to throw the paddles. She set them on their case. She began compressions again. "Give me fifteen second marks."

Leif kept his eyes on the monitor's clock, and said "Fifteen..." and again... "fifteen."

"Tell me when we've hit three minutes," she said. Strands of sweat-soaked hair stuck to her forehead and cheek. She continued the compressions.

After what seemed too long to Jeffrey, Leif said, "There's three minutes."

She repeated the procedure with the paddles, having the same result and returned to the chest compressions.

Jeffrey wondered how long she intended keep going.

In the spaces surrounding the compressions, she said, "My hope is, as the nanites complete their process, I might be able to revive him."

Jeffrey nodded even though her eyes were down.

"There's three minutes again," Leif said.

She tried two shocks. The spike on the monitor went flat. She returned to her chest compressions saying one word with each compression, "Get... beating... you... son... of... a...bitch. Come on!" she yelled, and then louder, "Come ON!"

She continued the chest compressions, and Jeffrey could see her arms trembling as the pressure lifted from them at the top of each compression.

"Dammit," she yelled, "Get going!"

Jeffrey reached over and took hold of her wrist gently, not interfering with the motion of her arms. His voice low, he said, "Caterina… it's okay."

Her eyes met his, furious. "It's not fucking okay." Taking up the paddles, she shocked Soy Bean's body twice. It lifted and went still each time.

She stared at it. Her expression hardened, lips narrowing. She threw the paddles into the side of the tent.

Sitting on the case beside Soy Bean, she put her face in her hands. Her arms trembled. After a moment, her back rose with a deep breath. She looked up. A mask of efficient professionalism had taken her over.

"Leif, please mark down time of death for…" she looked to the tablet beside the cot, "Lieutenant Brooks."

When she stood, Jeffrey reached out to touch her shoulder. She smacked his hand aside. As she walked out of the tent, she said to one of the nurses, "Get the body out of here."

Jeffrey looked at Soy Bean's face, mouth slack, eyes half-open. Right now, the kid should have been sitting on a crate pissed at Jeffrey for cutting him. In his rush to prep pilots as quickly as possible, Jeffrey had ignored his gut. The first dead Hammerhead was on him.

CHAPTER 39

Jeffrey sat beside the river, mesmerized by the fast water catching the moonlight in glittering whorls. Near him, the smoother surface reflected the stars, which spanned the gap in the trees like a cathedral ceiling between the buttressing branches.

"I heard what happened today."

Jeffrey looked behind him to find Samantha standing at the trailhead, as if respecting the space. She held her flashlight down, illuminating a circle at her feet. When he motioned for her to sit next to him, she clicked off the light and approached. Turning back to the water, he watched its dark mass passing and felt its similarity to his heart, black with slight sparks of hope now and again.

Arms wrapped around him from behind, and cool hair spilled across his neck. Her head came to rest gently on his shoulder.

"I'm so sorry," she whispered.

He nodded, feeling unable to speak with his grief lodged right up against his throat.

After a moment, he risked saying, "I called him Soy Bean… did it on purpose. He was so damn arrogant. I was trying to take him down a bit…"

"You couldn't have known."

"I should have." He let out a sigh. "It's such a waste."

"I suppose that's war?" Her tone conceded her lack of understanding.

"When we commit to face death against all odds," Jeffrey said, "we do so in the hope that, in fighting, we'll move those who survive forward. We comfort ourselves with dreams of an heroic end, one with some kind of impact. No one wants to die like he did. No stories get told about men like Nathan Brooks. We shove guys who die like that deep, and keep 'em down there."

Her arms came away. Stepping over the buttress root, she sat beside him and took hold of his hand. "I almost died once." She fell into silence, and he let that silence, in which the river slid by with silken sounds, remain as long as she wished. "It happened on a snowy mountain road. My ex-husband, driving too fast as usual, lost control and slid right through an already-damaged portion of a guard rail."

"We launched," she held out her hand as if it were the car, "into the sky. The river valley was about a thousand feet down." Her tone darkened as though the memory still troubled her. "To this day I can close my eyes and see myself hanging in nothingness. For a moment, the snowflakes went still around us and seemed to fall upwards as we accelerated." She looked down as if at the river valley below. "In that moment, I knew I was going to die… and I was… okay with it. It was a strange, peaceful moment."

Jeffrey asked, "How'd you survive?"

She smiled. "A huge pine tree growing out of the cliff face caught us like a baseball in a mitt. I was hanging off my seatbelt looking down into the valley through the branches. When I perceived even the remotest possibility that I was going to live, the sense of peace vanished."

"You were afraid then?"

"You bet I was… and furious with him. I remember hitting his shoulder. He yelled at me to sit still. Getting us to safety took sixteen hours after we called for help. They were so concerned the car would drop out of the tree, we had to wait for a military air lift. We sat there motionless for so long, I finally had to wet my pants. You usually don't hear details like that in those survival programs. They welded lines to the car and lifted the whole thing back up onto the road. Being set back down on the road we'd launched off of was surreal."

"One would hope your husband changed his driving habits."

"Ex-husband… and I wouldn't know. Putting me through that was the last straw. The moment the car touched solid ground, I threw

267

my wedding ring at his face." Her voice softened. "In the end though, I was glad he'd done it."

A bit shocked, Jeffrey asked, "Why?"

"Coming so close to death… Experiencing that complete peace… When I stepped out onto the roadway, I wasn't the same woman. I felt ready to be the person I was born to be. The whole world looked different."

"How so?"

"More beautiful."

"Beautiful," he said in agreement.

"The world is gorgeous." She held her hand out to the river and stars. "That day, freezing cold in wet jeans," she laughed lightly to herself, "I fell in love with life all over again… and myself. I suppose that's why I never remarried. In my line of work I'm surrounded by A-type assholes. Everyone I got close to wanted me to give up too much of myself." She looked to Jeffrey. "You know what I believe?"

"What's that?"

"I've looked through death's doorway, and I really do believe there's peace on the other side. I think Nathan Brooks is far beyond pain and pride. He holds no ill will toward you, and no regrets. He is at peace—true, wonderful peace."

Jeffrey drew a breath and let it out, feeling the pressure in his chest let off. He took hold of her hand, and they sat in silence watching the river flow.

CHAPTER 40

Jeffrey stood before the pilots he'd selected for the first stage. "While I'd love to let you rest, we don't have the luxury."

They looked horribly tired, their eyes bloodshot and shoulders slumped from the distress of the modifications. Still, the difference in their awareness was palpable.

"According to our intel, several squadrons of Lakota fighters are in storage at Turnbull Air Force Base in southwestern Arizona. You fifty are my collection team. We'll be transported to our location by Lieutenant Fields, Commander Zack's V.O. I'd like to get more, but Fields' Warthog has capacity for fifty... barely."

"Forty-six of you will bring back Lakota. That will afford us two backups, which isn't a lot. Because the Lacedaemon is not equipped to support aircraft, we have no fuel for algal-alcohol powered aircraft. To address this, we hope to bring back five, fully-loaded fuel tankers. I'll fly back one of the five."

"This mission is dine and dash. We go in the early afternoon and will reach our destination at sundown. That'll put our travel time out of alignment with the orbiting Sthenos destroyer. On our return leg, everyone but the fueler groups will break into pairs. At all times we'll fly low and fast to avoid detection. You'll each be assigned secondary return points. If anyone is followed, the hope is that the Sthenos will hunt down and destroy only that group. If we're lucky, they'll assume the aircraft were operating alone. When you reach your secondary points, you'll wait 48 hours before returning here. If, after forty-eight hours, a flight pair doesn't return, we'll carry on without you. If you are shot down, there will be no rescue attempt. Is that clear?"

"Yes, sir," the pilots said in a chorus.

"Upon your return, you'll find the majority of personnel gone. When the shooting begins, the Sthenos might seek out the Lacedaemon. Teams have already begun moving supplies to several separate camps a safer distance some twenty miles further down the valley."

"Now I'll assign flight groups." He pointed to the Norwegian. "Kodiak, you and Stump will pair off."

The Norwegian smacked the pacific northwesterner's back. "Utmerket!"

Scowling, Stump shoved him. "Lay off fisherman."

The Norwegian held his arms wide. "Who needs my hug?"

"Back off Kodiak."

"Never my friend." He shoved Stump's hands aside and wrapped his arms around him. Stump struggled but, realizing he couldn't free himself, went still.

Kodiak kept the hug on.

A slight smile formed on Stump's face. "You can let me go now."

"Tell me you love me."

"Gentlemen," Jeffrey said, "please." However, even as Kodiak let Stump go, Jeffrey felt glad of the banter. It would play a critical role in bonding the group.

"Once you've completed your layover at your secondary rendezvous point, you'll return to the Lacedaemon, not the new camps. On that day we'll form our attack groups. Our saving grace has been their apparent lack of interest in us. The moment we flick their nose though, their interest will spike. We can play our hand only when we're absolutely ready."

He pointed out through the trees. "I have to assume what's going on beyond those hills is bad. We have no idea what state humanity is in, but I'm going to guess there's no government, no law. As we travel, the Sthenos are not our only concern. People seeking to survive could cause problems. We must avoid everyone, no matter how desperate until our mission is done. At this moment, we can only help them by staying on goal."

He looked over the faces before him. "Questions?"

The hand of a pilot from Canada went up, who with his thin shoulders, reminded Jeffrey of Maco. "Yes, Blue Line?" Jeffery asked.

"When do we stand the chance to earn a new nickname? One like Whitetip's?"

Jeffrey said with a smile, "If I were named after a mark on a hockey rink, I'd want a change too."

Quiet laughter rose up among the pilots and even Blue Line smiled, his gaunt cheeks creasing.

"The truth of the matter is," Jeffrey said, "you'll earn them when you no longer want them."

CHAPTER 41

They lifted off in the early afternoon, Jeffrey sitting beside Marco. Strangely enough, Captain Donovan had argued that Jeffrey shouldn't go, saying they shouldn't risk the central authority. Jeffrey felt sure that Donovan would love to see him out of his way for a few days, but Donovan, while taciturn, could surprise. Jeffrey assumed Donovan didn't care about Jeffrey as much as he cared about overall success. He seemed fully committed to that. Yet still, there had been something beyond efficiency in his tone, something along the lines of personal concern. As Marco accelerated over the dense treetops, Jeffrey turned Donovan's motivations over in his mind.

Perhaps I haven't given him enough credit.

As Marco flew, Jeffrey watched the trees and rivers ranging away to the distant horizon. The deep-blue sky hung faultless above the sun drenched trees. For the first time in a month, looking on the broad expanse of the world, he realized how cooped up he'd felt.

Staying close to the tree tops, Marco flew below the speed of sound. Their flight would be just over 4300 miles and would take some six hours at sub mach speeds, but unnatural signatures, radio waves, sonic booms, anything, were to be avoided at all costs.

While Jeffrey felt positive about the mission, he regretted having to fly a heavy fueler home while his pilots returned in Lakotas. He'd never flown one and found himself seduced by aircraft touted to outperform Kiowas.

Looking into the mirror mounted on the windscreen frame, he looked down the short passage to the cargo/passenger area. He could see Whitetip talking to Springbok, her hands moving in arcs, one following the other. In the next few months, they'd both likely be dead. They said they were okay with it, but Jeffrey knew each harbored visions of the battles to be fought, and if they were anything like him, in their minds they'd somehow get the upper hand or they'd help someone else do it. Yet, that often wasn't how war worked. Like juggling bombs, even the brightest and best can keep them in the air for only so long. When they dropped, it was more often ugly than not.

Marco lifted the transport over the far ridge. More trees ranged away to the newly visible horizon. Flying in silence for some time, Marco's eyes scanned his instruments and the world beyond as his right hand gave light, endless adjustments to the flight yoke. Jeffrey hoped flying low would be a good tactic, but in truth, they understood little about how the Sthenos detected vehicle signatures.

Jeffrey drew a deep breath, let it out, and stretched his arms and legs, being careful not to touch the controls at his feet.

He felt sleep drifting into his eyes and had to do something to stay awake.

"Lieutenant Fields, where are you from?"

"I grew up in a mountain village about one hundred miles north of Mexico City."

"When did you emigrate to the United States?"

"When I was seventeen, sir."

Jeffrey put his hands behind his head. "Did you come stateside with your parents?"

"No sir, I ran away from home with my future wife."

Jeffrey brought his hands down. "Really?"

"It isn't a very interesting story, sir. I wouldn't want to bore you."

"We have six hours to kill, but if you don't want to talk about, I don't mind."

"Not at all, sir. As world population dropped, my village became isolated, which I didn't mind. It was a peaceful place. Quiet nights with a lot of stars, if you know what I mean."

"I do."

Marco, eyes on the blurring trees a few hundred feet below the belly of the transport, said, "I grew up wealthy. My parents farmed agave and ran a distillery. I had an easy life until the day she caught my attention. I'd known her my entire life, but that day it felt as though I'd seen her for the first time. Something had changed either with me or her... both of us I suppose. She was the daughter of the launderer, who had died years before, leaving her mother to struggle with the business. One day, she came out of her shop, my friends and I were kicking a football around in the street... a soccer ball, you know?"

"I understand."

"I stopped in the middle of the street, staring at her. I hadn't realized how beautiful she was until that moment."

As Marco spoke Jeffrey felt the darkening of his heart that came to him when he became familiar with someone. It had been that way ever since the first war and was the reason he had so few friends. One more person to know, one more person to grieve. Jeffrey glanced into the mirror again, back to the pilots. Maybe this time he wouldn't have to survive them.

"You all right, sir?" Marco asked.

Jeffrey patted Marco's shoulder. "Fine. Tell me about her... please."

But Marco didn't continue. His expression grew distant and Jeffrey understood he was wandering back to a time and place to which he couldn't return.

"You miss your hometown?"

Marco pursed his lips before saying, "Yes, but I haven't returned. My mother and father have disowned me for marrying Sofía."

"I'm sorry to hear that, Marco."

Marco asked in a frustrated tone, "Why must people have so much pride? Why can't they accept life as it is?"

"Because they don't understand how fragile it is. They believe they have control and feel angry when they don't get what they want.

If they knew what I know, they'd celebrate every moment of their lives just as they have it."

"What is it you know, sir?"

"When someone you care for dies, when you witness their last breath leave their body, all you want is another moment with them, one more word, an afternoon—" Jeffrey's words caught in his throat, and he fell silent.

"I'm sorry sir, I didn't mean to—"

Jeffrey held up a hand. "It's all right. People so often push their friends and family to be other than they are, but when they're gone we never miss the person we wished they'd been, we only miss them."

Marco lifted the nose of the transport to clear a ridge. Beyond it, the broad plane of the Amazon basin ended in rugged mountains.

"We're in Columbia now," Marco said, as he pointed to a large peak rising up beyond the horizon. Its rough-hewn sides ranged up to a domed, snow dusted peak. "That's Nevado del Ruíz. We'll cross the northern Andes soon."

Jeffrey leaned forward, squinting into the bright sunlight. "Tell me more about Sofía."

"As she walked to one of the vegetable seller's stalls, I could not take my eyes from her. She moved so gracefully... long legs." He laughed. "She's an inch taller than me. When we go out, she wears flats and makes we wear shoes with thick soles. She is very conscious of her height but shouldn't be. She says she looks like a stork, all knees and bones, but it's not true. She's like a white crane, beautiful..." at that he fell silent.

Jeffrey gave him time. When Marco still said nothing, Jeffrey said, "You love her very much."

"Yes." Marco's expression had gone flat. "When this," he held his hand out to the world before them, "happened, she was in Los Angeles. We had an apartment at the base of the Hollywood Hills..."

Jeffrey waited to see if he was going to finish the thought. When Marco remained silent, he said, "She's alive."

Marco looked at him with a mixture of worry and irritation in his eyes. "You can't know that."

"That's all there is to say, Marco. She's alive until you find out otherwise. If we lose hope, we lose everything." Jeffrey said the next words one at a time, "She—is—alive." He took hold of Marco's shoulder, "Clear?"

Marco said in an unsure tone, "Yes, sir."

"Now, what happened that first day at the vegetable seller's?"

"She was trying to buy vegetables, papas and such. I saw the woman fill her bag. I can remember that old woman like it was now. She had a broad nose and ugly teeth." Marco's tone turned regretful. "When I was younger, I judged her for that. She held up her hand to Sofía, who looked to her hands and said something. A truck pulled up, blocking my view. I walked to where I could see again. The woman took two cucumbers, an onion, and two potatoes out of the bag as Sofía's youngest brother Javier, maybe only eight then, came up to her. She was fifteen at the time, I was sixteen. As Sofía paid the woman, Javier tugged at her sleeve, pointing to a stack of oranges. As the woman gave Sofía the bag, Javier tugged at her sleeve again. She yelled at him, her voice coming over the sound of the idling truck saying, we cannot afford it. The old woman said something that calmed Sofía and handed a small orange to Javier. Sofía looked at the palm of her hand as if there might be some more money. When she spoke, the woman shook her head and closed Sofía's hand with hers."

"Sofía walked away with tears in her eyes. I had to do something. When she'd moved off, I ran to the old woman and asked what the girl had been unable to buy. She told me, and I bought the items. When she handed the bag to me, its lightness dumfounded me. How could she not afford such a small amount of food?"

"I told the woman to fill two bags with produce. When she had, I paid her. I knew my father would be angry with me for spending all my money, but I did not care. I ran after Sofía. As she left the market, she had her two brothers and one sister with her. The half-full bag in her hands seemed pitiful to me. I wanted to go to her, to say something witty, make her laugh. Up to that moment, I'd always had something to say, but I could not get myself to go to her. I worried that she might be angry with me or think I expected something for what I was offering her," his expression became serious, "which I did not."

"I'm with you."

"They did not notice me as I followed them to their house, a tiny thing with an ancient eucalyptus tree in the front," Marco held up his hand curling his fingers, "which hung over the front door as if it were trying to shelter the house from the world. As I stepped onto the porch, I heard her mother berating her for not having brought home enough. Sofía was crying, saying the lack of rain had raised prices. She'd bought as much as she could afford. Her mother asked about the orange, accused her of wasting money."

"I wanted to save her from the argument, so I knocked on the door as loud as I could, but the moment I did it, I felt as though my heart had stopped. I couldn't face her mother." He laughed. "Mothers always see right through young men don't they? I set the bags down and ran as fast as I could. Hiding across the street, I heard their door open. Watching through fence slats, I saw Sofía and her mother come out to find the bags. Her mother looked up and down the street as though something had been stolen from her rather than left, but she brought in the bags. Sofía remained a moment. When her eyes passed the fence, they stopped on me. I thought to come out, to show her who I was, but instead I ran."

Jeffrey began laughing. "That strikes me as evidence of humility."

Marco laughed as well. "More likely cowardice."

"How many times did you bring groceries to their house and run?"

"So many times, man," Marco said with a laugh, before his face snapped to a seriousness. "I mean, sir."

At that Jeffrey wanted to tell him to let it go, but he couldn't. The price of his authority was never being able to be just one of the guys.

"How many times?"

"All summer. I spent my entire summer's wages from the distillery on groceries for them. I had to go without lunch. It was no problem though, I'd eat as much as I could at breakfast and dinner. After work as I sat at the café with my friends, they'd asked me why I didn't buy a drink. I would tell them I was saving for something."

"You were spending it on a beautiful girl," Jeffrey said. "There's nothing wrong with that."

"If only I could have been that honest. If I'd been found out… my parents had other plans for my future and would have been furious at my interest in a lower-class girl. Once a friend stopped me with the groceries. I told him I was taking them to my mother. My mother once found me with the bags, and I told her that my friend's mother had asked me to carry them."

They now flew over high desert, fields of windswept brown grasses. Clouds hung over the shoulders of the mountains, and choppy air buffeted the ship. The high desert meadows and peaks made Jeffrey feel cold.

"That went on through the entire summer until school was about to begin. In September, in the shade of the market trees, the air was wonderfully cool. In the evening, I went to her house, set the bags down, knocked, and ran. I hid where I always had, behind the fence, and watched. The mother came to the door, took up the bag, looked around and went inside. Someone tapped me on the shoulder. With a shout, I turned to find Sofía glaring at me. She had me cornered. Having no idea what to do, I pushed past her to escape. As I did that, she took hold of my arm, pulled me close, and hugged me."

Marco's voice went quiet as he said, "There are moments in life we'll remember forever. We often do not realize their significance until years later. However, every so often we are actually aware the thing we are experiencing right then is going to be a treasured memory."

278

"I know that very feeling," Jeffrey said.

Marco snapped his fingers. "That's exactly how I felt at that time. She felt perfect in my arms, as though they had been measured out by God to hold her. The softness of her hair on my face… and the lavender… the scent of her was like a drug."

Marco fell silent, obviously off in the memory. Jeffrey let him sit with it for some time before saying, "…and?"

"Yes, of course," Marco smiled in that bashful way when drawn out of a private place. "I kissed her neck. I couldn't help myself. It was as though I was outside of myself. I can still feel the skin of her neck, warm and soft on my lips." He laughed now, shaking his head. "She pushed me away and slapped me so hard I lost my balance and fell against the fence."

"Holy hell," Jeffrey said. "That's not a traditional end to a love story."

Marco touched the temperature readouts for the reactors. "Thankfully that wasn't the end."

"I assumed as much."

"I felt devastated as she returned to her house, but as she crossed the street, she showed me how she truly felt. She had her hands in fists, but she glanced back at me four times. I can still see each time as if I'm watching it happen. On the fourth, I felt the greatest and most beautiful hope of my life. Her anger had gone, and I saw only the nervousness I felt."

"I knew then she had slapped me, not because she hated me or I had done something she didn't care for, but because it had scared her."

"So what did you do?"

"I would walk her home from school every day. I did not try to kiss her again, not until I had been walking her home for a month. I was waiting for her to tell me when it was time, as a gentleman should. In early October, she turned down an alley, stopping behind a wall where no one could see us. She put her arms around my neck, and I

279

kissed her for the second time. It seemed as though my heart had never beat in my life until that moment."

"I had fallen completely in love with her. So much so, I decided to risk telling my father about her. He became furious with me, forbidding me to see her. He had arranged a meeting with another rancher's daughter."

"Arranged marriages?"

"Not arranged as much as highly encouraged."

"What was she like?"

"I would never know. When he forbade me, I agreed with everything he said, went to my room, packed a bag, took all the money I had to my name, which was very little due to the groceries, and went to her house. I tapped quietly on her bedroom window she shared with her sister until she showed herself. Then I asked her to run away with me."

"And she did?"

"She wrote her mother a note, packed her bags, and we left town on the midnight bus to Mexico City. She also knew we had been destined to be together."

"You joined the military for citizenship?" Jeffrey asked.

"Exactly, and they were glad to have me. Apparently I am good at flying."

Jeffrey nodded, "Yes, you have very good flow on the controls."

They flew on for awhile, Jeffrey thinking to himself. He liked what he saw in Marco's flying. The man had a subtle touch, as if the craft were an extension of himself. Jeffrey wanted him for the project. But wanting him for the project was as good as wanting him dead. He thought of Marco and his wife, happy years from now.

She might already be dead.

Something in Marco's eyes made Jeffrey think that he was having the same thought.

"Marco…"

"Yes, sir?"

"I want to bring you into the Hammerheads."

Marco, nodded once. "I'll do everything I can for you sir, live or die."

"That's exactly why I need you Lieutenant. I'll discuss it with Commander Zack once we're back to base."

"Yes, sir."

CHAPTER 42

They flew on in silence for some time. When they reached the Caribbean Sea, Jeffrey took over, flying one hundred feet above the clear-blue water. An hour and a half later, Marco tapped the GPS screen and said, "We're passing into the Gulf of Mexico now."

In one hour, they crossed the pale-blue water of Texas' Matagorda Bay, and now the broad, dry expanse of the United States blurred below. In the back, a discussion on baseball had turned somewhat ugly, sounding to Jeffrey as though Whitetip had no love of the Texas Rangers while Marmaduke had grown up in Arlington. As they crossed into New Mexico, Marmaduke had moved onto which barbeque restaurants he missed.

All the while, as they flew, they avoided population centers. They saw some cars left askew on the shoulders of the highways, but few people. At one point, as a ranch house blurred by, Jeffrey saw a woman waving a white bit of fabric. Her face was turned directly to him, but they were moving too fast to see her expression. He imagined one of desperation.

That one woman broke something free in him. He imagined shackles, bloody wrists, thousands starving. He let the image go, but understood all too well the world was broken, farms ruined, transportation destroyed. Even if they stopped the Sthenos, millions more would die before the systems that supported the human race could be rebuilt. Right now there were no planes flying to the Arctic with supplies, no fuel coming from the algae farms, and no food coming out of farms. He wondered how the human spirit would cope. Most, he hoped, would come together, but some would turn to raids and warlording. If Jeffrey survived the initial resurgence, their next task would be to sort out those who had chosen the wrong path.

They reached Arizona as the sun touched the western Horizon. The speed of the plane chased it now, and it took thirty minutes to drop fully away. Marco took over, throttling down and turned the transport toward a broad runway among bleak mountains. Touching down next to large hangars which seemed untouched, Marco unlatched himself. Jeffrey did the same and walked into the back. The pilots were unbuckling from their jump seats and stretching their backs and legs.

"All right folks," Jeffrey said, "There may be service personnel here, so let's tread carefully. The last thing we need is to get shot by our own people."

"Yes, sir," they all said.

Kodiak flipped the side door latch, shoved the door open, and stepped out. Everyone followed him into the heat of the Arizona evening. Jeffrey found himself standing on a broad swath of old tarmac, and he felt at home there among the looming hangars with their hundreds of high, square-paned windows and towering, sliding-panel doors. None of the field lights had come on with the twilight. Jeffrey was glad of that as he listened to the airfield. The breeze caught in a windsock nearby flopping the nylon.

Jogging over to the nearest hangar, he heard one hundred and two boots beating the pavement behind him, which took him back to the good old days of service before the first war when he'd signed up for what should have been a quick four years before college. He'd get stronger, do something involving machines, and move on. But, the attack on Demos had changed everything.

Reaching the hangar, he looked to the tops of the towering doors and back down. The tracks for the massive doors were set in concrete. He gripped the handle and shoved. It shifted, but only just.

"Help me with this folks."

The pilots, putting their palms on the door, shoved together. The door slid sideways with a deep resonation. When it had opened a few feet, Jeffrey walked into the dim light, motioning for everyone to follow him The coming twilight cast a crosshatched shadow high up. Down low, all lay in darkness. There he saw the angled shapes of Lakota. An unsettling burnt stench pervaded the air.

Despite the disease the smell caused him, Jeffrey patted Whitetip on the back. "Step one of phase one is done. Now let's get some fuel and find the tankers."

"Where do you think everyone is?" She asked.

"There are a lot of possibilities," Jeffrey said as he walked over to the first Lakota, "They might have…" but his words faded away as the stench grew stronger, a smell he knew all too well, burned hair with a rotten back-note. Taking out a flashlight, he played it around the aircraft. Each and every Lakota's cockpit glass had been blown out, the edges melted away. Beyond that lay a dark pile. He walked past the ruined ships. The pile shown colorlessly in the light, grays, whites, and blacks. He saw long shapes with jointed ends and the half curve of a jaw bone. He played the flashlight over the expanse of bodies, the scent now overwhelming.

"Oh my God," Whitetip said beside him.

Springbok said, "Now we know where the personnel are."

Kodiak walked up beside Jeffrey, one of the few people Jeffrey actually looked straight across at, and said in his Viking heritage accent, "It would seem they were one step ahead of us."

"Which means we're jammed up," Springbok said.

"So what now?" Whitetip asked.

"We keep looking," Jeffrey said. "This hangar is destroyed, but that doesn't mean they all are." He looked around. "Our intel was for a classified installation of Lakota, but this is a well-known base out in the open. I wonder if there is another location nearby. Someplace that would not be known, not findable."

Jeffrey played his flashlight back over the corpses. "I want to check the administration offices." As they left the hangar for the cooling desert air, Jeffrey felt glad to be away from the stench of charred flesh.

He assigned three groups to search hangars. "Marco come with me to the admin building."

The door of the building stood partially open and half bent with a scorch mark on the outside. Jeffrey pulled it open with a metal-on-metal screech that echoed across the airfield. He listened for some time. He had no idea if there were Sthenos nearby, or if they had some kind of sensors on the base, but his gut told him, with an entire planet to dominate, they'd moved on.

Jeffrey stepped into the pitch-black office area, playing his flashlight across overturned desks, broken chairs, and a shattered water cooler. A glitter caught the light. Jeffrey walked over and crouched down over a woman's patent leather flat.

Marco said, "There's no power for the computers."

"No," Jeffrey stood beside him, "and we wouldn't want to fire them up if we could. That could bring the world down around our ears."

"So what do we do now?"

Jeffrey had his head down in thought. "I have no idea."

"There," Marco said simply.

"Where?" Jeffrey said looking around the room.

"I think we should check that shed."

"Shed?" Jeffrey looked to Marco who was pointing out the window. To the south of the admin building Jeffrey saw a simple sheet metal shed. Someone had spray painted the word 'HERE' on its side.

"That's odd," Jeffrey said.

"Exactly."

Going to the shed, they pulled open the door to find grounds keeping equipment. The interior, smelling of cut grass and algal fuel, still held the heat of the day. Jeffrey played the flashlight inside. The hand tools lay in a jumble against the back wall as though someone had thrown them there in great haste. Through the crossed handles of a shovel and a rake, Jeffrey saw more red spray paint. They both began throwing tools aside. Shovel heads clattered and rubberized handles thumped on the asphalt floor.

When they'd cleared everything away, they found two sets of words, but they were gibberish. The pattern was the same. Two nonsensical words, a degree symbol, two more words, then a minute symbol. Two more words and a seconds symbol.

"They're GPS coordinates," Jeffrey said.

"Exactly," Marco said, "Here you have 'ereht' and 'rofu' for the degrees. Anagrams. Three & four. Thirty-four."

"The Sthenos have little to no knowledge of our language, so it's a quick code to keep them from knowing what's what."

"Looks like they didn't even find it."

"So someone left us a location."

"Must be important."

"Let's hope it has what we need."

Marco played his flashlight down to the floor where a dark swath trailed away to the door. Jeffrey and Marco had been so focused on the interior of the shed, they hadn't realized they'd walked through blood. "Looks like," Marco said, "our code talker got caught."

...

Out on the tarmac, the twilight had faded to night. With no moon, the milky way arched over the horizons. Each team returned in the cooling air with the same report. All aircraft had been destroyed in all hangars.

"The first hangar appears to have been where all the personnel were gathered before being executed," Whitetip said. "No other structures held bodies."

When Jeffrey heard that, he knew something was wrong.

"How many people served on this base?" he asked the group. No one knew.

"Not enough bodies?" Marco asked him.

"Exactly, not nearly enough to account for a base this big, which means that a good amount were either taken or escaped."

Springbok spoke up again, "The burned bodies are higher ranking officers. I saw no enlisted insignia."

"Strange…" Jeffrey fell into thought. After a moment, he said, "That means they either didn't understand our ranking structure, which is doubtful, or weren't looking for hostages."

"Maybe they culled authority," Marco said. "Don't take anyone who'll rally the troops."

"Perhaps," Jeffrey said, "but I'm thinking more about age. Higher ranks go with longer terms of service. My gut tells me they're collecting the younger and killing off the older."

"Which lends itself to your theory of slavery," Whitetip said.

"Exactly." Jeffrey walked toward Marco's transport. "Let's get rolling."

"Where?" Whitetip asked as she jogged to catch up.

"To follow a treasure map."

...

After they'd loaded up, Marco flew into the darkness, his face glowing with the light of the instruments. The coordinates led them east into the mountains. Hills worn low with age lay shadowy in the rising moon, mottled with dark patches of mesquite and sage. After Marco touched down in a canyon, they filed off the transport. The walls of the canyon framed the night sky.

Looking at the mountains, Marco said, "I feel as though, at any moment, Sthenos fighters could come over those ridges and go to guns on us."

"They could," Jeffrey said.

In the dim light, Marco nodded.

Jeffrey said, "Scan the area folks. Look for anything unnatural, any evidence of an aircraft facility."

Fanning out, their shapes faded into the black. Deep-red flashlights came on one at a time and played through the scrub oak.

"We might have to wait for daylight to find it," Jeffrey said.

"I thought you wanted to be back in South America before morning."

"We work with what we have." Jeffrey clicked on his flashlight. "Let's take a walk."

After an hour of searching, Jeffrey called them back to the transport. When they'd all come aboard, Jeffrey lifted the ramp a few feet off the ground.

"That will keep the scorpions and tarantulas out. Now get some sleep."

After the pilots had settled down shoulder to shoulder, Jeffrey sat on the end of the ramp watching them. Some drifted off to sleep, others lay with the faint whites of their eyes glowing in the darkness. These were solid men and women, quick to settle down. Jeffrey stretched his shoulders as he considered that strength is as much the ability to stay calm internally, put emotions aside to find stillness, as it is the ability to drive forward and kill, perhaps more so. He lay down, drew his breath in through his nose, and let it filter out his mouth. His mind tried to draw him back to the Lakota, the Sthenos, Leif, Sarah, Stacy. Each time, he'd let his breath out and whatever it was on his mind with it. Soon he fell into a dreamless sleep.

CHAPTER 43

Leif sat in the darkness listening to the crick and drone of insects in the rainforest. Now and again, leaves shuffled in the darkness. He'd found he preferred the late hours of the night. Only in the quiet darkness could he settle his mind. He was used to ice samples and metallic casings, not projects that screamed and writhed… and died. Since his father had assigned him to the Hammerhead project, he hadn't been able to sleep well. He'd lay awake imagining all the things that could go wrong, and when those thoughts faded, he'd worry about what was happening to the human race. Every delay in his work felt as though he was responsible for the death or imprisonment of thousands if not millions more.

In the heart of the rainforest, with birds singing and a breeze shifting through branches, he could feel the world ending beyond the hills. On the second day of their project, he couldn't breathe. His hands went numb and he felt dizzy. Caterina had told him he was having a panic attack and given him a strong sedative. He'd woken at dusk drenched in sweat. How many had died from that delay? He spent the rest of the night working by the light of an electric lamp.

The next day, Caterina told him to rest. He hadn't stopped since the night before. He refused. There was no time. He woke to darkness, the pattern of the container he had passed out on stamped painfully into his forearm. Rubbing his arm, he stared into the darkness. A bat, pinging the air with sharp high-pitched cricks, flicked at his hair. As he breathed in the scent of rich loam, his heart stilled. His eyes became heavy, and he went to his tent, collapsed on his mattress, and fell into a dead sleep.

Each night since that time, he'd waited until others had gone to sleep, before turning out the lights and sitting in the darkness, letting ancient rhythms slow his mind. He'd slept well ever since. At first he'd considered it merely quieted his mind, but in truth he found a great comfort in the age of the things in the forest. Life had been going on for millennia, and it would continue to do so despite the Sthenos. Someday this would be studied by students as he had studied the sacking of Rome. He'd wake the next day feeling refreshed, but the thought of the Sthenos would immediately shove its way in and leaden his heart.

Tonight, he sat in the darkness on a crate, the humid breeze carrying the scent of rubber tree sap and orchids. A shuffling of leaves came from far off to his left, growing louder and louder. A person walking.

Moonlight, breaking free of the clouds, filtered in among the trees. He had the strange feeling he'd fallen asleep, that this was a dream. The figure of a woman came into the clearing, her hair in a pony tail. The moonlight glowed faintly on her white lab coat.

Leif's heart raced, and he felt cold despite the warm breeze. He could scarcely draw enough breath to whisper, "Sarah?" The specter shape of the woman continued toward him, seeming to float in the dim light on graceful, sweeping legs.

"Leif?" Caterina's voice, coming from the figure, shifted her into reality. What the darkness had allowed him to add, straight, red hair and a pale face where there were dark waves and olive skin, vanished. She sat beside him and put her hand on his back. "Why are you still awake?"

"I have to sit and let the day go, or I can't sleep."

"I am so sorry," she said. "Should I go?"

He wanted to be alone, but when she made no move to leave, he said, "No please stay, it's fine."

"Still not sleeping," Caterina said, brushing at his hair.

"Better than before."

Caterina's gentle, cool hands, took his face on either side. "You are working yourself too hard." The softness of her lips surprised him as they pressed into his. Her nails traced up his neck into his hair.

Leif took hold of her wrists and pulled her hands away, anger burning. He was a married man, at least he still felt like a married man.

A flare of desire boiled up through the anger. He'd worked with her for the last two weeks day in and day out, and had found her to be a warm and intelligent woman. Younger than him, but mature, and he more than once had been caught stealing glances at her, which undoubtedly had lead to her boldness tonight. This weighted his anger and desire with heavy guilt.

He folded her hands into her own lap. "You're wonderful Caterina, really amazingly beautiful, but…"

"But you do not like me? I do not believe I misunderstood how you look at me."

In that, Leif regretted not having told her about Sarah. He'd been unable to speak of her. Caterina knew only that he was Holt's son, had led the development of the singularity warheads, and had been one of two men to survive Europa base.

"My wife…" He fell silent, unable to say it.

"Oh my God," she whispered, hands going to her mouth. "She was on Europa with you."

He looked at his empty left ring finger. "I forgot my ring on the bathroom counter that morning."

She let out a sigh, and he felt the flutter of the air from her breath on the backs of his hands. "Oh Leif." She pressed her palm into his chest. "Your poor heart." She took hold of the sides of his face again, and she leaned close. He closed his eyes, hoping she wouldn't kiss him again yet wanting to feel that soft warmth at the same time. She tilted his head down, and her lips pressed into his forehead.

As he opened his eyes, she smiled and said, "I've never know anyone like you."

"Not too many strange men around your home town?"

"You are not strange," she said, a strictness coming into her tone. "You are intelligent, gentle, handsome, ugh..." Her hand flicked toward the darkness as if shooing something away.

"What?"

She let out a small laugh. "I've held flames before, but you... you are something different to me. It seems the flame might burn my hands if I hold it too long. I feel rushed, as if I have no time."

Leif had no idea what to say to that, so he went with someone else's words. "It can't be rushed Caterina. Love's not Time's fool, and doesn't change with its brief hours and weeks, but bears it out even to the edge of doom."

"Where does that come from?"

"A hack job on Shakespeare."

"What does it mean to you?"

"That I'll love Sarah until the day I die, and when we fix this," he held out his hand to the world beyond the dark forest, "there will be time for..." but he couldn't bring himself to say more.

She kissed the back of his hand, causing his chest to flush with heat.

Standing, she said, "I hope you sleep well, Leif."

Caught between wishing she would go and wanting her to stay, he said nothing. As she walked away, he felt he should say something, something about how much he enjoyed her company, how beautiful... but every possibility seemed a betrayal of Sarah.

CHAPTER 44

At dawn Jeffrey sent one team south and a second, which he joined, north. After they'd walked along the sandy floor of the steep-sided canyon a quarter-mile, Jeffrey stopped, crossed his arms, and stared at the wall.

"That's unnatural."

The cliff face, still in the cool shadows, met the canyon floor at a 90 degree angle. The wall had a huge, unshapely rectangular depression in it. As they walked up to the wall, the crunch of gravel vanished.

Crouching, Kodiak touched the ground.

"Concrete."

Jeffrey tugged at the leaves of a scrub oak. "These are artificial."

He pressed his hand to the cliff face. It was metal airbrushed to look like rock. He wrapped his knuckles against it. The surface gave the unyielding clack of blast-plate-thick steel.

Marco ran his hand along the wall. "That's an impressive paint job."

"I agree," Jeffrey said. "Now we have to figure how to get it open." Jeffrey went still. He'd heard the shifting of fabric. He looked up the canyon to where the western wall had collapsed creating a long scree slope spotted with scrub oak and mesquite.

Looking back to Marco and Kodiak, he slipped his fingertips across his neck to quiet them before focusing his attention higher up the scree slope. The sound had come from there. About two-hundred yards away, he saw a pile of mesquite and sage leaves—a gillie suit. In the center of the bush, muted by a high-end coating, he saw the tiny disk of a sniper's scope.

"I see you," Jeffrey whispered.

In a whisper, Marco asked, "You see who?"

"Him." Jeffrey waved his hand at the scope.

A voice called out, echoing off the narrow cliff walls, "Pretty good old man, but see me or not, I still have crosshairs on you. Time for you and yours to leave." The voice had a slow cadence and a depth that sounded Navaho to Jeffrey.

"I'd like to talk. We need your help."

"There's nothin' here for you. Now go find someone else to bother."

Jeffrey called out, "We've come for aircraft. I'm Fleet Admiral Holt of the U.S. Navy."

"What ship?"

"The last ship I served on was the U.S.S. Lacedaemon."

"Bullshit. The Lacedaemon was destroyed."

"I know," Jeffrey said. "We rode it into the ground."

The sniper made no reply, the dark disk of his scope remaining absolutely still.

"We need Lakotas," Jeffrey called out. "We went to Turnbull airfield. All the aircraft there have been destroyed. How many are you here?"

"Not going to give that up right now, sir," the man said. "What'd you want with Lakotas?"

"I'm willing to discuss that fully, but not in your crosshairs. Are you willing to assist us?" Jeffrey gave the man time to think. In the quiet, he heard a scratching sound at his feet. He looked down. A tarantula moved with slow, reaching legs over his boot. With a shudder he flicked it away.

He called out, "I don't have a lot of time, airman."

"Marine."

"I don't have a lot of time, Marine. I need to get back to our center of operations with aircraft and fuel within the next 24 hours. Do you have fuel?"

"Enough for me, sir."

Enough for me? "I take it you aren't as willing to share as I'd hope."

"The world's over, sir. I have water and food inside, enough to last me for years."

"So you won't let us in?"

"No."

"What if I give you my word that we won't touch your food and water supplies?"

When the Marine laughed, his scope shifted. "I won't let you touch the fuel either."

"That's unfortunate."

"Perhaps, but it's still time for you to leave. You're in the scope of an AX50, sir. You'll be the first to die."

"Easy Marine," Jeffrey said, lifting his hands. "I know this looks like the end of times." Jeffrey actually had no idea what it looked like. The current moment appeared to be a peaceful southwestern day, aside from the fact his chest was one finger pull away from being blown out.

"Get the hell out of here," the Marine said. "I won't say it again."

"Look," Jeffrey said, "do you really want to hide in this bunker and let the world burn?"

"Yes."

"Why do you say the world's over?"

"Everything's gone. The fleets are destroyed. The military bases scraped off the face of the Earth. The aliens flicked 'em away like a fly from their shoulder. It's hopeless."

"It's not hopeless."

"Sir," Marco said, "Maybe we should back off."

"It's okay, Fields," Jeffrey whispered, "He doesn't want to kill me. He's talking too much." To the Marine, he said, "I've seen them put in their place before."

"Yeah." A nervous laugh echoed down the canyon. "You'd be just about old enough wouldn't you? But I call bullshit. What would you know about the war?"

"I fought in it."

"What'd you do? Wax floors? Admirals never worked for a living."

"I was a Hammerhead."

The scope shifted down. Through the leaves he could see a small portion of the anti-glare surface of sniper's goggles.

"Not buyin' it. Next you'll be tellin' me… wait… did you say you're name was Holt?"

"Yes."

At that the pile of leaves sat up and resolved into the semblance of a human form. A tangle of sticks and leaves crowned the Marine's head, and a tan rag covered his face. As he settled into a reclined shooter's position, he retrained his rifle, draped with leaves, on Jeffrey. He lowered his head back into the scope. Jeffrey saw the rifle shift and stop, shift and stop.

"Who are they?"

"These are my Hammerheads."

The Marine came out of his scope. "No shit, really?" He brought the gun to bear on Jeffrey again. "So what do we do from here?"

Jeffrey shrugged. "That's up to you. You were protecting your installation as you should. You don't know us from Adam. But now that you do, lower your weapon and come down here."

The Marine stayed in his gun.

"Are you going to come down?"

"Not sure yet."

"Okay," Jeffrey said. The Marine didn't want to kill him. Looking over his shoulder to his group, Jeffrey said, "I'm going up there. No one moves. Is that clear?"

"Yes, sir," came their replies.

Jeffrey walked across the level area in front of the metal wall.

"What're you doing?" the Marine called down from his roost.

"Coming up to talk."

"Stand down, sir. I will fire."

"I'm banking you won't." Jeffrey made his way up the scree slope.

The Marine looked like a fat bush sitting upright in his gillie suit. Muttering something, he came out of his gun, the barrel lowering to the side.

Jeffrey reached the Marine, who sat with his knees splayed and the rifle's muzzle brake resting on his boot. He held his index finger on the trigger guard.

"We done?" Jeffrey asked.

The flat-black lenses of the Marine's goggles stared at Jeffrey through errant leaves. With a shrug, he shifted forward, stood, and shouldered the rifle.

As he began walking down the slope, the Marine asked, "How'd you see me, boss?"

"I heard you first. Then I saw the end of your scope."

Jeffrey watched the mask of goggles and fabric, but he could see in the downturned head that the Marine was thinking through his art. "The end of the scope? Bullshit." Appearing to realize the impropriety of his comment, he said, "Sorry, sir."

Jeffrey shrugged.

"You got pretty good eyes, sir. That part of what they did to you?"

"Exactly."

"I'd a' had you if I wanted you."

"That's a fact... What's your name?"

"Corporal Tsosie, sir."

"Navajo?"

"Yes sir."

When they reached the group, the Marine shifted his rifle to his left shoulder and pressed on the cliff wall. A panel turned over, revealing a touch pad. He pressed in a code and, leaning close, said something into the panel.

"When the door comes open," Jeffrey said to his people, "keep everything easy. Understood?"

"Yes, sir," the men and women said.

The panel rolled shut as Tsosie walked to Jeffrey, which Jeffrey took as a good sign. In an ambush, Tsosie would have stayed casually to the side, not joined them in the line of fire. Still he could bolt and run.

A bedrock-deep thump came through Jeffrey's boots followed by the low thrumming of a large motor. The wall split open along a vertical seam.

Inside, wire-basketed lamps hung from a high ceiling, illuminating the first ten yards or so of the interior. The lights beyond were switched off, and darkness reigned deeper in. In the deadness of the air beyond, Jeffrey sensed the space went deep into the canyonside. As the doors opened further, they exposed several Marines wearing helmets and ceramic, dragon-plate body armor. The gray-haired Marine in the center held a rifle at his chest, muzzle down. The others had their rifles trained on Jeffrey and his group. The gray haired Marine walked out into the sunlight.

"Master Sergeant Eric Mikelson, sir."

"Master Sergeant," Jeffrey said with a nod.

"So you claim to be Jeffrey Holt."

"I am."

He stared at Jeffrey, as if weighing him, before saying, "Not buyin' it."

Jeffrey offered no response.

"My father flew and died with Jeffrey Holt. If you're Holt, you'll know his call sign."

With that the name Mikelson shone in Jeffrey's memory like sun through storm clouds. Of course he'd known Mikelson. They'd all known Mikelson. Anyone who'd fought with the Hammerheads for even a short period of time had had their ass saved at least once by him. How could a gray haired master sergeant be the son of Nate Mikelson? But it'd been so many years… so many decades and time slips by so damn fast. Sure his son would have to be about this guy's age if he'd been born before the war.

"Did you know your dad?"

"No. I only have photos."

"He was… an amazing pilot and a good man."

"I didn't ask for generalities."

"Nate, his name was Nate Mikelson."

The hardness in the Master Sergeant's eyes diminished somewhat, but still he said, "I didn't ask for his name. I asked for his call sign."

"His call sign was Great White."

CHAPTER 45

Master Sergeant Mikelson motioned for Jeffrey to enter the hangar. As Jeffrey's eyes adjusted to the darkness he saw, parked row after row into the distance of the huge underground space, scores of Lakota. With them the glimmer of hope he'd felt, rushed into full life.

"How many do you have?" Jeffrey asked Mikelson.

"Two hundred Lakota and twenty C240 fuelers."

"Twenty?"

Mikelson nodded, his expression blank. Jeffrey took him by the shoulders. "That's the best news I've heard in the last three weeks." He looked over his shoulder to the some fifty Marines he saw standing behind him. "The only way it could be better is if you tell me that they're pilots."

"All, sir. The pilots remained here to utilize the Lakota if needed."

"They any good?"

"They're decent for Marine pilots," Mikelson said with a shrug, "but compared to Navy pilots they're amazing." With that a smile broke out across his face, and he laughed. "Admiral Holt, I'd like to formally offer our services to your command. I'm tired of hiding."

"I appreciate that more than I can say. You have," Jeffrey asked, "some fifty pilots here?"

"Here? Yes, fifty."

Jeffrey no longer had to split his force between Wraiths and Lakota. He'd have more in space for the final assault on the last Sthenos destroyer, and more for clean up.

As Mikelson said, "But," Jeffrey held his hope carefully, "this is only one group. I've got them on duty in shifts. I have another one hundred bunked down and fifty in the back at mess."

"Two hundred?"

"A total of two hundred one including me."

Jeffrey hugged him.

...

Mikelson walked out the main door of the base into the afternoon heat of the canyon. The day had progressed quickly with flight preparations, yet he felt drained. Like a boulder falling in a still lake, the sudden appearance of Holt had dashed his thoughts into a diffused mess.

Most young boys grew up interested in stories of super heroes. The only stories Eric Mikelson had grown up asking his mother to tell were of his father. She would tell him about meeting him, falling in love. She would tell him how strong he'd been and how sweet—he'd pick up roses for her on Fridays. None of that, however, is what Eric wanted to hear.

Whenever he asked about his father's military career, she'd find some distraction to pull her away. He'd resented her for it, but he'd been resourceful. At sixteen, he'd gone to the Navy recruiter's office in town. He told the recruiter he wanted to meet someone who could tell him about his father. The recruiter had taken his number and asked what he had planned after high school.

"No idea," Eric had told him.

The recruiter seemed satisfied with that answer.

A week later the recruiter called. "Your father's service records have been sealed."

"Who sealed them?"

"That's not for us to know."

That had been the end of it.

Now, after so many years, he'd found a man who'd fought beside his father, perhaps been with him the day he died... and he couldn't muster the guts to ask him about it.

CHAPTER 46

They'd finished prepping the aircraft as the sky darkened and the first stars came out over the canyon. Jeffrey went through flight plans with Mikelson. With the added Marines, they would be bringing all the aircraft home. The fuelers would have copilots, leaving only twelve Lakota with additional pilots in the navigation officer's seat.

When they finished their discussion and briefed the pilots, Mikelson called out, "Crack it open." With a ground-shaking vibration, a large section of the cavern's ceiling dropped several feet toward them before rolling aside, exposing the twilight sky. Air rushing through the side door flushed the cavern with a desiccated desert fragrance, heated rock and cactus.

They'd filled the fuelers from the base's deep reserve tanks. The fueler teams would leave fifteen minutes apart for the next five hours. The extra time was painful, but the gaps were necessary to prevent any large signatures or obvious flight paths. The paired Lakota's would leave after, and due to being smaller, only ten minutes apart. Still, flight groups would be departing throughout the night.

Jeffrey would leave with the last fueler group, piloting one of the heavy busses as had been the plan.

An approaching Marine said, "Sir, request permission to take your fueler from you. You should be in one of the Lakotas. With your abilities, should we need you, you'll need to know one inside and out."

Jeffrey nodded his approval, fighting off a smile.

Mikelson assigned Jeffrey a pilot called Hooka to ride navigation with him.

Just before dawn, he sat in a Lakota cockpit with the young Marine as the last of the flights left. He didn't ask how Hooka came by his call sign.

The pilot of the other Lakota in Jeffrey's pair was a Marine, call sign Obsessed. As Jeffrey lifted the Lakota off its landing skids, he felt the knife sharp flight characteristics right away.

As they rose out of the hangar, the Lakota slipped sideways as if on ice.

Hooka said, "These things hover like water on hot grease. To get them to calm down you have…" But he fell silent as the Lakota went table still, and Jeffery turned it 360 degrees. He'd only needed a few moments to feel the plane under him before he understood it.

"Looks like you've got it," Hooka said with a slightly disgusted tone. "Do you know how long I had to train to get a Lakota to settle down?"

"Do you know how long I've been flying?"

Hooka gave a slight laugh. "Fair."

Shoving the throttle forward, Jeffrey barrel rolled one hundred feet off the ground. Hooka grunted against the maneuver, but made no complaint.

As they flew just off the deck, Hooka walked him through the two weapons systems the Lakota had been armed with. "First, we have the fifty cal machine gun, still the best way to put the hurt on something at close range."

"Fully gimballed?"

"Yes, the crosshairs on your helmet HUD target it. Second are the mambo proximity missiles. As you know, guided missiles don't work air-to-air anymore."

"Yes," Jeffrey said, "Too many effective countermeasures."

"The mambos work like old anti-aircraft guns."

"Flack?"

"Exactly. You need only detonate one within five hundred feet of your target to inflict critical damage. A payload of grenade-sized cluster warheads with armor piercing fragments deploys in a sphere on detonation. You spread a few of those into a tight flight pattern, and the whole thing goes up in smoke."

"Do we have anything with a bit more precision?"

"Not at the moment. We're set up for air-to-air. Figured we wouldn't be doing much bunker busting. No matter the payload, a Lakota couldn't scratch a Sthenos destroyer."

"I like it, but friendly fire might be a problem."

"The FOF system assures the mambo is far enough away from friendlies before detonation. You can shoot it right over the head of your lead and into a swarm of enemy fighters, and it won't detonate until it's reached a safe distance from you and yours."

Jeffrey fell into silence as the scenario Hooka had painted began to draw up old memories, which Jeffrey shoved aside.

They made their way across the southwest and back over the Gulf, Jeffrey taking a heading which would bring him just under Cuba before vectoring back toward Columbia. His wingman, Obsessed, stayed to his four o'clock. As Jeffrey looked in the mirror at the bladed shape of the Lakota behind him, he wondered how the kid was doing. He wished he could key his mic, talk with him a bit. As he watched the shape of the Lakota, it bloomed into a ball of fire. Jeffrey, unable to understand what he'd seen, thought for a moment he'd had a full-blown PTSD reaction. He'd had a few incidents in his life, memories that stopped him short, but they'd never been visceral. He'd always known they were only memories. He'd heard of those whose memories came back so hard they found themselves literally reliving their worst moments, but not him... never that bad.

As Hooka said, "Bogies at seven, five, six high and six low, sir," Jeffrey's rational mind wouldn't take hold of it. They'd have died in that moment, as Obsessed had, but his lizard brain, reacting without rational thought, had the Lakota on its side pulling hard. Jeffrey clenched his legs and his belly as he huffed air and hauled on the ship. He heard Hooka say something muddy, then nothing. He'd gone out, while Jeffrey had pulled more than sixteen G's and had only developed perhaps a thirty percent visual tunnel.

He could kill unmodified Hooka doing that.

He throttled on and the airspeed rolled up from six hundred to eight and then a 1,000 and then 1,200 and then 1,400. Slowing, he curved in, his mind settling into the situation. The Sthenos had found them.

"What the hell?" Hooka asked in a confused tone.

"Grip it," Jeffrey said, and he heard Hooka huffing. Jeffrey pulled hard to the right. As he came around, he fired a missile blindly into the space he'd just occupied even before he saw the Sthenos fighters flashing through it. The lancing missile exploded in a football shape. Then, like a firework on the fourth of July, a series of secondary explosions flashed magnesium-bright. The flight of Sthenos fighters had been at the edge of that cloud, four... there'd been four in a tight diamond. Two bloomed black smoke and crashed in arcing white sprays into the clear-blue ocean.

There were two more. He scanned his instruments.

"Jesus Holt, quit knocking me out," Hooka said.

"You want to be conscious or alive?"

"Alive. Now let me target them before you do anything."

Jeffrey flipped the Lakota around and arced away at seven G's Hooka growling, to stay conscious in the back. He switched left, a bit up, crossed over. As the sun swept by his field of vision the helmet dimmed automatically.

"Nice."

As he waited for Hooka to paint him a target, an energy beam lanced through the space he'd jigged out of. Tipping the Lakota on its side, he shoved the control stick forward, almost redding out with negative G's as another bright-green beam lanced by the cockpit within a few feet. As they pulled away from it, Jeffrey flipped his ship on its left wing and slammed on the air brakes, turning hard, probably taking Hooka back into unconsciousness again. Jeffrey offered a silent apology for what he was doing to the poor bastard.

He let go of the G's a bit and Hooka came back to him. "I've got him," he said, sounding tired despite the moment's intensity.

Jeffrey gave him a lot of credit for being able to go completely out three times in a row and come right back to task. Most would have no idea where they were. "The trace is on your screen now."

Jeffrey saw his ship on the screen as a bright green dot and the Sthenos ship as a glowing red marker. Jeffrey flipped the ship into an inverted dive and a pen flew by his face and slapped into the top of the canopy. He flipped over, caught the pen with his left hand, and stuck it to his chest loop patch as he centered his reticule and gripped the main cannon trigger. Tracers lanced away from the cannon, meeting the Sthenos ship as it passed through where Jeffrey had guessed the pilot would go. A yellow ball of fire, born in the engines, ate the ship in a thousand millisecond bites, before pluming outward.

Jeffrey pulled away, searching for the final target.

"You must have hit something pretty vital for—"

"Where's the fourth bogey? Give me something to kill."

Jeffrey heard and felt the bang before he saw the dark shape whip right past his canopy close enough to touch. Scraps of metal scattered by with it.

In an incredulous tone, Hooka said, "He ran into us."

"Yep, that wasn't intentional or we'd be dead. He screwed up." Jeffrey'd never seen a Sthenos make an error like that. These guys were definitely limited in atmospheric dog fighting.

The stick shuddered in his hand. As the nose dropped, he pulled back. His artificial horizon stayed down. The entire ship began to shake as warning lights lit the dashboard.

"We've lost both engines," Hooka said, "Nothing left but to punch it. Get us slowed down."

The ship had already lost a lot of speed and Jeffrey waited for the indicator to go sub-mach before he hit the airbrake. His straps hauled on him. The airspeed dropped to four hundred, three hundred, two hundred.

"Punch it," Jeffrey said.

In the mirror, he saw Hooka's arms reach up over his head and haul down on the yellow and black handles. A bang was followed by a savage wind, which cracked at Jeffrey's flight suit and tore at his face sucking the breath from his lungs. He released the controls, pulled his feet in, and gripped his harness to keep his arms in place.

The cockpit filled with smoke as Hooka's seat rocketed away. Jeffrey had ejected once before. He thought he remembered how hard the acceleration was, but he'd been kidding himself. The seat crushed into him as the cockpit vanished, leaving blurring blue. Another bang and an ass smacking sensation was followed by his seat falling away. The wind stilled as he went weightless, hanging out over the broad, sun-glittering Gulf. As he began to fall, the air rushed around him again. A tremendous blustering of nylon surrounded him, crack-cracked, and his chute straps hauled on him.

He found himself floating in silence, the whine of the Lakota's sputtering turbines fading away before it crashed into the water with a concussion of spray.

CHAPTER 47

After cutting away from his chute forty feet up, Jeffrey had crashed feet first into the depth of the water and sank. His ears popped as he sank. The life raft did not auto inflate as it should have. As he fumbled for the location to the cord, his ears spiked with pain and the water became deeper blue. Sinking deeper his lungs began to burn and he felt panic tickling at the back of his mind. He stopped searching for the cord and went still, the weight of his flight gear dragging him down.

Where had the cord been? See it. Small rib. Left.

His hand went to his side, and he felt the marble-sized plastic ball attached to a cord. He yanked on it. A roar erupted behind him as he felt the shape of the back raft form a perimeter behind him. The water went lighter. He broke the surface, settling onto his back, gasping a deep lungful of air. When he'd cleared the saltwater from his eyes, he saw Hooka not far off, floating with his head back as if unconscious.

At least his raft had auto-inflated as it should have.

With a sweep of his feet, Jeffrey turned his back to Hooka and kicked his way over. In the paleness of Hooka's skin and the slight gap of his mouth, Jeffrey understood he was dead. As Hooka rocked, blood trailed away from him in the clear-blue water.

Jeffrey gripped Hooka's shoulder, pulled him close, and placed his hand on the young pilot's chest.

"I'm sorry I didn't fly well enough."

He went through the young man's pockets, taking his water and nutrient bricks. Turning the body around, he went through the other pockets, taking everything out and laying it on his own belly like a sea otter.

Lastly, he put one of Hooka's dog tags in his chest pocket, turned himself, and shoved off the body with both feet. Kicking away in casual, easy sweeps, he moved away from the plume of blood that Hooka had left in the water. He continued at an easy pace until Hooka was a distant shape. He didn't need any sharks finding him after getting worked up over the blood.

Sipping at the water, he considered his location. They'd travelled approximately halfway across the gulf, headed for the Yucatan Peninsula. Beneath his back lay nearly two miles of water. The depth felt malicious, the rocking of the easy swell deceptively pleasant, putting him at ease before it killed him.

Jeffrey had lived through so much that, when he told the young pilots that anyone lost could not be saved, he hadn't considered it would be him. But it was, and there would be no location beacon, no last known position, and no rescue team, as was the plan.

He thought of the Sthenos ships that had taken them down. He'd given somewhat better than he'd gotten, but had any of the other pilots encountered resistance? Perhaps all? It was possible the Sthenos had tracked them the entire way. The Lacedaemon crash site had been left alone, perhaps not because the Sthenos were unworried about the possibility of resistance, but because they'd had them in crosshairs the entire time. He thought back to how quickly they'd lost the first and second engagements and felt intense despair. Had the Sthenos swatted them aside once again?

CHAPTER 48

The Lakota pilots, after spending their allotted three days in secondary locations, began arriving in the Amazon at dawn, which relieved Leif and, he felt sure, the rest of the personnel. Captain Donovan had coordinated the clearing of small landing zones, but as more and more Lakota came in, they realized the cleared forest wouldn't be enough. Donovan ordered brush to be cut away and the uneven ground leveled with axes and shovels. The aircraft were rolled into those spaces under the canopy. After several hours, the men and women, backs soaked with sweat, had all the landing sites packed with aircraft.

When the slower fuelers came in on broad wings hulking downward as if great vultures with shoulders hunched up around squat necks, Donovan ordered the marine, who identified himself as Master Sergeant Eric Mikelson, to have the fuelers land in the clearings beside the Lacedaemon until more suitable landing zones could be cleared. As the fuelers' turbines faded beyond the tree tops, the forest fell into an ear-ringing silence.

Aiming his thumb at Leif, Donovan said to Mikelson, "This is Holt's son," then said to Leif, "Your dad's already briefed the master sergeant on the overall mission."

"Where is he?" Leif asked.

In an obtuse tone, Donovan said, "Don't know."

"I thought I heard someone say all the Lakotas were accounted for."

Donovan shrugged. "I can't help you with that."

Mikelson glanced at Leif and then to Donovan. "Sir, we have everyone accounted for aside from Obsessed, Hooka, and Admiral Holt."

"Three aircraft?" Leif asked.

Mikelson shook his head. "Two. Hooka was back seat with the admiral."

Leif looked to the sky beyond the wide circle of branches. Hooka and Obsessed didn't strike him as very good call signs. He hoped the pilots themselves were better than their names.

"What do we do?" he asked.

"Nothing," Donovan said. "If they show, they show. If they don't, we move on with our plans."

Something in the way Donovan said *our plans* troubled Leif.

Donovan looked to Mikelson. "Master sergeant. I want to discuss other possible locations of aircraft and pilots."

"We have more than we bargained for here," Leif said.

"I was speaking to the master sergeant Mr. Holt, but I agree none the less, and those additional forces have me wondering how much more might we be able to muster. 200 fighters, more than we bargained for as you say, is still an insignificant contingent against the Sthenos."

Leif quelled the desire to ask Donovan what the hell he was thinking and walked away.

"Where are you going?" Donovan asked.

"I've got to get back to work. I have vats of suspensions to check on. We have more pilots to modify." But he had more than enough supplies prepared. He'd be dammed if he was going to let Donovan change gears on him.

...

Leif searched the encampment until he'd found Stacy and her team resting near an ancient rubber tree, its root system half hanging in the air as if suspended in time. He asked her to walk with him. A young woman had told Leif she'd seen Delaney go down the trail to the river. As he and Stacy made their way down the trail, the sound of the waterfall increased.

As they came into the grove, the air cooled with the fall's mist. The ten foot high falls ran clear, water bending over the lip of rock. Delaney stood beside the pool wrapping her hair in a faded towel. She wore a white T-shirt and BDU pants.

Her expression grew worried when she saw them. "Mr. Holt, Commander Zack, how can I be of help to you?"

"President Delaney, please, just call me Leif. She," he pointed his thumb over his shoulder, "is just Stacy for this conversation."

Samantha's eyes narrowed as she said, "Okay, Leif... Stacy. Call me Samantha."

"Samantha," Leif said, "my dad's missing."

Her brow furrowed. "He didn't return with the rest?"

"No."

"Should we—"

"He's on his own." Leif held up a hand. "That's how it is. I need to discuss Donovan."

Delaney's chin came up as though bracing herself. "What's he up to?"

"The moment he realized my father hadn't returned, he began changing strategies."

"Excuse me?"

"Now that we have 200 new fighters, he wants to try and collect more, get as many together as we can."

"Are you serious?" Stacy asked, her tone a mixture of incredulity and anger. "What the hell's he thinking? We'll lose the only thing we have that matters."

"Surprise," Samantha said in a matter-of-fact tone.

"Exactly."

Samantha, her hands on her hips, faded into deep thought for some time before saying, "This is bad."

CHAPTER 49

Jeffrey watched icy cirrus clouds, perhaps five miles up, forming in the colder reaches of the troposphere. With the sea floor two miles below, the clouds miles above, and his head light from limited food and water, he felt disconnected from the world. He'd spent the last three days wandering through memories, all the while his emergency transponder off. If he had turned it on, the Sthenos would likely be on him in a few hours, if not sooner. It would be suicide… unless he could take just one with him.

He put the idea in the back of his mind. The Lakota should be arriving in the Amazon from their secondary landing zones today. They'd have more than enough for the assault… if they hadn't all been shot down as he had.

Jeffrey lay his head back, letting his hands sink into the water. His lips were already cracking, and his eyes itched. Through his life he'd imagined many different ways to die, but dehydration had never been one of them.

After floating for a time, his mind gone still, he leaned onto the right buoyancy bag to look into the deep-blue water. Sunlight stretched down in wavering fans. While he'd made peace with his coming death, the unfinished fight troubled him.

He drew his pistol from his thigh pocket. Water drained from its barrel. It would still fire. The smaller nine millimeter bore made him wish he had his 1911. Crossing his arms on his chest he drew a deep breath, catching the scent of the wide open ocean, which would be his grave. The 9mm could spare him a worse end. If he waited to die, he might live for a week. He'd either be found by sharks or, more likely, would die half crazy, thinking his wife was still alive, or that he was the King of England.

The sun sparkled on the water all around him.

Working the pistol's slide, he chambered a round and looked at the gun as though it were a foul medicine, bitter but necessary. He'd known several who'd taken their own lives after the war. He sighed. Those were, to him, the greatest tragedies. Having felt the suffocating weight of the mistakes he'd made and the unworthiness of having survived, he understood their choice but wished they could have found another way.

Samantha Delaney came to mind. Despite their rocky beginnings, he felt as though he'd missed something special in her, another possibility now lost.

In a different lifetime perhaps...

He rocked the slide back, leaving the pistol's hammer cocked and said to himself, "I won't let myself go insane. That leaves me only one option."

Reaching up to his shoulder, he snapped on his emergency transponder.

CHAPTER 50

Leif stepped into the command tent and found Captain Donovan sitting on a storage container beside Commander Holloway.

"You asked to see me?" Leif asked.

"Where's Zack?" Captain Donovan asked with irritation.

"I don't know," Leif said. "Shall we wait for her?"

Donovan nodded as though he couldn't be bothered to waste words on Leif and pointed to a container.

Leif contemplated not sitting. He felt sure Donovan was about to usurp everything his father had put into place. Deciding the moment to fight back had yet to come, he sat and waited.

In a few moments Stacy came in, eyes narrowed and jaw tight. She squared on Donovan and asked, "What the hell's going on?"

"Commander," Donovan said in a tone which weighed her rank against his, "you will be seated. The nature of this meeting will be discussed when all parties are present."

Stacy did not move. "Whom are we waiting for?"

"Zack," Donovan said, pointing to the crate beside Leif, "sit down, or I will have you put in your seat."

President Delaney came in.

"Good," Donovan said as he stood. He indicated where he would like Delaney to sit, and she did so.

"Thank you all for coming. I've asked each of you to be here because you all have specific interests." He looked to Leif. "Holt, you hold the reigns of the Hammerhead program, which we all agree is a critical part of our plans. Zack, you are the highest ranking officer for guerilla warfare in our group," He turned to Samantha, "You are our representative of the United States government."

"I'm a bit more than just a representative," Samantha said.

"A politician in a time of war…" He shrugged, not finishing the thought.

Samantha leaned forward. "I'm not sure how I feel about your tone."

Donovan gave an easy smile as he held up a hand. "There's no need for argument. All will be clear in a moment."

At that Leif felt any slight glimmer of hope fade into darkness. This would go down the hard way.

"I've gathered you here to ensure we are on the same page."

Stacy asked, "And which page is that?"

"I've considered the current situation, new forces having arrived, possible other forces available, and Admiral Holt lost… presumed dead."

"We've made no such assumption," Leif said.

"Your father instructed us to make that assumption for those who did not return. But I understand why you'd hold onto hope. That's precisely why those who are too close to an individual cannot be trusted to make good decisions, and you," he pointed to Leif, "the son, and you," he pointed to Stacy, "the daughter by proxy," he pointed to Samantha, "and you—"

"What is the point," Samantha cut him off, "you are doing such a poor job of getting to *Captain*?"

"You are all too close to him. You've bought into his plan too fully."

"It's a sound plan," Stacy said, "and if you'll recall it was *my* plan."

Leif nodded.

"In our opinion," he indicated Holloway, whose expression remained hard as her eyes met Leif's, "that plan is no longer our best option. We need a fresh approach. You," he pointed to Leif, "will continue modifying pilots." He spoke as though he'd given Leif a magnanimous gift.

"If we aren't moving forward with the singularity warheads," Samantha asked, "What do you propose we do?"

"We'll use the Lakota we have to seek out more military forces. When we have enough to form a full division, we'll begin an all-out attack on one Sthenos installation at a time."

Disgusted, Stacy slapped her hands on her thighs. "A war of attrition." She jabbed herself in the forehead with her index finger. "You've gotta get that big-war bullshit out of your head."

"Watch your tone Commander."

"I'll watch you get your ass beaten down before I let you run this into the ground. All you know is macro warfare. You're a fleet commander, and you," she said to Holloway, "what the hell are you doing backing this shit? You've already seen where it'll get us. Neither of you can think small enough to know how this needs to work. The Sthenos out tech us and now out mechanize us a thousand to one."

"I disagree," Donovan said. "I think—"

Stacy interrupted. "Do you disagree the last time we went head-to-head we got slapped across the ass hard enough to leave a mark?"

Samantha laughed at that.

Donovan eyes narrowed as he opened his mouth to speak, but Samantha held up a hand.

"As the president of the United States, I am the commander in chief of the military forces. While I appreciate your thoughts Donovan, we are going to move forward with Admiral Holt's plan."

Donovan yelled now, spittle flying from his reddening lips, "We will do *no* such thing. I refuse to recognize you as having any authority in this matter."

"Are you," Samantha asked, her tone calm, "refusing to obey your chain of command set forth by United States law?"

Donovan said through his teeth, "There is no more *United States*."

Leif saw doubt creep into Holloway's expression.

Stacy stood. "If there's no U.S. then there is no chain of command for me either."

"Stand down Zack," Donovan said.

She stepped forward. "On who's authority?"

Leif had had enough. He drew his father's Colt 1911 from his cargo pocket, ratcheted the slide, and leveled it on Donovan. "That's enough."

All eyes turned to him.

Stacy's eyes went a bit wide with surprise as she moved to the side.

Donovan said, "This is—"

"What?" Leif asked him, "Treason? You just refused a direct order from the president."

Donovan stood, a vein rising on his forehead. "Who do you think they'll follow? Power isn't based on a piece of paper or a gun, it's based on who they'll obey. You think that's going to be a technician who spent a soft four Army years at an electronics station?"

"So when my team doesn't follow you, and the Lakota pilots don't follow you," Stacy said, "you'll be creating a fracture that might lead to internal war."

"If it takes that, yes, but it will be you and yours creating the fracture."

"Excuse me," Leif said. "I'm the guy with the gun."

"I don't care if you have a—"

Leif yelled now, his voice finding its power and roots to his father. "You will when I label you a traitor and execute you. Now I want to know one thing right now, and know it fast." He looked to Holloway. "Where do you stand? Are you going to listen to the president? Or are you going to side with Donovan?"

Donovan looked to Holloway.

Holloway's jaw worked as her fingers gripped her knees. "This is a real problem." She looked at Donovan. "I've known you a long time and trust you. However, I've sworn an oath to support my country and obey the president."

"She is *not* the president," Donovan said. "She's just a skirt who thinks she's stepped into the game."

"Just a skirt?" Stacy said as though she couldn't believe she'd heard it.

Samantha said, with a nod to Stacy, "I never wear skirts."

Donovan gave a dismissive laugh, "Look—"

Stacy cut him off. "Donovan, I'll make you an offer. You kick my ass, and I'll give you airtime."

"Stacy," Leif said and twitched the gun as if to remind her that he had the situation in hand. When Stacy looked away from Donovan, he grabbed her. As he wrapped his arm around her, he drew his own side-arm.

Stacy said, "You have got to be fucking kidding me."

Popping both arms outward and her hips backward, she bumped Donovan's hold on her and fell straight down onto her back, curling her legs up to her chest. As Donovan's gun tracked downward, Stacy planted her left boot between his legs hard enough to lift him off the ground.

As Donovan doubled over, Stacy slammed her right boot into his face. He flipped backwards, his gun firing wild, and landed with his arms and legs askew.

Jumping up, Stacy picked up Donovan's gun.

"Oh my God," Holloway said, her eyes wide. She ran at Leif. Leif centered the gun on her, but it wasn't aggression he saw in her yes. It was fear. She shoved past him.

He turned to find Samantha on her back, her legs draped over the container she'd been sitting on.

Crouching down beside her, Holloway shouted at Leif, "Give me your shirt."

Leif stared at her hand, which was pressed over Samantha's neck, blood coursing through her fingers.

"Dammit Leif. I've got to stop the bleeding or she's going to die. Give me your damn shirt."

Leif tried to take off his shirt, but realized he still held the gun. He pocketed it, ripped his shirt over his head, and held it out to Holloway.

"Fold it up."

Folding it, he gave it to Holloway, who pressed it to Samantha's neck. Samantha's eyes searched the roof of the tent with a scowl as though she couldn't quite understand what she was looking at.

Behind him, Stacy had Donovan face-down, groaning as she tied his hands behind his back.

"Leif," Holloway said.

Leif looked back to her.

"Get Dr. Monti."

He nodded and leapt over a container. The tent flap pushed inward, and he had to slide to a stop as Whitetip stuck her head in.

"I'm sorry," she said, "but…" she trailed off as she looked at Holloway, hands and forearms covered in blood, the president laying beside her, paling.

"Holy shit," Whitetip said, her eyes going wide. "We heard a gunshot, but…"

"I need that doctor," Holloway said in a growl.

Whitetip nodded and said, "We just picked up Admiral Holt's emergency transponder in the Gulf of Mexico."

CHAPTER 51

Jeffrey lay with the pistol resting on his chest. The ocean swell rocked him gently. Several hours had passed since he triggered the survival beacon. No one seemed to care. The thought that his last stand might not happen made him angry. Perhaps, after settling in, the Sthenos no longer cared about emergency beacons.

As he drifted in half-sleep, he imagined the United States far beyond the broad, peaceful horizon, its freeways cluster bombed and skyscrapers tumbled into the streets among the jagged remnants of smaller buildings. He envisioned the Charles river in Boston clogged with debris. A sound at the edge of hearing caused him to open his eyes. High above, a white sea bird, its black-tipped wings held wide, descended in a broad circle. Skiing to a stop on webbed feet, it folded its wings and stared at him.

"I think you're a bit early for supper," he said and aimed the pistol at it. "Pop," he said and lifted the tip of the gun as if he'd shot. The bird turned with a sweep of its foot, visible in the clear water, and looked at Jeffrey with its other eye. A scream rose up as a flashing shadow was followed by a horrific wind, which chopped the water. The bird tried to fly away, but the wind caught its wings and swept it away. Jeffrey held his hand up against the spray of water, which pelted his palm like pebbles. A second shadow flashed by followed by another shriek. He wiped the water from his face and saw two Sthenos fighters moving away, arcing around for a strafing run.

So they came after all.

He'd found his final moment, and in it, he felt the profound peace Samantha had described, the acceptance of death. Soon, he could rest as the others had. As the lead ship turned and began its attack run, he aimed his pistol, sure it would do nothing, and fired four times at an opening on the port side. Drive-plate powered ships wouldn't have air intakes, but he hoped the bullets would ricochet down into something sensitive. The ship jerked downward, as if hit from above, and bloomed into a fireball. Without his firing another shot, the second Sthenos ship erupted into flames as well, its stubby wings falling out of the explosion and slapping the water. He looked at his pistol in confusion as three Lakota fighters screamed overhead, slamming him with the roar of their afterburners. He put his fingertips in his ears as the sonic boom thumped the water around him.

As the Lakota rounded on him, Jeffrey felt himself return to the world of the living, the profound peace melting away in a fire of anticipation. Lifting his fist, still gripping the gun, he screamed out with fierce joy and anger.

Two more Sthenos fighters came in from the north, and as they did, three more Lakota fighters streaked overhead, curving to engage.

The Lakota threw contrails as they arced around the Sthenos. Their flight characteristics wouldn't throw contrails in such warm air unless they were well above ten G's. In that Jeffrey saw something that made his heart thump hard against his ribs. Despite all the pain of combat, despite all the horrible losses and grief he'd faced in his life, as the Lakota destroyed one Sthenos fighter and the next as if they were nothing more than soap bubbles drifting in a summer sky, Jeffrey's heart overflowed.

The Hammerheads had returned.

The Lakotas turned, setting up a wide perimeter patrol pattern. From behind him, Jeffrey heard the ripping horror of a nuclear drive ship. Kicking his feet, he turned himself to see the special forces transport coming in low and slowing to a hover. In the cockpit, Marco held up his hand. Jeffrey would have returned the gesture had he not had his fingers in his ears due to the hurricane noise of the nuclear drive. The transport turned. Stacy stood on the open ramp, a safety line around her waist. Marco expertly dipped the end of the ramp into the water, and the man they called X threw Jeffrey a life ring. He'd hooked it with his foot, and they pulled him up onto the ramp. The ramp lifted and sealed, shutting out the screaming engines.

As the ship arced upward, turning toward the Amazon, Stacy gave Jeffrey a water bottle.

He drank deeply, and wiping his mouth with the back of his salt-crusted sleeve, said, "Thank you."

"Don't thank me," Stacy said. "Thank Whitetip. She'd have killed someone if we hadn't let her come get you."

He unzipped his flight suit and began pulling his arms out of the sleeves. "We have to move up our timeline. They'll start looking for us after this. Is Leif still modifying pilots?"

"Yes, but there's something else."

Jeffrey didn't like Stacy's tone nor the gravity of her expression. "What's happened?"

"We had a... conflict with Captain Donovan."

Jeffrey rolled his eyes. "What else is new?"

"This was worse..."

"What is it?"

"He shot Samantha."

Jeffrey felt his legs and arms go weak as he could find nothing to say.

Stacy told him about the meeting. "We have Donovan in custody."

"She's... not dead?"

"Not when we left."

"How bad is it?"

"I have no idea. When we left, Dr. Monti was prepping her for surgery."

"I'm so sorry Jeffrey," Stacy said. "If I hadn't gotten so close to him, or if I'd controlled the gun more effectively."

"I don't want to hear that," Jeffrey said. He wanted to say more, but the desire to comfort Stacy couldn't form itself through the wall of grief he felt, and he fell into silence.

...

After landing, Jeffrey ran as best he could on stiff legs to the medical tent. He found Leif sitting in front of it, his head in his hands.

"How is she?"

Leif looked up, dark circles under his eyes. In a matter of fact tone, as though he'd never expected anything otherwise, said, "You're alive." He glanced at the tent flap. "It's not all good news though."

"Is she?"

"I'm sorry dad."

Jeffrey entered the tent. Inside Dr. Monti was leaning over a figure on a cot, its feet splayed sideways. Caterina moved aside, exposing Samantha's pale face, mouth slack and eyes partially open. Her neck was wrapped in a bandage that seemed tight, as though it might choke her.

"Admiral," Dr. Monti said lifting her chin and inhaling deeply as though steeling herself.

He approached and touched Samantha's wrist. It felt unlike hers, too delicate. He gripped the relaxed hand.

"I'm so sorry," Dr. Monti said. "I did everything I could." She had a deadness in her eyes, which Jeffrey understood too well.

He remained silent for a moment, holding down the emotion welling in his throat before he could manage to say, "I know you did Caterina." He let go of Samantha's hand. "I won't have you second guessing yourself on this. Is that clear?"

Caterina tried to smile, but like a cloud of breath on a cold day, it failed to hold its form. "If it were only that easy."

Jeffrey nodded, remembering her fight to save Nathan Books, how personally she'd taken his death. She would have fought for Samantha like that. He wished there was something more he could say to help her but knew nothing would. Instead he said, "I need to see Donovan," and with a gentle touch on her shoulder left the tent.

Outside he said to Leif, "I need to go to my tent. Then I need you to take me to Donovan."

Leif followed him to his tent. Inside Jeffrey found his 1911, checked its magazine for rounds, released the slide to chamber one, and pocketed it. Coming out of the tent, he nodded to Leif, who took him back to the main camp, to a tent on the north side with Samantha's guards standing at the entrance. As they approached, both marines saluted. While their demeanor was strict, Jeffrey could see failure in their eyes. As with Caterina, he felt the need to say something supportive, but without the words, he returned their salute and entered the tent in silence.

Inside, he found two more guards standing on either side of a diminished Donovan, who sat on a container with his hands restrained behind his back, head down. Handcuffs had also been locked around his ankles.

When Donovan's head rose, his expression darkened.

Jeffrey pulled a crate from the side and sat in front of Donovan, close. When he drew the 1911 from his cargo pocket, the guards shifted their weight uneasily. Ignoring them, his eyes falling to the dark, scratched metal of the gun, he said, "It's treason you know."

Donovan's words came quick, "It was an accident."

Jeffrey looked up, trapping Donovan's red-rimmed gaze with his. "Was drawing your weapon on a Navy officer an accident?"

Donovan leaned away slightly. "What are you going to do with me?"

Jeffrey felt rage tickling in the back of his mind, back where his true reaction to Samantha's death lay waiting for him when he was ready to face it. "You intentionally undermined my plans, refused a direct order from our commander in chief, attempted to take a subordinate as a hostage, and killed the president of the United States."

Donovan's voice cracked as he said, "I never… I didn't—"

Jeffrey cut him off, anger growling in his throat. "This is a time of war captain. You are a traitor." He lifted the gun, finger on the trigger, and placed it between Donovan's eyes.

Donovan swallowed hard.

"I'd be well within my rights you know."

"Please," Donovan said, his lips trembling, "if I could go back…" A tear welled and, growing fat and glittering, slipped down his cheek, leaving a wet trail.

Jeffrey felt somehow the tear wasn't for Donovan's fear for himself, but for what he'd done. Still, he kept the gun barrel on Donovan's forehead as he said, "I need you to appreciate how close you are right now. Do you understand?"

Keeping still, Donovan said in a whisper, "Yes, sir."

Jeffrey lowered the gun to his lap. "Being a fool and an asshole is, in my opinion, not reasonable cause for execution."

Donovan exhausted his held breath, and as his head fell forward, he sobbed, blubbering "so sorry," and "thank you," now and again.

When he'd settled himself, Jeffrey said, "You'll be taken 1,000 miles away. We'll supply you with weapons for hunting, a filtration bottle, and a tent."

Donovan's red eyes rose now, fear again in them, "Alone?"

"You are, as of this moment, dishonorably discharged. You will stay clear of U.S. installations. If I see you again, I will consider you an aggressor and kill you. Understood?"

Donovan nodded.

Jeffrey stared at him for a moment, feeling as though standing was the signature on the pardon, and he felt unable to write it. His finger remained on the trigger of the pistol. He searched the man's dark eyes and willed himself to see the life they'd lived, the boyhood, the hopeful ensign, the years of faithful command to Cantwell. Only then was he able to stand, pocket the pistol and leave the tent.

Making his way to the edge of the encampment, Jeffrey walked down a solitary trail, coming to a rocky outcrop. He looked out beyond the canopy of trees. The valley lay in a broad curve in the bright sunlight. Branches swayed in the breeze. His thoughts swirled around Donovan.

Damn him to hell.

As he willed himself to let go, his mind betrayed him further, shifting to Samantha's cool hair draped across his neck that night by the river... then her lifeless eyes. He stopped himself short and willed his thoughts to the future. He imagined stepping down off the Lakota's ladder in Times Square into a profound silence. Fifty years ago, he'd been part of the team to offer coverage to escapees after the Demos attack. The Hammerheads had taken up the Mars Dome as a base of operations. There had been fewer than five hundred personnel in that city-sized dome. The shops and street fronts had been left as they were, some doors standing open, important belongings left out— pens, watches... all left untouched. Week after week, as those things remained in place, time seemed frozen. Small things were supposed to move, disappear, be used, stolen, wear out. The silence had been the most striking. When standing still, he could hear nothing aside from his own breath and blood coursing in his ears. The quiet seemed to collapse in on him. He imagined Times Square like that—shops left empty, a baby carriage sitting half off a curb, the canyons of steel and glass deathly empty.

What good was fighting if life was already destroyed? Would they find only silence? The hearts of major cities without the people... no arguments, no laughter, no footfalls, no traffic... would be nothing more than concrete hulls left to collapse as millennia passed.

He turned and watched the men and women coming and going in the forest. How many enclaves of human life remained? There must be thousands of small, isolated groups around the world. He understood why Donovan had wanted to bring them together, but it wouldn't work. Taking on the Sthenos head on was like trying to fist fight a grizzly bear. No matter how tough a fighter was, no matter how long he trained, even an old, small grizzly could tear him apart. Their only hope was to sneak up on the bear and kill it before it knew they were there.

CHAPTER 52

All Courtney Reynolds could think to do was shoot baskets in the side driveway. Her family hadn't had power in two weeks, and their pantry was thinning out. In the fields beyond the yard, the cornstalks, with no irrigation pumps to water them, had gone burned-brown in the intense sun. A few days ago, people had passed through scavenging the small cobs. She asked her father if they should offer some of their food. Without a word, he'd gone back into the house.

She lined up her shot and extended her arm. As the basketball rolled from her fingertips, she felt it was right. It arced toward the basket and cracked through the net with a satisfying chunk. She heard another chunk, similar but distant, which repeated and repeated. As it grew, a low vibration rose up, almost more a feeling in her chest than a sound in her ears. The chunking grew and became metallic. It came from the street. She ran to the front of the house. What she saw caused her to lose her step, and she fell to her hands and knees.

A huge transport, black as night, hovered down the road a foot off the ground. The air below it warped as if with swirling heat waves. Beside it walked a monster on four legs, which bent in opposing directions as it moved. Holding it's exoskeletal torso and a third pair of limbs upright like a centaur, it gripped a silvered rod in its three-fingered hand. The helmeted face, covered by an expressionless visor and jaw-piece, turned to her. She felt disconnected from herself, unable to so much as breathe, let alone run or scream.

It held up the rod, which caught a flash of sunlight. A flare of electric-blue leapt from it, washing over her vision. She dropped into darkness.

···

When Courtney woke, she tried to touch her hurting head, but her hands had been bound behind her back. She shifted her legs and ankle shackles clinked. The metal felt ice cold and foreign. She sat in her own yard still. Across the front lawn, near the steps to the house, four of the beasts sat on folded legs in a circle, their lower bodies prone in the grass. The lower face plates of their helmets hung open, exposing insect-like mandibles, which worked over something soft and red. Their hands reached to the center of their circle where a thing made of bright white lengths and wet redness lay. A body. They pulled away strips of muscle, eating. An arm extended from the near skeleton, her father's watch on the wrist.

Her mother came running from behind the house, their shotgun raised, screaming, "Get away from him."

She fired at one of the things as it put its arm up. As the shotgun concussed and a flick of fire and smoke blew from its barrel, the monster's arm vanished, spattered against its body. It turned away, the ruined stump of its arm pumping red gushes. The lens of its helmet had been blown away on one side. Beneath, she saw a corpse-white eye, laced with red capillaries, lolling. The monster screamed, and she thought her ears would break against the two-tone high and low sound, a mixture of shrill pain and thundering rage.

Her mother pumped the shotgun. A shell came cartwheeling free from the ejector port as one of the monsters whipped a glittering metal rod at her. A bolt of lightning clawed its way across the yard and ran up her mother's leg to her chest. She dropped as if she were a bag of skin filled with gelatin. As she hit the ground, the shotgun fired into the air. The echo of the blast settled away across the fields.

The monsters moved to her mother's body, making low thundering sounds at each other.

"Leave her alone," Courtney screamed at them, but they gave her no heed.

They tore her mother's clothes off, exposing pale skin, which they pulled away as if a second set of clothing. They stripped the

330

muscles from the bone. One took its helmet off, exposing a smooth skull and white eyes, marshmallow puffy, with no pupils, looking like diseased flesh.

Stuffing the meat into their wide-opening mandibles, they ate until all the major muscles were gone. Rising, they put their helmets back on, leaving the two skeletons with bones still attached by ligaments and tendons, arms and legs askew, rib cages and hips like baskets filled with organs. Her mother and father's faces had remained untouched. Both had slack expressions, mouths agape. Only after it had ended, her parents skin laying strewn aside like bull hides, did Courtney consider that she should have looked away.

She began trembling as a guttural growl rose in her throat as if by its own will. When it reached her mouth, she screamed. She screamed until her throat hurt and when one of the beasts came to her and thundered at her, she screamed at it with fear and grief and rage. She spit her scream at the obsidian black visor as if she could break it with her voice. Even as it thundered again, raising its rod high, she screamed.

Only the brilliance of the electric-blue light silenced her.

CHAPTER 53

Afternoon sunlight glowed through the roof of Jeffrey's tent as he lay on his cot lost in thought. Since Samantha's death, Leif and Caterina had worked long hours modifying the remaining pilots. A second pilot, a young woman from Mikelson's group, had died, and another young man had been left unable to speak. Jeffrey had, as best he could, and as he'd done so many times before, brought up an emotional numbness to shield himself from it. Still, regrets plagued him. If he'd dealt with Donovan when they first crashed, or if he hadn't allowed himself to be taken down by the Sthenos fighter… she'd still be alive.

Stacy called from outside his tent flap, "Jeffrey?"

"Come in," he said, sitting up onto the edge of his cot.

The flap drew aside and Stacy entered. More than a decade older than the twenty-something she'd been when they first met, she still looked young and beautiful despite the scar on her face, which he'd created with his rough stitches. She wore her hair slightly longer than the pixie cut she'd had then, but still, she had a playfully dangerous look, which reminded Jeffrey of Puck from A Midsummer's Night's Dream. That thought lifted him slightly from his self-imposed darkness.

She sat on a container and leaned forward, elbows on knees. When she looked at him, he saw a profound sadness in her eyes.

In a concerned tone, he asked, "What's going on?"

Giving a slight shake of her head, she said, "Nothing. Leif asked me to come get you… said he's done with the last pilot."

He took hold of her hands. "Stacy, I know you well enough to see when something's bothering you. Talk to me."

She looked to the side, appeared to be considering speaking or not, and said, "I can't stop thinking about President Delaney… that it was my fault. If I hadn't gotten in Donovan's face…"

"Stacy," he fell silent trying to choose his words perfectly, which he knew to be impossible in such a moment. "I've been having the same problem."

She looked at him, hopeful.

"We can only offer our best try at life, faults and all. We'll make mistakes, and those mistakes will sometimes haunt us."

"For how long?"

"Sometimes a day… sometimes a lifetime… Stacy, I'm sorry for what you're about to go through. I regret that I'm the one who has to ask you to do it."

"I'm not worried about the fight."

He squeezed her hands. "As crazy as it sounds, the fight's not the hard part. It's the living afterward that's hard. If we get through this, you might just understand what I mean. Hell…" He looked off through the half open tent flap, "I hope I'm wrong. I hope nothing worse than Samantha's death gets under your skin."

"It can get worse?" She said with a sarcastic laugh.

"A lot worse." He touched the side of her face.

Lowering her eyes so he could see only her chin and nose, she asked, "You've dealt with things like this in the past. How'd you keep going then?"

"Hope and duty?" he asked, sincerely unsure. "Maybe stubbornness…"

"How do you keep a sense of duty after what they did?"

Jeffrey looked at his hands, turning the question over in his mind. "I don't know. Why ask something like that?"

"Fifty years ago, when you came home, they turned their backs on you."

"Not all of them did."

Anger glowed in her voice. "A lot did."

Jeffrey laughed heartlessly. "I do it… *we* do it because we're not bankers or lawyers. Whether you like it or not, you're a fighter. I know you don't necessarily want to be, but when you're needed, and now's one of those times, all the bankers, lawyers, and elementary school teachers need you to do what they can't. There are horrors they can't face emotionally nor physically, so you and I have to do it for them."

Stacy said, "And when the dirty work's done, they can claim we don't matter. They can say the war never happened at all."

"Not this time, not if I have my say. But even if you knew they would, you'd still fight for them."

She looked at him with her intense, hazel eyes. "Why should we if they don't care?"

"Because it's how we're built. When someone goes after those who can't fight for themselves, we don't have an off switch."

A smile drew up the right side of her mouth.

He stood, pulling her to her feet and hugged her.

"Thank you," he said.

She looked up at him. "What are you talking about? You're helping me."

"And you reminded me that I'm not alone."

When she smiled, he said, "Do me a favor."

"Sure."

"Don't die."

"I'll damn well try not to," she said, with a sincere laugh, "but I hear my long term odds are pretty bad."

CHAPTER 54

That night Jeffrey dreamt he was sitting alone in the ready room of the U.S.S. Argalus, a ship long since decommissioned. His hands were young, unscarred; his right pinkie still had its last joint. Dim light came from the small reading lamps among the rows of seats. Maco walked in with his slow, sweeping gait, shoulders narrow, eyes wide like a bird of prey. Sitting down beside Jeffrey, he put his hand on Jeffrey's forearm, fingers warm. On the left shoulder of his flight suit was the Hammerhead insignia, a shark with ghostly eyes, mouth open, tail curved under.

Jeffrey felt the long-dead pilot had something to say, but Maco, as had been his way, only nodded once. There seemed to be a contentment in his expression, an acceptance of the inevitable. As the ready room and Maco faded away, Jeffrey found himself in the pitch-black night filled with the sounds of insects and the falls. His heart settled into a rare tranquility as he drifted back into a dreamless sleep.

He woke with the glow of dawn, fat rain drops pattering across the tent's fabric. Remembering the dream, he felt he understood. It hadn't been his mind spinning with stress that had brought his dead wingman to sit with him. Against all logic, Jeffrey felt it really had been Maco, as though he'd come to give Jeffrey permission to send more to be with him.

As he dressed, he felt as though Maco's spirit, calm and reserved, was still with him. When he left his tent, the rain had faded to intermittent drips, but the plants remained speckled with moisture. The air smelled clean. High up, strips of blue shown through the clouds, which the sun undercut, illuminating the sky fire-red. As he walked among the tents, the smell of boiled oats and coffee drifted in the cool air.

Lost in thought, he came into the ready room clearing and found himself standing in front of more than two hundred pilots, twenty-two special warfare operatives, and the support staff.

He squared his shoulders as he looked over their faces, young, some pretty, some strong, some closed-off, others nervous, all venerated by him.

Conversations faded as all attention became focused on him.

"Those who've gone before you gave their lives so the world could live. Make no mistake, your odds of following them tomorrow are high. I know you've signed on for no less. In that you give of yourselves wholly and completely... and selflessly. Because of that willingness to sacrifice—" Emotion welling in his chest cut him short, "you are the true north I set my will by, and I am proud to call you all Hammerheads."

Kodiak stood, punched his fist in the air, and gave a deep, resounding whoop, which the entire group echoed. Jeffrey held up his fist as well, but made no sound as he was overwhelmed at the pride he felt in them, and the grief already growing for what he knew was coming even if they found victory.

He remembered something Admiral Cantwell had said to him years before. *Wars are not won, they are survived.*

As he scanned the faces of these new Hammerheads, ready to face the horde one more time, he said, "You've all had the chance to test your new limits with short flights, and I'm impressed with how well you've adapted to them. Now on to business. When we fly out tomorrow one pilot will have a Special Warfare operator, the other will have a second singularity warhead. You must stay dark and undetected, so fly low. By low I mean within feet of the ground. We have no precise recon, so you'll have to scout your own landing area. This stage contains the largest risks to the mission. You must remain undetected until the warheads can be triggered. Passively scan for vehicle and airborne signals and avoid them at all costs. If you fail here, we all fail. One Sthenos destroyer in orbit is already more than enough for our Wraith pilots to have to face."

"All singularity warheads will be hard triggered." He looked to special warfare. "At 5PM tomorrow GMT, correctly placed or not, they'll activate. We can't risk manual triggering. If upon arrival at the location, no hiding location can be found, you'll keep the warhead on your back so it remains stealthed and wait with it. You let it take you. Is that clear?"

"Yes sir," all the special warfare operators said without hesitation.

"Good. Thank you all."

"If," he looked back on the pilots, "the Sthenos destroyers are not disabled at 5PM GMT, you are to go live and kamikaze the second singularity warhead in. That's forty-four singularity warheads dedicated to this attack. We have only nineteen more. Those will be with the Wraiths.

"The Lakota pilots who aren't assigned attack groups are on clean up. You'll be assigned one of two staging points, one in south eastern New Mexico, the other in Luhansk, Ukraine. From there you'll wait until 5:01 PM GMT before attacking Sthenos forces in Denver and Moscow respectively."

"Once the Sthenos destroyers are taken out, break radio silence to confirm. We will *not* respond. At that point, all surviving Lakota fighters will move to join forces in Denver or Moscow. From those locations we'll begin working through remaining Sthenos forces. If our current experience in atmosphere holds true, you'll be able to readily outfly the Sthenos fighters."

"You'll move from one former Sthenos destroyer location to the next. After Denver will be L.A. When L.A. is clean, move on to Tokyo. You'll have to scavenge your own fuel and supplies along the way. You'll run out of ammunition. When you do, you must find more. Success tomorrow will not bring us to the end. The Sthenos will be on Earth for a long time to come. There will be issues with the human populations as well. Warlords may rise up. If we're successful tomorrow, we'll see the best and the worst from human society over the next several years. Those who live will help rebuild the world. Are you ready to do that?"

"Yes, sir!"

"Good. Now I hope you said your goodbyes because as of right now your asses belong to me. When Holloway has assigned your group and destination, prep your aircraft and get the hell out of here. I want all flights outbound at dusk."

He stared at them for a moment before asking, "Do you all understand?"

"Yes, sir," came the booming chorus of pilots and special warfare.

"Does anyone have any questions?"

"No, sir."

As the area cleared, Stacy walked up to Jeffrey, gave him her winning smile as she said, "You ready to make history?"

Jeffrey returned her smile as best he could manage. "Yeah." But his heart wasn't in it. Win or lose he already grieved for her. He'd seen brilliant souls worn threadbare too many times before.

CHAPTER 55

Stacy had to cover eight miles in a few hours with a fifty-five pound pack on. Her legs burned. To keep herself going, she picked small points along the road to reach. Ahead she saw a stoplight, blinking red, somehow still powered.

Get to that in ten minutes.

The clock on her HUD ticked down. She reached it a few seconds late. The traffic signal tilted in the breeze. She looked ahead for her next goal. Her back and shoulders hurt. The main weight of the pack rested on her hips as it should, but the straps still dug into her shoulders and she felt her balance weakening as she put miles behind her.

At the drop off point, when she powered up the suit, her arms had disappeared save a slight shadow thrown by her HUD to show her body position. She'd given the suit the command to shut the ghost off. She felt exposed when she could see her outline even if no one else could. She'd waved her hand in front of her eyes, marveling at the efficiency of the suit, which masked her visually, on radar, the electrical and heat signs of her body, and cooled her exhaled breath to ambient temperature. Ten years earlier Jeffrey had defeated special ops mercenaries equipped with stealth suits by reading the CO_2 which had been exhaled. Since that time, CO_2 scrubbers had been added, which left her effectively invisible. She could only hope the Sthenos didn't have some form of detection they hadn't considered.

At her back, the suit's small fusion power source gave off a tiny whine. A seed-sized hydrogen sun burned behind her shoulder blades. Without its electromagnetic shielding it would simply burn out, but not before cutting her in half. The shielding was programmed to fail first away from her, but a catastrophic failure, immediately cutting power from the back up battery, would kill her. Everyone who wore the suits tried not to think about it.

In the distance, she could see the spire of the over mile-high Sthenos destroyer towering above dark-green oak trees. As she walked out of the empty streets of Clifton NY, she felt unsure. She'd expected the interstate to be jammed with cars. There were none. The Sthenos had either let those on the freeways go, or had stopped them before they could fill the roads.

Soon she saw the towers of the NY skyline catching the sun. She was right on schedule. As she walked, the sun hung in a brilliant ball straight above, but she didn't feel the warmth of the day nor the wind. The suit kept her at a comfortable temperature. She did feel the burn in her thighs and sweat running down her back. She drank now and again from the tube at her jawline, which she could use without lifting the face mask. The suit had been designed for an operative to remain stealthed for days, only needing to shut down the shield to eat or relieve oneself. She would hope to need neither in the next few hours.

In another tiring but steady hour, she reached the edge of the Hudson River and the mouth of the Lincoln tunnel. As she approached, she found a large structure with matte-black, armor-plated walls had been constructed around the mouth of the tunnel. She assumed the other bridges and tunnels had similar defenses or had been destroyed.

Scaling the ivy-covered embankment to her left, she climbed over a concrete barrier into an industrial area. She walked among the buildings—all dead quiet. Cars remained neatly parked, a few with their doors or rear hatches open. She touched the hood of a black sedan where it seemed an electrical arc had burned the paint.

Where have the people gone?

As she considered it, she guessed she didn't want an answer. A deep humming rose up from behind her. Returning to the barrier, she looked down to the four lanes of concrete, which would have led into the tunnel if not for the armored obstruction. She rested her chest on the barrier to relieve the weight of the pack. The humming grew to a rumbling. It seemed to be coming from the direction she'd come. The ground and the barrier began to vibrate. To the west, a massive vehicle came into view, rounding the final bend in the highway. The night-black transport hovered a few feet off the ground on a warping energy field. Approaching the tunnel entrance, it stopped perhaps 100 yards from the metal wall. The rumbling faded away as it set down. Between seams in the armor, the side of the transport dropped inward and slid to the side. Something moved in the dark interior.

CHAPTER 56

As the thing emerged into the sunlight, it brought back a long forgotten memory of a black widow Stacy had found in her garage as a child. The spider had looked as though it were leather-wrapped, shining and vicious. This quadruped had a similar sheen, but with two arms making six limbs total. The long legs, thin at the joints, bent backward as it walked. Its waist was narrow and the chest curved inward, giving the creature a stalking appearance. The arms, like the legs, were thin and pitch-black. It held a long metal bar, most likely, Stacy assumed, some kind of weapon. Its narrow head and long jaw gave it an almost hatchet-like appearance. Its dark visor caught the sunlight with a flash of light. Stacy understood she wasn't seeing the creature but a helmet and environmental suit, or perhaps defensive armor. Two hoses ran from the sides of the face to a finned backpack. Waves of heat came off the pack as the creature moved forward.

They're cooling arrays.

Glancing at her HUD she saw that the ambient temperature was 84 degrees.

...and yet they still need to stay cool.

Two more Sthenos emerged, holding the metal bars as if a street gang armed with lengths of high-tech pipe. As they gathered at the end of the ramp, the first swept its arm in command and a keening sound punctuated by clicks and a low vibration sounded out, resonating in Stacy's skull.

A young man emerged from the darkness. A metallic bar bound his hands together, and a cable between his ankles caused him to take short steps. A woman, perhaps twenty years old, followed him. Another cable connected them at the waist. Another woman appeared and then a young man. As the chain gang grew from the side of the transport, the first man tripped, falling forward. A Sthenos made low sounds laced with menacing clicks as it held out the bar. An arc leapt away from it, stuttering from the young man's heel up to the base of his skull. The arc left its ghosted memory on Stacy's eyes as the young man convulsed on the ground. The Sthenos let out the low resonation as it pointed toward the building.

Stacy's trigger finger curled closed.

The man pushed himself up to kneeling. As he tried to stand, his legs trembled, and he crouched back to his knees. The woman behind him said something to him. Coaxing the man to standing as best she could with restrained hands, she helped him walk toward the building, the chain of people following in a single file.

As Stacy watched the people come from the transport, she noticed there were none overweight, none younger than teenagers, and none older than perhaps forty. This group had been processed elsewhere, distilled from the general population. They were young and strong. But why?

The Sthenos weren't here to destroy humanity. They wouldn't have transported these people here in that case. This wasn't just about water and ore. Jeffrey's theory on slavery came to mind again, but something she couldn't pinpoint told her it didn't fit.

She counted in tens until the last person emerged from the doorway. Two hundred in total. The last was a girl of perhaps fifteen, tall and thin but athletic. She still had a touch of a little girl in her cheeks. Her shoulder-length, dark hair shone in the sun, reminding Stacy of her own sister. The girl's head rose and scanned the top of the wall where Stacy crouched. When the girl's eyes passed her location, Stacy wished she could uncloak for a split second to give the young girl some hope that someone had come, that she wasn't alone, but the girl's eyes, hollow as if they'd been cried empty, swept past.

As the chain of people approached the structure, a tall doorway slid open. The metal was at least a foot thick. More Sthenos came out, these wearing red suits with a similar leathery sheen. As the young man and the woman, still helping him walk, approached, one of the red Sthenos held up a metal rod, it's end sparking. Stacy's gut tightened and her shoulders glowed with adrenaline with the desire to step in, but there was nothing she could do. Live or die, those people were on their own.

The chain-gang moved into the tunnel, disappearing from view one at a time.

They might have turned the tunnel into a prison, which would be smart. Only two points to guard and no way to effectively blow doors without sending shockwaves down the tunnel or drowning the prisoners.

Still, something about that felt wrong to her as well. She guessed the chain gang's destination was in Manhattan. She looked up to the Sthenos destroyer towering over the skyline, clouds catching on its upper reaches.

The rumbling rose up again, but it did not come from this transport. Looking up the highway, she saw another come around the distant curve.

She backed away from edge of the road, stepping carefully among the debris, and turned east toward the river. With no tunnel access, she would have to swim. When she reached the water she stepped in and visually confirmed the suit was correctly throwing holograms over the holes she made in the water.

Inflating small airbags, which ran down her chest from shoulder to hip bone, she settled into the water. The airbags compensated for the weight of the pack as she quietly breast stroked across the river.

The current carried her downstream as she swam. She would now be swimming directly over those prisoners walking down the tunnel. When she reached the island, she climbed out of the water over craggy boulders. Crouching low, she waited for excess water to cascade from her. While the suit covered over anything close to it, the water falling off would leave a visible signature. Shaking off the remaining excess water, she held her hand up. The suit compensated for the wetness still on her leaving her invisible again. Hopping up the boulders, she climbed a short concrete seawall to the pavement and made her way up 34th street, but when she reached 9th Avenue, she looked north several blocks to where the Lincoln tunnel emerged. A bit ahead of schedule, she felt if she could learn something more about the Sthenos and their intentions, anything, then the time spent would be worthwhile. As she approached 38th street, she saw something she didn't understand.

CHAPTER 57

Down the street, a tall barrier shimmered in the late morning sunlight.

"Suit-Con," she whispered to activate the suit's voice recognition, "zoom five times."

Her view of the barrier leapt forward. It had a similar pattern to cyclone fencing, but glittered as if crystal.

As she approached the fencing, she whispered, "Suit-Con, eliminate zoom."

Beyond the fencing, emerging from the mouth of the tunnel, were a group of prisoners. Not those she'd seen earlier. They'd probably already moved into the city. These, freed from their chains, walked in a loosely formed group. Their faces held hopelessness.

As she approached, she found the entire length of the street lined with the glittering barrier. Its uneven lattice seemed to be more of a natural spiderweb of clear, thin tubes. The tubes appeared to be melting in the sun, just about to drip, but never did.

She watched the people move by. A Sthenos passed within a few feet, walking on its rear legs, monstrous in its height of perhaps ten feet. The middle appendages hung at its sides, while its elongated head swept back and forth scanning the prisoners. The creature wore a suit the color of fresh blood, which creaked as it walked. It stopped, dropped down onto four legs and looked in her direction. Stacy held her breath. Despite the stealth suit, she felt as though she were fully exposed. The Sthenos looked back to the men and women as it let out the low resonance again, imbedded with sharp clicks. The resonance vibrated in Stacy's chest, and the clicks made the back of her neck sparkle with animal terror. At that moment, she understood in her gut why they'd come.

Prey.

She waited for the Sthenos and prisoners to pass before she moved on with quiet steps.

One block south of the barrier, she turned east on 37th Street. As she walked, the weight of the warhead burned into her legs. At each intersection, she looked north to see that she was keeping pace with the prisoners, who had continued along 38th Street, it's entire length seemingly blocked by the glistening barrier. As she closed in on the Sthenos destroyer, its great spike towering against the blue sky, she guessed it had landed near the New York Public Library, perhaps in Bryant Park, squarely in the heart of Manhattan Island.

At 6th Avenue the barrier on 38th Street turned north. She decided to continue down to 5th Avenue before turning north as well.

The empty street felt alien. She'd been in Manhattan before. Coming from small-town Colorado, she'd been unprepared for the crowds in one of the few areas on Earth that had maintained its density as the world's population ebbed. People had walked shoulder to shoulder on sidewalks in a great river of humanity. The streets teamed with cabs and delivery trucks, the chords created by their variant fusion engines filling the air with resonant music.

Now she walked alone and invisible among the towering buildings, feeling as if she were surrounded by ghosts. Looking to her invisible hands, she felt a ghost herself. As she looked at where her arm should be, a loud clank sounded beside her. The bottle she'd kicked skittered out into the street, fell from the curb, and shattered in the gutter. Flushing with adrenaline, she crouched down.

Dammit Stacy.

A deep thrumming rose up in the distance. She ran to the crook of a staircase, knelt down, and waited. As the sound grew, a small, black ship, hovering on the same warping heat the transport had, sailed around the corner.

They'd wondered how sensitive the Sthenos would be to intruders this close to the landing zone. Now she knew.

Very sensitive.

The small transport hovered up to the area where the bottle had broken and green laser lines scanned in a grid across the sidewalk and walls of the building, spreading out and rotating. Stacy was caught dead center in the scan pattern. She looked directly at the Sthenos pilot, who wore a distinctly different helmet than the prisoner handlers.

Here's where I find out how good these suits really are.

She became hyper aware of her breathing, remembering how Jeffery had detected Maxine King's mercs. Even though the CO_2 flaw had been dealt with, she wondered what faults the engineers hadn't considered. The Sthenos pilot seemed to stare directly at her. For all she knew, it was trying to understand why she was sitting still and not running for her life.

Pulsing with the ship's power source, the air filled with the sharp, clean scent of ozone. After a moment, she dared think that, if it could sense her, it would have done something by now, killed her or attempted to communicate. The grid of lasers appeared again and scanned over her. Beneath her and behind her she saw the grid land unhindered on the brick wall as the suit bent the laser light around itself.

The Sthenos turned the ship to the west and flew away, kicking out paper and dust from the gutters as it went.

She wasted no time in moving her position. She'd allowed herself to become distracted, which was totally unacceptable. She couldn't fail to place the warhead, and she almost had.

Reaching 5th avenue, she looked north. Two blocks up, a wall of debris two stories high blocked the street. As she approached, she saw it consisted of loose brick, metal ducting, and other materials. It couldn't be climbed in silence. Her HUD told her she had thirty minutes to plant the singularity warhead and begin her return trip. She could try and climb the pile slowly, but one broken bottle had the Sthenos on her in seconds. If they cornered her up there, the shifting

348

debris would easily give her away. Climbing over wasn't an option, and she couldn't leave the warhead here, as it was still too far away to assure destruction.

Her gaze tracked up the ten story building to her left. The debris lay halfway up its side like a swelling wave, frozen in time.

If I can't go over, I go up.

She walked around the back of the building. She wouldn't be able to climb with the weight of the pack. Giving the street a quick check, she took it off. The pack became visible as it came away from her torso. Taking a flat disk from a cargo pocket, she drew a filament cord from its edge and attached it to the pack's top strap. She clipped the spool to her hip and began climbing. The broad window sills made for a straight-forward ascent, but even so, as she gripped the sixth floor sill, she felt her fingers slide. The empty air behind her back loomed. She adjusted her grip and held herself to the wall. If she fell she'd die, or at least break something bad enough she would wish she'd died. Worse than that, would be the failure of the warhead. Where it sat, it would cut a crater in the hide of Manhattan but nothing more.

Reaching the top floor of the building, she had to lean her head back to look at its overhanging cornice. She felt her gloves pulling at the skin of her fingers as her grip slipped by micrometers. Looking down at the street over one hundred feet below, she saw the line of the thin cord pulling in the breeze. She turned her attention back to the stone cornice. Climbing was not her strong suit, and an expert *dyno*, as rock climbers would call the leaping transition, was well above her skill set. She looked to see if she could go around the cornice, but it ranged all the way to the building's edge. She looked into the tenth floor window. She saw office furniture and a design table, now only a black sheet of glass without power. Breaking the glass to get inside wasn't an option.

Do or die.

She looked up again, picked a target between two buttresses, huffed twice, and leapt.

Her heart went airborne with her, and she felt her entire body go effervescent with thrilling fear. Her hands caught the stone, and the gripping surface of her gloves held. Her body swung out and back, causing her grip to slip slightly. Her foot kicked the window, which thumped but did not break. Her forearms began to burn. She had to move fast. Her grip would last only a few seconds under her full body weight. Pulling herself up, she shot her arm forward, praying for something to grip. Her fingers brushed an edge, but couldn't hold it. She slid back to hanging, her arms extended. Her shoulders began to burn. Gritting her teeth, she pulled with everything she had, reached with her right arm, and caught the edge with the last two joints of her ring and middle fingers. Her ring finger slipped free, tearing the nail away from the bed. As her middle finger began to slip, she pulled as hard as she could. The palm of her hand exploded with pain as she reached with her left hand, caught the edge, and brought her right leg up stomping into the buttress to create friction to hold herself up. Sliding her right hand forward, she locked a solid grip on the stone edge, pain flaring up her arm. Hauling herself over the ledge, she rolled off to the roof where she collapsed on her side holding her right hand. She held it up to look at it, but could not see it. Telling the HUD to throw a ghost of her on the display, she bent her fingers. The ring finger trailed behind the others, and pressing on the palm of her gloved hand, she could feel the tendon knotted in her palm. She'd snapped it.

She lay for a moment longer, drawing slow breaths. It would be no use to lean over the ledge to recover the warhead if she became dizzy and fell. After several slow, meditative breaths, she shifted to her feet. Staying off her right hand, she leaned over the edge. Pulling on the cord with her left hand, she tried to lift the pack, but with only one good hand, she couldn't grip to pull it straight up. She drew her left forearm under the rope and pulled it left. Then she drew her right forearm under the line and drew that right, lifting the pack off the ground, the cord now passed from her belt, behind her left bicep, around her left forearm and over her right. Twisting to maintain the distance between her arms, she swept her left forearm under the extended cord again, and now had two wraps of the cord around her forearms. She twisted her body and swept her right arm under the cord, now three wraps and had lifted the warhead up four feet or so. She began going back and forth like a taffy pulling machine, wrapping the cord around her forearms and lifting the pack. By the time she had it within grasp of her left hand, she had her forearms wrapped in a thin sheet of the cord. She gripped the top handle and pulled the pack up and over. Sitting on her butt, she unwrapped the cord from her arms, laying it out in a careful ribbon so as not to tangle it before rolling it back up on the flat spool.

She pulled the pack on and walked across the silver weather-sealed roof. When the base of the Sthenos destroyer came into view, she whispered, "Oh my God," and felt her willingness to place the warhead vanish.

CHAPTER 58

As the hour of departure approached, Jeffrey walked among the Wraiths. Ducking under a stubby wing, he ran his hand down its smooth belly, wondering how long its life would be. Would they succeed or fail? If even one Sthenos destroyer survived, it would likely come here. The crash site of the Lacedaemon would be an obvious source of the attack. Despite their encampments being distant from the crash site, Jeffrey assumed it wouldn't take the Sthenos long to locate them. He'd already set plans in place in that contingency. They would break into small units and disappear into the wild, the last major military force splintered to nothing. In that state, he had no idea how they could possibly rise up to fight again.

As he stepped out from under the Wraith's wing, he saw, spray painted in flat-black letters under the cockpit sill, *Lieutenant Lila "Springbok" Okoye.*

Those like Springbok caused him the most worry. Sending men like Master Sergeant Mikelson against such poor odds was easier. He, like Jeffrey, had at least lived the majority of his days. Most of the new pilots, however—

Hearing something shift above, he leaned back to see a crown of dark hair in the cockpit. He climbed the ladder and found Springbok staring at her instruments with haunted eyes.

"You okay?" He asked.

"I feel as though this is my last day."

"And how does that hit you?"

She kept her eyes on the instruments, clearly not wanting to answer.

"On the Lacedaemon, when I asked you why you fly, you told me it was for the love of it, but there's something else…"

Her luminous, dark eyes turned on him. "To prove my mother wrong."

"Did it work?"

"I don't think so. She said I wasn't a warrior."

"You're not?"

"No. Warriors aren't afraid."

"You sure about that?"

She looked at him with suspicion.

Crossing his arms on the sill, he said, "When I was your age, I admitted to my flight commander, a pilot named Reggie Olds, that I was afraid. Holt-he said to me-," he let his voice grow as gruff as Olds' had been, "My great-great-some-such-damn-thing grandfather was a Brigadier General and a triple ace through World War II, Korea, and Vietnam. I'm gonna tell you something he passed down, and you damn well better not forget it." Jeffrey let his voice return to normal. "You want to know what he said?"

"Something about fearlessness?" she asked in a forlorn tone as if disappointed in herself.

"Not at all. He said anybody who doesn't have fear is an idiot."

Hope glowed in her eyes. "You?"

Straightening his back, he looked away. "Yeah. I'm afraid of what's coming, more for those like you than myself, but I've learned to keep going despite it. It's a kind of liar's dance. If we let fear lead, we'll fail before we begin. We have to grip its hand, turn it, and shove it where we need to go."

Her gaze returned to her instruments, her hand shifting the flight stick as if absently going through maneuvers in her mind. "I always thought bravery was fearlessness."

"No." He took hold of her shoulder. "Bravery can't exist without fear. Facing what we're *not* afraid of takes no will. Only when we're scared to death do we show our true selves. Bravery isn't about afraid or unafraid, it's about what we do when we are unequivocally scared shitless."

She laughed in an unsure way as she patted the instrument panel. "I wanted my mother to be proud of me."

"Have you given this," he touched the cockpit sill, "everything you've got?"

"Yes, definitely."

"Well then, I can't speak for her, but I'm damn proud of you."

CHAPTER 59

Stacy should have had one more block of buildings between her and the New York Public Library and Bryant park, but all structures in nearly a quarter-mile diameter had been razed to the ground, leaving only foundations and rubble-filled basements. The trees of Bryant park were gone, either having been scraped aside or crushed into the earth by the wide stern of the Sthenos destroyer. Halfway up the ship, already twice the height of the tallest building in Manhattan, the mist of clouds had descended down to what appeared to be secondary engine nacelles. Beyond the mist of clouds the ship narrowed and became vague in the high, colder air.

She looked back down to its broad base and felt dizzy. Large stabilization arms extended from the sides of the ship perhaps five hundred feet up. One was stabbed into the street near the building she stood on.

Surrounding the park boundary was the glittering, liquid fencing. In the fencing milled thousands of people.

"Suit-Con, five times zoom."

She watched the faces of the people.

"A human shield."

A human shield she had to ignore, if she could. She scanned the ruined foundations below and saw no suitable attachment point for a zip line. Not that she could if she wanted to. A fixed line might be seen, and she had no way to deliver it.

Several Sthenos walked among the people. With their metal rods crackling, they directed individuals toward a white wall, which had been erected against the side of the ship. If individuals did not comply, they were shocked. Sthenos at the wall moved the people through a doorway set in the, perhaps fifteen foot, metal wall. The walled area had no roof, only serving to partition the crowd from the interior.

After passing through the door, the people moved down a hallway where Stacy could just make out the tops of their heads. She saw a blue spark. A man's arms came up as he took off his shirt. Nothing more. Her eyes scanned down the hallway where several Sthenos guards twitched metal rods, directing the unseen people along. At the end of the hallway Stacy could just make out the blonde crown of a woman's head. The last Sthenos guard lifted her hair and swept a blade through it, leaving her with a spiked scalp. The Sthenos dropped the hair to the side.

The next doorway led to a larger, square area. One man stood in its center completely nude. A Sthenos touched its rod to his chest.

"Suit-Con," Stacy whispered, "Zoom in ten times." The HUD's magnification leapt forward. Now she could see the man's face and the rod at his chest. The tip of the rod pulsed a brilliant white, and he fell, either unconscious or dead. As she watched though, she saw his eyes move, wide with fear now, not dead, but paralyzed and aware.

The Sthenos hooked metal shackles onto the man's feet.

"Suit-Con, zoom out two fold. The image backed away until she could see the man's entire body as the Sthenos picked him up by the shackles, the man hanging upside down, his arms limp over his head, wrists and elbows loose, eyes wild with fear. The Sthenos hung him on a rack with moving hooks. She'd seen that type of rack before... in a meat processing facility in Greely, Colorado.

The sliding hooks moved the hanging man, swaying slightly, toward the wall. The wall shifted open, and he passed through. When the doors closed, the blonde woman with her hair cut short, was allowed into the space. The Sthenos guard touched the rod to her chest and the pulse flashed again. She fell. He shackled and racked her as he had done the man, and the woman, hanging upside down, moved off.

Stacy remembered a memoir of World War II in which Jews were told by Nazi guards to fold their clothes carefully and put them where they could find them when they came out of the showers. To lead people to the slaughter one must simply give some hope of survival until the last moment. If the people in the pen around the Sthenos destroyer knew what was happening inside those walls, they would not go quietly, they would revolt even if it meant death. At least she'd like to believe they'd rather die fighting than strung upside down.

The rack snaked through the area. Biped creatures with long, delicate limbs—smaller than the Sthenos—worked with shrimp-like speed. They wore white garments, spattered red. Men and women hung from the rack every few feet, all moving with a swaying grace. The first creature cut a circle around the ankles and the wrists of the man, whose eyes remained wide but facial muscles slack in paralysis.

Stacy wanted to look away, but a mixture of duty to report what she'd seen and target lock prevented her.

Another of the creatures, working beside the first, slit from the first cuts up the insides of the arms and legs to the torso. At the next station another slit the skin from groin to throat, gripped it at the ankles, digging with clawed fingers, and tugged the skin from the body in one large sheet. The sheet of skin was thrown onto a pile.

The man, now a body of muscle and tendon, his face lined with runnels of blood, moved to another creature, who sawed open the breast bone, and slit the belly wide. As it worked the blade inside the torso, bowels and organs fell out. Another creature threw the entrails into a pit dug into the ground. Around the edges of the pit Stacy saw lengths of gut, small wet things she thought might be kidneys, and other gore.

Only then did a creature cut the man's throat with one quick motion. As blood poured in a great torrent out of the neck, the life faded from the man's eyes. Stacy felt grateful for it going.

The next creatures removed major muscles. One took the thighs, another the calves, another the glutes. One creature worked down one side of the back while another did the opposing side. The chest was worked through. Fat and sinew were tossed into pits while the larger wet, red muscles were set onto conveyors, which carried the meat through openings in the side of the ship.

When they'd finished, the man's body was nothing more than a skeleton with full head, hands, and feet. As it passed over a dark pit, the final creature whipped a broad blade through the ankles. The remainder of the man fell into the pit. The shackles still held bare feet. The creature took them from the hook, tossed the feet into the pit, and re-hung the shackles, which moved out of view through an opening in the wall.

Finally, Stacy was able to look away.

"Suit-Con, eliminate zoom."

As her view returned to normal, she realized with some disappointment in herself that her hands were trembling. She gripped them into fists.

Get off this roof and do what you came here to do.

Leaning over the edge of the building, she saw the pile of rubble not only blocked the streets, but had been shoved up along the side of this building. If she rappelled down from here, she'd end up on it, which would make far too much noise.

Walking to the corner of the building, she looked down, scanning the place where she'd stood looking up at the rubble. She lay down and leaned over. The overhanging cornice ran around the top of the building here as well. That's all she needed.

She felt along the small seam where the stone slabs met. Sitting up, she looked around the roof and found a thick steel grate set in the floor. She pulled on the grate. It lifted out readily.

No use.

She looked to the stocky legs of the water tank. Walking over to it, she tied her line to one of the angle-welded legs. As she returned to the ledge, she played out the line. Taking a small, black plasma cutter from a chest pouch, she ran it along the mortar seam between two stones. With a huffing sound, it vaporized the mortar six inches deep.

She sat in silence to see if the sound of the cutter had attracted attention. Her timer said she had twenty minutes to her target turn-time.

Setting the rope into the gap she'd created, she found it wedged nicely.

She'd done a swing-out descent before, but not with an extra fifty-five pounds on her back. It had to be done that way though, as there was no way to lower the warhead down. She simply had to go for it. Stepping up onto the cornice, she walked away from the destroyer playing out another sixty feet of line, which should give her five to ten feet of clearance over the rubble. She set her auto-braking belay device on her suit's center harness clip and ran the line through it. As she entered her height from the ground, the estimated height of the rubble she needed to clear, and her current distance from the pendulum source, she hoped the belay device would pay out line correctly. Too slow and she'd swing back and crash into the rubble, making a hell of a noise and surely exposing herself. Too fast and she'd hit the ground at a dead fall, break her leg or worse. Again, screwed.

No time for the timid.

She pulled the rope snug against the gap in the cornice. When she activated the ATC it clamped down on the rope. Fighting the urge to grip the free line, she drew a deep breath as she positioned her boot toes at the edge of the cornice. A pigeon flew by eighty feet below. Crouching down she exhaled as she leaned forward, face first out over the street, and as her weight pulled her forward, she shoved hard with her legs, pushing herself as far away from the ledge as possible.

Her guts went electric with the zero G, and the wind roared in her ears. As she arced downward, she held the line loosely in her hand, just enough to keep herself head up.

As she fell, the line remained taught, pulling her in an arc. She groaned through gritted teeth as the heavy pack strained at her back, threatening to pull her upside down. She gripped tighter on the line as she swung toward the rubble. As it came racing up at her, it appeared she wouldn't clear it. The building also felt far too close. The rope swept her forward. The rubble blurred under her feet, and she was arcing out over the ruined street. The belay device came alive, whirring, and she had reflexively gripped the line, which now flashed a burning pain in her hand from the friction as it played out. She relaxed her hand, willing herself to not let it go entirely. As the length of line extended, she did not go upward, but moved parallel to the ground like a casted fishing lure. Slowing to a stop, she fell. The ground slapped a sharp pain into her feet through her boots. Her eyes followed the line from her hand up to the roof ten stories above.

"I can't believe that worked," she whispered to herself.

Remembering the rope was hanging out like a flag, visible to the Sthenos, she removed it from the belay device. She'd played out all but four feet of the line.

When she let the line drop, it slithered back to lie across the rubble pile, it's dark gray and brown mottled surface disappearing in among the urban colors. She moved quickly away from where she might have made noise. As she approached the liquid-mesh fencing her back ached from the weight of the pack coming down on her at the end of the descent. She crouched down on her heels. The burning pain in the palm of her left hand told her she'd cut through the glove but couldn't afford to evaluate her injury. No blood dripped from the hand and she still had full, if painful, use of it. Not as much as she could say of the right hand with its snapped tendon.

She looked to the thousands of people beyond the fencing.

CHAPTER 60

Some sat on overturned stones, others on the dirt-crusted stumps of trees. As with the prisoners she'd seen earlier, they were all younger than perhaps forty, most in their twenties. Here and there she saw teens. Sthenos walked on their four legs among the people, who stayed well clear of them. The Sthenos from time to time would let fly a bolt of current from the rods.

To her left, she saw where a pit had been dug. Boards hung out over it. A woman sat on the board relieving herself, totally exposed to everyone. In her face, Stacy saw someone who had lost everything, given up all hope. On the other side of the park, Stacy saw people eating out of metal bowls.

As the wind shifted, the scent from the pit reached her, causing her to gag. The rancid smell shocked her back to her purpose, the weight of the pack on her back. In a best case scenario she was to mount the warhead up against the ship, but the fence appeared to border the entire area where Bryant Park and the New York Public Library had stood. While she couldn't see beyond the towering base of the Sthenos destroyer, she assumed the fencing circumnavigated the space. She didn't have time to recon the entire fence-line. The fence had been erected perhaps three hundred feet from the ship. If she planted the warhead at the fence line, it would cut out the entire bottom section of the ship reaching up halfway along its length. There would be no recovering the destroyer at that point. The entire drive section would be ripped away into the singularity.

Pushing against the weight of the pack, she got to her feet and walked to a nearby building foundation. There a gap into a service tunnel lay exposed. She dropped down into the low tunnel to find a broken pipe extending from the concrete wall. Pulling the pack from her shoulders, she hung it on the pipe.

That's that.

Pulling herself slowly and quietly out of the hole, she felt a massive relief at no longer having to shoulder the pack's weight. She would be able to move much more quickly without it. She looked at her HUD and saw that she still had twelve minutes until her designated turn-time. Extra time was always good. When she looked out on the people beyond the fencing, she saw the girl from the transport, who had reminded of her of her sister, sitting near the fencing in a patch of grass and daisies. Stacy walked quietly over and stood watching her. The girl, completely unaware of Stacy, sat with a blank expression.

She plucked a dandelion and held it out to the fence. Stacy crouched down and watched the girl touch the flower to one of the glistening webs of the fence. The flower smoked and melted in half. Several petals dropped on to Stacy's side.

Acidic?

As Stacy settled into a cross-legged position, her boot scraped along the ground, pushing a small rock aside. The girl stared at the rock and then directly at Stacy's chest. Her eyes scanned through her, focusing on nothing. She looked back to the rock. Her eyes came back to Stacy, but focused too low, missing her eyes.

"Hello?" the girl whispered.

Stacy's chest flushed with electricity. She should go, *now.* Instead, she leaned forward, close to the acidic webbing. She wanted desperately to talk to this girl. To tell her she was there, that they were going to put things right. But she wouldn't put things right by her. She was going to kill her.

Stacy looked out on all the people beyond the fencing. She was not here to save them, but to destroy the destroyers. They didn't have the ability to do both. She remembered what Jeffrey had said. *No matter what you find, plant those warheads. Keep them on your back if you have to.*

All dead.

362

"Is someone there?" the girl whispered again. "Hello?" She said louder.

If she draws too much attention, they might sweep the area, find the warhead.

"Shhhh," Stacy let out before fully weighing the risks of speaking. The girl fell silent. As Stacy watched the girl's dark eyes, large and pretty in her delicate face, she wished she'd not come over to her, wished she'd never seen her.

"Who's there?" the girl whispered.

Unsure of what to do, Stacy said nothing. No contact had been her orders. She'd already broken that and now found herself backed into a corner. She had to figure out how to get out. Standing, she took a step.

"If you leave, I'll scream," the girl said a bit louder, "Please—" her voice choked for a half beat, "don't leave."

Stacy settled back down and whispered, "Okay. Just don't make any noise."

The girl put her hands to her face, the half burned dandelion still between her fingers. When she lowered them, tears had wetted her cheeks.

Stacy's HUD told her she had to begin her return journey in eight minutes.

The girl whispered, "You're here to save us right? Please tell me you're here to help us."

I'm here to kill you all.

"Yes," Stacy said, and had to clench her teeth after the lie.

"Who are you?"

"Special Warfare."

The girl sobbed at that and covered her mouth. She looked over her shoulder at the nearest Sthenos guard who walked through the crowd of people quite a distance away.

"They let you sit this close to the fence?"

"They don't care. When we got here a man tried to take one of their weapons. They threw him into…," she held out her hand to the glistening tubes, "whatever this is. He passed through it without so much as slowing down." She pointed toward the sewage pits. "You can still see him down at the end."

Stacy did indeed see a scattered pile of something where the girl pointed.

"We can't touch the fence, can't overpower them, can't do anything. Please, you have to help us."

"I will," Stacy lied.

Just get the girl calmed down enough so you can get out of here.

As she imagined herself walking away, living while the girl was left to die, she considered sitting here beside her. It would be better to die with them than live having killed them. She would have done her job... but what of what she'd seen? Jeffrey had told them to make careful note of Sthenos interactions and, if possible, report back.

Someone else will report it from one of the other locations... maybe.

Still, she knew she had to leave if she was able.

"Everything's going to be okay."

"My parents are dead," the girl said, as her eyes brimmed anew. "They electrocuted them and..." She fell silent.

The girl's tears reminded Stacy of the heavy weight of losing her own father. The image of him slumped in Maxine King's reeducation chair came to her. The suddenness of the memory caused her to gasp. She shook her head and muttered to herself, "Let it go."

"What's that?" the girl whispered.

Stacy remained silent.

"Hello?" the girl whispered, her eyes going a bit wider as she leaned forward. "Are you there?"

"Yes. I'm here."

The girl's head dropped and she exhaled. She looked so pitiful, Stacy said, "I'm going to get you out of here," and wished with all her heart it wasn't a lie. At least the quick death Stacy would give her was better than what the Sthenos would offer.

The girl's back and shoulders trembled with crying. After a moment, Stacy heard a quiet, "Thank you." The girl lifted her head to face what Stacy knew was only an empty street. The girl's eyes, red from crying almost caught Stacy's but shifted lower like a blind person's. "Please hurry. There isn't much time."

"Why do you think there isn't much time?"

"They're butchering us."

CHAPTER 61

"It wasn't here," the girl said, her eyes falling back to the dandelion in her hand. She tossed it toward Stacy. Passing through the fence without resistance, it fell into smoking pieces. "They ate my parents in the front yard, right out in the open. My mom shot one of the fuckers' arms off before she died though."

The foul language coming from the young, pretty girl seemed the worst thing the Sthenos had brought to the world in that moment. As the girl pantomimed her arm blowing off with her fingers flicking wide, Stacy found it strange how, through all the dark things she'd seen, one harsh word could have such an impact on her.

"I couldn't look away as they—"

When she faltered, Stacy said, "My father was beaten to death," surprising herself in her bluntness. She hadn't spoken about it in years, having finally put the ghost to rest... as much as it would rest.

The girl's eyes rose again. "I'm sorry," she whispered. "I'm so sorry."

"I understand how hard it is."

"Did you have to watch?"

The question did not strike Stacy as cruel or dark, but hopeful as if searching for someone who would know her own pain.

"No, but the woman who ordered it made me look at his body afterward."

The girl said nothing.

Stacy, in her early twenties at the time of her father's murder, had already had her mind steeled by the military. This girl was nearly a decade younger. She should be planning for her first dance, worrying over who would ask her to go, not watching her father being eaten alive.

"You don't have to tell me if it's too much."

"No," the girl said, wiping her nose with the back of her hand. "You have to go tell them what they're doing here."

"I know what they do," Stacy said, hoping to spare the girl the grief of having to recount it. "It's…" but she fell short, not wanting to tell the girl what was happening on the other side of the wall.

The girl's chin puckered and her face tightened, "It's beyond that wall isn't it? They're processing us like cattle aren't they?" She let out a gasping sob.

Noticing her sob, the nearby Sthenos guard turned to her.

"I'm sorry—"

"Shhh" Stacy cut her off and fell silent as the guard walked up to the girl. In that lowered, centaur-like position it still towered over the girl. Lifting the rod, which crackled with blue arcs, the guard let out a deep thrumming mixed with the skin-chilling, variant clicking.

The girl stared hatred at it as she plucked a dandelion and tossed it at the guard's feet.

The thrumming tones increased, vibrating Stacy's chest and legs, and the clicking grew sharper. The Sthenos stood on its hind legs, its middle appendages folding around its waist. She caught the scent of ozone most likely coming off of the cooling unit on the back of the suit.

"They won't do anything to me," she said with an angry growl at the guard, "because they don't want to damage—" she ripped up a handful of dandelions and tossed them at the guard, "the meat."

As the dandelions fluttered to the Sthenos' broad, multi-clawed feet, Stacy found herself amazed at the girl's boldness. This girl was much stronger than she'd been at that age. Stacy had been a coward, nervous on the stage of the world. This one however, captured and sentenced to die, still had a great deal of fire in her heart. Stacy wanted to put a hole in the Sthenos' smoked face shield with the pistol on her hip, use the small length of det-cord she carried to blow down the fence, and take the girl with her.

The rod in the Sthenos' hand crackled. Whipping its arm, it sent a blue bolt crackling into the girl. Back arching, she fell, her hands locked into claws. The Sthenos settled down on all fours and walked away. The girl lay on her back, her arms relaxed, one in the grass and one across her belly. Her empty eyes reflected the pale-blue sky.

As she regained consciousness, she blinked and whispered, "Are you still there?"

"Yes."

The girl kept her eyes on the sky as she said, "They had me shackled when they ate them. They skinned my mother like a deer."

The girl patted her hands on her belly casually, as if she were discussing her weekend with a friend. "They want the good meat. They killed the older ones, burned the bodies. I've thought about it a lot. I think they ate my parents because they're only allowed to eat the older ones... maybe the ones that fight back. I think they're exporters. They're butchering us and," she pointed to the sky, "they're going to sell the meat to whoever is out there." Stacy's eyes followed the girl's finger up to the cirrus-streaked sky.

The girl sat up and held her head as her face winced with pain.

"Please don't leave me here."

Stacy looked to her HUD. She should have left two minutes ago. She could make up the time, but it put her at risk.

"I can't stay now, but keep your head down. I'll be back." The lie burned.

The girl looked over her shoulder at the Sthenos walking among the people, their rear legs bending unnaturally backwards. As she looked back, the fear in her eyes broke Stacy's heart.

"I can't help unless I leave. If they try to take you through those doors..." She took her K-bar from its sheath and shoved it tip-first through the fence. As the knife left her hand, it materialized and fell to the dirt. The handle smoked where it had brushed the fencing. "...do as much damage as you can."

The girl covered the blade with her hands and slid it under her thigh.

"I have to go," Stacy said.

The girl nodded, eyes down. "You'll be back right?"

"This will be over soon enough."

As Stacy stood, she felt something more needed to be said, but couldn't find the will to lie further. Instead, she walked away, haunted. She made her way with quick gliding steps to where her line hung down the building, draped over the rubble pile. She had yet to strategize how to get back up the rubble pile. Without the weight of the pack, and already having a line set, it would be easier.

The rubble at the front of the building consisted of everything from roofing tiles to concrete slabs to pieces of sinks and toilets. Large slabs of concrete made up this side of the rubble. Her eyes tracked up the slabs, as she visualized herself jumping from one to the next, but each path she picked ended in wide swaths of tile, bricks, loose stone, insulation, and glass. Far too noisy to disturb. Her eyes scanned up the line to where it disappeared over the cornice. If she made a noise and attracted the Sthenos now, they would see the line. They would know someone had infiltrated. They might launch the destroyer. Scanning the rubble all around, she found no place that would allow her a quiet escape and nowhere she could hide which was outside the singularity's range.

She was effectively trapped. She thought of going to sit with the girl until the warhead triggered, or she could hunker down in the hole where she had set the… the hole. In the corner of her memory she recalled there had been a half buried door in the low tunnel. She ran back to the hole and dropped down. There she found a metal door half covered with a slab of concrete. Pulling on the steel handle, she found the slab too heavy to move on her own. Taking out a new length of line from a second spool, she wrapped it around the slab. She tied a trucker's hitch in the rope and ran it up to a half exposed pipe on the far side of the hole. Wrapping the rope around the grating and then back to the hitch knot, and again, and again, she created a series of pulleys. She pulled on the rope slow and steady, and the slab shifted out of the way, dragging a path in the accumulated dirt with a ceramic sound. She sat listening to the street above and watching the clock on her HUD count how many minutes she'd overridden her departure time.

The street above remained quiet.

A few more minutes.

Still nothing.

Okay, time to fly.

She stuck her head into the doorway to find total blackness.

"Suit-Con," she whispered, "infrared." Infrared lamps mounted to her helmet lit the area. In her HUD, a narrow shaft, running down to a landing some thirty feet below, glowed in a ghostly green. A steel ladder had been bolted to the far side of the shaft. Stepping out onto it, she lowered herself down the rebar rungs to the platform.

A short passage opened into a subway tunnel. The end of a subway car sat somewhat tilted in the quiet tunnel. She looked over the side of the train, into the windows, and along the narrow concrete walkway. Finding nothing of interest, she began moving west along the foot-wide walkway. Counting her steps, she maintained an estimate of how far she'd come. She'd need a subway station or access shaft beyond the fenced area.

The tunnel turned northward. She walked on until she felt she'd moved well-away from the rubble perimeter, but found no access shafts nor stations. With each step north, she added to her distance to the rendezvous point. She began a low, quiet jog, again grateful to no longer have the weight of the pack.

Her HUD began pulsing red. She was now forty-one minutes past her departure time. She should be swimming the river now.

A loud clank of metal on metal sounded out ahead of her. She stopped and scanned the tunnel. The tracks lay to her right. Out ahead, perhaps 100 yards, a small frame of brilliant-green glowed around a doorway.

CHAPTER 62

"Suit-Con," Stacy whispered, "infrared off."

The tunnel fell into darkness. A rectangle of electric light now illuminated the doorframe.

Moving in the darkness with quiet steps, she slid her hand along the tile wall. Nearing the door, she listened. Voices murmured. No deep resonation or clicks. One was high pitched, nasal. The other deep, but not alien. They might be able to lead her out of the tunnel. It was a risk, but her gut told her to take it, so she turned the door knob and shoved the door open.

The light extinguished. She heard shuffling followed by the slip-clack of a gun-slide.

"I'm Commander Stacy Zack with U.S. Navy Special Warfare. I'm here to help."

"Show yourself."

With a loaded weapon trained on me? Good luck.

"Suit-Con," she whispered to her suit, "Infrared on." The world came back to her glowing green. She leaned around the door frame. The room was a storage area of some kind with shelving units along the walls. Two men in jumpsuits hunkered at the back beside a cluttered desk. The larger aimed a shotgun on the doorway. Moving quietly on the balls of her feet, Stacy stepped through the doorway and to the right, out of the line of fire.

"Gentlemen, I need you to remain calm."

As she spoke, the larger man's eyes went wider, searching the darkness.

She moved further right, now up against the shelving.

The smaller man flicked on the light at the same time the larger man fired the shotgun blindly right where Stacy had been standing. While her suit had muffled the blast, she knew their ears would be ringing.

This is not how I'd hoped this would go down.

The electric light overwhelmed the infrared and her suit automatically cut out the display. She stood seven feet or so from the men, both unwashed and unshaven with eyes narrowing against the bright light. They wore stained, orange jumpsuits with black letters stencil-sprayed across the chest, "Property of Allegany Co."

Prisoners.

Stacy wanted to leave, but before she could, she had to deal with the shotgun. Even an errant shot in the right direction of a sound could severely injure her if not cut her in half. She cursed herself silently for having come in the room.

The man lifted the shotgun to his shoulder, finger on the trigger. He tracked the barrel left and right, sweeping it momentarily across Stacy's chest.

When the barrel tracked away from her, she leapt forward, slapping the gun to the side. It went off with a concussion that left even her ears ringing. She whipped her elbow over his shoulder and caught the side of his neck with a heavy thump. His eyes went vague as he dropped. She snatched the gun's receiver and pulled it from his hands as he fell. Foot-long sections of the gun vanished as the suit attempted to cloak it, but it was too long to fully vanish.

The man had fallen to his knees, and to assure he wouldn't lunge for her, she kicked him in the chest, knocking him backward. She threw the half visible shotgun out the door. It clattered to the tracks in the darkness.

The smaller man was staring directly at her so she moved sideways with cautious steps out of his sightline. The larger man groaned and rolled over, holding his neck.

"What do you want?" he asked, his voice sounding vague after being nearly knocked unconscious.

"I don't want trouble," Stacy said. "I need to know how to get out of here, fast."

"Uncloak yourself and I'll tell you."

Stacey laughed. "Tell me, or I'll kill you and have your friend tell me."

"Then get the hell out of here. This is the Broadway tunnel. You got stations in ten blocks either way."

"Which is closer?" But in that moment Stacy had underestimated the big man. He lunged forward, not at her, but for the doorway. He slammed the door shut with an echoing bang of metal and turned to generally where she stood. At his full height he was over six feet tall and well over two-hundred pounds.

"I know you're still in here, and I can tell by your voice you're a sweet little girl." A wicked smile drew across his face. "We're gonna have ourselves a little *talk*."

Stacy said, "So that's what it comes to. We make all this progress for thousands of years and in a few days and a few missed meals this is what we fall to?"

"Oh not *we*, honey," the big man said, rubbing his hands together, "I never been any good. We ain't all raised with silver spoons in our mouths."

Stacy was about to make her move on the man, when something in the back of her mind came forward. "Where did you come from?"

"Allegany County Pri—"

"I can see that. How did you get here?"

"The eaters brought us."

"Eaters."

"Well, that's what they doin' ain't they?"

"I suppose."

"It's true. So when they got us out of the prison and moved us all around, they cut up the old ones and burned 'em. Meat must be no good. No matter, those old guys have nothin' but bullshit stories anyway. They spent their whole lives behind bars and then think they have somethin' to tell me." The man laughed, "Those spider things can't have me though, and not Shay here neither."

Stacy looked to the smaller man Shay, who touched his forehead in a flippant salute. He smiled showing darkly yellowed teeth.

The larger man continued, "I'll be damned if I'm gonna be some freak's meal. At night Shay and me dug under the fence. We know what to do. Spread the dirt out across the yard, so there's no evidence, dig it in between bushes and fill it with branches. We worked slow and took turns. If the guards looked too close, one of us would cause a distraction, pick a fight or somethin'. You know. It only took us a week. Stupid fuckers are useless guards."

"Is the hole still there?"

"Yeah... why?"

Stacy looked at her HUD. She had thirty minutes before the singularity went off.

I only want to get one out.

"No matter though," Shay said behind her. He smiled. "It's the end of the world, and you sound pretty."

"Are you sure?" Stacy asked.

Shay hesitated at the question.

"Oh we're sure," came the larger one's response. "We're absolutely sure. Now I'm gonna go ahead and cover the exit while Shay here swings a metal pipe around. IF he hits you and we get our hands on you, then you gonna regret it. Why not just shut that fancy cloaking device off and let us have a look at you?"

Stacy said, "I don't have time for this."

Shay took a three-foot pipe from the desk and swung it like a baseball bat. When he stepped forward, Stacy stood right in the strike zone. As he swung it again, Stacy dropped into a pushup position. The pipe whipped over her head.

The big man said, "Looks like you gonna have to make time."

Stacy pulled her pistol and trained it between the big man's eyes. "Last chance to step out of the doorway."

The pipe whipped the air again.

"Sorry boys," she said and pulled the trigger. The gun's grip bucked into her palm as the small silencer reduced the report to a crack, still pronounced in the confined room. A hole appeared between the big man's eyes as dark material splattered against the door. He tilted forward and slammed face first to the ground, dead.

She asked Shay, "Where's the tunnel you dug?"

Shay dropped the pipe mid swing. As it clanked to the floor, he said, "I…"

"The tunnel. Save your life Shay, talk quickly. If you lie, I come back and hunt you down. How did you get out of the fence?"

Shay did speak quickly, almost too quickly for Stacy to understand. "There's a transformer with three bushes around it near the latrine. It's between the bushes."

"Where does it come out?"

Shay looked to the door as if he might make a run for it.

Stacy shot the light switch behind him and all fell into darkness.

"Suit-Con," she said, "infrared."

"Now Shay, you're standing in complete darkness and I can see you as clear as day. If you want to live, tell me where it comes out."

"I don't know… about ten feet away from the fence there's a big hole in the street, a big crack where a foundation was. We dug out there. There's a cab next to it, smashed flat by a street light."

"North or south of the fence?"

"North… ten feet north."

Stacy watched Shay's frightened eyes. Here she had a man compliant in fear, but a few moments ago, he'd been ready to hit her with a pipe and do what he liked. He was a killer and a user. If they succeeded in stopping the Sthenos, the next step would be to save the human race from those like him. If she let him live, if he found someone defenseless, he'd use them just like he'd said he wanted to use her.

"I'm sorry Shay."

"No, no, please," he said as if reading her mind. "You need to know how to get out of here, and I can help you do that. The next station is ten blocks away. It'll take a long time. I can have you on the surface in two minutes."

"How?"

"Give me your word you won't kill me, and I'll tell you."

Stacy thought for a moment before saying, "Okay. Tell me."

A look of relief washed over Shay's face, and he side stepped. Stacy kept her pistol trained on his skull as he moved. He pointed behind him to a metal door that Stacy had taken for a closet. "That's the exit right there. There's a ladder up to a manhole cover."

"Open the door."

Shay walked over and pulled the door open. It moved readily on oiled hinges and clanked to a stop on the wall. Stacy could see the rungs of a ladder on the far wall.

"That won't do me any good Shay."

"Why not?"

"There's a pile of rubble where I need to go I can't climb. I have to go back the way I came."

"The pile they made? No, on the north side, there's a pathway over it that's just concrete blocks, you can climb it without making noise. It's right on 6th Avenue. That's how we got out. It'll bring you right over to the tunnel we dug."

Stacy considered her options, go back and have to arc around to the south side of Bryant Park because the subway tracks didn't go straight to the park. She didn't have time for that. She'd have to trust a convict's word.

"Okay Shay, get out of here."

Shay began to step through the door.

"Not that way. Go into the subway tunnel and walk down the walkway. I'm going to watch you. If you stop, I kill you."

"H-How far do I have to go?"

"I'd suggest not stopping."

Shay stepped forward, but crashed into a metal shelf. "I can't see nothin'."

"What would you prefer, walking in pitch dark and turning an ankle or having your skull sprayed all over the subway tracks like your friend?"

"You gave me your—"

"Don't push me. I'm out of time."

Shay nodded and began to move toward the outer door with sliding steps, hands out in front of him. As he passed her, she stepped aside. Her boot shifted the pipe Shay had swung at her. His eyes turned toward her. Holding the tip of her pistol a few inches from his skull, she would have killed him if she sensed aggression of any kind, but all she saw was stark fear. He had to kick the big man's legs out of the way to pull open the door. Leaning out into the tunnel he looked back at her.

"I can't see nothin'."

"Just follow the wall."

"Which way?"

"Go left, away from where I'm going. If I see you again… you die. Got it?"

He nodded. "Thanks for not killin' me."

"My guess is that you'll be dead soon enough anyway."

Shay's eyes, glowing green in the IR light, gave him a soulless look. "Ma'am, you're probably right." He walked into the darkness. Stacy moved to the outer door and watched him moving away down the narrow walkway his left hand tracing the wall.

"Keep walking. I'm watching," she said as she holstered her pistol and went to the doorway at the back of the room. Stepping inside the closet-like space, she looked up. Shay had been truthful. A rebar-rung ladder ran up some thirty feet to the disk of a man-hole cover laced with little circles of brilliant-green light. She was not excited about lifting a man hole cover for the noise it would make but had few options.

She climbed the ladder quietly, not wanting to reveal to the convict she'd already stopped watching him. The space smelled of loam and fungus. At the top, keeping a grip with her good, left hand,

377

she shoved on the manhole cover with the top of her head and her right hand, the torn tendon spiking pain into her palm. The cover resisted for a moment, but with a pulse of effort she dislodged it from the sediment around it's rim, which fell with little clatters into the hole. She lifted the cover. As the shaft filled with sunlight, the suit cut the IR, leaving her in natural daylight.

Balancing the cover on its side, knowing full well what would happen if she dropped it, she shimmied herself butt first onto the street. Coming to her feet, she moved around to the other side of the cover, stuck her fingers through its inner holes, and set it down in its circular depression.

Her HUD showed her she was fully an hour behind schedule and had only twenty-five minutes before the singularity would trigger. She should have been at least three miles away. She looked beyond the tops of the buildings to the towering Sthenos destroyer, standing like a shard of obsidian lanced into the city's hide. The clouds had faded from the higher reaches, leaving the ship stark against the sky.

Time to get moving.

She ran into the afternoon light angling between the towering, empty buildings.

CHAPTER 63

Jeffrey stared at the Nav-Con's dark disk with Leif and Holloway. At 5:01 GMT they'd turn everything on. Only then would he know their fate. He had no idea where his teams were and felt he might lose his mind in that vacant space. He wanted to go hands on, to strap into a Lakota and fight, but that wasn't his role anymore. He would sit and wait, listen and coordinate as his men and women fought… and died. He dreaded standing aside as they did, knowing what would come over the com channels in the next few hours would likely haunt him until his dying day.

His thoughts turned to his pilots. Who were they really? He hoped they were strong enough, but he'd missed the mark with Nathan Brooks. It was easy enough to be bold before the fight.

When death grips their shoulder, who will they prove to be?

Jeffrey had heard arrogant men crying in their last moment. He'd seen the bold run when the odds shifted. Then there were those like Maco, who when death came for him, without words put his arm around destruction's shoulder.

Fifty years he's been dead. I wish he were with us now.

Jeffrey looked at his watch. 4:40 GMT.

20 minutes.

•••

Stacy's HUD said she had twenty minutes until singularity initiation. She'd found the concrete slabs which formed a staircase off of 6th Avenue just as the convict had said. Across the field, she saw the grassy area where she'd talked with the girl. It lay empty.

...

Marco sat in his Wraith. He hadn't flown a fighter in a few years, but if he could survive being chased by Sthenos in a transport, he felt sure he'd do fine in this. He could see the hulking engines in his rear view mirrors. Even with the modifications, which had left the back of his left index finger numb—something he hadn't told the doc—he knew this ship could beat the hell out of him, knock him out and snap his neck. He felt as though he were in a bull-pen chute, sitting on a broad, twitching back.

"GMT 4:45 folks," came a call over the radio, "Fire 'em up."

Marco's stomach tensed as he initiated the firing sequence. The nuclear engines spooled up with a turbine like whistle, rising in volume and deepening in pitch until his ship rumbled like a volcano, the engines thump-thumping as they warmed and settled in. As the seat resonated behind him, he wondered if Sofía was alive. He hadn't let himself think much about her or his children. Downtown L.A. had a Sthenos destroyer spiked into it, and after Denver, the war would go there. He prayed she'd been able to get away. He wished he'd never taken her from her quiet home in Mexico. She'd have been better off poor but safe. His thoughts turned to his parents. He wondered if they'd find forgiveness for him now.

As he adjusted his seat straps, he looked up beyond the opening in the trees to the high clouds. In less than fifteen minutes he and the other Wraith pilots would launch through them and into the starry void—thirty-three against thousands. He wished somehow he could get one last message to his wife, to let her know he loved her, and just before his death, he wanted only to think about her dark, beautiful eyes and warm smile.

...

Stacy had run on light feet halfway around the fencing. She'd spotted the place where she needed the girl to go, two bushes on the

380

far side of the Sthenos destroyer's broad base, but no girl. She would stop every twenty feet or so and scan the faces.

There are so many… Have they already taken her through the wall? …processed her?

The thought of the girl passing through the slaughterhouse made her stumble.

She looked up the reach of the destroyer, a vertical cliff-face glittering in the sun, its prow invisible in its height. When her gaze returned to the crowd, as if by fate, it landed on the girl. Stacy inhaled, checking her elation. The girl stood among several others, her eyes hollow, skin pale.

The girl's gaze shifted in a slow arc. Her eyes looked like those of a corpse, as though she'd given up so completely on life that her inevitable death had already sidled into them. She seemed terribly thin standing up, hip bones showing through her pants, the joints of her elbows larger than her biceps. Stacy ignored the rest of the crowd, unable to bear acknowledging them. If she could save just the girl, that might mean something in the years to come.

Stacy picked up a small stone and threw it at the girl. The stone arced through the air against the backdrop of the monstrous ship and landed at the girl's feet. One of the people standing beside her looked around.

Stacy threw another small stone. This one sailed through the air and cracked right between the girls eyes. Blood bloomed there. Stacy winced.

"Ow," the girl shouted and clapped her hand to her forehead. A Sthenos guard looked in the direction of the girl. The girl held her forehead as one of the adults asked if she was all right. The Sthenos guard walked over, towering above their heads on its hind legs.

The girl said something to them and, holding her face trickling with blood, turned from the Sthenos guard and walked toward Stacy on the fence line. The Sthenos guard's attention remained fully on her as she sat down. Stacy moved over to her, watching the guard as it continued to stare at the girl.

Give up on her. She's nothing but a weak girl ready to die. Just look away.

But the Sthenos guard did not look away. He walked over to the girl.

Stacy had run out of time, she had to hope the girl understood. "Do you see the transformer with three bushes around it?"

The girl said, almost inaudibly, "Yes."

"Go there when the guard stops being interested in you. There's a tunnel dug between the bushes under a stack of branches. I'll meet you at the other end of the tunnel."

The girl gave one simple dip of her chin to acknowledge.

The Sthenos guard lifted its silver rod, which scattered blue fans of electric sparks.

Stacy now had nine minutes to get the girl through the tunnel and move at least a quarter mile away.

• • •

In the hills north of Los Angeles, Sofía Fields ran as fast as she could up the slope carrying Luciano in one arm, and fairly dragging Emilia. Stealing one look over her shoulder, she saw the black transport had stopped at the edge of the trees. Beneath it, the air warped and pine needles and dirt floated in its shadow.

Sprinting around the trees with the weight of her children on her, the burning in her legs became numbness, and she felt they might give out at any moment. She gasped for air. The dawn light, angling in under the trees, threw the long shadows of her racing legs out ahead of her. She glanced back again. The rising sun framed one side of the ship in brilliant light. The side opened and a dark shape emerged. She could not see clearly due to the bright light, but it seemed to have too many legs. She did not look back again.

As she ran she heard the transport begin thumping again. It was moving. When she came out onto the gravel access road, cut into the ridge crest, she saw its broad, dark shape coming around the hillside on the road. Despite her exhaustion, she sprinted across the road, but her legs finally did betray her and she fell spilling Luciano from her arms. Landing head first on the gravel, he began to yowl. She turned him over, blood began pouring from a cut on his smooth cheek. Without a word of comfort, Sofía picked him up and ran on, Emilia's little legs barely keeping up.

She dropped down into the forest on the other side, now barely able to breathe, her legs feeling as though they were filled with lead shot. She had to find a place to hide. She wouldn't be able to outrun them much longer. Luciano howled in her ear as blood dripped warm on her neck.

Finding a narrow ravine, she slid down into it. At the base of the ravine she found drifts of pine needles, which she threw over Emilia.

"Stay perfectly silent Emilia, no matter what you hear. Do you understand?"

"Yes mama."

She covered over her face loosely. "No matter what, you stay still."

She tried to bury Luciano in the same way, hoping to run off again, drawing the things away from her children, but his screaming wouldn't be quelled, so she dug a larger pit in the needles and buried herself with the boy. Covering herself over as best she could. In the dim light under the needles she tried to hush him. He screamed louder his eyes wild with fear.

"Mijo, I need you to be calm, to help me protect your sister."

At that his cries quieted. He gave her a silent nod in the dim light under the needles.

The thumping rose up and she heard scuffling and… not footsteps… but almost hoof-falls coming near. They'd been found. She'd have to keep running.

Sitting up out of the needles, what she saw caused her to freeze with fear. Perhaps ten yards away stood a red monster, a mirrored, faceless head with a centaur's body, but insect-like in its sheen and segments. It's head turned on her. Leaving Luciano behind, she took up a branch and ran at the beast, screaming bloody murder.

The beast raised a chromed pipe. As the pipe caught the sunlight, the light seemed to jump out of it. Crackling into her, it wrapped her in darkness.

...

On the other side of the world, Whitetip sat in her Lakota waiting. The vast swath of Tokyo's lights shone through the shadowed shapes of branches, which blustered on a heavy breeze. The city's fusion generators had somehow stayed online. The monolithic spire of the Sthenos destroyer towered over the sea of silvered, multi-story buildings. Nearby, an island of darkness marked the imperial palace. Somewhere between here and there was X and the singularity warhead. He'd told her he'd be back with hours to spare, and in his confidence, she'd felt hope.

But he hadn't returned. Her Lakota's clock read 4:51 GMT. In 9 minutes she'd know her fate. If the stern of the destroyer wasn't consumed, if the massive ship failed to tip over and crash into the city, she'd have to take it down herself. It would be easy in the night. She'd come over the tops of the buildings fast, follow the ship up into the sky as it launched, and trigger the singularity just as she had when she took out the first destroyer. Yet, this time she wasn't piloting a drone. She'd go with it, crushed into the space in the back seat where the backpack lay with wires running to a switch beside her.

She was willing to do it, knew the destroyer couldn't be allowed to launch, but as she thought of dying, she felt the scarcity of her twenty-two years. As a Navy pilot, she'd lived an amazing life but had so much left she'd like to do. She spent those final moments visualizing the destroyer falling, imagined X coming back, and her hugging him.

At 4:52 GMT, she gripped the control yoke with her right hand, and with her left pressed the switch to release the compressed air. The air hissed as the Lakota's turbines spooled up, fired, and built to a whine. Beside her, the Norwegian called Kodiak's Lakota fired up.

•••

Sofía opened her eyes to see pine boughs against a blue sky. Her head hurt, and at first, she couldn't remember where she was. She sat up with a start, finding her arms shackled behind her and legs bound together.

"Luciano, Emilia!"

Several meters away one of the monsters held her children, Emilia by the upper arm and Luciano by his shirt front. Emilia tugged violently against its grip, while Luciano wailed. The monster had its helmet off exposing white, irisless eyes, which seemed half-rotted out. As it lifted Luciano, screaming, over its head, it's wide mandibles opened, exposing a second set of scissor-like inner jaws, flicking at its upper pallet.

"Leave him alone!" she screamed.

The thing looked at her.

"Let them go!"

Rolling to her knees, she hopped to her feet, and jumped toward it.

It looked at Luciano and then Emilia. It could not draw its weapon and maintain hold of the two children. If she could get it to attack her, perhaps it might release them.

It lunged at her, slamming her with its chest. Heavy ozone and the scent of a rotten-sea overwhelmed her as she fell. When it stomped on her leg, a loud crack sounded out. She screamed against the pain. Keeping its weight on her leg, it held her children up.

"Please... no," Sofía said in gasping breaths.

Its mandibles opened as it let out a low, reverberating sound, which tickled at the hairs on her neck.

•••

385

Seven minutes to go and the Sthenos guard seemed unwilling to move away. He'd continued staring at the girl. Wolves would single out a weak member of a herd. Stacy wondered if the girl had somehow triggered a predatorial instinct. If the Sthenos shocked her, knocked her unconscious, there would be no way to save her. Stacy leveled her pistol on the dark, glassy lens of the Sthenos' helmet. The helmet might be armored, but very few things that allowed light to pass could stop a bullet.

Steadying her breath, she shifted to a solid base on her knees, sitting on her heels. Her heart thumped in her chest. She exhaled slowly as she increased the pressure on the trigger. Before she could fire, the girl drew the knife and leapt high, slashing at the arm which held the rod. The Sthenos guard let out a piercing scream as it dropped the rod.

The girl ran. On the other side of the fence, Stacy ran with her.

The next closest Sthenos guard dropped to all six limbs and came sprinting at the girl at perhaps forty miles an hour. Stacy stopped, leveled her gun at the shifting visor, and fired. The Sthenos' head whipped back, and it tumbled forward, skidding head first to a stop in the dirt. The left side of its visor lens blown out. Dark wetness pumped through the shattered glass.

Stacy looked back for the girl, who still ran full-tilt toward the bushes.

"Good girl," Stacy said.

Two more Sthenos guards had focused their attention on the running girl. Stacy stopped and fired at each of their visors. Neither shot found its mark perfectly, but caught one in the forehead with a metallic spark and the other in the throat, which seemed to do no damage. But the impacts caused them both to stop and scan the fence-line. Stacy ran to the taxi with the light pole buried in its roof, just as the convict had described. The girl was almost to the two bushes, but the second Sthenos closed on her in a full gallop.

Stacy aimed her pistol with both hands at the Sthenos' visor. *Make it count.*

386

She fired, and the Sthenos' head snapped backward as the visor shattered. It fell in a jumble of limbs.

The girl reached the transformer and disappeared between the shrubs. Sticks flew up in the air. Stacy scanned the area. The third guard had stopped coming on when the second had died, appearing now to cautiously survey the street beyond the fence-line. In the distance, other Sthenos were galloping across the field, knocking people down as they ran, but they were running toward the fallen guards, not toward where the girl had disappeared. Stacy came around behind the taxi.

Sure enough, she found a gap in the concrete. A narrow tunnel had been dug out of the side wall. With nothing to do but wait for the girl, she looked over their escape route. She needed a quarter mile at least from the point of singularity, and more would be better.

As she scanned the open ground up to the concrete slabs on 6th Avenue, she heard the thumping growl of a patrol ship. It came around the side of the Sthenos destroyer and rushed up to her. As it passed, the girl emerged from the tunnel covered in dirt, standing up waist deep in the hole.

The patrol ship slowed and turned.

"Get down," Stacy said, and the girl crouched as the patrol ship's main gun tracked to the taxi and fired. Stacy leapt aside as the concrete in front of the hole exploded and dust obscured the patrol ship, the hole, and the taxi.

Sprinting at the patrol ship, Stacy holstered her pistol and, pulling a thin cylinder-grenade from her hip, pressed its trigger, arming and magnetizing it. Leaping onto the nose of the ship, she slapped the grenade onto the metal below the cockpit glass.

Sliding back down the nose, she ran for a small pile of debris as fast as her feet would carry her. She flipped sideways over the debris and landed on a concrete block, which cracked into her side. A sharp flash of pain told her she'd broken a rib. Gunfire erupted over the pile of debris a moment before a concussion shook the ground followed by thumping secondary explosions.

Stacy lifted her head to find the ship lying on the asphalt not far from where the girl hid, it's cockpit blown out and black smoke roiling up into the sky. As she stood, a sharp spike from her rib made her gasp. She felt light headed, but as Jeffrey might say, she'd have time to feel the pain later. Looking to her HUD for her time, she found it blank. She looked at her hands. They were in full view, either her fall, the shots, or the grenade had shut down her stealth.

She ran to the gap behind the taxi as the girl stood up, her entire body powdered with concrete dust and asphalt chunks. She looked like a statue.

Stacy pointed to the stair-stepped rubble. "Run!"

The girl hopped out of the hole and ran. Looking over her shoulder, Stacy found all the Sthenos guards staring at her.

"No matter bastards. Stay there a few more minutes and you'll be dead." Her eyes shifted to the people, thousands of them, all looking at her. One man shouted out, raising his fist in the air in victory. The hope she saw in their eyes would haunt her the rest of her life.

A voice screamed behind her. Turning, she saw the girl already at the base of the rubble holding out her hands as if asking if she was going to run. The thumping of another patrol ship rose up. Stacy sprinted toward the girl. "Go!" she screamed waving the girl up the pile. The singularity would trigger in a few seconds.

The girl was half-way up the rubble.

If I can see her get over the pile, if I can just believe that she got out of here it will be okay. I just need one.

The girl scrambled over the pile and out of sight, but the rubble was still within the quarter mile distance to the singularity warhead.

Stacy didn't look back as the thumping increased behind her. She sprinted up the rubble pile on hands and feet, her palm and rib screaming pain at her. As she came to the top, she saw the girl running down the street. Stacy leapt off the last half of the debris, rolled on the asphalt and came to her feet sprinting, the broken rib stabbing her in the side as she gasped for air.

The thumping behind her became louder and the roof of a car beside her flashed with green light and melted away. The heat threw a concussion that knocked her over. Skidding across the street, her helmet crashed into a curb. Rolling to her back, she saw the patrol ship, now coming off the rubble pile, racing toward her. Beyond it stood the spire of the Sthenos destroyer against the sky. A heavy wind picked up sucking dirt and loose papers toward the debris pile, which chewed away from behind, until it had vanished.

The singularity's triggered.

The patrol ship fired again, and the green beam, lanced into the asphalt a few feet away and raced toward her, the chunks it knocked free flying away on the wind. Then the patrol ship was shredded to nothing in a blink. The beam vanished, leaving a shattered line in the asphalt, which ended a few centimeters from her feet. The wind intensified, pulling her toward the destroyer. She snatched the iron bars of a gutter drain.

The street began tearing away as the event horizon raced up on her, the buildings on either side peeling away.

Stacy wasn't outside the blast zone, but the girl had made it. Knowing that made Stacy's death okay. She'd saved one and felt she deserved no less than she'd given to the people in the fence. The event horizon flashed up to her feet and her boot tugged on her leg as though a powerful animal had gotten a hold of it, and then… nothing. The wind swirled around her and fell into silence. A haze of dust hung in the air. The buildings on either side of her rained down sheets of glass and papers, into a half mile void gouged out of the island's hide, which she now lay at the edge of.

Torn pipes hung from the walls of the cavernous bowl. Dark subway tunnels yawned. A spray of water whipped away to a black mass, where everything within the event horizon had been crushed to its atomic mass. A perfect sphere about the size of a medicine ball. The sewer water misted as it raced to the sphere and meshed with it, wetting the dark surface. The stream of water fell as the singularity died away. The sphere fell as well, crashing down into the great bowl.

A moment later, the crack of it landing reached her, followed by a shockwave in the ground.

Stacy looked up to the Sthenos destroyer, its entire stern gone, floating high above, the last two thirds of the ship suspended in the blue sky with a great, curved bite taken out of it. It began to fall, tilting toward her. She leapt to her feet and ran. She felt as though she had a knife jammed in her lung, but she gave everything she had.

A great shadow blocked out the sun as she sprinted between the buildings. Looking over her shoulder, she saw the prow of the destroyer tilting out over her line of escape. The buildings pinned her in to the north and south. She had no way out. Sliding to a stop, she stuffed her fingers into a sewer cover and hauled on it, her injured hand and broken rib searing with pain as she pulled it free. The destroyer crashed through the tops of the buildings above her. She hopped into the circular pit of darkness and let herself fall straight down into the unknown. If it was a few feet deep, she'd be killed by the falling ship. If it was deep enough to survive the ship, she might break a leg or worse. The wind roared around her as she fell into the pitch black. The unseen bottom of the hole slammed into her feet. Her right leg and ankle exploded with pain as the ground crashed into her arms and face.

With her last ounce of will, she rolled into what she hoped would be open space. She found it, rolling over and over until she heard concrete and dirt crash down where she'd been. As the floor jolted, she turned face down with her arms over her head, waiting for the unseen ceiling to crash down on her. It didn't. A moment longer… silence. She took a small flashlight from her chest and flicked it on. Grayness surrounded her. She could see nothing save swirling dust.

Shutting the light off, she lay back and finally allowed herself to scream against the pain of her broken leg, ruined ankle, injured hand, and cracked rib.

CHAPTER 64

The engines of Whitetip's Lakota whined as they rose to operating temperature. She stared at the clock on her HUD. Beyond it, looming in the darkness above Tokyo some ten miles off, she could see the spire of the Sthenos destroyer. The digital display ticked from 4:59:59 to 5:00:00 GMT, and the seconds continued on. Her eyes shifted to the base of the destroyer. Having no idea what a detonated singularity warhead would look like, she imagined a deep blackness growing into a sphere.

But nothing happened.

The clock moved on through 5:00:30 GMT. At 5:01:00 she was to launch if there was no damage to the destroyer. Its base still glittered in the lights, and… nothing.

Her eyes moved to the clock. 5:00:45. Fifteen seconds to live. Eyes back to the destroyer… nothing. Something had gone wrong. At that moment, a dark sphere formed, not at the base of the ship, but in the sea of city lights halfway to the destroyer. It expanded in a few seconds to half a mile across before collapsing back down, leaving a circular void in the lights. X had failed. In his failure, her time had come to an end.

...

"What are we looking at?" Jeffrey asked, leaning over the Nav-Con operator's shoulder, as he shielded the bright sunlight from his eyes.

Leif, Dr Monti, and Commander Holloway all stood behind this one operator.

In a calm, focused voice, the kid said, "I won't know for a few more minutes."

Jeffrey looked at his mission timer. 5:02 GMT now. It should be on now. The destroyers were either falling to the ground or launching into the stratosphere.

Jeffrey looked out to where the Wraiths should be taking off out of the valley, and as if he had awakened them with the thought, a horrible roar rose up among the trees. Flights of snow-white birds lifted away across the valley. The Wraiths ascended after them, stubby delta wings and canard-bladed nosecones. As they leaned back on their main engines, the roar grew, thundering across the valley. Thirty-three ships shot into the blue sky, their thunder fading into resonant thuds.

As the glow of their engines turned to specks of light, the thunder grew distant, as if a far off storm that might never realize itself.

"God speed friends."

A hand touched his shoulder. He looked to find Leif pointing to the displays.

The operator had live screens, but the Nav-Con was still dark.

"What do you have?" Jeffrey asked.

"It's a communications satellite operating at a geosynchronous position over the North Pole. I've located the space-borne Sthenos destroyer and am sending coordinates to the Wraiths now."

"Is there only one?"

"As far as I can tell."

Jeffrey felt a rush of relief. The possibility that more Sthenos destroyers had come during their blackout had been eating away at his confidence for weeks. Looking up, he found the Wraiths had disappeared. He imagined what the pilots were seeing, the ground dropping away, the blue deepening to violet as the first stars came out. The Earth's broad horizon curving. He wished he could be up there with them. He'd never realized how difficult it was to be a mission leader, to be absolutely responsible for those men and women, and when the most important part came, to have to sit and wait, to watch them burn.

"What about the ground-based destroyers?"

"I'm gathering data now sir," the Nav-Con officer said as he adjusted the controls and entered commands. In a moment the globe of the Earth appeared on the Nav-Con the size of a basketball.

Jeffrey leaned forward as the markers for the twenty-two ground based Sthenos destroyers appeared. As the image of the Earth rotated New York came into view. The green fleck of light that marked the ship Stacy had been sent to destroy flicked to red. The globe kept turning and Denver's light flicked red. Los Angeles flicked red as did Mexico City.

"Sir," the operator said, "we have the ships all where we expected them. Twenty-two planet side and only one in orbit." He listened for a moment, gripped his fist in a quiet celebration, and reached out, spinning the globe with a swipe of his fingers. With quick, excited words, he said, "We have confirmed kills on all destroyers... save Tokyo." He zoomed in on Japan, where the destroyer's marker lay nestled in the belly of the Tokyo sprawl. As the image zoomed in, the ship began lifting away from the city.

Whitetip's assignment.

"We have about half of the special warfare operatives back to their origin points," the Nav-Con officer said. "The other half are unaccounted for."

"Have the fuelers arrived in New Mexico, and the Ukraine?"

"Yes, sir," the operator said. "We have only one Lakota down with a mechanical malfunction in Mexico. Everything else is in place."

As Jeffrey watched the Tokyo based Sthenos destroyer lift away, he asked, "Current altitude?"

"5,000 feet and climbing at Mach 2, sir."

...

She was halfway across the city of Tokyo now. While they were invisible in the dark sky, on her IFF display red sparks of light swarmed across the sky as Sthenos fighters poured from the upper reaches of the destroyer. The destroyer itself glowed a brilliant, ruby red at the center of her HUD. She began to jig and turn, barrel rolling and twisting as she crossed the open space. A beam of green energy lanced by to her right.

"Got him," Kodiak said over the radio. Yellow fire bloomed in her small kidney-shaped rearview mirrors.

"These guys really can't keep up with us," Kodiak said.

She understood why not. With each jig she was pulling G's which should have blacked her out. She had to will herself to go beyond rational limits. As she curved over, her vision tunneled only when she pulled 16 G's. She felt as though her brain was a fusion reactor, a smoldering glow of awareness. She felt she could keep every single element on the IFF in her mind at once. She sensed the space around her aircraft as if it was her own skin and could imagine multiple pathways from each moment as clearly as if she'd had hours to draw them out on a flight plan board.

Kodiak continued to strip Sthenos fighters off of her as she kept up a scattered pattern, assuring both she and he kept their six clear. Racing across the blurring sea of city lights, she leaned the Lakota onto its mains and shoved the throttle to its stops, growling against the crushing acceleration. Beyond her HUD, the Sthenos Destroyer's glowing volcano-red engines lifted into the sky. The delta between her acceleration and the destroyer's cascaded from 1200 to nothing and then into negative hundreds as she passed into Mach 3.

As she passed the destroyer's engines, their blast buffeted the Lakota. She fought the stick to keep her line close and true. She could have triggered the singularity then, but Kodiak was right behind her, well within the quarter mile radius. Also, there were too many Sthenos fighters outside of it. At the top of the destroyer, fighters still poured out. If she could destroy that portion, the fighters would be gone as well. But what if the destroyer could achieve orbit with only the back half?

Slowing, she let the ship slide back by, so she flew just beside it, the air coming off the ship shaking the Lakota's wings.

Kodiak flew 100 meters behind her.

She keyed the radio, "Get out of here Kodiak."

"I'm—"

"Get the hell out of here… please."

His ship dropped away and when he had moved more than a quarter mile away Whitetip flicked open the plastic switch cover. She wondered for a moment if she would feel herself be crushed. In that moment she would have given anything to have just a bit more time. One more love affair, one more day on a warm beach, one more snowfall. But so that others might have them instead, she threw the switch.

…

Kodiak hadn't seen the singularity form. He'd turned away, taken a Sthenos fighter, barrel rolled out of another's sights, and when he came back around, the ship was simply missing it's lower half… and Whitetip was gone. The destroyers prow slowed to a stop, seeming to go weightless for a moment before dropping back down into the sea of light that was Tokyo.

As the ship crashed into the lights, dark swaths forming as it hit, he felt no victory, only emptiness for the young woman now gone. Turning toward a large group of fighters, he throttled on. The fighters seemed for a moment lost, unable to respond to the loss of their destroyer, and he fired into the poorly formed group, taking ten with as many shots. He fired again, and again.

…

The Nav-Con operator shouted out as though he were at a baseball game when the red marker for the Sthenos destroyer over Tokyo winked out. Beside him Dr. Monti hugged Leif and kissed him—not passionately, but with the unrepentant joy of a victory wholly unexpected.

"Give me the status of all other ground-based destroyers," Jeffrey said.

"All destroyed, sir," the officer said and gave a whoop of innocent joy.

Jeffrey was glad to let him have it. They'd done nothing but lose until this moment, and even Jeffrey had to admit he felt... vindicated. To turn the tables this much... However his thoughts turned to Whitetip, who now, he knew, had to be gone, and the Sthenos destroyer in orbit, which could still ruin them. The hardest fight remained. Dealing with the Sthenos fighters in atmosphere had proven simple. In the vacuum of space, the advantage was largely washed away. He had only thirty-three Wraiths on an intercept with the goliath ship. Thirty-three chances to take it down, and nothing more. The Sthenos had thousands of fighters in the air on Earth, and Jeffrey assumed hundreds were pouring by the second from the Sthenos destroyer in space. The modified Hammerheads could pull more G's and if history rang true, outthink their opponents, but thousands to thirty-three...

The Spartans at Thermopylae hadn't survived, but they'd made enough of a difference...

In that, Jeffrey felt hope rise. The Sthenos were more advanced. They had incredible numbers and powerful weapons, but they weren't accustomed to losing, and right now they were, badly... again. This time the Hammerheads and Special Warfare had done more than bloody their nose. This time they'd cut their damn arms off. What would a fighter do with no arms?

They'll run.

He looked to the Nav-Con. "Get me a close up on the Sthenos destroyer in orbit."

"Yes sir," the young officer said.

...

Kodiak spun and fired. He jinked. On his IFF two Sthenos fighters behind him winked out of existence as they collided. He fired again into the darkness. Two yellow blooms rose ahead, and he had to swoop around them, grunting as he braced himself against the G's.

Another Sthenos fighter, unable to follow his turn, winked out on the IFF as it passed through the cloud of debris.

He'd lost count of how many dead, but he felt now, as he arced upside down and looked to where the hulk of the Sthenos destroyer had landed in Tokyo, fires burning around its dark outline far below, that he'd done enough. He would kill as long as he could, but if he died now, it would be all right. He'd paid them back for Whitetip.

He chased down one Sthenos after another, never staying more than a few seconds on each target. He used short bursts and, as he shot another and another without missing, began to laugh. He felt almost god-like in his ability to see a target and turn it to a blooming cloud of yellow fire and streaking debris. He had a Sthenos on him now and a green bar of energy lanced below him as he turned. He turned so hard the tunnel came on deep and pacifying. For a moment he was unsure where he was. He found himself surrounded by an electric-blue field. Had he been shot? Had he died? The field faded. He was in the Lakota, still turning hard. He'd blacked out. As he came to his senses he realized he'd come all the way around on the Sthenos who'd been on his six. He flicked his trigger. Nothing. He'd run out of ammunition. He switched to rockets, targeted the Sthenos, and launched a needle-thin mamba missile. Lancing away on a trail of smoke, its bloom of cluster warheads missed the Sthenos. He fired again, but the mambas wouldn't track.

"Too bad," he said and turned the Lakota toward the largest concentration of Sthenos fighters, all vying for position on him. He fired off all of his mambas in a spiraled pattern, sweeping the nose of the Lakota in an outwardly increasing spiral. All twenty were away and several found lucky hits. Those explosions caused a few other crashes.

He was done. No more weapons.

He considered what to do as he spun away from lancing green energy beams. He could harry them. Fly among them until they shot him down, but he was growing tired. He could crash into one, try and pick out one of the best and take it out, or he could run, get refitted, and kill more later. He hated to run from the fight, but that was the right choice.

Kill as many as you can if you get the chance had been Holt's final command to him, and he had. He'd run his guns until the barrels glowed, run them empty.

He slammed the stick forward, and dove for the deck, jigging and swooping. Beams from the pursuing Sthenos lanced around him, striking the ground. Buildings and streets scattered into flame and cloud where the beams struck, leaving smoking craters in the lights.

He came down low over the city, flying between buildings, and the Sthenos followed him, shooting. When beams came straight down, he realized he'd gotten himself caught with too many bogeys and not enough options. By being this close to the ground, he'd taken away a full dimension of flight. Here their greater numbers could pin him down and grease him. The beams from above rained down as fighters descended and cycled out. He knew he was done, knew one final misstep had caught him up. He now realized when he'd engaged the horde, he'd bought into it body and soul. There was no way to disengage that many fighters. He could stay in it, could out fly them well enough save accidental shots, to stay alive, but to move away took too much singular linear motion. He was doomed. Still, there would be others to kill those who'd killed him. The Sthenos couldn't stand against the Hammerheads; he felt sure of that. He wondered if the Sthenos understood that.

He would never know.

...

"They're leaving," the Nav-Con operator said.

"What do you mean?" Jeffrey asked.

The Nav-Con operator held up his hand, waving away his previous comment. "I don't mean leaving... All Sthenos fighters have disengaged ground targets and are space-bound... vectors indicate an intercept point with the final destroyer, sir."

Jeffrey felt his heart beating in his throat. That was the right tactic… to put all resources into preserving the final destroyer. And it meant even worse odds for the Wraith pilots. He'd hoped the Sthenos would be devastated and not think clearly, but they had. Taking their fighters to orbit, took all his atmosphere-bound Lakota out of the fight.

Jeffrey said, "Inform the Lakota forming up in Denver to hunt for any Sthenos installations or personnel on the ground. Tell them I want prisoners."

The officer's fingers flew on the keyboard. "Yes, sir," he said.

Jeffrey's attention turned back to the Sthenos destroyer in orbit. The Wraiths were almost on it. The swarming red sparks of Sthenos fighters had moved several miles away from the destroyer, creating a defensive barrier.

"Tell the Wraiths to go straight through the fighters. Tell them to fly like hell."

"Yes, sir." He typed for a moment, watched his screen, and said, "Flight commander Springbok's response is: *Yes sir, like hell sir.*"

Jeffrey smiled as he imagined the young woman, heart on fire, racing toward her own death. Again, he felt the regret of not being able to be with her.

...

Despite knowing he was a dead man, Kodiak still flew hard. He wasn't going to make it easy on them. He came down as low as he could, snaking down the streets of Tokyo, making sixteen G turns on the street corners between the towering offices. The IFF showed that the Sthenos stayed high and tried to pot shot at him. Some shots came close. At any one time ten or more beams lanced down. It would only be a matter of time until he ran out of luck.

A beam lanced down a few feet in front of his nosecone, filling the cockpit with green light. As it faded, the sky, which had been lit with the beams, went dark. He looked to his IFF display and, in shock, almost hit a building. He arced around it, lifting away from the streets as he did. As he came up out of the city, he saw the blue-violet glow of hundreds of thrusters turned on him, all leaving. He wished he had something to throw at them. He had nothing to kill them with, and they were moving up away from him in a straight path. They were going to fight the Wraiths. He had one last chance. He could take one last ship, if that made the difference in orbit, it would mean something. He shoved his throttle forward, and the power of the Lakota slammed him into his seat. But the Sthenos fighters pulled away, moving from supersonic to hypersonic speeds. While they couldn't outmaneuver the Lakota, they could out accelerate them. As he reached 60,000 feet, their thrusters became small points of light, fading into the now brilliant stars. His fuel warning light came on. Breaking away, he arced upside down and looked up at the ground, at the dark outline of the Sthenos destroyer far below. He wondered how many he'd taken, felt it hadn't been enough.

He dropped the nose of the Lakota to bear on the city, freefell to 10,000 feet. Gradually he leveled off at 1,000 feet and turned around the ruined destroyer, the smoke from the fires rushing over his cockpit glass. With nothing left to do and his fuel indicator pulsing red, he touched down on a tall building's landing pad. The Lakota's engines spooled down. Releasing the cockpit, he climbed down, removed his helmet, and walked to the edge of the building. Fires around the hulk of the destroyer filled the air with the smell of burning wood and metal. The great swath of Tokyo lay in perfect silence.

CHAPTER 65

Springbok led the charge. She clicked her radio twice to signal the all-ready and the channel lit with the clatter of mic clicks. No words, just quick confirmations, they were all ready.

She was familiar with the ship but not herself. A peregrine strength coursed through her. She'd flown Wraiths before. They scared the hell out of her because she could barely keep up with them. Now she felt stronger and faster than the Wraith, as if a flowing river of energy ran from her mind down her limbs, connecting her to the twitchy beast, reining it in.

The message passed across her screen, *Admiral Holt says to fly like hell.*

She confirmed, *Yes sir, like hell, sir.*

"A-1 check in," she said into her mic.

"A-1 here," Repo Man, the marine whose father had been Great White, confirmed. Springbok felt strange to be calling the shots over someone like Master Sergeant Mikelson. When Jeffrey assigned them their commands, she'd argued that Mikelson should lead. Holt insisted she'd do fine. He needed someone who knew the pilots well. That was her.

Her IFF showed the nineteen Wraiths with singularity bombs as bright yellow flecks among the three flights of green markers.

You have the last destroyer, came the message on her screen.

She responded with a dry *acknowledged,* but a thrill ran through her. They'd succeeded. The surface-bound destroyers were gone.

Now it was up to them. As the destroyer came into visual range, hanging among the stars beyond the curved earth, she and the rest slowed. The destroyer showed on her IFF as a broad red blade.

Hundreds of smaller, red markers poured from the prow, moving outward in a barrier between the Wraiths and their target.

"Everyone spread out. Keep the warhead Wraiths at least a quarter mile apart."

Now swarms of red markers on her IFF began rising from the planet. The Sthenos were boxing them in.

Looking back to the wall of Sthenos, she decided there were far too many. They'd never break through.

"Delay, delay," she called out and turned hard. The Hammerheads followed her, arcing around to fly across the face of the wall. The swarm from the planet raced up behind them.

They had nineteen singularity bombs. Her mind raced. With each she could take out a half mile sphere of Sthenos fighters. With twelve she could clear a hole in that wall of fighters nearly four square miles wide. Then she could take the last seven bombs right up the middle.

"What are we up to?" Repo Man asked over the comm.

Springbok keyed her mic. "I want twelve singularity-carriers to create a lotus formation. Create a combat spread of one-half mile. She called out six pilots with singularities to stay out of the formation. The others formed up quickly. "The remaining fourteen without singularities, follow the leads in. The last six and myself will pretend to play support roles, come through last looking unimportant. When leads are within range, trigger your warheads. The rest will come through the gap they create in the barrier."

The radio went live with either a simple click-click or brief confirmations.

The lotus formation of Wraiths turned and accelerated at the wall of Sthenos. The second group of fourteen folded in behind it, their titanium skins glinting in the unshielded sunlight. She, as part of the final seven, layered in last. As she shoved her throttle forward, the nuclear-plate thrust ruthlessly crushed her into her seat.

As the first Wraiths reached the Sthenos, green beams lanced at them. Springbok wondered what sort of particle/wave technology could create visible beams in the vacuum of space. She felt as though the tech she and her fellow Hammerheads were bringing to the fight was like rocks swung on leather thongs in comparison.

On the IFF, as the Wraiths joined with the wall of Sthenos fighters, twelve circles of Sthenos fighters were sucked into nothingness, ripping a hole in the defensive wall nearly two miles across. Only then did she register that she'd given an order that twelve men and women, twelve friends, had without question followed to their deaths. The second flight came through the hole, and as she and the other six, the last seven singularities in the game, passed, it closed behind them. They'd made it through. The destroyer was only six miles away, ten seconds time at her current speed.

She jinked left a moment before a beam lanced by to her right. A millisecond slower and she'd be gone now. A few Sthenos had remained near the destroyer. As they closed on her, she picked a line through them, hoping the other Wraiths were able to do the same. She ripped around a Sthenos ship, pulling more G's than she ever had in her life. She saw no tunnel.

"Amazing," she said to herself.

It's so sad to be this good for only a moment.

Wraiths began winking off her IFF. They were now down to seven non-singularity Wraiths. Three of her final flight were gone as well.

Only eleven ships left.

"When we get within 100 meters of the destroyer, I want all non-singularity Wraiths to break away."

As the Sthenos destroyer filled her forward cockpit glass, a Wraith exploded above her.

"Keep your movement up folks," she said. Another of the yellow-marked singularity-carrying Wraiths winked out.

Three warheads left.

They came in close, and as was expected, a huge, blurred beam from the destroyer turned the two lead Wraiths into clouds of gas and metal. Another behind her vanished. Now just two warheads remained... two miles away. One and a half. The other yellow marker vanished. She was it. Everything she had ever dreamed to be now balanced on this moment. As the proximity marker came to one mile, one half, 300 feet, she thought of her great-grandmother and how much she'd loved the old woman. When Springbok flipped open the singularity's trigger cover, she heard the wavering yet sure voice in her memory, "Lila, you can have what you earn. If you want the name of a shark, you go and take it."

She pressed the switch.

...

Jeffrey stared at the Nav-Con, watching the sparks of light twirling around each other. At first, when Springbok had them pull off he'd yelled out, "What the hell is she doing?" He thought she'd lost her nerve, but as he saw the lotus of ships form up, he whispered to himself, "That's genius, Lila."

When the lotus cut a hole through the wall and the remaining Wraiths moved in on the destroyer, Jeffrey watched with breath held. A fan like energy weapon took a third of the remaining Hammerheads out in one sweep. In a few seconds Lila was left as the only singularity.

"She's ordered them to break away from her," The Nav-Con operator said, "but they aren't."

A Sthenos fighter bore down on her as she reached 100 meters. Her wingman took that Sthenos fighter out and was drawn into the singularity. In his rebellion against her final order, staying with his lead instead of abandoning her, he'd saved them all.

The center section of the destroyer collapsed in on itself, more and more of it being consumed by the singularity as the two massive ends of the Sthenos destroyer were pulled toward each other. The singularity shut off before the entire ship could be consumed, leaving only small portions front and back to collide with each other.

"Three Hammerheads remain sir," the Nav-Con operator said. "Shall I have them engage the Sthenos?"

"No. Get them in atmo," Jeffrey said. "Send them to Denver to connect with the Lakotas moving there. Feed the Sthenos fighters to the buzz saw."

"Yes sir," The communications officer said and gave the commands.

The Wraiths arced away from the remains of the destroyer and began racing Earthward, jinking and dodging as they flew. The Sthenos took one more, leaving only two to trace a line of smoke across the sky as they entered the atmosphere.

Looking up, Jeffrey saw the thin trail heading north followed by the streaks from the Sthenos. "Who's that final Hammerhead?"

"Repo Man is one sir."

Mikelson… the old man lives while the young pay with everything.

"The other?"

"Lieutenant Commander Fields sir."

Marco.

Mikelson and Fields dropped down into the waiting Lakota, which rose up with a fiery plague of fifty caliber hell-fire, ripping the Sthenos fighters apart.

Jeffrey looked at his clock. 5:46 GMT. In the span of forty-five minutes, David had risen up and ripped out Goliath's heart with a black hole.

"How many are left?"

"I have seventy-eight Lakota in the Denver formation, sir. …and the two Wraiths."

"Sthenos?"

"I have… the number detected is dropping too quickly."

"Locate me some ground based Sthenos."

"We've been tracking several ground transportation vehicles on the surface."

"Are there some near Denver?"

"Yes sir."

"When the Lakota are done with the fighters, get them on those ground transports. I want them alive."

Finally, Jeffrey was going to get to look one of these bastards in the eye.

He fell quiet for a moment, feeling empty. Everything he'd built himself up for had played through. He'd assumed they'd lose, that they'd give their all because that's how it was done and fail …but they'd won. After the rush he was left, as he always had been, empty. A thought pushed the emptiness aside.

"Has there been any report from the New York Special Warfare Operator?"

"None sir. I've received confirmations from all operatives aside from Tokyo and New York."

"Do we still have a Lakota here?"

"One, sir."

"Is it functional?"

"Yes, sir."

"Good, get it prepped for flight. I'm going to New York myself."

CHAPTER 66

It had taken an hour to prep the Lakota for flight. As it was fueled and armed, Jeffrey loaded supplies—a tent, rations, first aid—into the rear seat.

After strapping in, firing the engines, and going through his preflight, he throttled on and lifted the Lakota off the deck. It rose through the dark leaves, the sunlight growing in intensity until he broke out over the heavy canopy into its full brilliance. Rolling the throttle on, he shot out across the treetops, grateful to be airborne again. He stayed at five hundred feet as he passed Mach 3.

At that speed, he'd soon crossed the Gulf and entered the Caribbean Ocean. With Cuba rolling below him, the Lakota's heart rate monitors triggered on thousands of survivors. Along the Atlantic coast's small towns, he detected similarly high concentrations.

As he neared the city however, the monitors showed fewer and fewer human signatures until only the scattered signals from small animals remained. He decelerated as he crossed the Hudson river and came over Manhattan, where the monitors began picking up scattered three-beat, syncopated rhythms.

Sthenos.

As he scanned the streets, the monitor blurred and flicked to darkness.

"Not now," Jeffrey said, thumping the display.

It remained dead. Without the monitor, trying to locate her in the darkness would be impossible. He crossed the length of the island a few times in the hopes she might see him and fire a flare.

As he came back over the southern end of the island, a green beam lanced out to his left. He jinked away from it, cursing. He'd have to wait until first light.

Circling a tall building, its glass still catching the last rose-tints of the fading sunset, he set down on its landing pad. Unstrapping, he unscrewed the heart rate monitor, unplugged it, checked its fuse, and reinserted it. He powered it on. Nothing.

Taking a welder from his emergency kit, he went to the roof access door and welded its seam shut. Now no one could get to him without an aircraft or climbing gear.

Above, stars had begun to emerge en masse... stars which, in his youth, had struck him as beautiful now felt menacing. How many Sthenos were among them? And what other horrors did they hold?

He considered sleeping in the Lakota, but sitting upright was a sure way to have a rough night, so he set up his tent under the Lakota's wing, crawled into his sleeping bag, and lay in the darkness listening to the silence of a dead city.

...

That night he dreamt of Stacy sitting on the side of a mountain, her face crusted in frost. He woke with a start thinking he'd heard footsteps pass the tent. He listened beyond the sun-glowing nylon. Nothing. After breaking down the tent, he made himself take time to eat and drink water, his breath billowing in the damp morning air.

After packing up his supplies, he strapped himself in. Closing the cockpit, he fired the engines. As he let them warm, he pressed the power switch on the heart rate monitor. Nothing, but the switch felt loose. Taking his pocket knife, he pried the switch cover off and pulled it out. Cutting the wires off, he stripped them and twisted them together. The monitor glowed to life.

Lifting off, he began scanning for human heartbeats. Finding one, he closed on it to find a man wearing an orange jumpsuit standing on top of a rubble pile, waving both arms in desperation. He would have to wait. Approaching a second heart signature, he found nothing

408

in the center of the street where it should have been. It must have been underground. But it was on the eastern side of the island, well away from Stacy's mission path. Turning west, he passed the dead hulk of the destroyer and the half-mile wide pit Stacy had created.

He flew down the length of the ruined Sthenos destroyer, finding no heart signals. The Sthenos inside had either evacuated or been killed in the crash. On the northern side though, the heart rate monitor picked up a Sthenos' strange rhythm. A block beyond that, his display showed a human signature. The Sthenos was moving toward it.

Dropping between the buildings, Jeffrey rounded a corner to find the Sthenos with its back to him. They'd haunted him for fifty years and, before this moment, he'd only seen their destroyers and fighters. He hadn't expected six limbs.

Turning, it lifted its hatchet-like head and held up its front-most limbs in a universal sign of surrender. Jeffrey had often wondered what deep-seated emotion might rise up when he saw one for the first time. Now he had his answer… nothing. He remembered how adamant Gerard Schodt had been that they were misunderstood, intelligent beings.

"I have no misunderstandings," he said and fired. The fifty caliber rounds blew the body in half, a leg flying away. He could find prisoners for study later. Right now he needed this area clear.

He flew down the block beside a half-toppled building. Coming into the next intersection, he slowed to a hover, and turning, found two figures in the street. One sat upright with the other laying in its lap. Yet, there was only one heart signature. As he approached, the woman, who wore dust-coated body armor, held up her hand to shield her eyes from the Lakota's turbine wash.

Stacy.

Jeffrey touched down and gave one last look to the monitors to assure no heart signatures were nearby before shutting down his engines.

She sat cross-legged with a teenage girl in her lap, turned toward Stacy's belly as if for protection. Stacy ran her fingers through the girl's shoulder-length hair, which was infused with scraps of concrete. The girl's arm was peppered with small cuts.

As Jeffrey approached, Stacy kept her attention on the girl. He sat down cross-legged in front of her.

"Stacy?"

She seemed to not hear him.

He touched her knee. "Stacy."

She said, as if not to him but to the girl in her lap, "I'm so sorry…"

She looked up at Jeffrey. Her eyes, hollow and red from crying, broke his heart.

"I thought if I could save just one…" Her voice went quieter, trembling. "I killed them." Her chin tightened as she looked back down to the girl. "All of them."

She gripped the girl's hair as a gut wrenching sob overcame her. Gasping her next breath, she said, "I thought she was safe…" She lowered her eyes, and tears began falling from her chin as her shoulders trembled. Gently, she set her hand on the girl's shoulder. "I did this."

Jeffrey took Stacy's fingers from the girl's shoulder, pressing his hands around hers. "Stacy, I know where you are right now."

Her hand tugged with her sobbing.

He said, "I'm here and I understand. Okay?" He waited, but she said nothing, "In the months and years to come it will be important to remember that we do the best we can, but we can never do it right… not all the way. That's impossible. You'll be consumed if you try to go back and figure out what you could have changed." He gripped her wrist as if bracing to pull her up off a ledge. "There's no glory in what you had to do. There's the chance at life for many others, but in giving those people that chance, you've paid a price few can understand. The dead get to rest, but we still have work to do and lives to live."

She kept her head down.

"Stacy... look at me."

She did not at first, but he waited, gave her the time.

When her eyes finally rose, they were pitiful and tired, not the clear, cutting gaze of the Stacy Zack he'd known.

"Stacy, you're a strong woman, and this is another challenge you'll have to face, but you don't have to face it alone, okay? I'm not going to let you have to hide in a scrap yard like I did. I'm going to be here for you whether you like it or not."

She looked away, and he reached out, took gentle hold of her chin, brought her eyes back to his, "You did the best you could. There's no way you could have done any different. Do you understand that?"

Stacy pushed his hand aside and, looking down at the girl, shook her head. The corners of her mouth turned down. Anger came growling into her voice, which Jeffrey knew she directed at herself. "No... I could have gone back sooner. I could have saved her if I hadn't taken so damn long to get back."

He took hold of her hand again with both of his, "Stacy, make me one promise..."

She said, her anger now shifting toward him, "What?"

"No matter what you feel, I want you to promise you'll talk to me, okay?"

In the pitiful trails of tears crusting from her auburn eyes, Jeffrey felt hope. She was willing to let it out even so early, which was the highest bravery he knew and the first step to healing.

"Stacy, you're strong," Jeffrey said, "but this is too big to face alone."

Stacy nodded in silence.

Jeffrey put his hand on the dead girl's side, the fabric of her shirt smooth and her skin stiff with rigor. "Now it's time for her to rest..." he looked to Stacy, "okay?"

Stacy nodded again.

Jeffrey said in a quiet voice, "Will you let me help you prepare a grave for her?"

411

Stacy ran her fingers through the girl's dark hair as she said, "Yes. Thank you."

CHAPTER 67

A month later, operations had moved on surprisingly well. The Lakota pilots had cleared many regions and located several isolated military forces. Commanders were placed over those regions as governors.

Jeffrey had moved the central command from the heat and humidity of the Amazon, to the cool, dry summer air in the Rockies west of Denver, where he now sat in an office with sun-heated pine scent filtering in the open window. He looked out on the high peaks, barren aside from a few swaths of snow. A knock sounded on the door.

"Yes?"

The door opened, and Master Sergeant Mikelson and Commander Holloway came in.

"Commander, Master Sergeant, please sit."

They did as he asked.

"What can we help you with Admiral?"

"We have unfinished business with someone."

"Sir?" Mikelson asked.

Jeffrey pressed the com link on his desk. "Bring him in."

Mikelson and Holloway turned as the door opened. An MA entered holding a thin, dark-haired man by the upper arm. He had disheveled hair and a full, twig-laced beard. Jeffrey indicated the man should sit as the heavy scent of body odor filled the room.

"I should have had you clean up before we met."

The man nodded, keeping his eyes on the floor.

Holloway said, "Oh my God… *Captain Donovan?*"

Donovan glanced at her before saying in a quiet tone, "I'm not a Captain anymore." His eyes flicked distrustfully to Jeffrey. "You said you'd leave me alone. Why'd you bring me back in?"

"The war's over Donovan," Jeffrey leaned back, "and I need good commanders."

Donovan gave him a sidelong look.

"I don't believe you'll ever cross me again. True?"

Donovan shook his head, "I wouldn't. You could have killed me, would have been justified…"

Jeffrey gave him time to continue. When he didn't, Jeffrey said, "I need expertise in fleet operations. Expertise you have."

Donovan kept his eyes on the floor.

"Donovan… *Captain* Donovan… look at me."

Donovan's eyes rose to meet Jeffrey's.

"I'm offering you command, a return to civilization, a chance to make a difference in what needs to be done." Jeffrey touched the center of his chest. "I'm offering you my forgiveness."

At that tears welled in Donovan's eyes and trailed clean streaks down his dirty face.

Jeffrey looked to Mikelson and Holloway. "Do either of you disagree?"

Donovan looked to them as though they might take from him something precious.

"Not at all," Holloway said touching Donovan's shoulder.

Mikelson nodded his agreement. "Like you said, sir, we need experience."

"Walter," Jeffrey said to Donovan, "it's over. Go get cleaned up and get some sleep. We'll meet again tomorrow."

Donovan, seeming unable to raise his eyes to Jeffrey, nodded at the floor. "Th-thank you." His eyes did come up then. "I'm so sorry… She was…"

When he faltered, Jeffrey said, "It's done. Go rest."

With one final, quiet, "Thank you," Donovan rose and left the room.

Holloway's jaw flexed. She seemed to Jeffrey to be angry.

"Something you'd like to say Holloway?"

Holloway lifted her chin, pressed her lips together, and said, her voice cracking slightly, "Just that I sincerely appreciate you, sir."

Jeffrey gave her a slight nod before saying, "And I you. But we need to discuss the future."

Holloway and Mikelson looked to each other, a question forming between them.

Mikelson voiced that question with some doubt, "I thought we had already, sir. We have infrastructure recovery well ahead of schedule, and other proj—"

"Not immediate plans… plans beyond our lifetimes."

Holloway and Mikelson waited.

"We need to determine the next step for the Sthenos. As I see it we have two choices."

Mikelson said, "We either prepare for the next attack…" He looked to Holloway.

Holloway said, "…or we go on the offensive."

Jeffrey nodded. "Which path do you two prefer?"

Mikelson said, "I prefer the offensive, sir."

"I feel the same, sir," Holloway said.

"Then we begin from here. This will mark the beginning of a dramatic shift for the human race. Our purpose over the last two hundred years has been to live in peace, to seek out recreation and leisure, health and higher learning. It must now, sadly, shift to war."

"Put that way, it sounds wrong, sir," Holloway said.

Jeffrey leaned back. "It's not… ideal. But the necessary path often can't coexist with the ideal. In studying conflicts amongst ourselves, we find the majority are a result of cultural misunderstandings. Those should primarily be dealt with through diplomacy, but even in human history we have many examples of what can only be described as evil. When that arises, there's only one answer. The malignancy must be cut out."

He eased back in his chair and looked out the window. "I think the Sthenos considered the first engagement a fluke. They're not accustomed to losing. That means they've done this time and time again," he pointed to the blue sky above the peaks, "out there."

Mikelson said, "You think we're the first race to offer them real opposition?"

"That's my guess."

Holloway said in a grave tone, "So you're suggesting there are other intelligent races in the galaxy subjected to life as cattle."

"Or extinction," Jeffrey said. Leaning forward his tone became more energized, "And we're going to be the ones to set it right."

"But," Mikelson said, "predators have a natural place in any ecosystem. Who are we to say it shouldn't be that way?"

Even as he said it Jeffrey knew he was playing the devil's advocate.

Jeffrey smiled as he said, "Eric, we're the wolves, not them."

Mikelson nodded and a smile flickered across Holloway's face as she said, "Yes sir."

"Go to your groups," Jeffrey said, "and discuss the possibility of an offensive against the Sthenos. I already have teams attempting to glean the technology from their ships. I give us twenty-five years before we need to be bound for war."

"Yes, sir."

"Dismissed."

As they stood and left the room, Jeffrey found himself considering the future beyond his lifetime as the people of Earth dredged up their warring roots. However, instead of fighting for land, skin, gold and salt, they would fight to stop a race of killers. While he couldn't say why, Jeffrey felt sure that, rising up from its primal bed the human race would venture to the stars and set them free. All the loss and pain he'd experienced in his life seemed somehow worthwhile as the great purpose of stopping something as yet unchecked materialized before him. For so long he'd felt tired and old. Now he felt regret that he wouldn't live long enough to see the greatest acts of the human race.

...

Stacy sat outside the base watching a magpie hop among boulders, turning its head to the side, listening to the ground. Pouncing, it came up with a dark insect and flew away.

Neither the bird, the warm sun, nor the summer breeze had an effect on her mood. She'd been unable to rise beyond an overwhelming sense of failure. As days progressed, she did the work she had to do, but when nothing was required, she'd find a quiet place to sit, and speak to no one. While Leif and Caterina had formed a close bond in their success—Stacy could see them growing closer as wounds closed—she felt her own troubles opening wider. She felt anger at them for moving on. They hadn't been forced to the edge of the blade. She'd tried to discuss her feelings with Jacqueline and Horace, who had both killed thousands as well. However, when they spoke, she couldn't make herself bring it up, and she feared they felt the same, wanting to move forward but unable to face what they must to do so.

Jeffrey often came and sat with her. She knew he was waiting for her to talk, but even with him, she couldn't. Not yet…

Today he walked up to her but didn't sit down.

"You need to come with me Stacy."

Beyond him, near the entrance to the base, she saw Marco shifting his weight back and forth as if worked up about something.

"What's going on?"

"Not saying," Jeffrey said, "but it's good. Now come on." He walked back toward Marco.

She didn't feel she wanted to face *good* today, but when the fleet admiral of the navy says to come with him…

She followed to the hangar where an old Kiowa transport sat on a launch pad prepped for flight. Jeffrey directed her to climb the open ramp, and as she strapped into one of the jump seats, he did the same beside her.

As Marco went to the cockpit along with a copilot she didn't know, she asked Jeffrey, "Now can you tell me where we're going?"

He shook his head.

Throughout the flight, he stayed true to that. They spoke a bit, but each time she asked about their destination, he would simply shrug. Her curiosity peaked with every passing minute.

After an hour, the transport went vague with hovering. The decking thumped as it touched down. The rear ramp came open and lowered to the ground, letting in a wash of hot, dry air.

Stacy unstrapped herself and walked off the ramp into a high mountain forest of tall, narrow pines. Among the underbrush stood dark-green, broad-leafed plants and here and there the flat paddles of prickly pear cacti. Under the scant grasses, the soil was the color of faded terra cotta.

"Where are we?"

Jeffrey put his hand on her shoulder. "Mexico. In the mountains about a hundred miles north of Mexico city."

Marco pushed past them running toward a group of people. A young woman Stacy felt she knew shoved her way through a few others and ran to Marco.

Reaching each other, they embraced as if they might fall off the face of the Earth if they didn't hold tightly. Two small children came through the crowd. Of course. Marco's wife Sofía and the daughter and son, both more grown than when Stacy had last seen them. Marco picked them up like sacks of groceries and spun around.

Jeffrey said, "She hid with them for days before being found. Apparently the Sthenos had her shackled and were about to kill the children when the attack commenced. When rescue forces found her, she asked to be brought here. It seems Marco's parents have had a change of heart about her."

"I can only imagine," Stacy said in a whisper.

"If we hadn't attacked the moment we did," Jeffrey said placing his hand on Stacy's back, "They'd be gone."

Stacy's heart, which she felt had faded to nothing, spilled over. As her vision blurred, she felt weak. Fearing she might fall, she knelt as tears began streaming down her face.

Jeffrey crouched beside her, took hold of her hand. "What we've lost is gone. We have to focus on what's been saved."

Marco's little boy, no more than three years old, caught Stacy's eye. Brow furrowing, he pulled his hand free of his mother's and ran to her. He touched her face with delicate fingers.

"Su nombre es Stacy, sí?"

She smiled as best she could and nodded.

"Por qué está triste?"

As Sofía walked up, Stacy looked to her, a beautiful woman with delicate shoulders and kind eyes.

"I am sorry if he is troubling you, Commander Zack."

"Please Sofía, call me Stacy. He's not at all, but I don't know what he asked me."

Sofía said to her son, "Ella no habla español. She is one of the soldiers who saved us."

He nodded, looked to Stacy, and said, "I didn't think heroes cried."

Stacy, barely managing a whisper, said as she took hold of his small shoulders, "Yes, Luciano, we do."

"Why are you sad?"

"I'm not sad at all."

The boy scowled, asking his mother, "Por qué está llorando?"

A heartfelt smile came to Sofía's face. "He asks why you are crying."

Stacy drew the boy in, hugging him close. As she held the little chest in her arms, hair soft on her cheek, she whispered into his ear, "Do you ever wonder who rescues the heroes?"

He pushed away from her, his expression worried. "Who?"

"A few moments ago I thought no one would," she wiped her cheek with the back of her hand, "but now I think you and your sister will."

CHAPTER 68

As Kevin Bradshaw held up the sharpened pipe, a hunk of blood-dripping meat hanging from it, he asked, "Why are we feeding this thing?"

"Admiral Holt wants it alive so we can learn from it," Gabriel Hernandez said as he gripped the handle on the sliding metal door as though it were the spring on a bear trap. "You ready?"

Kevin blew out a breath. "Wait just a minute."

But Gabriel had already pulled open the door. He ran a few steps aside as the weld-laced metal wall, the south side of a large enclosure, concussed as something big collided with it. A spiderlike arm with four claws whipped out of the small opening, searching the surface of the wall.

"Oh crap," Kevin said, backing away.

A bellowing rose up through the open steel mesh, which made up the top of the cage.

"Don't back away," Gabriel said as he ran around Kevin, shoving him forward. "You have to give it the meat, but whatever you do, don't let it take the pipe."

"Oh hell," was all Kevin could say, eyes locked on the searching arm. He had spent countless hours with his friends, discussing what they would do to a Sthenos if they got their hands on one. Now, with one right in front of him and an angle-cut pipe in his hands, all he wanted to do was back away.

The Sthenos let out a clicking sound, vibrating Kevin's ear drums.

"Get it done," Gabriel said. He shoved on Kevin again.

"Get off me. I'll do it."

Drawing a deep breath, Kevin lowered the pole and stepped forward. As he did, he could see white-rotten eyes looking out at him through the pass-through. He felt dizzy as the arm reached, the four fingers held wide, ridged claws curling.

"Don't let it get hold of the pipe."

"How the hell am I supposed to keep it—"

The Sthenos snatched at the flesh, sank its claws into it and pulled. The pipe lurched, and the meat came free. Kevin stumbled backward, falling to the dirt.

Gabriel laughed at him as he took the pipe and used the end to shove the panel shut. Tossing it back to Kevin, he said, "Welcome to the zoo, rookie."

The sound of wet chewing came from beyond the wall.

"Yeah," was all Kevin could say as he got to his feet.

They walked out of the courtyard past the hulking shape of the Gorilla.

"What the hell's that thing for?"

"That?" Gabriel said with pride. "That's a Gorilla. Holt used it to capture this thing. They're so aggressive it was the only way to restrain…"

They walked away, neither noticing the figure with a shag of blonde hair standing in the twilight shadows behind a pine tree. The man remained there for some time, seeming to wait for darkness to fall.

When night had come on, moonlight belied the darkness, throwing silvered shadows across the courtyard. Leif Holt, wearing the metal-ring-jointed jumpsuit, which controlled the Gorilla, stepped out from the darkness and looked to the officer's offices to the north. Seeing no one in the windows, he approached the enclosure. His breath came in short huffs as his surging adrenaline made his arms and legs feel electric.

He placed his hand on the metal. Only a quarter inch of plate steel separated him from one of them… those that had taken his wife and child from him. The moonlight reflected off a half-mad smile as

421

he smacked the metal with his palm, causing the wall to ring like a massive drum.

Running hoof-falls thundered up to the wall. Leif stepped back. The wall crashed and reverberated. Claws scratched down the metal as a sound like a buzz saw razed the air.

Leif laughed quietly and said, "I see you're ready."

He walked into the darkness under the Gorilla, mounted the ladder, strapped himself to the back rest and closed the cab door. He powered it on, and as it stood, he pulled the VR headset on. Now his sight line stood almost as tall as the cage wall. Walking up to it, he brushed his hands together, the Gorilla mimicking him, and threw the cage door open snapping the chain.

While he could have changed the cameras to infrared, he wanted to see it in natural light, and the moon offered enough, especially in the camera's sensitive optics. The thing shied away from him, back to the other side of the space.

"Hey buddy," Leif said as he moved into the cage.

He stepped aside. "There's the door. All you have to do is run for it."

The Sthenos watched him a moment before turning in a circle, kicking dust toward him, and spraying something out its thorax.

"Not as advanced as you'd like to pretend."

Leif became suddenly cognizant of the risk he was taking, not for his own life, but others. If the Gorilla shut down or the thing got past him, he'd have let free that which his father had worked months to catch. But, somewhere deep in his psyche, Leif knew he needed this. He wouldn't sleep right until he had it. He'd seek forgiveness later… if his father would grant it

"Come on you chicken shit." Leif knew that if he moved away from the door, it, being faster and more agile than the Gorilla, could run around him and be gone. It would kill before being killed. Those deaths would be on Leif. He stayed by the door. "Go for it bastard."

As if on command, the Sthenos dropped to all six limbs and sprinted at the open gate, startling Leif how quickly it crossed the space. As it passed him, Leif reached out, shouted a curse as he felt he would miss it, and caught it by its back leg.

The Gorilla jolted sideways, and Leif feared it might fall, but it settled down, and he lifted the thrashing monster up. Turning, he pulled the gate shut and regarded the oversized insect-like being.

"Intelligent. That's nice."

He gripped, crushing the leg.

The Sthenos let out a horrific scream.

That will bring the base down on me.

He had limited time, but wouldn't go too fast. Europa had been their time. Now this was his.

It clawed at its leg, now chewed on it. Just as the leg came away from its body, Leif gripped an arm, then a second arm, and plucked one off. Threw it aside. Its head thrashed with the pain.

"Yes," Leif said, his heart fluttering against his ribs. "That's what it feels like." He pulled the other arm off. "Do you see now what you've been up to?"

Darkness coursed from the arms.

"Not yet… I want more time. Cutter." The Gorilla's hand folded back, and the cutting bar lifted out. Leif pulled his trigger finger, sending arcs of blue electricity across the bar. Touching it to the bleeding sockets, he cauterized the wounds. The Sthenos writhed against his grip biting at the armor-plating.

Leif laughed and, for the first time, understood how much he'd held in.

Over his earpieces, he heard a commanding and familiar voice, "You in the Gorilla. Stop at once!"

He turned to the gate, which remained closed.

"This is Admiral Jeffrey Holt. Acknowledge my order."

Leif's eyes scanned the dark office windows.

"Down here, in the feeding port."

Leif looked to the small rectangle, framed in scratches, and saw his father's face illuminated by a flashlight.

"Hey dad," he said over the Gorilla's loudspeaker.

"Leif?" Jeffrey asked in an incredulous tone. "What the hell are you doing?"

My times up.

"This," Leif said as he pinned the Sthenos to the ground, looked into the white rot of its eyes, and punched the Gorilla's fist down, and down, and down again, until all that remained was a crater in the dirt with the lower half of a Sthenos extending from it.

He heard the scraping of metal and looked to see the gateway coming open. Several men ran through. Powering down the Gorilla, he swung sideways out of the cab, climbing up to sit on its back.

Jeffrey jogged up to the crater, stared at it. "Leif... I don't understand... You *know* how hard I worked to capture this thing."

With his eyes on the depth of the stars, Leif said, not to his father, but to the glittering reach of the Milky Way, "You like death?" He laughed to himself. "That's good because I'm bringing you genocide."

A closing request…

As an independent writer (and I plan to stay that way) word of mouth is the main engine I must rely on. To that end, I humbly ask, if you should find my work to your liking, please tell others and consider leaving a review wherever suits you best.

I would also love to hear from you at jason@jason-bond.com.

Jason grew up in Oregon and currently lives in Washington State with his wife and son. He holds a Bachelor of Arts in English Literature, an MBA and an MLIS. When his first novel *Hammerhead* unexpectedly reached bestseller status, he realized its success was founded in the word-of-mouth recommendations of combat veterans from around the globe. Jason takes a hands-on approach to writing. When SCUBA research couldn't wait for summer, he found himself certifying in Puget Sound's frigid January waters. Outside of writing and his family, martial arts are an important part of his life. At eighteen years of age, he entered an Aikido dojo for the first time, and has since trained in Jeet Kune Do, Kali/Escrima, Taekwondo, Shudokan Karate, Kobudo, Goshin Jutsu, Judo, Muay Thai and Brazilian Jiu-Jitsu.

For more about the author, future novels, and events, please visit:
www.Jason-Bond.com

26186752R00236